Praise for Michele Hauf

"Hauf delivers excitement, danger and romance
in a way only she can!"
—*New York Times* bestselling author
Sherrilyn Kenyon on *Her Vampire Husband*

"With action-packed excitement from start to
finish, Hauf offers an original story line full of
quirky, fun characters and wonderful descriptions.
And the sexual tension between CJ and Vika
sparkles. Readers won't want to put this one down."
—*RT Book Reviews* on *This Wicked Magic;* Top Pick!

"This quirky story has a fair amount of humor
and a lot of heart as well."
—*HarlequinJunkie.com* on *The Vampire Hunter*

"Nothing at all tame about this book. Lots of
messy, dangerous sex, complete with teeth, the way
vampire sex should be. Along with the romance,
there's quite a bit of action, several fight scenes."
—*BrazenReads.com* on *Beautiful Danger*

"I love the world building this author creates
in her books."
—*RomancingtheD...*

"*Kiss Me Deadly* i̶ ... on't
be put down u̶ ... ."

D1398669

MICHELE HAUF

Michele Hauf has been writing romance, action-adventure and fantasy stories for more than twenty years. Her first published novel was *Dark Rapture*. France, musketeers, vampires and faeries populate her stories. And if she followed the adage "write what you know," all her stories would have snow in them. Fortunately, she steps beyond her comfort zone and writes about countries she has never visited and of creatures she has never seen. Michele can be found on Facebook and Twitter and at www.michelehauf.com. You can also write to Michele at P.O. Box 23, Anoka, MN 55303.

BEYOND THE MOON

AND

GHOST WOLF

Michele Hauf

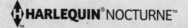

Recycling programs
for this product may
not exist in your area.

ISBN-13: 978-0-373-60672-6

Beyond the Moon and Ghost Wolf

Copyright © 2014 by Harlequin Books S.A.

The publisher acknowledges the copyright holder
of the individual works as follows:

Beyond the Moon
Copyright © 2014 by Michele Hauf

Ghost Wolf
Copyright © 2014 by Michele Hauf

Printed in U.S.A.

www.Harlequin.com

CONTENTS

BEYOND THE MOON

This one is for me, because Rook is mine.

Prologue

Verity Von Velde's mother, Amandine, had the ability to determine the origin of a person's soul. So when Verity was born in the 1860s, Amandine had known her child's soul had once belonged to a witch—who had died twice.

Knowing she possessed a reincarnated soul helped Verity to understand the strange compulsions she experienced on occasion. The first time, at fifteen, had been on that horrible night she'd been compelled to rush to the forested village of Clichy, just outside of Paris, and had spied the bonfire. Amandine Von Velde had been betrayed by the witch hunter to whom she had unknowingly promised her heart. "Witch!" the crowd had shouted, and they'd laughed and clapped as the flames had consumed her mother's screams.

That night, left alone in the small cottage she had shared with her mother, Verity had fallen into a deep sadness. Years later, the compulsion had once again led her to the aqueducts beneath Paris where her grandmother, Freesia, had apported out of a Faery portal to hug the granddaughter she hadn't visited for years. Freesia had been born with a faery soul. Of all the witches in the Von Velde family, she was the only with sidhe ichor running through her veins.

Freesia had carried with her the quilt Great-Grand-

mother Bluebell had made for Verity's mother. Because
Bluebell had decided not to prolong her immortality and
had died a natural death (which was rare for witches,
even in a time when the burnings had begun to fade), her
compassion lived on in the quilt. As Freesia had wrapped
the quilt about Verity's shoulders, she'd felt the hugs her
mother and great-grandmother could never give her again.

"I know your mother begged you never to trust a man,"
Freesia had said as they'd stood beneath the city beside
the gently flowing aqueduct waters. For men had been
Amandine's curse and death. "But I would bid you trust
the right man."

Verity had liked the sound of that and had nodded,
promising her grandmother she would give it consideration. When she began to protest that she did not know
what to do all alone, Freesia had added, "Stay in Paris. It
will take care of all you need. Trust your soul's compul-
sive ways. It is your birthright."

Freesia then fluttered through the portal, and Verity
would not see her lavender-haired grandmother for a long
time.

Years after Grandmother Freesia's visit—Paris, 1908

Verity tripped through the field grass that the city at-
tendant had not scythed, for this swath of land that edged
the forest was kept wild. Tourists did not venture off the
paths or cobblestone roads that cut through the Bois de
Boulogne. She would not normally skip through the overgrowth in a long skirt and button-up chemise, scratching
at the buzzing insects, had she not been compelled.

Sometimes Verity's soul insisted so profoundly, she had
no choice but to listen. And follow.

Now, she raced toward a massive tree stump that pushed

up from the earth, its serrated edges jutting like castle crenellations. Thick, verdant moss coated the south side. The rowan tree must have fallen naturally from age or perhaps a lightning strike. The stalk, branches and leaves had long been cleared away, most likely for firewood.

Arriving at the grand root base, Verity sighed in awe. She had great respect for nature and knew all living things were connected, be they human, paranormal, animal or botanical. Kneeling before the trunk, she laid her palms on the cool moss coating and smiled. It must have taken four men to clasp hands and surround this tree when it had once proudly held court here at the forest's edge.

The wood pulsed with life. And there, in the center of the stump, which had been dug out by animals and insects over the years, grew four new shoots of life. All things renewed and lived on.

Much like her soul.

Reaching down, she played her fingers over the wood where it was wet from yesterday's rain and smelled earthy and sweet. Insects had not chewed through this part for it was solid and strong. The heart of the rowan. Verity felt the pulse. She curled her fingers within the core of the tree, and it pulsed again.

And yet…

She tilted her head, her dark, unbound hair spilling across the stump. The pulse felt familiar. Human? Perhaps, and long lost.

"A soul?" she wondered.

And then she knew, indeed, that it was. This is why *her* soul had compelled her here.

Sliding her fingers inside her ankle-high leather lace-up boot, a gift from her mother for her fifteenth birthday, Verity drew out the silver-handled athame. Her mother had always chastised her for carrying it about. One must honor the sacred tools of magic and keep them wrapped and tucked away until required to conjure a spell. Silently mocking her mother's nagging words—may she rest in peace—Verity tapped the wood core with the blade tip. "If I had kept this tucked away, I wouldn't be able to free you now."

She worked at the wood, carefully carving around the core, which was about as wide as her fist and shaped like a *pain de campagne*. An hour later she'd set the core free. Verity turned and sat against the mossy base of the stump between two thick, twisted roots, smoothing her hands over the rough, moist core of the rowan tree.

"I know you belong to someone. What did he do to lose you?"

She pressed the wood against her chest and felt the subtle resonance of the long-lost soul and knew, without doubt, a man had sacrificed this soul in great sadness. She also knew that the man yet walked this realm.

Did he seek what he had lost?

"I'll keep you safe," she promised. "Someday he will come for you."

Chapter 1

Paris—now

King laid a manila folder on Rook's desk and then stepped around to stand beside it, arms crossed.

"Got time to take a look at this?" King asked Rook. "I'm getting itchy about Slater with the Zmaj tribe. He's been acting out through others. Over the past six months the tribe has turned sour. Too many murders linked to their vamps, and the increase in their numbers is disturbing. Slater is creating vampires without regard. I think it's time the Order stepped in."

The Order of the Stake policed the vampires across Europe and took out the ones who proved a danger to mortals. One of the Parisian tribes, Zmaj, had been peaceable since its inception early in the twentieth century, but recently the Order's intel had noted a shift in power within the tribe. And a disturbing penchant for violence.

"I'll put our best knights on it." Rook, King's right-hand man and the figurehead in control of the Order, tapped the keyboard to boot up the computer screen. "I might even scout them out myself. Been feeling the need to return to the field lately."

"Is that so? I thought you'd grown accustomed to your cozy office chair."

"That's just it. Do you know what happens when a man rests?"

King shrugged.

"He rusts," Rook replied. "I haven't trained a new knight in months. I need to do something physical. Go beat in some vampire skulls and get the death punch out of the bottom drawer."

The Order's knights called the specially designed titanium stake the death punch. Standard gear—no knight went on the hunt without three or four in his arsenal.

King, the founder of the Order, had recruited Rook about a decade into his project. They'd known each other since the end of the sixteenth century and had been friends and brothers through the ages. Rook loved and admired the man. He would do most anything he asked, and he knew the respect was reciprocated.

While King watched over his shoulder, Rook scanned through the Order's database on tribe Zmaj. Their computer network kept detailed records on all known vampires and tribes in Europe and the surrounding nations. Although they focused on vampires, the Order also recorded information on all other paranormal breeds because their work tended to overlap.

They'd been keeping an eye on the vampire Frederick Slater for more than a decade, since his creation in the early part of the twenty-first century. Before that, he'd been mortal for thirty years. The sick bastard had asked for vampirism. The tribe leader was aggressive and devious, yet used others to do his dirty work. And he had entitlement issues. Took things that didn't belong to him, such as expensive cars and nightclubs. And innocent mortal women he then turned into vampires. A nasty habit the Order had overlooked because he hadn't been killing them. Until now.

Rook opened the manila folder, a recent file on Zmaj. The first picture was a crime scene photo of a young woman lying in an alley, her neck torn out. Dead. A bloody handprint marked her cheek, a common indicator in the other photos that followed.

"Zmaj is marking their kills," King noted, tapping the handprint. "Why?"

Rook had no clue. "Vampires tend to be secretive and hide their mistakes." He shuffled through the photos, each flashing bloody handprints. "These kills are bold and blatant, as if they wanted someone to discover them. Or, rather, to know they are the tribe responsible for the death."

"They've captured the attention of the mortal authorities."

"Which means," Rook said, "it's time the Order shut down tribe Zmaj before Tor has his work cut out for him."

Torsten Rindle did spin work for the Order. He was a master at convincing the mortal press that a vampire bite on a dead body was simply deranged fandom at its worst.

Rook closed the manila folder. "I'll take care of this personally."

"See that you do." King strode out of the office as silently and unexpectedly as he'd entered.

From the drawer at the bottom of his desk, Rook drew out a titanium stake. With a squeeze of his hand to compress the paddles, out pinioned the deadly stake from the sleek column. Pressed against a vampire's chest, the weapon pierced the heart and reduced the vamp to ash. Rook had created the stake centuries earlier, and as technology had improved, so had the original design. He took pride in the implement.

He spun the weapon smartly, slapping it solidly into his

palm. A bloody palm print? "You just signed your death certificate, Slater."

He stood and, with a keystroke, put the computer to sleep. In the closet at the back of his office hung a long, leather cleric's coat with a bladed collar and reinforced Kevlar panels on the chest and back. Leather pants, a cotton undershirt and a Kevlar vest hung inside.

Stripping off his crisply ironed gray dress shirt, he tossed it aside and caught a glimpse of his bare chest in the mirror inside the door. He proudly fisted the raised brand of the Order of the Stake on his left shoulder and announced, "Tonight I'll turn this city gray with vampire ash."

With full intel on the Zmaj tribe, Rook had headed toward the seventh arrondissement, where most of the attacks marked with the bloody handprint had been reported. It was an affluent quarter where old money mingled with the new. The Eiffel Tower and Les Invalides attracted tourists, which led Rook to believe Zmaj was hunting either unknowing tourists or the established, yet oblivious, rich.

His steel-toed boots took the cobblestones swiftly, quietly. His senses were alert for sounds beyond the incessant traffic noises. The city never slept. It was something he had in common with Paris. The air was crisp with imminent autumn, a season he enjoyed because it softened the city's harsh odor as the ominous dread for winter settled in.

As the principal trainer and supervisor for the Order, Rook took knight trainees out in the city on the hunt, but he hadn't hunted alone in years. Not for lacking desire to stake some longtooths. He had simply been too busy training and running the Order. The paperwork involved in keeping their secret order an actual secret was ridiculous. He never could have imagined, four centuries earlier, fill-

ing out computer database profiles or making duplicates
over an office copy machine.

The vampire population in Paris was high, but most of
them enjoyed their anonymity from mortals and worked
hard to keep it that way by not killing humans and thus
raising the Order's ire. Best way for a vampire to ensure
immortality? Avoiding a stake to the heart.

Yet there would always be the young and reckless
vamps who deemed the world their playground and enjoyed the kill. They never survived long. And although
the Order served only to protect mortals from vampires,
Rook knew many breeds appreciated the work they did
because keeping all vampires mythical in the eyes of the
mortal population benefited everyone.

Some mortals believed in vampires, werewolves, faeries
and all the other breeds that shouldn't exist. Those mortals were few and were rarely considered a problem. It was
those who did not believe but then had been attacked by a
vampire—forcing them to believe—who Rook wanted to
keep far from the fangs of hungry vampires. Those victims who would scream, raise a holy stink and invite investigation, and Rook wanted to avoid that.

And the only way to do that was by ashing the culprits.

Closer.

Directing his attention inward, Rook questioned Oz's
statement.

Something feels...familiar.

Rook always paid attention to the entity within him.
Asatrú, an incorporeal demon, had been trapped within
him for four centuries, accompanying him through this
thing called life.

"What seems familiar?" he asked Oz. Sometimes he
spoke aloud to the demon, but he could think the question
and the entity would understand just as well.

It is a feeling. You are close...to something important.

Not far ahead of him, a female cried out.

Rook fitted a stake into both hands and ran toward the harrowing sound. It was before midnight, yet this section of the city was quiet and dark with only intermittent vehicle traffic. Ancient buildings that had seen war, revolutions, and the rise and fall of monarchies closely paralleled the street. The alleys in between buildings were claustrophobic. Street lighting was at a minimum. Not the optimal place for a lone female to go walking.

Nowadays mortals had lost their sense of danger. Their naïve complacency never ceased to astonish Rook. One must always be vigilant.

He spied a crowd of young men looming around something, or someone, he could not see. Yet he could feel fear in the air as tangibly as he could read a person's truth by placing his hand over their heart. Had to be the woman who had screamed.

One of the men hissed dramatically and exposed fangs.

"Thought so," Rook muttered. He picked up his pace.

What was that?

A fireball, small and tight and flaming orange, zipped through the air and singed one of the vampires on his bald head. The vamp yelped and batted at the flame, hissing and cursing at the one who had lobbed the attack.

Was the woman they had surrounded a witch? Had to be to throw fire like that. A rare witch, though. Few practiced such magic because fire promised a witch's sure death.

Another ball of flame looped in the air but fell onto the cobblestones like a deflated balloon. Sparks sputtered, and the flame hissed to smoke. She didn't have control. Had her hands been shackled by an attacker?

Rook shouted, catching the vampires' attention. Four charged toward him. He took one out with a plunge of the stake to his chest. Ash formed in the air in the shape of a man. The remaining three vampires scattered in the inky darkness.

Rook ran through the ashy cloud toward the woman clinging to the brick wall. In the confusion of having one of their comrades ashed, the vampires had left her alone. Fire burned in patches on the ancient cobbles before her, finding tinder in the dry autumn leaves littering the ground. She huddled against the wall, her dark hair spilling over her face and wide eyes taking in the scene. Hands out before her, her fingers shook, and he thought perhaps the flames on the ground danced at the command of those shaking fingers.

Rook lunged to kneel beside her, laying a hand high over her breast to feel her frantic heartbeats. It was a conditioned touch. He could read a person that way, but—not this time. What the hell? Perhaps her fear blocked his read.

"You okay?"

She nodded frantically.

He was getting nothing from her. Not the clear read of truth he always did when touching another. Yet he felt a strange sensation of recognition surge through his system. Something familiar but so distant he couldn't touch it. He'd lost it so long ago.

That is it!

He winced at Oz's inner outburst. Looking into the woman's shadowed eyes that flickered with small red flashes from the flames, he wondered aloud, "My...soul?"

"Get him!"

Jerked away from the woman by a vampire's claws, Rook switched from the sudden, overwhelming knowing that clenched about his heart to fierce and ready fighting mode. He twisted at the waist, swinging out an arm and slashing the stake across a vampire's face.

Behind him, three vamps lined up. He caught a glimpse of the woman. Now on her feet, she ran away from them.

Get as far away as you can, he thought.

No, we need her! Oz said.

Perhaps, but right now he stood his ground surrounded by vampires. All thoughts focused on getting the job done. This night, no longtooth would walk away from him alive.

Verity ran down the dark street, her heartbeats racing her strides. A short skirt and heels were not optimal running attire, but when her ankles threatened to buckle, fear pushed her.

After a long night at the gym practicing her performance piece for the Demon Arts Troupe, she'd looked forward to strolling home in the crisp night air to walk off the strain in her muscles. Her mind reviewing the new routine she'd been perfecting, she'd walked right into the gang of vampires. Though she'd never feared them in numbers before, immediately she had known they hadn't wanted to chat.

She'd thrown fire at them, but there had been too many. Two had wrangled her wrists, stopping her from casting more flame balls. They'd begun to reason out who would bite her first when the hunter had charged onto the scene, stakes swinging like some kind of samurai warrior.

Though he'd worn the coat of the Order of the Stake, the long leather jacket had not concealed his muscular physique. His movements had been skilled and swift. Nothing like having a knight in dark leather rush in for the save. Verity had swooned a little when he'd held his hand against her chest and their gazes had locked. When he'd said "My soul," she had gasped.

Could it be?

She clasped the wooden heart that hung from a leather

cord around her neck and ran faster over the cobblestones, her heels clicking too loudly. So long she had wondered about what she held in her hand, and—could he have finally found her?

Sensing someone was quickly gaining on her, she couldn't risk turning back for a look. One of the gang must have escaped the hunter and now pursued her, a panther hot on the rabbit's tail.

She dodged to the right down a narrow alley, seeking the streetlight some hundred yards ahead and cursing the fact that she didn't know where she was. She needed a moment to reorient herself with the neighborhood.

Testing her magic, with a thought she sent out a spurt of fire. That was all she could manage, a tendril. She'd expelled most of her fire during practice. She needed a night of rest to properly recharge and restore her magic.

And although she was skilled in gymnastics, this running in heels business was quickly taxing her after hours of exertion in the gym. In proof, she stumbled on a loose cobblestone, but instead of her body floundering, she felt a hand sweep around her waist, turn her and slam her shoulders against the concrete wall. Impact jarred her teeth. Her ankles wobbled. Verity could barely hold herself upright as she faced the bald vampire with fangs revealed and menacing eyes.

"What the hell do you want?" She tried to say it with command, but without any magic to control, she had lost her only defense.

"Your blood, witch." The vampire slammed his hands to either side of her shoulders and leaned in to sniff at her hair. "You burned me, so now I'm going to make you scream before you die."

Before she could reward him with the scream he sought, the vampire sunk his fangs in her throat. Instinctively, Verity jammed her knee upward but only managed to connect with his thigh. The bloodsucker didn't even groan. She beat his chest with her fists, but he easily wrangled her hands with strong, pinching fingers.

The teeth in her neck tore at her skin. It hurt like nothing she'd ever experienced before. She'd never been bitten. Would not suffer a vampire to be so intimate with her, despite having once dated one. The creep sucking at her vein drew out her blood. He moaned as if in the throes of orgasm and—

A yell from down the alley stopped the vampire. He tore out his teeth from Verity's skin, twisting his head to pinpoint the origin of the shout. The wounds hurt so badly, the pain manifested as a scream. Slapping his hand to her cheek, the vampire mimed a goodbye kiss, but thankfully, his bloody lips did not touch hers.

As the vampire ran off, Verity sank against the wall. Grasping her neck, her fingers slipped in her blood.

The hunter lunged to a diving kneel before her and lifted her chin to peer at her neck. He inspected her cheek and swore. "Damn it. I didn't see that one get away!"

Eyelids fluttering, Verity tightened her jaw to keep back the tears that threatened. She wanted to beg him to save her, to make it all better, but she knew it was too late. She'd been bitten. And the vampire couldn't have had time to seal the wound. If the wound was not properly sealed, the victim risked becoming a vampire.

"You a witch?" the hunter asked quickly.

She nodded.

"Impressive fire magic back there. Are you going to be okay?"

"Of course," she gasped. Dragging her knees up, she hugged her arms about her legs. "Just a little nibble." It hurt to conceal the pain, but she was an expert at hiding her weaknesses.

"I think I got here in time." The hunter stood.

He scanned down the street. She knew he wanted to go after the vampire—and he should. But he squatted again before her, drawing her in to his overwhelming presence. An easy authority that felt not too harsh and not too hesitant. When he wrapped his arms around her shoulders and pulled her against his chest, she sank into the comforting embrace.

How strange that he gave her the comfort she had craved, yet had thought to skillfully conceal that need.

You must get home and find a spell to counteract the bite!

But right now Verity could only tilt her head against the hunter's shoulder. She felt so good in his strong arms. He smoothed a hand over her hair. Perhaps a teardrop spilled down her cheek. Or it could be the repulsive heat of the blood the vampire had taken from her vein and smacked onto her cheek.

She clutched his jacket, and he suddenly tugged it away from her face. The Order knights wore blades at their collars to deflect vampire bites. Verity wished she'd worn more than the comfortable slip dress. Like full armor with a neck guard.

Get to safety!

She was safe in this man's arms. She knew it without doubt. That was her mother's voice prodding her to flee. *Never trust a man. Most especially a hunter.*

"Who are you?" she managed between sniffles and gasps for breath.

"Name's Rook," he offered. "I'll see you home?"

"No, go after the vampire. He could harm someone else.

And I need to fix this. To find a spell to stop the vampire taint from changing me."

He bent to meet her eyes. Compelled to look into his eyes, Verity's breathing calmed. Despite the frail light from the distant streetlamp, she clearly saw his irises were blue. Intense, bright and true. Yet something about him was as far from the truth as it could ever be.

She had no idea what that meant.

"I felt…" He looked at her chest where he'd touched her earlier. "But not now." He shook his head and stared at his hand, as if battling with an inner argument. Then he touched her cheek where the vampire had slapped her. "Zmaj."

She knew that tribe. How did he know? He must have been tracking them.

"You sure you'll be okay if I go after the longtooth?"

She nodded fervently and looked at her shaking, bloody fingers. "Yes, you've a job to do."

"I will—uh, what's your name?"

"Verity."

He gave her the oddest look. "Your name means truth, yet…" Now he laid his hand against her chest again, and she wanted him to hold it there forever, imbuing his surprising coolness into her very being and stealing away her fears. "I can't read you. Strange."

"Go," she said against the screams from her heart that begged her to swoon into his arms so he'd have to carry her home.

He nodded and, helping her up, walked her to the end of the alley. "You live around here?"

"I—yes. I need to orient myself. Where is Les Invalides?" The military museum, which was also a hospital, always served as a navigation point for her.

"That way."

"Then I can walk home in five minutes. I'm good now. Thank you, Rook. You're with Order of the Stake?"

"Yes." He took out a metal stake and spun it between them. His body shifted as he stepped from foot to foot, eager to return to the chase. "Start walking. I want to make sure you can so I don't have to worry about you."

Taking directions, she meekly turned the corner and scampered homeward, finding adrenaline carried her to the front door. Once inside, she raced upstairs to her attic bedroom and through to the bathroom.

Flicking on the light, she leaned toward the vanity mirror. A bloody handprint dripped down her cheek. But that wasn't half as disturbing as the actual bite mark. Panic rose at the sight of her bleeding neck—and then she adjusted that unnecessary fear into more helpful focus. She twisted on the faucet and sloshed hot water on the wound. Cleaning it wasn't important. Vampires rarely carried disease or anything communicable—save vampirism itself. Stopping the vampiric taint from entering her bloodstream was paramount.

Verity raced out into the attic bedroom, half of which was her spell area. The lofty room was dark, save for moonlight that beamed through the cathedral window on the south end and across the gray floorboards and walls. Silvery light glittered in the dozens of grounding crystals she'd strung from the ceiling beams, like stars to capture the night's enchantments.

Grabbing the centuries-old grimoire that she'd been writing in since she was a child and slamming the massive tome onto the floor, she then knelt over it and paged through the spells.

"Please let there be something in here to stop me from becoming a vampire."

* * *

The bald vampire tossed the bloodied necklace onto the table before Slater.

"You did it?" Slater asked. He stood before the window, looking out at Sacre Coeur's multiple travertine domes, lit from below by spotlights.

The vampire nodded. "She's dead."

"What's that thing?"

"A trophy. Ripped it off her neck after I bit her."

Slater studied the simple wooden heart, stained with blood. A worn leather cord had been run through a small metal loop at the top. It felt warm, almost as if it possessed a pulse. He recalled Verity's skin had been warm and soft, electric against his skin. He inhaled the blood scent but didn't want his tribemate to see him devour her essence.

And then he remembered. She'd always worn this necklace. Had once even said something curious like, "I'm keeping it safe."

For what, he often wondered. Heh. Guess she hadn't succeeded.

"That'll be all, Clas. Thanks."

"No problem. Let me know when you need another favor."

"You know I will."

The vampire left, closing the door behind him, and Slater lashed his tongue over the bloodied heart. Verity's taste burst on his tongue. She'd never allowed him to bite her. He'd always known she'd taste sweet. Pity he only got to experience her sweetness postmortem.

"This is what happens when you piss me off, witch," he muttered and tucked the necklace in his desk drawer.

Chapter 2

A beam of morning sunshine prodded at Verity's eyelids. She popped upright from lying on her side in the middle of the hardwood floor. Looking about the attic bedroom, discombobulated by the sudden awakening, she winced as sunlight flashed through a crystal suspended overhead and lasered her directly in the eye.

With a yawn, she stretched her arms and legs, curling her toes inside her boots. She still wore her ankle boots? And her clothing from last night.

Her fingers landed on the open grimoire, a thick, centuries-old book that had been in the Von Velde family for six generations. Bound in blue leather, it was two feet long and almost as wide. Beside it sat black and red candles, both guttered to wax puddles that would leave a stain on the painted floor. Beside that lay a dead dove that she'd deftly eviscerated to get to the beating heart. The heart lay embedded in the guttered black wax.

The grimoire was opened to a blood-spattered (from the dove) page that detailed the spell for Fending Off Imminent Vampirism in Mortals. She wasn't mortal by any means, but it had been her only hope. In desperation she had recited the ancient Latin incantation and torn out the dove's heart.

Once bitten, the vampiric taint entered the victim's system. If the wound was not properly sealed with the vampire's saliva, the victim could then turn vampire by the next full moon if one of three things did not occur: the victim killed the vampire who had bitten them; the victim refused to drink mortal blood before the full moon (which generally resulted in madness because the blood hunger was relentless); the victim committed suicide.

Verity had walked through one and a half centuries and had not been bitten once. Hell, until two decades ago, vampires would have never dreamed of biting a witch because of the Great Protection spell enacted a thousand years earlier to safeguard witches from vampires enslaving them for their magic. It had made all witches' blood fatal to the vampire.

And then the spell had been lifted as a means to bring peace between the two breeds.

"Idiotic plan," Verity muttered. "What witch had thought that a good idea?"

When the vampire she recently dated but had not allowed to bite her had turned on her after a month, she'd realized he'd been grooming her to steal her magic all along. The only way to do that was with bloodsexmagic. Lots of sex and biting and drinking blood imbued the vampire with the witch's magic. It also left the witch's magic drained and lacking.

Verity would have none of that and had broken it off with the vampire. She would never rule vampires out completely as dating prospects, but she would be much choosier next time she fell for a fanged one.

She rarely went beyond the three-date mark. It was safer that way. It was difficult to shake the mantra her mother had ingrained within her soul: Men were not to be trusted.

But the three-date minimum had been stretched to a few more with the last guy. Rules were not meant to be rigid.

Her ex-vampire lover had stalked her for months after their breakup, but she'd thought he'd finally given up when she had been forced to move two months earlier. He hadn't found her new address.

Or had he? The hunter had said the vampires last night were from tribe Zmaj. Same tribe as her ex-lover.

"No, if he wanted to hurt me, he'd do it himself," she said, stroking the rough wounds on her neck. "Blessed goddess, I hope the spell worked. What am I saying? It *did* work." She tapped the grimoire. Never did her spell-craft fail her. "I'm fine. Just a little bite mark that should heal within a few days."

As a witch, she didn't heal quickly—perhaps only fifty percent faster than a mortal. The healing arts had never been her talent. That was her friend, and fellow witch, Zoë's forte.

As she studied the wound with her fingers and trailed them over the dried bloodstains on the dress neckline, she realized something was missing.

"My necklace."

The vampire must have torn it off as he'd ripped his teeth from her neck. Why would he take that precious bit of wood and leather from her? Or could it have simply fallen off during the attack? She'd had the necklace since early in the twentieth century. Had been waiting for its owner to come and claim not only the wooden heart, but also the very soul within.

"I have to go back and look for it."

She had protected and cared for that soul too long to give up on it now. And because of what the hunter had said last night. Rook. She couldn't get his startled exclamation out of her head.

"His soul?" As bedraggled and exhausted as she felt, Verity couldn't help but smile. "Could he be the one?"

Sure she'd find the necklace lying in the alley near her dried bloodstains, she pushed to a stand and wobbled. Weak and drained, she felt as if she'd run two marathons. Curse her girlie need to always wear high heels.

"First a shower," she muttered. Making a beeline for the bathroom, she stripped off her clothes along the way. "And then back to the scene of the crime."

The Order had intel on the majority of vampires across the world. Rook wasn't a computer expert—he employed a team of IT techs for that—but he did use the database frequently. Actually the IT team was one man, and he was currently in the States setting up operations because the Order didn't have an official US headquarters yet. He and King hoped to open the New York base within a few years.

In the database, Rook located the *Other* section, which detailed all breeds not vampire. It was more a way to keep tabs on who was living where and associating with whom than a complete archive of every breed that trod mortal ground. Their files on faeries were sparse. Those creatures lived in an entirely different realm, yet the knights had occasion to deal with the sidhe who lived in Faery-Town. Mortal vampire sympathizers also were kept under close watch.

Under *Witches,* the database didn't list any more on Verity beyond her name, believed to be Veritas Von Velde. Or so he assumed she was the only witch named Verity who lived in Paris. Records guessed at her age as more than two centuries. Because she was associated with the Demon Arts Troupe, a known address was listed for her. A recent move within the past few months?

He made a note of her address and headed out. Half an

hour later he stood in front of a pretty little walk-up town-home with a vast and lush herb garden out front, enclosed by a wrought-iron fence painted deep purple.

He clanked the greenman brass door knocker and after five tries decided she was either not home or not answering a hunter's raps. He didn't sense anyone inside; it wasn't a magical skill, he just felt as if the place was empty. So he scribbled a note and tucked it under the mat.

He'd wanted to see that she had survived the attack last night with little wear and tear and check that she had found a spell to counteract the bite. The last thing he needed on his watch was a witch turning vampire. The double-whammy of magical skills and the hunger for blood tended to make such a creature deadly and place them on top of the Order's *Most Wanted* list.

The field trip to search for the necklace resulted in disappointment. But stocking the pantry had been successful with a quick stroll down the Rue Cler.

"Wanted to know that you are okay," Verity read from the note she'd found fluttering up from under the doormat. "Need to talk to you. Please meet me at the coffee shop on Quai d'Orsay at eight p.m. Rook."

She fanned the note over her lips as she strode inside and set the reusable grocery bags on the kitchen counter. Drawing the multicolored silk Hermes scarf away from her neck, she touched the bite wounds. She'd applied her great-grandmother's ointment on the punctures, and the swelling had calmed nicely.

After putting away the groceries, she cut a head-sized watermelon into chunks, which she transferred into a glass container. She ate a few pieces, then picked up the note again and marveled over the precise, squared letters that reminded her of an architect's writing style.

It was already evening. Dare she meet the man? She had an idea what he wanted to talk about. Couldn't tell him she'd lost the thing, could she? No, she had to be certain of his identity before she started worrying about that.

And she did want to learn more about the man who had saved her. Sort of saved her. It would have been a hell of a lot better had he staked *all* the vamps before the bald one had bitten her. And she was just snarky enough to let him have it for that omission.

But should she meet a strange man out of the blue? Especially a hunter?

Though her mother had been dead for more than a century, her warning words still resounded clearly in Verity's memory. Amandine Von Velde had been betrayed by a hunter—a betrayal that had taken her life.

Sighing, Verity popped another watermelon cube in her mouth. Yet grandmother Freesia's entreaty to find the one man she could trust dallied with the learned maternal diatribe. Verity had lived alone for more than one hundred and sixty years. She'd had many lovers and a few boyfriends, but never had she allowed herself to completely let down her guard. To trust. Even her male friends she kept at a comfortable distance. A witch had to be cautious.

She wanted that trust. That moment of releasing her breath and just accepting. And she wanted love. What woman did not? Yet would she recognize it when finally it entered her life?

"I hope so. I don't want to die alone. Companionship sounds…lovely."

Yes, she would go see the hunter named Rook. Because she wanted to look at him in the light and see if he had been as handsome as she'd remembered while in her fearful, panicked state. And if he embraced her again, maybe gave her a welcome hug, then her night would be complete.

Because his hug had made her feel safe. And that feeling was all too uncommon of late.

Rook paused mid-sip of his espresso. The witch striding across the street toward his table positioned out front of the café was the sexiest thing on two legs.

Shod in shiny black patent leather high heels, her long legs stroked the air sensuously. Those sexy gams were sheathed in sheer black thigh-high stockings that stopped about four inches below her skirt, and those four inches of skin made his mouth water.

He finished the sip and winced at its heat. Or was that the heat suddenly moving over his perpetually cool skin?

A miniskirt flirted with black ruffles at the hem, and above that, a plain white T-shirt emphasized her pert nipples as the swing of her long, curly, purple hair brushed over them. An unbuttoned gray sweater slouched off one of her shoulders and hung longer than the skirt length, giving her a tousled bedroom look. As if she'd just been given a sound tumbling between the sheets.

Fuck, she was gorgeous.

The dark eggplant hair was curious but not shocking, the color of a lush bloom one would nuzzle to their nose to smell the fragrant perfume. Something he wanted to push his fingers through and clutch to his face while he was giving her the tumble her sensual allure demanded.

And with that thought, Rook straightened and set down his coffee before he spilled it on his lap and singed the erection that had suddenly tightened his pants.

He stood and offered his hand, which she shook before sitting down in an elegant glide and crossing her legs beside the chair instead of under the table, giving him a great view of her gorgeous gams.

"Purple, eh?" he asked stupidly.

She swung thick ringlets over a shoulder. "It's natural." With a gesture to the waiter, she confidently summoned him.

"I wasn't sure you'd come," Rook offered, inwardly admonishing himself for his sudden timidity. He didn't do insecurity. He'd overcome that weakness, at the least, three centuries ago. "I'm glad you did."

"I had to come. I wanted to thank you in a more coherent manner than I must have done last night." She patted his hand before releasing it. "You're cold. It is a bit chilly this evening, isn't it?"

"It's the way I am. I've always been cooler than most. But I warm quickly when..." He stopped himself from saying *stroked properly*.

Just met the chick, Rook. Dial your lust down a notch.

This one he did not want to scare off. She could help in his investigation.

The waiter stopped by, saving him from having to finish the sentence. Verity ordered mint tea and two vanilla macarons.

"So, thank you," she said when the waiter walked away. "Did you stake the vampire who bit me?"

"I, uh..." He didn't want to answer that question but had known it was coming. "He got away. I'm sorry. By the time I left you, the longtooth had given me the slip. I searched the Order database but couldn't find him. I didn't get a good look at his face. All I know is that he's bald."

She nodded and looked aside, tugging down her skirt in a nervous gesture. On her fingers glittered copper rings clasping amethysts. Witches were into gemstones and precious metals. He'd once known the meanings of the stones and how they could be utilized in magic. That had been so long ago.

"It's fine," she offered sweetly. "You took out four others."

"Were you able to find a spell to prevent the bite from…?" No way to put it gently so he would not even speak it.

"Performed it last night as soon as I got home. I'll be fine."

Fluttering her fingers over the glass tabletop, she grasped the creamer with one hand while the other tugged up her sweater collar to hide the bite marks Rook managed to note with a glance.

"So, Order of the Stake. How long have you been a knight?"

"A long time." And leave it at that. He never revealed the details unless he felt it was worth the trouble of helping the person through the shock. However, she was a witch and nothing should shock her when it came to paranormal particulars. "I'm actually the trainer and leader of the knights, just under the founder."

"Impressive. Now I feel special. The big man on top saved me?"

Her flirty lash flutter captivated him. Her blue eyes were tinged with deep violet, almost as purple as her hair. As if some kind of rare jewel, they briefly stole attention from her soft, plump lips. But not for long.

Tea was set before her, and she stirred the tea bag about with a spoon. A nip at the macaron summoned a purring approval from her kissable lips.

"I love macarons. If you want to know the way to my heart?" She held the pale ochre pastry up. "This is it. I can tell you which patisseries in Paris sell the best macarons, which offer the crispest, softest and most unique in flavors. And which ones to avoid."

"Duly noted. It's always helpful to know the way into a woman's heart."

She lowered her gaze.

Rook sipped his espresso and took in the graceful lines of her hand wrapped about the teacup and the flick of her tongue as it dashed out to lick off a flake of pastry from a fingertip. Every move she made was sensual; he fought to not lean in and kiss her.

But what he desired more than a kiss? He wanted to lay his palm over her chest and read her, as he could read any person. He'd gotten such a strange read from their brief contact last night. All night he'd wondered about that flash of knowing that had washed over him as if heat had flooded his nervous system.

Oz had also been distracted through the night. In fact, the demon had been the one to prod him to visit Verity's home and invite her to this meeting.

"I have to ask you something," he started.

"It's about what you said to me last night, isn't it?"

Her eyes brightened and, compelled, Rook leaned across the table. To be nearer. In her aura of lush flowery scent and sweet sugary macarons. He wondered if her perfume was rose. He wanted to remember her scent when he returned home alone.

She added, "About your soul?"

He sat upright. So she had heard him utter that last night. Even shivering with fear, she'd been coherent and so brave. "Yes. I…felt something when I laid my hand on you."

"You mean when you grabbed my boob?"

"I didn't grab it."

Not purposely. He'd been in a rush to ensure she was all right while the vampires had closed in on him from behind. But her flirtation amused him. She wasn't afraid of him. In fact, the woman exuded an engaging confidence. Maybe she was interested in more than a chat over tea. He certainly wouldn't rule it out.

"You felt me up," she said, drawing her tongue along the jagged edge of the second macaron. He didn't know her well enough to guess if that tone had been a tease or if she was actually offended.

"It was an accident," he offered. "I wanted to touch you, to make contact, and let you know you were not alone at such a harrowing moment."

"Sure." She tapped the spoon against the plate and sipped her tea. "Admit it. You got a free feel."

"Well, sure. And what an appropriate time, when four vampires were on my ass."

"Touché."

Her lips pursed as she sipped, and Rook sat up straighter, easing his leg to the right to allow some room in his rapidly tightening pants. Damn, she was gorgeous. And a witch. He held great respect for witches. Even when considering his not-so-illustrious history with the breed.

You are not here to flirt but to find your soul. Ask her!

Oz had the worst timing, but like it or not, the demon had always been more forthright than Rook's conscience.

"Do you…" he started, not sure how to ask such a thing. "I mean, the touch. It felt familiar."

She set the teacup down and tilted her head. Her assessment of him delved a bit too deep to remain a simple flirtation. She looked into him, beyond the suit and tie and the well-groomed jaw stubble. Beyond his vain need to slick back his hair in an attempt to coax the tufts of gray behind his ears. Her look felt as much like a touch as if she'd actually laid her palm over his chest.

"I need to tell you a story," she finally said. "About something that happened to me, oh…a hundred and ten years ago. It was around 1908, I believe. A few decades after my mother died."

Rook sat back, wondering where this was leading but

content to listen to anything this sultry vixen wanted to tell him, even a story. "1908? It was a good year, if I recall correctly. The tale end of bohemia."

She nodded, their shared history refreshing. Rare did he meet someone who could remember the history he did—that is, someone he didn't want to stake.

"So, there I was, in bohemia—actually, it was more the Victorian era coming toward an end. I remember the stuffy long black skirt I was wearing. Wool. Ugh. So gothic. Anyway, I was wandering the edge of the Bois de Boulogne."

The park that hugged the modern peripherique road that surrounded the city had once been a forest—and still was—though by the nineteenth century it had already been commandeered by less upstanding citizens for midnight liaisons and occult rituals. Not that Rook would admit to knowing anything about such rituals firsthand. Some things a man liked to keep close to his vest.

"Have you lived in Paris all your life?" she asked.

"I've traveled France and Europe and stayed in some countries a year or two at a time, but Paris has always been my home."

"Then you'll know that the forest had some wild parts. And I'm not talking about the illicit parties."

Perhaps she also kept a few dangerous liaisons close to the vest. The thought that he may have passed by Verity Von Velde while wandering in a sex-blissed haze at a midnight orgy dialed Rook's lust up another degree.

"It was near a field," she continued, "and I saw a fallen rowan tree. Actually, I was compelled to the tree. My soul does that to me sometimes. Makes me go places and do things I would never intend to do. It always works out swell, though.

"The trunk had split away from the stump and had fallen with old age, but the wood revealed in the split smelled fresh and alive. I was lured closer to inspect, and I ran my hands along the jagged wood and down inside where the deepest parts had been reduced to soft decay from insects.

"At the core it was solid and hard, and I felt something there." She looked at him, her bright gemstone eyes waiting for him to respond.

"A soul?" Rook's heartbeats thundered as he began to grasp the hope he was aware Oz had tread for ages.

She dipped her head and gazed up at him. "Is that what you believe?"

"Don't you know?"

"I do. I also knew the soul belonged to a man. A sad man. And that it needed to be kept safe. I can recognize things like that. A person's heritage and, well, I can generally tell if that person has fathered children or been reincarnated. I have a reincarnated soul. And you…" She twisted her lips as she studied him from tufts of grey to the perfectly knotted tie at his throat. "Yes, you've fathered a child."

"Sorry to disappoint, but I have not."

"Hmm…I'm usually never wrong. My intuitions are like my magic. Spot on."

"There's a first time for everything, eh?" Her blatant confidence appealed to him. "But let's get back to your tale about this soul in a tree."

Rook's memory flashed to the end of the sixteenth century, that fateful night he'd stood in the open field near the edge of the Bois de Boulogne, where he had made his home with Marianne. That cruel, dark night that the devil Himself had stood before him and presented an offer Rook had not refused.

"My soul was taken from me and buried in the ground," he blurted out. "Very near the forest."

"Hmm, that makes sense. If it was buried, a tree could have grown up through and around it, encompassing it in the core of its structure."

A thick violet curl fell over Verity's shoulder, and she cupped her hands around the teacup, lifting it just below her chin to inhale the spicy aroma.

"I couldn't walk away from it," she said, "so I dug out the core of the tree. Took me all day because I had but a small athame with me. *Maman* always berated me for carrying it around. One must revere instruments of magic," she said in a haughty tone, obviously imitating her mother.

Rook chuckled, but he wanted her to continue, so he didn't speak.

She set down the teacup. "The chunk I took away was about the size of a baby's head." She formed the shape with her hands. "I took it home and carved at it for months until I felt I'd carved to the essence of it. I made it into a heart shape about this size."

She pinched her fingers together to represent something the size of a half golf ball.

"I polished it and strung it on a leather cord and have worn it around my neck ever since."

Rook found words impossible. That she had done such a thing. Actually found his soul? It had to be his. The devil Himself had placed his soul in the ground, a wicked remuneration for the bargain they'd agreed to. A foul bargain that no sane man should have made.

What man could ask for such a thing?

He had. And he lived with regret even now. Never would he have forgiveness. Yet it was all he desired.

"So you have it?" he asked, tapping hope with his tone.

Verity took another sip of tea and looked aside, rubbing a hand along her sweater sleeve. She shook her head.

"You don't have it? But you said you've worn it since. Protecting it?"

"I was wearing it last night. It must have fallen off during the struggle with the vampire. I went looking for it this afternoon, but…maybe I need to look once again."

"Yes, you must. I'll go with you."

Rook stilled as she placed her hand over the back of his. Not clasping but simply calming his desperate need to rush into action. "How can you be sure it was yours?" she asked.

"How many times does a man have his soul stolen at the edge of the Bois de Boulogne and then watch it be buried? It can't be anyone else's soul. And like I said, I felt it when I touched you last night. It was a brief knowing."

"Yes, I had a moment of knowing when you touched me, too. I think we're connected, Rook."

"Maybe." He certainly felt some compulsion toward this beautiful woman. But it could simply be that she was gorgeous and appealed to his desires. "I'm sorry, but…could I touch you? Just to see if I can feel it again."

"My boob?"

He chuckled. "I'd like to put my palm above your breast because that's where I can feel your heartbeat. I, uh…can read people. Not like you claim to know things about people—I can actually see their truths."

With a sigh, she turned on the chair to face him and propped her elbows on the wrought-iron chair back. "Fine. But don't perv out on me."

Much as he'd love to do that, he was a gentleman. Until he was not.

"Trust me, when I cop a feel, you'll know it."

Verity tugged the sweater open wider, and the soft T-shirt beneath revealed nipples so hard Rook could already feel them against his tongue.

Gentleman, remember?

He placed a palm above her breast, spread out his fingers over the shirt and closed his eyes. The heat of her was delicious; it spread up his fingers, up his arm and through his system like waves of rose blossoms shushed by a breeze.

At the sound of her sigh, he opened his eyes to see she had closed hers. Her lips were slightly parted. Long dark lashes dusted her cheeks. If they weren't sitting out in the open with tourists and Parisians passing by, he'd kiss her.

"What do you feel?" she whispered in a breathy tone, eyes still closed.

Nothing.

Nothing?

Hell, he felt absolutely nothing. He couldn't read her truths as he could do to any person or creature in this realm. It was an odd gift he'd had since the incorporeal demon had landed inside of him. Oz was a truth demon, after all.

Really? he asked inwardly.

A mystery, Oz answered. *One you must explore further. I need you to get your soul back, my friend. My wife waits for me!*

Yes, Oz's faery wife, who was soon to give birth to their first child. He owed Oz his freedom. And there was only one way to do that—find and restore his soul.

Retracting his hand, Rook stared at his palm a few seconds before wiping it along his pants leg. Nothing. What was that about?

"That bad, huh?" she said, remarking on his actions.

"I didn't get the same feeling as I did last night. But if you lost the necklace, then what I felt last night could have been true. And now with it missing, it makes sense I would not feel it."

"I'm so sorry. I will find it. I've had it so long it's become a part of me. And if it was your soul, well…"

"It's not your problem anymore. I'll track back to the site of the attack and have a look around. Your neck." He gestured to the bite mark. "It's healing? I did feel latent traces of vampire when I touched you."

"Like the shimmer?"

The shimmer was the subtle vibration of connection vampires felt when they touched one another. It was the only way they had to know one another, unless, of course, fangs were down.

"A bit like the shimmer, but I'm not vampire. I just know that feeling."

"You have been bitten?"

"Many times." He wouldn't tell her it had been voluntary. And that it always delivered erotic pleasure. That was another of those secrets he'd take to the grave. "Part of the profession. Like I said—"

"You can read people."

"Except, apparently, you."

Tilting her head down, she looked up through her lashes. "I've a bit of intuition about people."

"Still never fathered a child."

"Maybe. But I do sense something about you. Your touch is cool. I thought the knights in the Order were mortals?"

Oops. "They are."

"You're not mortal, Rook. Especially because you seem to recall the bohemian period at the beginning of last century. What are you? There's…something inside you."

Her intuition was surprisingly on the mark.

"What are *you* that you can read me so well?" he countered.

She shrugged and sipped her tea. "My mother always said I had a keen sense of place in this world. And that I could place others too. Though I'm a bit of a mystery to myself. Thanks to the reincarnated soul, don't you know? It's a demon inside you," she stated suddenly. "Am I right?"

Rook nodded, finding the centuries-old lie to protect his identity did not come forth with the usual practiced ease. What sense was there in lying when she had so cleverly figured him out?

Yet why couldn't he see her truths? How annoying.

He toyed with the porcelain coffee cup. "A truth demon," he offered. "Asatrú has been with me for centuries. Allows me to read people's truths."

"But not mine?"

"I'm not sure why that is. Oz is as baffled as I am. You're the first person I haven't been able to read. And your name is Verity. How ironic is that?"

"I'll count that as a good thing. A girl can't give up her secrets too quickly. A little mystery is a good thing, yes?"

As she drew her tongue along her upper lip, Rook decided that yes, mystery was indeed good.

"So you call the demon Oz?"

"Asatrú is his full name, and he is pleased to meet you," Rook offered, though Oz made no whisper that he cared about the witch one way or the other. The demon was pouting because she did not have his soul.

"I don't understand why the vampire would want my necklace. It's just a wooden heart and of no value to anyone else. I don't think vamps can detect souls, can they?"

"I'm not aware that they can. He may have claimed it as a sick kind of trophy. Did you get a good look at him?"

"I was frantic and more upset that I'd expelled all my fire magic and was feeling helpless. He was bald, but you already know that."

"Right. The one you blasted with fire. Good shot."

"I've expert aim, but unfortunately using so much fire

magic depletes my stores quickly. And I had been rehearsing earlier."

"Rehearsing?"

"I've a fire act with the Demon Arts Troupe."

"Interesting. It was a good thing I happened along last night. I need to find that vampire. If he has the necklace with my soul in it—"

"If it is your soul."

"I think it is."

"You want to believe it is."

"Is there anything wrong with wanting to believe?"

"Not at all."

Her mouth curved so prettily, Rook thought surely, if it had been his heart stolen by her, he'd let her keep it for as long as she wished to wear it around her neck on a leather cord.

"Would you mind taking a look at some mug shots at Order headquarters?"

"I, uh…hmm." She twisted the teacup around on the saucer.

"If you're unsure about what you saw…"

"It's not that. I'm not particularly fond of taking sides within the paranormal community. I let the vamps do their thing, and they tend to leave me alone. If I should dabble in their affairs…"

"You fear reciprocation. What if I could promise you protection?"

She shook her head. "No. I'm sorry. I just…"

"That's fine." He didn't want to push, though he couldn't understand why she wouldn't want to catch someone who had harmed her, no matter the breed. If he had been mortal, would she have helped him?

He wouldn't dwell on it. He had other ways to make the woman talk. And he didn't really mind what the topic of conversation was, so long as she didn't walk away from him now, never to be seen again.

"Would you have dinner with me?" he asked. "I find I don't want you to walk away from me. I'd like to get to know you better."

"Where would we have dinner?"

"The location hinges on your decision?"

"Of course. If you suggest a seafood restaurant, I'd have to refuse. I'm not much for slimy cuisine."

"My place," he said. "I want to cook for you."

"I've never had a man cook for me." Her eyes brightened as she pushed aside a thick curl from her face. "It's a date. Right now?"

"Have you other plans?"

That smile would undo him. "Not at all. Do you live close?"

"On the Ile St.-Louis. My car is parked just down the street."

"I am at your beckon." She took his proffered hand and followed him down the street.

That had been too easy. Yet disappointment weighed down Rook's shoulders. He'd been so close to his soul, and now it was gone. Possibly taken by a vampire. He had to get it back.

Because he owed Oz for four centuries of imprisonment.

Chapter 3

The buildings on the Ile St.-Louis where Rook lived were old, and Verity knew anyone living here had to be wealthy. She suspected Rook was rich, judging by the stylish suit and Italian leather shoes he wore. She wasn't into brand names, but she could pin a designer label merely from the way it made the man stand, erect and proud, elegant and tailored. Right with his place in the world and not afraid to take on any challenge.

Of course, that could be the hunter in him, too.

And he smelled like something worth more than a quick spritz from a cheap bottle of cologne. Like burnt peaches and tobacco. The idea of tasting him effervesced in her core and warmed her skin.

Occupied by a truth demon, eh? Yet he couldn't read the truth in Veritas Von Velde. Interesting. And definitely worth further exploration.

After shedding her sweater and handing it to him to hang, Verity sat at the kitchen table with a goblet of Bordeaux to watch her host work culinary magic. Admittedly, cooking was not in her arsenal of magical or just plain practical household skills. She ate simple whole foods that required little preparation, but that was only because she'd never taken the time to learn to cook. She had always been busy with her magical studies. And when a woman grew up with a grandmother, great-grandmother and mother who always cooked, why bother? So to watch this gorgeous man move about with such ease as he concocted food for her was a dream.

Rook was tall and sleek. Beneath the gray dress shirt flexed steel muscles, and the very sinews of him conformed against the fabric as he reached for vegetables or high on a shelf for cooking oil.

In her imagination Verity glided her palms over his cool skin, mapping his contours and memorizing his hard angles. She bit the corner of her lip to contain a squeal of glee.

His slicked-back dark brown hair touted tufts of gray near his temples and a few sprigs of salty strands mixed here and there throughout. Dark brows commanded her attention to his gaze when he regarded her. While sitting at the café table she'd noticed a tiny scar above his left brow and fancied it from a rapier or even a vampire fang.

The groomed stubble that edged his jaw as if to frame his façade begged her to touch. A small triangle of stubble sat beneath his lower lip, and along with the mustache, it gave him a swashbuckler appeal. She loved facial hair and wanted to feel his mustache tickle her upper lip as he kissed her.

All in all? The man possessed a brutal beauty that she wanted to trace and learn.

Rook's frequent glances over his shoulder acted as if invisible touches shot through the atmosphere and made it impossible for her to relax because her entire body hummed with desire. Tracing the inner curve of her lower lip with her tongue, she tapped a fingernail against the crystal wine goblet.

"You like quinoa?" he asked over a shoulder.

"I'll like anything you offer." Including a tickling kiss

from that sexy mustache. "It's a treat to have a man cook for me."

"I've been cooking for myself for centuries. I hired a chef for a few years in the early twentieth century but decided I prefer doing things for myself."

"You like the control," she guessed.

He nodded, conceding with a guilty grin.

"That's the difference between the two of us," she said. "I prefer people doing things for me."

"It pleases me to do this for you." His wink caught her as if a hand about her heart clasped ever so gently.

Verity swore under her breath. The man was sexy. But she'd only just met him. Cool the fire, and calm the jets. She didn't need to trust him at this stage, but learning a little more about him would prove wiser than leaping blindly into lust. And after her last disastrous relationship, she was skittish.

By all means, she wanted to help him find his soul. Because—and this was just occurring to her now—if this hunter could find the vampire who may have stolen her necklace containing his soul, then naturally, he'd slay the longtooth. Then, if for some strange reason the spell she'd worked last night hadn't been effective, she would have a backup reassurance that she'd never transform to vampire.

Not that she needed backup. Her spells were always effective.

She wandered over to the stove and peeked around Rook's arm to inspect his creation. Bright chopped vegetables glistened in the frying pan. Scents of lemon, pepper and rosemary teased her nose.

"Looks delicious. Mind if I snoop about while you create?"

"Go ahead. The bathroom is through the bedroom if you need it."

"Thanks."

As she strolled into the living room, her heels clicked on the parquet flooring. A vast ballroom-sized area, it was sparely furnished with only a massive turquoise velvet couch and a sleek glass coffee table that harbored a laptop and precise stacks of mail and books. Even the man's clutter was controlled.

Along the far wall stood various large artifacts that drew her interest. A marble sculpture of a nude woman stretched backward in an impossible bend intrigued Verity enough to glide her fingers along the cool white curve of her torso. The creation felt as cool as Rook's skin. Was he cold because of the demon within? Had to be. She studied the smooth stone. It had been carved especially for Rook. She knew it as she knew things about living, breathing people. It was that thing she had about knowing a person's place in this world.

Touching the small brass knobs on the unstained apothecary's cabinet next to the sculpture, she wondered at what might be inside the dozens of tiny drawers but respectfully did not pull any open.

Her heels clicked on the spotless wood floor as she crossed to the floor-to-ceiling windows that looked out over the Seine. Although the sun was setting, the gray sky was illuminated from all the unnatural light that burst forth from a city that never slept. Across the river, lights inside the four-and five-story buildings formed a pixilated artwork against the cityscape.

Verity performed a twirl right there because she felt light, despite the events of the previous evening. She didn't want to think about that darkness. Tonight she would enjoy spending time with a handsome man.

Her mother would turn over in her grave.

"Just in it for the adventure," she reminded herself,

knowing her staunchly warned heart would never allow
~~her to actually fall for a hunter. Any man, for that matter.~~
Because just when she began to let down her guard and
welcome in love, she had gained a stalker.

She walked on light feet to a door impressed with ro-
coco carved wood scrollwork. She decided it must lead
into Rook's bedroom. Glancing over a shoulder to ensure
he was still in the kitchen, she pushed open the door and
stepped inside.

A bedroom was a person's thumbprint of their person-
ality, and what an interesting study of the stoic knight.
This was his sanctum.

Grays and blues designed the room's color scheme, with
the parquet floor painted a soft gray, much like in her attic
bedroom. Calming and serene. Verity released her breath
and then inhaled the subtle blend of cinnamon and myrrh.
Exotic scents for an equally exotic man.

She decided suddenly that Rook was chocolate yuzu.
She had a tendency to assign macaron flavors to the people she knew. *Crisp and delightful on the outside, with a
surprising tang on the inside.*

Smiling at her assessment, she wandered inside the
room. Again, little furniture, as if to collect possessions
would somehow clutter the man's vita. She liked that. Some
who lived many centuries tended to collect hoards of material things. This home showed restraint. Control was
certainly Rook's mien.

A large turquoise velvet tufted ottoman—must be a
match to the couch—sat near the window. Next to that a
cloth yoga mat was spread out before an altar that featured
a stone Buddha with tumescent belly and a gleeful grin.

"Disciplined," she further assessed the man. "Yet also
open, and…" her eyes fell over the bed "…so sensual."

The middle of the room offered a peek beyond the

tight-fisted control. A king-size bed sat beneath a fall of turquoise fabric tied up to allow entry to the innermost sanctuary. It resembled a harem hotspot, a post where illicit and exquisite pleasures could be had.

Verity tapped her lips. Such fantasies she could entertain beneath that gossamer fabric.

Keeping to the wall that hugged the living room, she tiptoed over to the wardrobe. Drawing her fingers along the steel front, she decided the modern-styled piece felt out of place in the room. A hinged door was open a crack.

Chewing the corner of her lip, she vacillated between whether or not to peek inside. She hadn't done so out in the living room, but here, so far from the kitchen…?

She slid a finger between the crack in the wardrobe, and the heavy steel door glided toward her to reveal not clothes but—

Bloody Hecate, it's an armory.

Must be the weapons he used when engaged in hunting. Dozens of titanium stakes were lined along the back of the wardrobe. Pistols and a crossbow and an assortment of blades. She marveled over the throwing stars she'd only seen used in movies. Ninja stuff. Did he use all this in the fight against vampires?

Daring to draw her fingers along the cool column of one of the stakes, she took it and held it, finding it was much lighter than expected. A flashlight was twice as heavy. Careful with it, she knew that the actual stake part came out of one end with some kind of release mechanism—

"You take that snooping thing seriously, don't you?"

Startled, Verity squeezed the titanium column. The stake sprang out, jerking her arm back to hit Rook in the chest with her elbow. He wrangled her wrist and spun her around, an expert offensive move that he may have only practiced on vampires previously.

"Uh." She gasped and looked from the deadly stake, pointed toward his chest, to his smirk and those laughing blue eyes. "Sorry?"

"Be careful. That thing could take out an eye."

"Or a life," she whispered, releasing the weapon to him. He extracted it from her shaking fingers and set it inside the cabinet. "I'm sorry. It was open a little, and I—well, I did say I was going to snoop."

"You should be chastised for such daring." He looked at her over his shoulder. "And I'm of a mind to do that."

"But I was just…uh…" She sighed and lifted her chin, losing all powers to reason as she fell into the depths of his intimately delving stare.

The man answered her astonishment with a kiss that landed on her mouth as softly as a butterfly. But as their lips joined, the too-gentle pressure demanded they seek one another more forcefully. Pulling her body against his, he claimed her in that moment. His fingers moved along her hip and curled, forcing her closer. His other hand swept through her hair and clutched it aside her cheek. He tasted like the herbs he'd used to season the meal, which mingled with the wine lingering on her tongue. His mouth seared fire against hers, teasing her to match his urgency.

And she did.

Every part of Verity shimmered, seeking, grabbing, wanting this delicious connection to never stop. It was as though she had not been kissed for centuries, and finally, exquisitely, she was being fed the life she had never known she needed.

Rook's hand swept down her derriere and his fingers traced along the ruffles that hemmed her miniskirt, his fingertips every so often touching the bared skin between skirt and thigh-high stockings.

Verity pressed up higher onto the tips of her toes, clinging to his shirt collar to keep him at her mouth. She needed his breath. Their connection made her feel as powerful as she did when throwing fire. Combustible, that was the word for this embrace. And if she could, she'd melt right into his arms. May he lay her across his vast bed of untold exotic pleasures and continue his exploration with a million more kisses.

Suddenly the kitchen buzzer tinged, and he abruptly pulled away from her. Verity gasped, stepping on her tiptoes to maintain balance at the loss of such utter sensual strength. The kiss had completely discombobulated her in the best way possible.

He bracketed her face with his hands. "Dinner's ready."

Screw dinner. Another kiss, please?

Seeming to completely dismiss that he'd just kissed her silly, Rook closed the wardrobe doors, secured the latch, then strode out of the room.

Verity obediently followed him into the kitchen and sat when he pulled out a chair for her. Her body was still in the bedroom, crushed up against his powerful build. Her mouth was at his...

Licking her lips to savor the taste of his chastising kiss, she pressed a palm over her heart. So fast, it rushed toward something she hadn't thought to ever know. Excitement, adventure, romance. It all sounded deliciously decadent.

Yet he'd walked away from the kiss as if it had meant nothing more to him than, well, peeling away the rind from the lemon as he'd prepared the meal. Perhaps he was not as enamored of their embrace as she had been. Or maybe it had simply been as he'd stated: a punishment for her snooping.

If so, then what other kinds of mischief could she get into that required such admonishment?

Play it cool, Verity. It hasn't been that long since you've been kissed. Why the silly swoon this time? He's just another man. Take it slow or you'll end up in another wacky relationship with a stalker.

But Rook wasn't any other man. They had met for a reason, and she wanted to learn why.

When he offered white wine, she held up her goblet. Its scent was ridiculously strong, and she picked it out, even over the herbs and cooking aromas. "Raspberries?" she guessed.

"Very good. A friend of mine owns a vineyard in the south of France. They plant raspberries and peaches within the vines."

After a sip, she said, "It's delicious."

"You may claim an epicurean mastery of Paris's macarons, but I challenge anyone to match me at wine."

"I bow to your sommelier skills. But is wine the way to your heart?"

"No."

"Then what is?"

"You have your unreadable secrets. I have mine."

He set a plate of quinoa and vegetables before her. Verity closed her eyes, drawing in the crazy-good scents, until Rook touched her shoulder to sweep her hair back.

Meeting his gaze, they shared a smile that said everything she had wanted that kiss to mean to him.

"This meal won't be anything to talk of after that kiss," he said.

So he had been affected by it.

Smiling to herself, she forked in a bite. True, his kiss had been delicious, but the food was nothing to sneeze at. "I've only known you a few hours and already you're spoiling me. If you keep feeding me like this, I may never leave."

"Is that a promise?" He winked and poured a goblet of wine for himself.

* * *

While Rook loaded the dishwasher, Verity wandered into the living room. She didn't feel compelled to help. Domesticity was not tops on her list. Admittedly, she spoiled herself with maid and catering services. She could afford it. An immortal witch with a mind to living many centuries compiled a nice portfolio over the years, and a cache of seventeenth-century gold given to her by a former lover who had taken infatuation to new levels was something she would appreciate for centuries to come.

The sudden awareness that Rook was behind her made her bow her head and smile. He was so quiet. Stealthy, like a hunter. But a sexy, cool stealth that disturbed her need to remain cautious around him. She was normally not so quick to jump into a man's arms, let alone allow him to kiss her, but with Rook all her personal boundary rules seemed ridiculous.

Trust? Certainly not. But trust had nothing to do with lust.

He wanted to touch her? Bring it on. And don't stop, pretty please.

He raked his fingers up through her hair, clutching a good portion of it, and tugged her head and shoulders back until she bent at the waist. Looking down at her and holding her firmly before him, he traced a finger down her neck and the vee décolletage of her T-shirt, leisurely skimming the mounds of her cleavage. To be held like this—controlled—excited her.

"Your skin is soft." With a twist of his hand, he righted her to stand straight. His fingers never left her cleavage, and they felt like a cool summer breeze against her warm skin. "Your skin is like the flame you seem to have mastered. I've known witches over the years, and most avoid fire."

"Because it can bring our death."

He nodded, his jaw tensing. Burning a witch at the stake, or in any other manner, was the worst and most assured way to end their life. Had he witnessed such a travesty? Verity got the impression he suddenly wasn't in the present moment, so she sought to lure him back.

With a teasing dip of her tongue out the corner of her mouth, she held up her palm, and with nothing more than a thought summoned a fireball the size of a plum to hover above her fingers.

Rook's eyes alighted with the flame's reflection, and his smile grew. "Marvelous. And so controlled. May I?" He opened his palm as if he wanted to hold it. "Can I?"

"If I allow it, you should be able to hold it a few seconds without getting burned."

She tilted her palm, and the ball of ensorcelled flame rolled onto his hand without touching skin, only skimming above it. Her magic kept it from settling onto his palm, and she had to concentrate to make it stay there. He didn't flinch at the heat, and she gave him credit for that. Perhaps his cooler skin also made it possible to hold it as long as he was.

Lifting his hand before his eyes, with his other fingers he touched the top of the ball. "Incredible." The flames licked at his fingertips and he hissed, retracting and shaking out his palm and dropping the fireball.

Verity bent to sweep a hand through the flame, extinguishing it before it hit the wood floor.

"Sorry." He studied his fingertips. "I'll leave the fire magic to you."

"You had to try it," she said, taking his hand to inspect the damage. "I sense you are a man who likes to control whatever you can. You exude power."

"Is anything wrong with that?"

"Not at all. So long as you don't corrupt that power with

greed or malevolence." She kissed his fingertips, which were warm but had not touched the flame long enough to receive more than a red blush to the skin. "You want to play with something dangerous that'll warm your hands?"

She stepped back, teasing her fingers along the neckline of her shirt. A dip of her head, and she looked up through her lashes at him. The hunger in Rook's eyes brightened. He followed her as she backed across the room, nearing the Buddha statue. Only when the windowsill behind her stopped her progress did he smirk. Triumph. She was now trapped by the hunter, unless she dodged to the side.

Verity planted her feet. She preferred the capture.

Rook did not disappoint.

He swept a palm along her thigh and hooked her leg with a hand, coaxing it up along his hip. Pressing her back against the window frame, he placed a hand over her head as he leaned in and captured her mouth with another of his devastating kisses.

Verity tugged him closer with the leg she had wrapped behind his hip, and he nudged his erection against her Hard and ready. Goddess, but she could unzip him and take him in hand if she could get beyond the fact that this was happening so quickly. They'd shared a drink at a café and then supper, and now…

The devouring. Which she didn't mind at all if she didn't think about all the reasons to mind it. Reasons that included the fact that she knew nothing about this man and generally she was a bit more prudent when it came to intimacy.

His kisses tickled along her jaw and up her cheek, where he nuzzled into her hair and his breath hushed across her ear. The touch sent shivers up and down her skin. Verity coiled against him, wanting to pull him into her and become one with his powerful distraction of masculinity.

"You were right," he said at her ear. "You are as hot as the flame but infinitely more interesting to play with."

He slid a hand over her chest and she gasped, tilting back her shoulder to fit her breast against his palm. A squeeze of her nipple stirred up a moan, and in response he bent and mouthed her roughly through the fabric.

"Rook," she gasped. "This is…"

"Fast?" he guessed, nudging his nose along the neckline of her shirt. A finger dragged the stretchy fabric aside. A dash of his tongue traced the rise of her breast. So sensitive there. "You want me to stop?"

"Uh…" Did she?

Hell no, and blessed be, yes.

She grasped behind her, and her fingers landed on the carved woodwork coasting a windowsill. Leaning away from him only thrust up her breasts and offered him more of what he wanted.

Yes, this is too fast, her conscience finally blurted at her. She and the hunter should take it slowly. Couldn't give him everything he wanted so quickly. Bad things happened when she gave in—like stalking.

Verity shoved at his chest.

Rook stepped back, putting up his palms. "Sorry."

"Don't be," she said quickly and offered him a sheepish smile. Swishing a curl of hair over her shoulder, she took a much-needed breath of air. "I didn't want to stop you, yet I needed you to. It is a bit fast. Not that anything is wrong with fast. I just think—"

"I got it." He dashed a hand across his lips and flicked a wink at her. "You're right. I tend to take things that I want when a little prolonged desire is best employed. We should savor this."

She nodded eagerly. "Savoring is good."

At the same time she wished she wasn't so prudent to

hold him off, and instead, could grab him by the shirt and pull him back for more.

"Any way I can convince you to go along with me to headquarters tomorrow to look at mug shots?"

"Still don't want to take sides."

"The victim chooses her own side. Very well. I won't push you to do anything that would make you uncomfortable."

Being labeled a victim did not sit well with her. She had merely been in the wrong place at the wrong time. Yet the idea of missing out on his coercive sensual skills made Verity drop her shoulders. Should she reconsider helping him? What if she refused to help unless he kissed her?

"Come. It's time we called it a night."

He tugged her hand into his and led her through the living room and into the kitchen, where he promptly helped her on with her sweater. Gathering her long hair into his hands, he pulled it from the sweater and let it fall across her shoulders. He nuzzled his face into her hair and wrapped a hand around and across her stomach from behind.

"You have gotten inside me, Verity."

"And yet you claim an inability to read me."

"Frustrating, but the mystery of you is as sweet as a vanilla macaron."

He'd guessed it right. She had always considered herself a vanilla macaron.

"Mmm…your hair. I want to lose myself in this." He bunched up her tresses against his face. "You'd better leave now before I decide to keep you here against your will."

Sounded rather adventurous, actually.

But Verity declined her lusty imagination. With a nod, she turned to give him a quick kiss. "Thanks for a lovely evening."

He stroked her neck over the vampire bite. "This should be gone by tomorrow, yes?"

"We witches take a little longer than most paranormals to heal. Give it a few more days."

"Sure. That'll give me an excuse to see you again. To make sure you're looking as good as new. *Bonsoir.*"

Closing the door behind her, she exhaled and shook her head. Damned vampire bite. Did it bother him? Surely, as a hunter, he wouldn't like to look at anything left behind by a vampire. She'd have to practice her cover-up skills with makeup before she next saw him.

Date number two couldn't arrive fast enough.

Rook caught his hands on the back of the kitchen chair and listened until he could no longer hear Verity's heels tapping away down the outer hall. They'd been so close to stripping away clothing. He certainly wouldn't have stopped it. When the hell had he been such an animal around a woman?

Besides always? He did have a tendency to take and then push them aside, never to see them again. Easier that way. When a man lived this long he couldn't dream to have real, lasting relationships. Such a connection would only result in heartbreak. He'd been there and done that enough times to have learned his lesson.

Verity had bewitched him; that was it. Because he couldn't imagine not touching or kissing her. He wanted to put his hands on her. Constantly.

Are you forgetting why you need her?

"No," he muttered to Oz.

She can help you find your soul. End of story.

"Why can't it be the beginning? I like her, Oz."

She will muddle everything if you do not treat this as a business arrangement.

Could be true. Oz was the wiser of the two of them. If Rook became further involved with Verity, his brain would certainly not be *en pointe* and he could not expect to have the focus required to hunt Slater *and* find the bald vamp who might have his soul.

It was all tied together in some way. Zmaj, Slater and the vampire who had stolen his soul from Verity.

Ah, but he hadn't felt this way about a woman in a long time. A little muddling was all right, wasn't it?

Rook, you are not thinking straight.

"No, I'm not," he whispered. And the smile that followed spread up to his eyes and into his heart.

Chapter 4

Verity slipped her feet into thigh-high black suede boots. A fitted blue sweater dress stopped above the boots. With winter, she'd have to switch to longer skirts, but she was holding out with the shorter, more flirty skirts as long as possible.

Strolling through the house, her thoughts admonished her silly need to take sides yesterday. Because really? By not helping Rook to identify the vampire who had attacked her, she was taking the side of the vampires.

What could it hurt to take a look at a few pictures? Especially if it meant seeing the handsome knight again.

"I'm not a victim," she said. "And I'll prove it by doing the right thing." She touched the cell phone sitting on the kitchen counter. "I should have gotten his number."

The doorbell rang, startling her from her thoughts. Dashing down the front hallway, she opened the door and, stepping out, walked right into Rook's arms. He slipped her into his embrace with an ease that didn't give her time to comprehend that he was also kissing her until her shoulders hit the door frame behind her. And the man's tongue slid across hers.

He certainly knew how to kiss. Forget "Hello, how do you do?" or even "*Bonjour, mademoiselle.*" She'd take this silent yet intimate greeting any day. His entire body fit up against hers, feeling the shape of her, speaking his command with the jut of his hip to hold hers against the doorframe.

Verity tucked the toe of her boot around one of his ankles, wanting to draw as much of him against her as possible. His tongue lashed hers. He tasted like espresso, the dark, bitter kind that she'd never dared try—until now. A sigh ended the surprise connection.

"Namaste," he said.

"Right back at you. To what do I owe this pleasure?"

"I thought I'd make one more attempt at coercing you to look at mug shots today."

"Oh, well—"

He put up an admonishing finger. "I have a bribe."

Verity lifted a brow. A bribe sounded promising. Far be it from her to confess she was just considering helping him.

From behind his back, the man produced a pretty sky-blue box embossed with white lettering.

"Ladurée," she whispered with glee.

She recognized the signature Bonaparte box; it was filled with eighteen macarons. It was a treat she never indulged in because so many at a time felt too decadent. She dashed her tongue across her lips and reached for the box.

Rook pulled it away. "It's yours if you accompany me to headquarters and look over some mug shots."

Wasn't he a sneak using macarons to coerce her? If she told him she'd had a change of heart, surely she'd spoil his perceived success and the prize would be reneged.

She nodded. "Agreed."

He lifted a brow. Had she agreed too quickly?

"Uh, well, you know, I suppose it couldn't hurt to take a look at a few photos. But I'd be doing it against my original convictions."

"Of course, your convictions can remain strong. Let ~~it be recorded that I coerced you and you fought might-~~ ily to the end."

Smiling, he stepped back onto the walk, paralleled by flowers and vines and, box held out as a lure, began to step backward. He crooked a finger in beckon.

Verity closed and locked the front door behind her. Following the bait, she took delight in Rook's little-boy grin. He thought he was being so clever. Far be it from her to reveal otherwise.

Once through the purple iron gate, she saw the car parked in front of her property and her attention diverted from sweets to something even sweeter. Oh baby. The sports car's curves were obscene. The paint color resembled the inside of a crushed pomegranate. Verity actually wanted to lick a vehicle. She'd bet the interior was soft, creamy leather that a person could absolutely melt into.

The knight had expensive tastes that she could appreciate. And just because she could take care of herself didn't mean she couldn't get behind a man with money.

Forget behind. She preferred a man to stand alongside her or even allow her the lead on occasion. Date number two?

Wait, no. Today wasn't a date. This was work. Which meant she still had two dates remaining on the three-date rule.

"What do you call this sexy contraption?" she wondered as he held the car door for her to get inside.

"It's an Alfa Disco. A little out there in style, but I love the curves. You like?"

Her eyes darted from the interior of the car to the little blue box he held.

"Oh yes." She liked everything about this man.

She slid onto the passenger seat and he shut the door,

taking the box of macarons with him and placing it on his lap as he got in and revved the engine. A pulse of his jaw momentarily switched the playful man over to focus. Certainly he had a dark side that he seemed to guard as precisely as he ordered his home. The heart was a home, after all.

"Want a sip? If I had two cup holders, I'd have picked you up a cup." He handed her a paper coffee cup and shifted into gear.

The espresso was dark and commanding, much like Rook. Verity sipped the bitter brew while the crushed-fruit Alfa Disco glided through the city as if on air.

Settled into the leather seat that was as soft and buttery as she'd guessed, she observed her dashing host from the side. So intriguing, that tuft of gray hair above his ear. Immortals tended to age slowly. How long had he lived?

A furrow in his brow made her wonder if he concentrated too intently when driving. Cool, calm, yet ultra-aware. A hunter to the core. She wanted to reach over and trace the triangle of stubble that underlined his mouth, but instead she curled her fingers into her palm.

"What?" he suddenly asked after they'd driven ten minutes. He turned, navigating the car into an ill-lit underground lot. "You've been staring at me since we left your place. Do I have my shirt on inside-out?"

No, but if he had, then he'd have an excuse to remove it and give her a look at what she felt sure were sexy abs. The shirt in question stretched snugly across his pecs and about his biceps.

"Is this normal business practice for the Order of the Stake?" she wondered as he stopped the car and dashed around the front to open her door.

She stepped out. "Inviting witches into headquarters?" she reiterated. "It feels sneaky to me."

"We're not being sneaky. Just clandestine."

"Mmm, clandestine appeals."

"Everything about you appeals, Verity." He nudged her hair with his nose as he tucked a kiss behind her ear. Stepping back and pressing his palms together as if to remind himself to keep his distance at work, he then said, "It is rare an outsider is invited into the inner sanctum, so to speak. So forget everything you see inside, will you?"

"Or you'll have to kill me?" she joked, handing him the espresso as he led her toward an elevator.

"I don't kill witches."

She wanted to trust that statement but could never get beyond the distinct scent of burning flesh reminiscent of her mother's death.

"But you've killed female vampires?" She followed him into the elevator.

He tilted his head at her, his eyes seeking but probably not seeing what he wanted to see. He couldn't read her? Good.

"On occasion I've had to stake a woman," he finally said. "It's never easy. But my job, first and foremost, is to protect humans, and I do it no matter the costs."

She nodded. The man was a killer, and she didn't want to get on his bad side. But only a vampire could do that. She hoped.

The elevator doors slid open to a limestone-walled hallway. It appeared as though it had been carved from the stone beneath the city, much like the hundreds of miles of labyrinths that coiled under Paris.

"Cozy," she commented, following Rook's sure strides past a few steel doors that looked out of place nestled within the stone walls. The air was humid, the light thin. "What's above?"

"Don't ask me to reveal the exact location of this place,"

he said over a shoulder. "I probably should have blind-folded you."

"You had me at clandestine escapades, but I'll swing for the blindfold, too."

She walked right into his embrace. The man slid his mouth along her jaw, and at her ear he whispered, "That can be arranged. But not here."

"Of course, not at your place of business. Don't worry. You can trust me to keep a closed mouth about this visit," she said.

She tapped the blue box, and the knight swung out of the embrace and into a stride. Verity picked up her steps to keep his pace. And to keep the box in eyesight.

Excitement scurried through her system. She had been invited into the inner sanctum! There was something cool about that. A bit like playacting the spies she'd seen in movies. Too bad the man didn't keep a blindfold in his desk drawer. A little kink never hurt anyone.

Rook arrived at a door. "Ready?"

So much unsaid in that word. An invitation to much more than was exposed on the surface of the sultry look he cast her.

"Always." And that was a yes to both helping him and the lascivious deeds his eyes promised. "Anything I see while I'm here will go to the grave with me. Promise."

He spread his hand before her chest, as if to touch, then did not. Must have remembered he couldn't read her. "I believe you. My office."

He opened the door and gestured her inside. Expecting hi-tech cyber décor with blinking lights and secret pass-keys, Verity let out a sigh of disappointment as she entered the room. It was plain and spare, much like his home, with only a marble-topped desk and a few ancient weapons hung on the limestone walls. Not a retinal-eye-reading device in sight, nor a green laser security beam threatening to cut her off at the knees should she make the wrong step.

"Collected over the years?" she asked and tapped the cold iron spike protruding from a mace. The tip of it was blunted, no doubt from repeatedly connecting to stone or perhaps skull.

"Yes, and used in battle more than a few times."

She imagined Rook swinging the mace at a vampire's head, and then—no, she didn't want to consider the gory details. Besides, beheading a vampire wasn't always the trick to ending its life. The heart had to burst to guarantee sure death.

Rubbing her palms over her sweater skirt, at Rook's direction she took a seat in the office chair, while he stood beside her and booted up the computer. Tilting her head closer to his chest, she picked up his tobacco and peaches scent. Wonder if she could lick that delicious scent off his skin? She would certainly like to try. And she'd start… there, just under his jaw where it formed a square corner of his face.

"Verity?"

Had he said something to her while she'd been imagining dancing her tongue over his body?

"It's yours." He placed the box on the desk next to the mouse pad. "Thank you." He winked.

"Always willing to help. Uh, for macarons, of course."

"Of course. You'll find we have a few photos. Some vamps photograph well enough, but many do not, so there are sketches mixed in with the photos. Click the right arrow to scan through them. Let me know if you find a face you recognize. Are you cool with this?"

"Oh, yes." She sat up to the desk and palmed the mouse. "I like a good adventure."

"Then I'm going to leave you a few minutes to check on operations. I'll be back with more espresso, yes?"

"Sure. Cream, too, please!" she called, still tasting the bitterness at the back of her throat.

As soon as he had left the office, she lifted the top of the box. Inside nestled colorful jewels that smelled like heaven. If a witch were to believe in heaven, Verity felt sure her ethereal diet would consist entirely of macarons (and the occasional cup of hot chocolate from Angelina). She strolled her fingers over the soft yet crisp pastries and landed on a deep golden jewel that she then drew out and bit into.

"Mmm, chocolate yuzu. I love that sneaky knight."

She smirked at how easily it had been for the man to win her over. So he'd won this round. She wasn't at all ashamed of the loss. And really, it wasn't an official loss considering she'd decided to help him before the bribe had been revealed.

Focusing on the faces before her, she clicked rapidly through the first half a dozen or so because they all had hair, but then she stopped herself.

"He could have shaved his head recently. Better look at them all," she cautioned.

Again, her gaze swerved to the macaron box. Such a distraction would prove this a most challenging task.

Smiling to himself at the forethought to purchase the macarons, Rook strode through the locker room and checked in the gym to see if any knights were using the facilities. Most days the headquarters was quiet, and without any current trainees, he usually had the place to himself.

"Kasper," he said to the man who sat on the weight bench. Clad in sweatpants, his formidable biceps shone with sweat. "How'd it go with the Magic Dust situation?"

Recently vampires had discovered a new drug. Although faery dust was a vamp's favorite drug, the past few months Paris had been hit with a much crueler version of the stuff that drove vamps insane. And to feed their cravings, they went in search of anything that sparkled. That had resulted in innocent humans getting their necks ripped out as the vampire clawed for the diamond necklace they wore. Even rhinestones had attracted them. Nasty stuff.

"We've seen the last of Magic Dust," the hunter said, standing and grabbing a T-shirt to pull on. "I can promise that."

"Excellent."

Kaspar Rothstein was one of Rook's best knights, and he had recently hooked up with a pretty little witch who made her home on the edge of FaeryTown. Kaz had been recruited into the Order when he was seventeen, the youngest knight to take vows. Tor had found him.

"I'd appreciate it if you'd take some time to update the database with the information you gleaned regarding the sidhe while on the investigation," Rook said. "You had a few close calls with the Sidhe Cortege, yes?"

Kaz rubbed a hand over a hip where Rook suspected one of those close calls had landed. "Oh yeah. But Zoë fixed it up for me. She's an amazing healer. You know, the Order should consider having a healer on staff."

It was a good idea, and Rook was surprised he'd not considered it over the centuries. Probably because he had a way of healing that was more appealing than being tended to by a physician or healer.

"I'll take that under consideration. I'm conducting a private investigation in my office. Keep your distance, will you?"

He left the knight nodding and probably wondering at that statement. Rook knew he had an abrupt manner, but it was a powerful tool for a trainer and for a man who had centuries of secrets to keep under wraps. He'd learned that less talk and more action was the optimal way to teach, learn and guide. Because he wasn't much for small talk, the method suited him well.

In the lounge where a full kitchen was kept stocked, he brewed fresh espresso, found some cream in the fridge, then wandered back to his office.

He found Verity gazing at a sketch on the screen. The box of macarons was open to reveal three missing treats. Good girl. Rook walked up behind her and recognized the face on the monitor.

"That's Johnny Santiago," he said. "It wasn't him."

"I know. He's too pretty to be the creep that bit me. Thanks," she said, taking the cup from him and sipping. He'd poured in a lot of cream after noticing her wince in the car. He liked his brew tough. "I've seen him before, though."

"Hanging with his glamour tribe, no doubt."

"Glamour tribe?"

"Bunch of young vamps who strut around the city like they own it. Call themselves the *Incroyables*. Shambling in their wake are human women who all want to give blood to the pretty vampires. Surprised they don't sparkle."

"You don't like him much, do you?"

Rook laughed at the ease with which he'd allowed his bias to show. "I think it's silly, actually. Johnny's a good kid. Sings in a rock band, too. I'm familiar with his father, Vaillant, and his mother—"

"Is Lyric! I work with her. That's why I recognize him. Huh. I had no idea he was so handsome. Looks a lot like his dad."

"You mentioned you work for the Demon Arts Troupe."

"Yes, I have a fire throwing act. Go figure, eh? Do you have anything against the troop?"

"Not a thing. It amazes me that they perform for the general public, and the humans never seem to catch on that they are watching actual paranormals. Risky."

"You speak of humans as if you are not one of them."

"I am human. Yet Oz makes me immortal."

"If you got your soul back, what would happen?"

He propped a thigh up on the desk and set his cup down next to hers. "After four centuries of entrapment inside me, Oz would be free."

"You want the demon to have that. I sense you two are… well, close is the obvious word, but more…"

"Friends. When you live with a demon inside you like I have long enough, it's bound to happen."

"And what about you? What will a soul mean to you?"

He shrugged. "I'll be the same as I ever was, just without Oz and without the ability to see others' truths."

"All except mine." Her eyes twinkled. She liked that he couldn't read her, and he would kill to know why he could not.

I have no idea.

Thanks, Oz. I'll figure it out.

"And you'd then be merely mortal," she said as her concentration flicked from sketch to sketch on the screen.

And he'd then be mortal.

Rook wasn't sure how he felt about that. He'd lived so long he couldn't imagine facing final death. Yet, every time he faced a vampire he stood before probable death— or a close facsimile of it. He could take a lot of damage, and he always seemed to survive. It was Oz's presence that made him something more than human, able to heal rapidly and impervious to most damage inflicted, be it by blade, bullet or bite.

Could he handle mortality?

You can.

And so he would.

"Other than Johnny Santiago, did you find any other familiar faces?"

"I…no."

Verity's shoulders slumped. Her gaze lingered on the Ladurée box.

Rook's eyes outlined the curves of her breasts beneath the low-cut dress. Despite his warning to her earlier to keep business, well, business, he decided he wasn't going to let her leave his company until he'd touched those utterly soft, alluring breasts. And kissed them, too.

"I'm sorry," she said. "I thought I got a good look at the creep, but now I'm not so sure. There *was* one face." She scrolled back a few pictures to a sketch Rook recognized as a drawing done by Lark, the Order's only female knight. Lark did detailed drawings; she was meticulous in all her actions. "He's similar, but I don't know. I think the eyes are wrong. They were narrower. More…shifty."

Rook noted the vamp was a known Zmaj tribe member. No name attached to the sketch, though. One step closer to Slater? The vamps he'd slain the other night had to have been Zmaj because the bloody handprint Verity's attacker had left on her cheek. He was still so far from learning where, exactly, they gathered.

"A possibility, though?" he asked.

She nodded.

"I'll check him out."

"Thanks. If you shaved his head, then maybe. I'm not sure. I'm sorry I couldn't have been more help. I need you to catch this guy."

He caught the desperation in her tone. "You need me to?"

"I uh…well, you know. Can't have a crazy vampire

running about Paris. Who knows who he'll go after next? Might be a human woman who doesn't have the ability to throw fire to scare off his buddies. I don't even want to think about it."

Yes, and he should be more focused on finding the vampire. Not compelled to lean closer to Verity because she smelled so good and because he wanted to figure out the exact shade of her hair. Aubergine or eggplant? Violet? No, not bright enough. It was like the deep folds within rumpled purple satin.

She smiled at him over the brim of the cup. "Now you're the one staring at me."

"Best view I've had in ages," he offered. "I wish I could look longer, but I do have some follow-up work to do now that you've given me a lead. I'll give you a ride home."

"That's okay. We're close to where I practice for the troupe. I'm going to walk to the gym. Got a show tonight, and I want to make sure the routine is perfect."

"Where are you performing?"

"In a theater near the Seine. It's a para show. No humans allowed. So that means we can pull out all the tricks and be real. I'd invite you, but you'll be out looking for the vampire."

"I will. Should I tell you to break a leg?"

"You can, but I'd prefer to stay in one piece and hope for some wicked fire instead."

"To wicked fire, then."

He leaned in and kissed her nose, and her lashes fluttered against his cheek. A sweep of his fingers along her collarbone, and he moved down to trace the tops of her breasts. That she thrust back her shoulders in reaction pleased him. Her body sought his touch.

"I'd keep you here longer, but I don't think the Order

would appreciate what I have in mind to do with you if you did stay."

"Sounds promising." She stood and hooked her purse over an arm. Again, her gaze strayed to the macarons.

Rook strolled his fingers over the curved rows of colored cookies and paused above the pink one. He glanced to Verity. Her face revealed neither want nor disgust. It was probably raspberry or cherry flavor. Too sweet. He tapped the edge of a pale green treat and took it out.

"Pistachio," she offered. "Good choice."

"Not for me." He held the macaron to her lips and she bit into it, closing her eyes as she did. Such pleasure she took in the taste—he wished he could know the same delight as her mouth tasted him. "But not your favorite?" he guessed.

"How did you know?"

"I assume you've eaten the favorites already."

"I could be saving them for last." She leaned in, and he fed her another bite. "I like pistachio, but I love chocolate and vanilla."

"The most common flavors. Interesting."

"Ladurée's chocolate and vanilla. Now if you had brought me macarons from Paul, you'd best be sure to bring lemon."

"I'll make a note of that."

He held up the last tiny bit of macaron and Verity tongued it, tipping it into her mouth. Her eyes held his as she chewed and swallowed. Then she dashed out her tongue to lick off the tiny crumbs from his thumb. He'd been hoping she'd taste him. The slide of her tongue along the side of his thumb electrified his nerve endings and made all things on him stand up at attention. Yes, all things.

She smiled and tucked her hair behind her ear. A quick kiss to his thumb, and she made show of placing the cover over the box and tugging at her skirt hem. "Should we make another date?"

"Let's play it by ear." He knew a woman would prefer a definite time and place, but if he were going to focus on the job, he didn't want to disappoint by breaking that date if he did find the vampire she'd pinned. "I know where you live. And now that I've gotten a taste of you…" He traced her lip with his thumb. "…you'll have a hard time keeping me away. You'll see me sooner than you expect."

"I like the sound of that." She touched him over his heart, as if she were him and was attempting to read his truth. A tilt of her head spilled that gorgeous hair over her shoulder.

"Can you read my place in this world?" he asked.

She frowned and nodded. "You're exactly where you should be, but not entirely all there. Must be the missing soul. You believe I'm wrong about you having a child, though, so who knows if I can read you correctly or not?"

"You can't be right all the time."

"I usually am. And that frustrates me. Still, I feel connected to you in a way that I've never noticed with anyone before. And that's not because I'm hot for you."

He took her hand and kissed it, holding it against his cheek to savor her natural warmth. "You are?"

"You're the sexiest hunter I've ever known. You've cooked for me. And your kisses make my toes curl. What's not to be hot for?"

"But the connection is different?"

"Yes. I'll figure it out. I always do. I'll see you sooner than I expect."

She was going to leave him with a quick kiss to his mouth, but Rook hooked an arm about her waist and changed her intentions with a long, deep joining that stirred every part of him alert and made him question exactly what he was getting himself into.

A connection to a woman who had once held his soul?

Interesting. If only he had been there to protect her from the vampire in the first place, he might have his soul right now. And then he could release Oz.

And become mortal.

He pressed harder into the kiss but only because he needed to stop thinking about the what-ifs and take it day by day. Today, he got to kiss and hold a beautiful witch.

It had been a long time since he'd done that.

Reaching behind him, he palmed the box and tucked it into her hand. "Thanks, Verity."

Chapter 5

Verity hung upside down, her knees bent over the bottom of a four-foot-diameter steel trapeze hoop. The stagehands had pulleyed her above the stage, which loomed thirty feet below. Seated in a half circle of tiered bleachers, the rapt audience watched her juggle fireballs. This was her final trick, and she'd practiced months to perfect it.

Most would claim it impossible to conjure fire from out of thin air. A combustible material and some sort of oxidizer exposed to a heat source were requirements to make fire, according to the scientists.

But within the realm of the unseen and the paranormal, fire could be coaxed from elementals. And Verity had built a trust with the fire elementals. She never used fire as a means to destroy or harm (unless she was forced to defend), so it was always on hand when she needed it.

Closing her eyes, she focused inward and clutched the fireballs gently as she slowly began to grow them. From each ball—about the size of a softball—she began to send out smaller golf-ball–sized flames. They fell slowly and as if tethered to the larger fireball and would not reach the stage until she wished them to.

A shift of her hips twisted her body in the air, and the steel circle began to slowly spin. She used her body weight to increase the speed as her hands fed out more fireballs. Spinning out below her, the fire formed a tornado of blaze down to the floor, where the flames landed in a steel circle designed to contain them and keep all the fire controlled.

On cue, the trapeze began to lower, and she shifted her hips to swing wider, around the blazing column. This was the hard part because should she skim the flames, they would burn her skin where she did not wear the protective cream. She covered as much of her skin as she could with a specially blended fire retardant she made herself, but there was always a risk she'd miss a spot.

Spinning above the flame tornado, she thrust out her arms, ceasing to release more fire but working to control the column, expanding it and narrowing it. Then, with a grand clap, the trapeze was dropped dramatically. She spun through the flames, dispersing them into the air where fire spittles fizzled to embers and then ashed out.

Flipping her body upright, she jumped onto the stage at the appropriate time that her head would have hit had she still been upside down. The audience cheered madly, and Verity took a bow.

Beneath an old-fashioned circus tent canopy he stood in the darkness on the planked walkway between two sets of bleachers set in a half circle in front of the Demon Arts Troupe stage.

Earlier, out on the hunt, Rook had taken a knight along to case the area for vamps from tribe Zmaj and had found nothing. Word couldn't have gotten out that the Order had a target on the tribe, so he'd call it a Sunday night lull. He'd left Aaron to check one final nest spot but didn't expect the new recruit to report any findings.

Passing the old theater, he recalled this was where Verity had said she performed, so he had purchased a ticket from the box office. The vampire selling the tickets had given him a once-over—before approaching the ticket booth Rook had folded his blade-lined coat over an arm—asked him what he was and had been satisfied with Rook's mumbled "demon."

He hated claiming that title. He wasn't demon. He was a human man with an extended life thanks to the demon who existed within him. They were two separate entities. He even let Oz out once a month because otherwise the demon would go stir crazy. But only once a month because it took a lot out of Rook to go through the transfer and release of Asatrú. Though separate, they were always connected. And until Rook reclaimed his soul, Oz would always be tethered to him, even on the night of the full moon.

He'd arrived as Verity took the stage. Flames danced at her fingertips, and she performed gymnastics in a skimpy leather costume enmeshed with chainmail. Her hair was braided and up, he figured, to keep it from catching fire. Up and down her arms and legs coiled gold jewelry to draw the eye and catch glints from the flames. The glow of fire across her skin undulated over belly, breasts and shoulders. He'd never thought he could find a woman surrounded by flame sexy.

And then he began to think about it a little too much. Flames whipping deviously around a beautiful woman. *A woman he cared for.*

Rook clutched a hand over his heart and winced. Fire and witches? What was she doing? Did she not fear death?

Stumbling backward, his shoulders hit the bleacher wall. He slammed back his head and closed his eyes, struggling against the bleak memory. Images of a brutal fire enveloping Marianne exploded into his skull. He could feel the heat of the flame singe his skin. And her screams, oh, those wretched screams that no living being could make unless under extreme torture.

Memories he'd buried deeply roiled to the surface. He didn't want them to push through, to be bared to the world. Fire had destroyed the one thing that had meant the most to him. She had been reduced to ash.

And then he had unburied those ashes and had naïvely requested further torture, until finally he'd had to erase from the earth the abomination he had created.

But never from his heart. He'd closeted her away so deeply and kept her memory shadowed. He'd been good with that for more than four centuries.

Why now did the awful memories have to resurface when he was beginning to find an interest in someone new?

It is the fire.

Indeed. It had tortured Marianne mercilessly.

Fire makes Verity strong. That is the difference.

Truly? Rook twisted his head to watch as Verity was raised high above the stage while she dangled from a steel trapeze. Flames tornadoed out from her fingers in a fiery column below.

"She frightens me, Oz," he muttered.

That is a first. One should always face that which they fear.

"I can't. I…do not like this. So much fire."

The small flame ball she'd shown him the other day had been easy enough to watch. To be curious about. It hadn't roared and whipped at her clothing or eaten away her skin and hair.

The audience clapped uproariously for Verity's performance. The clatter chased away the vicious memories, yet left Rook panting for breath. He shouldn't have come here. She had told him she performed with fire. Fool. He should have <u>known what to expect.</u>

Turning to leave, Rook passed by a man struggling against chains as he was led toward the stage Verity had exited. He sensed the chained one was human and the man leading him was vampire.

From the stage, a rousing announcement was made. "Are all the vamps sitting in the front row? Because it's going to get messy!"

The crowd again cheered, and Rook swallowed down his bile as he could only imagine the macabre display that would follow. This was no place for a vampire hunter.

Verity shared her backstage dressing room with Lyric Santiago, a vampiress, along with two others who were currently onstage assisting Valentin. The vampire's act was bloody, but it was popular with their paranormal audience. The human prop wasn't killed, though he was brought close to death. Some of the troupes' acts were very dark, and others mingled blatant eroticism with the macabre. Verity preferred to keep her act lighter.

Lyric—tall, blonde and gorgeous—was removing the heavy makeup they wore under the lights. The vampiress couldn't see her reflection, so it was all done by skill and experience.

Verity didn't wear a lot of makeup. The fire usually melted it, causing it to drip down her neck, mix with the flame retardant and make a sticky mess. She took a baby wipe to her arms and exposed skin to remove the majority of the sweet-smelling cream.

"Great performance," Lyric said as Verity removed the decorative metal stomacher designed more to protect her from the flame than to suck in her gut or look pretty. "The crowd was hooting."

Yes, and she'd been compelled to scan the crowd as she'd stood to take her final bow. She'd seen him, even standing in the darkness. It was as though her soul could see no one but him.

The vampiress was trying to work the zipper down her back.

Going in for the save, Verity unzipped her friend. Then she started to unbraid her hair, pulling it out and over her shoulders. "Tonight I saw someone in the audience I know."

"A man?" Lyric asked gleefully.

"Yes."

"A lover?" Lyric coaxed.

"Not yet."

"Do tell. The last time you had some delicious gossip was when you were dating that creep Slater. On second thought, it wasn't so delicious after he turned on you. What kind of macaron did you call him?"

"Pierre Hermé's tea matcha and sesame noir. Ugh."

Both women shuddered. Verity had described the flavor to Lyric as an evil surprise. She'd expected sweet, and upon the first bite she had gotten savory and just plain awful. Not what she wanted from a macaron. Or a vampire, for that matter.

"This new guy is not a vampire. Though you know I would never rule one out in the future."

"Every breed has their assholes," Lyric said. She pulled on a soft red jersey dress and looked about for her Louboutins. "Is the *not yet* because you've just met the guy or because you're not sure about him?"

"Both, I think. I can't wait to have sex with him. He is a fine specimen, Lyric. He's a—"

"Sweetie!" A dark-haired vampire slipped inside the dressing room and pulled Lyric into a kiss.

Verity admired the couple who had been together near-ing three decades. They still acted as if they were on their first date every time she saw them. Strapped across Vail's chest hung a baby in a carrier, Lyric's second child, a sweet little girl named Summer. Vail took that baby everywhere; he insisted on watching her when Lyric was working.

"Hey, Veritas," Vaillant offered. He slipped a hand into hers, beringed fingers flashing as he brought her hand to his lips to kiss. "How are the hexes?"

He would never understand that she did not work hexes. Only dark witches did that.

The baby strapped across the vampire's chest giggled and gave Verity bright eyes from beneath the pink knit skullcap. Vail slipped close to kiss Verity's cheek, then paused and sniffed near her neck. "What's that? You've been bitten?"

Lyric flashed her a look that screamed, *You didn't tell me.* "I thought you were over vamps for a while? Was it this new guy?"

"No, he's not a vamp."

Verity rubbed her palm along her neck. She shouldn't be surprised that another vampire could detect the bite, even though the wound was now but two small red marks that she had used a bit of pancake to conceal.

"It wasn't my choice," she offered.

"What?" Lyric grabbed her hands and peered into her eyes. "Some vamp bit you without your permission? Are you okay? Verity?"

"I'm fine. I...yes, fine." Was she? Why did she suddenly feel shaky and not in her right place? It was all cool. The spell had worked, and life went on.

Right?

"The vampire sealed the wound, yes?" Vail asked over his wife's shoulder. Summer cooed and kicked her pudgy legs.

Verity shrugged.

"Oh fuck." Vail punched the wall. "Who was it? I'll rip the bastard's head off!"

"Vail, chill," Lyric said. "And watch the language around Summer." She hadn't let go of Verity's hand, which now trembled. "Sweetie, he didn't seal the wound?"

"I was attacked. And a hunter scared him off, so no, I don't believe the wound was sealed."

"I can't believe I'm going to say this," Vail said, "but thank the human's God for the hunter."

Lyric rubbed Verity's hand between hers. "Did you perform a spell to counteract the vampire taint?"

"I did." Verity sighed. She hadn't wanted to get into this with her friends and didn't want them upset. "It's fine. My spells never fail."

"You may be sure of your track record, but that shake in your voice tells me you're scared, sweetie."

"Me? No."

They'd just caught her off guard. As the bite marks faded, she hadn't given it much thought or felt the same worried urgency as the vampire couple did.

"Really?" Vail ducked his head to meet her eyes.

Okay, maybe not. Until now she hadn't considered— okay, so she had considered her options, but only because it was the smart thing to do.

"Guys, you know me. I do have a backup plan. I have someone helping me to find the vampire. I'm sure he'll get him before the full moon, so if the spell didn't work, then he'll stake the bastard and be done with it."

"Who's helping you?" Vail asked.

"The hunter who chased the vampire off."

"You're hanging with hunters now?" Vail paced behind them, his disgust over hearing she'd befriended a hunter more obvious than his concern that she'd been bitten. "Then why the hell didn't he stake the asshole *before* he bit you, huh? You wouldn't have this problem if the guy had been a little faster—"

"Vail, leave," Lyric said firmly. "Verity doesn't need you going all six-guns right now. And I'm sure Summer needs to get some sleep."

Leave it to Lyric to know exactly how to handle her cocky husband.

But as Vail opened the dressing room door, he stepped aside to allow another man entrance.

"Rook." Verity stood, a smile unstoppable. She hadn't expected he'd come backstage, but then again, why not? "I thought you had…" She exchanged eye contact with her vampire cohorts. "…business."

Vail crossed his arms over the baby and tilted his head, eyeing the new man. Did they know one another? Earlier, Rook had recognized Johnny, Vail's son.

"Lyric and Vail, this is Rook. Rook, well, I assume you know them already."

"He does?" Vail prompted. When Rook held out his hand to shake, Vail kept his arms firmly crossed. "Who are you? Wait. Are you the hunter who is supposed to be protecting our Verity?"

"Protecting?" Rook looked to Verity.

"I didn't tell them you were protecting me," she said. "Exactly. He's looking for the vampire who bit me, and that's enough talk of that. Really, I don't want to get into this. You're making it sound much more dire than it really is. Vail, could you leave? And, Rook, could you wait outside while I change?"

"Of course." With a wrinkle of concern to his brow, he stepped aside to allow the vampire to exit first. "Vaillant. You're friends with one of our knights, Kasper Rothstein, right?"

"Depends on how you define friends. Let's talk, man." Vail strolled out.

Rook gave Verity a wondering glance and then a wink before he closed the door behind him.

"Mercy, he is handsome." Lyric fanned herself with a hand before her face. "Oh, I'm sorry, sweetie. I don't mean to discount what's happened to you—but, damn."

"He is incredible."

"He was surprised about the mention of protecting you. Does he *know* you need him to help you?"

"Not exactly. Like I said, I know the spell worked. When has my magic ever failed me?"

Lyric shrugged.

"Rook is my backup plan. I'm helping him to track the vampire because he thinks it will lead him to tribe Zmaj, who are on the Order's hit list. Oh!" Verity put a hand to her mouth. "I wasn't supposed to tell anyone that."

"Don't worry. I have no love for half the tribes in Paris. What the hunters do is their own business. So long as they stay away from my family." She tilted Verity's head against her shoulder. "I thought your mother had ensured you were all about avoiding hunters."

"She did, and I am. But you know I always like to give a man a chance."

"Until you dump him like a rotting corpse after two dates."

"Usually they get three."

"Maybe you should have Vail go after the vamp for you. The hunter is handsome, but good looks do not equal trust."

"I don't have to trust him. I just need him to trust me while we work together to find his soul."

"His—what?"

Verity clasped her fingers at her throat, missing the solace of the warm wooden heart. "Remember the soul in the heart I told you about?"

"Right, you dug it out of a tree back when the women wore those frumpy long skirts and billowy shirtsleeves. It belongs to the hunter?"

Verity nodded. "We think so. But it was stolen by the vampire who bit me. Lyric, I know Rook and I have been brought together by forces greater than we can imagine. And the soul has been close to my heart all these years. I feel as if I know it. Which is how I felt when I first met Rook. As if we have known one another or, at the least, belong together."

"Wow. This coming from the three-date maximum chick?"

Verity could only shrug. How to answer that one?

"He is cute," Lyric offered, "but be careful. Take your time, sweetie."

"I plan to. But you know, my grandmother Freesia once told me that I shouldn't stop trusting all men. That I should recognize when the right man to trust comes along. Lyric, I think he's come into my life."

The vampiress hugged her and rubbed her back. "I certainly hope so. But to be safe, you keep my phone number with you at all times. If the hunter turns on you, I'll sic Vail on him."

Vail strolled in front of Rook as they waited on the back loading dock for the women. The baby strapped to the vampire's chest slept peacefully, head bowed and hands tucked beneath her pudgy chin. Her father was in classic vampire black from coal-dark hair to the black suede boots studded with silver. Silver rings glinted on his fingers as he swung his arms casually.

"So," Vail said, "you and Verity have a thing going on?"

"A thing?"

"Yeah. A thing. You getting all up in her business?"

The vamp had an uncouth manner about him, but Rook knew from Kaz's reports he was not to be feared and was a trusted informant to the Order. Still, that didn't mean he had to bump fists or sing "Kumbaya" with the longtooth.

"We've known each other a few days. I like her. She likes me. That's all you're going to get."

"Fair enough." Vail cradled the infant possessively, likely unaware how unthreatening a vampire with a pink-clothed toddler strapped to his chest appeared. "You going after the vamp who bit her?"

"That is my intention. But it's not because Verity is worried about transforming. She performed a spell to counteract the bite. She's fine. I just don't like it when vamps pick on pretty witches."

Vail nodded, looking down his nose at him. Trying to decide whether or not to like him. Rook preferred he did not. He had enough longtooth friends. One, to be exact. He needn't any more.

"Verity is my wife's friend. If anyone hurts her…"

"I get it," Rook said. "We won't be coming to arms over the witch. I promise you that."

"Good. So who is this vamp you're looking for?"

"I don't have a name, only the tribe. Zmaj."

"Zmaj. Johnny was mixed up with that tribe a while back. They were an okay bunch."

"They've changed. Frederick Slater is now their leader."

Vail sneered, revealing fangs. "That bastard dated Verity a while ago."

Rook tilted his head. She'd dated a vampire? That was new to him. But he wouldn't show Vail his surprise.

"She's not anymore," Rook stated as a means to verify his guess.

"'Course not. The guy is an asshole. Tried to enslave her. Uh, she told you that, right?"

Rook nodded. This investigation just got a whole lot more personal.

Chapter 6

Verity found Rook waiting outside the backstage door. A smile glinted in his eyes when he saw her. From her stash of clothing she kept in her dressing room, she had slipped into a soft heather dress that ruffled above her knees and was cinched with a deeper purple velvet bow at the waist. Add to that the black suede thigh boots and a few moonstone bangles on her wrist, and she felt presentable. But it was chilly out this late, and she wished she'd brought along a sweater.

After Vail and Lyric strolled off with Summer, she asked, "Did you like the show?"

Rook pulled her into his arms and kissed her in the shadows against the limestone wall. The chills she'd been feeling? Gone *like that* as his hands burnished across her skin, seeping his slight coolness against her until they alchemized warmth between the two of them.

She melted against his solid form as she stood on tiptoes to capture his intensity. The man never simply kissed her. He devoured her. He also left an indelible mark on her that she knew she might never erase. And for that she must be cautious.

Lyric had been right. Three times was her limit. But they hadn't fallen into bed yet, so she would extend this tête-à-tête as long as possible. And perhaps the definition of date should be altered too.

"Your performance was amazing," he said as he pulled back and brushed a thick hank of her hair over her shoulder. But his smile fled too quickly. "Witches and fire." He smirked, and she sensed he wasn't completely behind her act and was probably just saying nice things.

"You didn't like it."

"I did. It just…surprised me." His brow furrowed, and the scar tugged up the end of the brow. A sinister arch. "Lots of surprises tonight. You're quite the gymnast."

He was changing the topic, but she would grant him that because she sensed something was off with him. "Lyric taught me the gymnastics. Her act involves acrobatic silks. She literally flies on a couple strips of bright fabric. It's amazing."

"The two of you must be the beauty in a show that offers all sorts of dark and wicked things."

"You saw the act that followed mine?"

"I didn't hang around to watch, but I'm guessing I wouldn't like to hear what that was about."

"The human is not killed."

"Would it be a mercy if he was?"

Verity sighed. She didn't want to discuss the morality of an act that wasn't hers. Not taking sides was the wisest way to remain alive. Unless, of course, she'd been seduced by macarons.

"Sunday night shows are paranormals only," she said. "I'm surprised you were allowed admission."

"When asked at the ticket counter, I said I was demon. Though I don't like to make that claim. Ever."

"How does Oz feel about that?"

"He is in agreement. I am not him, and he is not me. Yet we are one another. If you can understand that. Let's walk."

He wrapped an arm about her shoulder and they walked, as if lovers. It thrilled Verity that he was so easy with her. And it wasn't in a covetous, ownership way as some men were wont to behave. Rook subtly claimed her, but he also allowed her the distance and independence she required. He wouldn't force her to do a thing, yet any opportunity to stand close to him she would take.

"Was Vail's baby wearing a bedazzled skull on its cap?" he asked as they strolled a cobbled street away from the river.

"Yes. That was Summer, their second child. Vail is proud of his children. They won't know if the baby is vamp until she reaches puberty."

"Don't all children of bloodborn vamps become vampire?"

"Not always. A rare few are completely lacking in blood hunger."

"Interesting. I had no idea. I'll have to…"

She squeezed his hand. "You're making notes in your head, aren't you, hunter?"

"So I am. I marvel after living so long that I can still learn new things. Let's detour through the Metro. I don't want you walking so far in those high heels."

Fine with her. The heels were high, and she appreciated that he'd noticed. Each slid their Metro cards through the turnstile, and they caught a train heading to her neighborhood. Only one stop. A quick ride. Rook secured a steel pole for the two of them. Verity had to stand close, chest to chest with him to avoid stepping back and stumbling up against the pregnant woman seated behind her.

The hunter's eyes were blue and speckled with dark, almost appearing freckled. He smiled at her intense curiosity, and she tapped his chin with a finger, tracing the stubble. Tilting up onto her tiptoes, she placed her mouth close to his, but instead of kissing him, she held his gaze.

The innate coolness of him simmered to an eager warmth, as if she rubbed flames against his body. His was an invisible fire that sought her skin with a brush of desire. To kiss him in front of everyone on the train would be too simple and blatant. And it would spoil the tease.

Dashing out her tongue across her lower lip, she then dipped her head and looked aside, unable to control the wide smile as she met an old man's eyes across the rows of faces. The man nodded to her and winked.

Rook's hand slid around her waist, and his thumb fit against her spine. Verity closed her eyes and tilted her head against his shoulder, sinking into his burnt peaches and tobacco scent and allowing the train to rock her gently against his hard chest.

As it had felt when she had spotted him from the stage, her soul sighed and relaxed.

She didn't know Rook well enough to judge whether or not he'd make a good boyfriend. Yet she did feel like a certain emptiness had crept into her heart over the past several decades. She desired a lover, a relationship, and yes, she could even see herself saying vows to another someday in the future. That was why she had allowed herself to stay with her previous lover so long. But she wasn't going to start shopping for a veil and party favors. This was a new and exciting adventure with a handsome, sensual man.

And it was difficult to erase her mother's voice from her brain. But she did have Freesia's suggestion to push her toward at least trying to allow the man into her circle of trust. She wanted to.

But did she need to?

Once off the train, they emerged beneath a streetlight amid a spill of passengers that flowed out to all directions of the compass under the velvet night sky. Verity tugged Rook along toward her home, a five-minute walk from the station. She felt light and not at all worried that the moon was waxing gibbous. Swinging his hand in hers and skipping down the street, she raced him toward something she'd never known—a blissful surrender.

Once inside the purple wrought iron gate, Rook swept Verity into his arms and twirled her on the cobbled walk. Her heels clipped some of the tall growing herbs, releasing rosemary and thyme into the air.

"Just felt like doing that," he said, setting her down on the steps. The surprise on his face was genuine. "Must be something in the air tonight."

Indeed, something like lust and romance and all that sparkly, frilly stuff that made Verity's insides giggle and stretch and then coil in anticipation.

"Maybe it's all the flowers." The knight in black duster coat looked around the front yard.

"It does smell gorgeous, doesn't it? Like an exotic elixir designed to intoxicate. But you look out of place."

He spread out his arms and his coat opened to reveal a flash of deadly stakes. "The coat does come off."

"That's a start," she said and turned as she skipped up the steps to hide her irrepressible grin.

She opened the door, pushed it inside and turned to find Rook, sans coat, swing in from the threshold and plant a kiss on the underside of her jaw. He nuzzled his nose along her skin, drawing it up and landing on her mouth with another kiss.

"Your performance was incredible," he said between kisses.

"You've never been to a Demon Arts performance before?"

"Not much time for shows of any sort. Usually busy with work."

"You're very disciplined."

"Something you can understand, yes?" He kissed her eyelid. "The work you do with fire is amazing. And yet…"

His sigh and sudden letdown of his body against hers prompted Verity to wonder what was wrong. "Rook?"

"Sorry. Some weird stuff came up watching your fire magic. Memories."

"You knew a fire witch before?"

"No, not like that. Uh, well, now that I've said it, you should know. I've witnessed a witch being burned at the stake. So to see a witch in the vicinity of fire doesn't sit well with me. Makes me nervous." He inhaled, then exhaled heavily. "And with that confession, let's move beyond the uncomfortable topic and taste each other again."

He had fallen into some bad memories and was desperately trying not to get lost in them. Verity could understand. She'd watched her mother burn at the stake. Now was no time to relive that horror. But she respected fire and the elementals who provided it to her, so she did not fear its harm.

She'd explain it to him some other time. The mood they'd conjured did not welcome such a heavy conversation.

Circling Rook in the open doorway, she pushed one of his shoulders against the foyer wall. Moonlight beamed across the parquet flooring and their legs while their upper bodies remained in shadow.

"I can make you think of better things," she said. "But it requires your cooperation." He lifted a curious brow. "Put your hands on me."

He clasped her hips and squeezed, pressing his fingers to urge her closer. Led forward by his expectant lifted brow, Verity stepped between his splayed legs. A full head taller than her, he shuffled down the wall to a bent-leg stance until their faces were level. She lashed her tongue across his lower lip. The man moaned appreciatively.

Burying her nose into his soft hair felt like the finest luxury. She could get lost in this man. "You smell like burnt peaches and tobacco smoke. Makes me hungry for you."

"You smell like—"

"Don't even try to guess. I still have traces of the flame retardant on my skin. It's homemade and completely natural. It's not too awful, is it?"

"It's spicy. Smells like cloves and…"

"Lemon thyme."

"I like it. Flame retardant, eh? Does that mean I'm safe from getting burned by you?"

"Do you want to be safe?"

His grin turned wicked. "Never."

He tilted her hips against his loins and trailed kisses from her mouth and downward. As she lifted her chin, he traveled down her throat with soft, tender touches and scintillating licks. Tenderly, he slayed her inhibitions. Sliding her leg up along his hip, she hugged his abdomen with hers, delighting in the rigid muscles that spoke of strength and discipline.

Pushing her fingers through his hair, she gripped it tightly and kissed him deeply. Getting lost in him was a perfect way to end the night. Bodies melding, tongue dancing, heartbeats drumming a wanting thunder. She needed this man. She needed the intimate connection.

Just once or twice. Or maybe even three times. And then, never again.

"Uh, Verity?"

"What?"

"A cat is watching us."

Without glancing toward the threshold, she pulled his head back down to make sure his kisses at the base of her neck did not stop. "That's just Thomas. You know where the food is, Thomas."

"Me-OW!"

"Was that a snarky meow?" Distracted, Rook leaned back and eyed the calico feline that traipsed down the hallway toward the kitchen.

"Thomas has an attitude." And she hated cats who interrupted intense make-out sessions.

"He yours?"

Seriously? He wanted to chat about the cat instead of kiss her? "That alley cat belongs to no one yet claims every female he encounters. He's a Casanova, but he'll never get more than a few kitty treats and food from me. Enough about the cat."

She kissed him, silencing further pointless questions.

Mouths touching and opening against one another, they dashed tongues in intimate swordplay. He plunged in deep, tasting her. Making her forget about snoopy cats. All that mattered was the two of them, crushed up against one another, giving and taking as much as they could offer.

And what he offered was dark and delicious. Mysteriously enticing. Verity didn't want to learn all his secrets—only the ones he wanted her to know. It was a fair trade for the secrets she was willing to share.

Of course, she didn't have any secrets. So there was that.

Ten minutes later, the cat strolled around Verity and Rook's entwined legs. He meowed again, following with a purring flutter of cat sounds.

Rook paused from their kiss and followed the feline's exit across the threshold, where the cat made a leap over his abandoned Order coat. "Now that was definitely cat laughter."

"I think you're right." She closed the door behind Thomas and buried herself in Rook's embrace. "You know any familiars in your line of work?"

"Cat's a familiar? Uh, no. I stick mostly to vampires."

"Speaking of vampires, did you and Vail have an interesting discussion?"

"Interesting is the exact word for it. He cares about you and made it clear he will protect you at any cost. You know…it's some kind of crazy that I found you," he said, stroking the hair from her face.

"What do you mean?" She wanted to kiss, not talk.

"I was stalking Frederick Slater that night we first met. Yet who would have thought I'd run into the one person on this planet who had my soul?"

"Slater?" She stepped back from the embrace, absently touching her kiss-plumped lips. "You were after Freddie Slater? I thought you were out hunting."

"You call him Freddie?" She saw the mental note-taking flash in his blue irises. "Do you know him, Verity?"

"I, uh…he's with Zmaj, right?"

"Yes, their leader. He's our most-wanted vamp right now. I mentioned the tribe to you. You didn't tie that in with Slater?"

"That is a strange coincidence."

Verity stepped back until her shoulders hit the wall opposite where Rook leaned. Her body slumped and she looked aside at the moonlight glinting in the glass on the front door.

That she could be so connected to this man through another was remarkable. And that so many coincidences had occurred was not haphazard—or coincidence. Nothing in life was coincidence. She believed that with all her heart. Everything happened for a reason. Like finding a man's buried soul. And getting bitten by a vampire who worked for the very vampire she had dumped months earlier.

"How do you know Slater, Verity?" He stood up from leaning against the wall, losing the sensual looseness that her body so desperately craved and assuming a stern demeanor. The hunter emerged, serious and ready for action. "Do you have information that could lead me to him? If so, it would be a hell of a lot easier than trying to track him through the nameless vamp who bit you."

"Slater, uh…we dated for a while. Not long. Well, longer than I usually allow…"

The man's brows dove together, and his jaw pulsed. He didn't like that statement. But she wasn't as offended by vampires as most hunters would be.

"Vail mentioned as much," he said.

"He—you already knew? So why this angle of questioning?"

"I wanted to see if you would admit to it."

Pissed that he would use such tactics on her, Verity slapped her arms across her chest. He was definitely all hunter now. And he had no right to the details from any of her former romances.

However, his investigation had become inexplicably entangled in her life. And she had no right to conceal information that could aid his work.

With a sigh, she confessed. "It didn't work out. I generally only date guys three times, though we did stretch it a bit further. I realized he was grooming me to steal my magic, so I broke it off with him. He's an asshole, though, and I expected retaliation. He stalked me for a few months, but I'd thought I'd lost him when I moved a few months ago."

"You had to *move* to get away from him?"

She winced and said softly, "Yes."

Rook fisted the wall beside her head. "That vampire is one of the most dangerous in the city right now. You should have told me you knew him!"

Setting back her shoulders, she lifted her chin. "My dating history is no concern to you."

"Verity." He huffed.

"I'm sorry!" Her confident posture softened. "I hadn't a clue it was important to you. I thought you were after the one who bit me."

"I told you I was investigating the whole tribe. Hell, Verity, do you think Slater sent those vamps after you?"

"I don't know. It's possible. But they weren't following me that night. I was walking home and turned a corner, and there they were."

"Doesn't mean they didn't plan it to go down that way. Damn it!" He shoved a hand over his head, rubbing at the back of his neck as he paced before her. "Did Slater ever bite you?"

"No! Never. Not that it's any of your business."

He smirked. Nodded once. "Just wanted to know if you were a fang junkie."

"A fang—how dare you?"

He put up a hand to stop an angry protest. Really? Talk to the hand?

Verity marched down the hallway, away from him. "Get out!"

"Verity, don't be angry. I—hell, I slipped into hunter mode. It's what I am more often than just a man or friend or even lover. I needed to know if you had been hurt by him—or bitten."

"Yes, well, I have been bitten, no thanks to you!" She turned on him, stopping him in his tracks only a few feet from her. "If you would have done your job the other night, this would have never happened!"

She slapped her neck but then realized the angry re-action was not like her. She did not rage at others for her own misfortunes. And she could handle this by herself, thank you very much. And she had. The spell to stop the vampire taint had worked. End of story.

"I think you should leave now," she said, trying to keep the anger from her voice but failing. "There's nothing more to say. I don't know where you can find Slater."

"You must know where he lives if you dated." He scratched his head. "Only three times?"

That tidbit had just flown out. She shouldn't have told him that.

"I'm not in the mood for an interrogation, Rook."

"Please, I...I'm sorry. You're right. This was supposed to be romance and kisses, and now..." He blew out a breath and again raked his fingers through his hair in frustration.

He was doing his job, Verity reminded herself. And if he didn't investigate all the angles, he'd never get his man or the tribe.

Hell, she didn't want him to leave. She wanted to re-sume the romance and kisses, and...was it too late to try for the sensual mood that had ignited sparks between them?

Maybe if she gave him something, anything, to appease the hunter, he could set work aside for the rest of the night.

"The last time I saw him, he lived on a barge," she offered.

"On the Seine?"

She nodded. "But he'd put it up for sale right after the breakup. I'm sure it's sold. You could check, though. Maybe trace the sale if he's no longer there. He lived south-west, past the sixteenth."

"Thank you. That could help my investigation."

He stroked her hair, which was wavy from the braids she'd taken out after the show. She wanted the intimacy right now. Yet she did not. She wasn't sure what she wanted. Trust? He'd muddled any burgeoning feelings of trust she'd felt toward him tonight.

"I'll go," he said, "but I don't want to leave you angry, Verity. Please. I'm sorry. I didn't mean to offend. I want to keep you safe."

"I am safe. I have wards against vampires on this home. Werewolves also. Perhaps I should put up a ward against demons?"

Rook heaved out a sigh. "Fine. I guess I was wrong about you. I should get back out there on the hunt. Wasted enough time already on…"

He didn't finish the sentence, but she filled in the last part herself. He'd wasted his time on her. Because he'd been wrong about her?

Turning away from him, Verity listened to his boots tromp the floor toward the door. It opened and closed. And she raced up the stairs to the bedroom where she grabbed her great-grandmother's quilt, wrapped it around her shoulders and pressed a palm to the window to watch the hunter's retreat into the night. The quilt hugged her, but she took no comfort in the memory of the women who had come before her tonight.

She was alone in this world. And she didn't want to be alone anymore.

The argument with Verity had served to clear his brain. What the hell had he been thinking to get involved with her when right now he needed to focus on tracking Slater and taking out the longtooth? There was no room for error, no time for extracurricular activities. An Order knight must give all to the cause.

Live to serve. Serve until death. Die fighting.

That was the vow he and all knights lived by. And he

took his vows seriously. It had been he and King who had penned those very words.

Rook had served the Order for four centuries. He could mark countless thousands of vampire kills to his stake. He'd witnessed evils no man should ever have to relive in his nightmares. Now was no time to go soft and start chasing some woman's frilly skirts because he was horny and she had a soft, kissable mouth. And even softer hair that he liked to tangle his fingers into.

Punching a fist into his opposite palm, Rook marched down the sidewalk toward the Metro station.

Three times was all she was willing to give a guy? How many times had he seen her now? Twice? The time in the café didn't really count. Maybe. Hell, had he used up all his chances already? So did that mean she didn't date?

Apparently she'd dated the vampire Frederick Slater. And the asshole must have warranted more than the standard three-date maximum.

The idea of Verity kissing a vampire put a bad taste in Rook's mouth. Though he shouldn't hold her past against her. He'd certainly had his share of questionable flings. A man can't always be particular when he's spent centuries on the prowl. Nor had he a bias to breed, save werewolves. He kept his distance from them, mainly because the males fiercely protected their females with claws that could slice a man in half.

It is not her familiarity with a vampire that troubles you. It is her fire.

"Shut up, Oz."

You need her to find your soul, and you know it. I will be damned if I am going to let you pout and stomp your boots because the woman had a life before she met you.

"You're pushing it, Oz."

And why is that?

"I can find my soul without Verity's help!"

Fine job you have done of it thus far. The witch can identify the vamp who stole your soul. You need her. Do not fuck it up.

Ignoring Oz's rant, Rook paused at the corner of a utility building and pressed his spine against the sharp brickwork. When was the full moon? He wanted to let the demon out to work off some of his steam. Less than a week, if he judged the shape of the waxing moon correctly.

Spinning the stake at his side, he sharpened his focus and stared down the street, seeing nothing yet feeling the city crush up around him. So much in Paris had changed over the centuries. The pace was faster, the air dimmer, the people more varied and the noise constant. Tourists wandered every nook, street and sidewalk. Yet very much, such as the buildings, the streets and the river, hell, even life and the ever-present hum of humanity, remained the same.

Much like him?

Oz was right. It wasn't the vampire ex-boyfriend who poked at his ire. Verity's performance with the fire had stirred up memories of Marianne. He had loved her like he had never loved another person. She had been his world.

And he had destroyed her.

Setting his jaw, Rook struggled to pull away from the memories that wanted to tear out his heart, a heart he'd only managed to bandage and hold together over the years because he did not have a soul to fill it with the emotion and compassion upon which most humans thrived. But had it ever completely healed?

Did he deserve another chance at such bold and blissful love?

Did he want it?

Why was he asking himself such questions? This *thing*

with Verity was a flirtation. A tango of lust and desire. And Oz was right. He needed her knowledge to do his job.

Hell. Truth? He wanted Verity. For reasons beyond what she could do for him and the Order. He wanted to sink his fingers into her long hair and pull it over his face, to lose himself in the violet darkness and find a place next to her body. To slip inside her mouth and indulge her taste, her heat, her whimpers of desire.

He simply wanted Verity Von Velde.

Slamming a fist against the brick, he pushed off from the wall and marched back in the direction from which he'd come.

Twenty minutes later, he knocked on Verity's door.

When the witch opened the door and her royal blue eyes flashed wide, Rook took her head in his hands and kissed her soundly. She didn't resist, but she didn't quite succumb as compliantly as he desired. In fact, she was the one to break the kiss.

"Really?" she asked, her tone still tight from their argument.

"Sorry," he said, "but I'm not leaving this anger hanging between us. Tonight we're going to learn things about one another we may not want to know. But damn it, we're both going to enjoy the ride."

And he tugged her hand and walked toward the stairs because he guessed her bedroom was up the stairway at the end of the hall.

Chapter 7

Verity knew exactly what the hunter had in mind as he strolled past her bed, then over to her spell area. He glanced across the table scattered with spell accoutrements but didn't linger in curiosity.

She was still angry with him. And she was not. He'd accused her of being a fang junkie. Sort of. Kind of? Okay, so he'd had to ask. Their argument had been stupid. He had no right to get upset over any man she had dated. Yet she could understand a hunter having trouble with her having dated a vampire.

So what next? Did he seriously think he could march into her house and toss her across the bed and ravage her?

Sounded…not awful.

She teased a strand of hair across her lips, eyeing the handsome man who paced before her spell table. He wore Order gear, from the sleek black leather coat with a bladed collar to the steel-toed boots. He was some kind of knight in black armor. And she wanted a peek beneath that armor. Hell, she wanted to see the man exposed, skin bared and muscles flexing.

"Why me?" she asked.

Rook tilted his head and smiled at her. It was a smoldering, knowing grin that delved beneath her clothing and tickled her skin. She warmed to his catty tease and straightened her shoulders, awaiting an answer.

"You want me to answer that?" he asked. "If I do, then you have to take off those boots."

She looked down over her thigh-highs. "You planning to do strip twenty questions?"

"Sounds like a good way to get to know each other better."

Oh, that sexy smirk! In her mind Verity was already peeling the zippers down her boots and kicking them off. But only if he reciprocated.

"Okay. But I don't think I'm wearing twenty things."

"We'll stop when you want to stop. Agreed?"

That sounded like an adventure she was willing to take. "Fair enough."

"The blanket doesn't count," he added.

She tossed the quilt to the bed and asked again, "So why me?"

Shoving his thumbs in his front pockets, Rook wandered toward her but stopped between the bed and where she stood at the top of the stairs. Moonlight beaming through the windows twinkled in the crystals that hung like raindrops frozen mid-fall above their heads. The pale light also glinted in his hair and eyes, a wicked challenge.

"I didn't choose you," he said. "Some kind of weird destiny brought us together. But I liked you the moment I laid my hand on you."

"Of course, you *were* copping a feel."

He raised an admonishing finger. "You're not allowed to protest the answer. I answered your question. Now, off with the boots."

"If this is going by the officially sanctioned strip twenty questions rules, then it's only one item at a time." Not that she was aware there *were* any official rules, but it sounded good to her.

Verity bent and unzipped her left boot and toed it off. She stood on her other boot, balancing on tiptoes with her stockinged foot. "There."

"Fair enough. My turn to ask the question."

"This is going to be good. Oh, but so you know, the official rules of the game also states that all weapons are counted as one item."

He mocked a shocked look, then swiped away the look with a rub of his hand. Behind his fake alarm a smile emerged. "If the lady insists."

"Just game rules. You understand."

"Of course. It's a good thing one of us is up on things like rules on intimate games. My question, then. Why would you date a vampire if you had no intention of letting him bite you?"

So he couldn't let that one go, eh? Verity considered calling the game to an end. But no. If he wanted to play dirty by going straight for the personal stuff, she could go there too.

"I was attracted to the man, not the fangs. He was—and is—a smart man. I like intelligence."

She wasn't about to mention that intelligence was also tinged with malice, something she hadn't clearly understood until they'd gone weeks into the relationship. That's what happened when she broke her three-date rule. Nothing good.

Rook's jaw pulsed, but he nodded subtly, accepting her answer. That muscle at the back of his jaw was his tell.

"Off with the weapons," she said.

He spread his coat open to reveal the inner lining, crowded with assorted weapons. Pulling out a stake, he stepped back and set it on her spell table. Another stake and two more from loops inside the coat. At his back, he pulled out a curved blade, and from the top of his left boot emerged a stiletto. Hooked at his hip was a garrote, which he pulled out to display to her, eyebrow lifted gleefully, before setting it aside. A hand-sized crossbow also had been fitted inside the coat.

When he finally displayed a syringe, capped with a steel tip, Verity had to ask, "What's that?"

"Is that one of your questions? If so, you'll have to remove something since you deem to ask out of order."

She sighed. "I suppose."

He smiled widely and set the syringe on the table. "Holy water. Works on unbaptized vamps. The other boot, if you please."

That had been a wasted question, but Verity didn't mind at all as she unzipped and toed off the other boot. She wandered closer to the man who had revealed an arsenal to her as if it were nothing more than jewelry adorning his body. So many dangerous items sat upon her spell table. A sacred place that she hoped wouldn't draw out the bad vibes that surely existed within the weapons. He had laid them there with playful and good intention, so she wouldn't worry.

"What's with the cat?" Rook asked next.

On to the questions. "Thomas? Oh, he's a good friend. He's a familiar."

"You mentioned that."

"He stops in once or twice a week for food and sometimes a chat. He's quite the lady's man."

"Has he ever been your man?"

"That's two questions."

"I'll remove two things."

Running her tongue across her lips, Verity nodded her agreement. "Coat."

He shrugged off the long leather duster, folding it inward to ensure the bladed collar was concealed, and tossed it over the weapons on the table.

"And..." she prompted.

"Answer the question first."

"Me and Thomas ever get it on?" She shook her head. "Strictly platonic between us. There's something about shapeshifters that does not appeal to me. Boots."

The man bent to unbuckle the straps about the ankle of one boot and heeled it off. He stood there in one boot and waited for her to insist he remove the other.

She could play fair. Though it killed her that this was going so slowly. What did she want to know about the man that she dared ask? Favorite color or car? She didn't care. Favorite sexual position? Oh, baby.

"Do you often play such games with women with the intended outcome resulting in nudity?"

"Not often." His tone teased that she should have asked exactly what sort of games he did enjoy.

Rats. She should have worded that one differently.

"Stockings."

Verity took her time rolling down the black sheer thigh-high stocking, bending and giving the man a side view as she pulled it from her toes and tossed the sheer slip to the end of the bed. "Happy?"

"Immensely. And that was another question. The other stocking, if you please."

Shoot. She had slipped. And she was rapidly losing her clothing, whereas he had a lot to go. Verity slipped off the second stocking with as much élan as the first, and this time she didn't ask about his emotional state.

"What's your favorite way to spend time with a man on a date?"

Now that was a good one. And she appreciated that he was attempting to learn how to please her.

Verity tapped a finger to her lips as she considered for a moment. She'd gone on many dates over the decades. Some wonderful, some worthy of Alka-Seltzer and a rewind. Others, well, having to pack up her belongings and physically relocate to get away from Slater topped her list of worst relationships ever. But Rook was only wondering about the good stuff.

"Any kind of interaction that involves paying attention to one another," she said. "I like it when a man shows me that it is me he's interested in. If you whip out your cell phone and start texting at any time when we're together, then forget it. The other boot."

"I don't do the cell phone thing," he said, "save to check in for work." He removed the remaining boot.

Damn it, he was wearing socks. He also had the vest, shirt and pants remaining. Whether or not he was wearing Skivvies beneath the pants, she was now determined to find out.

Gripping the hem of her dress, Verity tiptoed across the gray-painted floorboards in front of the bed, sat and leaned back to study the handsome image of calm, sex and slayage.

"How often do you have sex when you're dating a woman?" She had to know. He looked like a man who needed it often. Certainly he would have no difficulty fulfilling that need, either.

"As often as she desires me," he replied.

Oh mercy. That left the interpretation wide open. Verity instantly narrowed it to *every day*.

"Dress," he said on a husky tone that brushed her skin indelibly.

Verity stood and, fingering the dress hem, decided she was all in. This night could end only one way, and she wasn't about to lose the game. Curling her fingers one by one under the hem, she tugged it up slowly, gliding her hands along her thighs and over her hips to reveal her black lace panties. Rook's intake of breath delighted her. Up a few inches higher, and she exposed her stomach. She could feel the heat of his gaze follow the skim of the fabric as she pulled it to the bottom of her matching lace bra.

The man's hands opened and closed near his thighs, anticipation drawing down his head so he watched her from an expectant downcast stare.

Finally pulling the dress off, she tossed it aside without a care, swished her hair over her shoulders, turned to the side and glanced coyly at him from over her shoulder.

"Gorgeous," he said. "Would you make love with me, Verity?"

"Is that one of the questions?"

"It is."

"I, uh…." A bold question. He should know the answer. Yet if he did not, and she daren't speak it, then she'd never get another item of clothing off him. "Yes," she whispered.

Her heartbeats thundered and she smiled, growing into the answer as quickly as the titillation of revealing her desires stretched through her body. Nipples hardening, she remained facing sideways to him, unwilling to give him the full tease just yet.

"Socks," she said, then when he only removed one, she added, "I believe the official rules state that socks always come in pairs. Unlike a woman's hosiery or shoes. It's sort of universal that one must do them together."

He gave her a doubtful quirk of brow but then bent to strip off the other sock. And Verity exhaled quietly, stunned he'd allowed her that silly made-up rule.

What to ask him next? She desperately wanted to know about the witch he'd seen burned to ash, but she didn't want to take this teasing moment in that direction. So instead, she approached him, taking note that his eyes traced her breasts. Such regard made her nipples tighten even more. She basked in his admiration.

"What part of me would you like to touch first?" she asked.

"Your breasts," he breathed out quickly. "I want to touch them with my tongue and squeeze them against my palms. Then I will suckle them until you moan and squirm against me."

Verity blew out a breath and stepped back from him. If she stood too close, she'd touch him, and that would bring the game to an end she didn't want to see happen yet. She had to keep her wits about her and not fall to her knees like some silly wanton.

"Vest," she directed.

The man unsnapped the tight-fitted vest and dropped it to the floor, where it hit with a startling thud.

"That thing must be heavy. What's it made of—wait!" She thrust out a hand. "Nix that question."

"You sure?"

She nodded. "I have better things to ask."

"It's lined with Kevlar," he offered freely. "Comes in handy if I encounter a werewolf with claws out."

"You fight werewolves often?"

He narrowed his eyes at her, and Verity realized she'd used another question. "Yes, let that be an official question," she decided. "I didn't think the Order slayed wolves."

"We don't, but sometimes a pack gets out of hand. It's not unlikely to encounter a wolf while out hunting a vampire. I have to protect myself, no matter the circumstances. And no, I've not slain a werewolf. Yet."

She sensed his desire to do so was strong. Hmm…

With an accepting nod, she waited for his next request. Either one would reveal so much, yet she was ready to expose herself to this man. To take in his gaze and feel it glide across her skin as if it were the fire with which she so often danced.

"Bra," he said in that sex-laced tone that she could feel drip across her body. *"S'il vous plaît."*

Verity turned and walked toward the paned glass cathedral window on the other side of her bed. It was shaped like something you'd find in a church but without the colored glass. Slipping her hand behind her back, she unclasped the bra with a smart twist. She let the lace bra fall from her arms and tilted back her head, loving the feel of her hair across her back. Skyclad was always her preferred attire.

Air, skin, breath, vita. She thought the words to a reawakening spell. She whispered it often as a means to lift her spirits and bolster her vitality. Right now, she felt desire simmer across her skin, and her pores sought touch.

Putting her hands down at her sides, she turned to face Rook, knowing the moonlight spilled across her skin and flashes from the crystals danced in her hair.

The man bit his lip and gripped a fist before him. But he didn't look ready to punch someone; rather, he was trying to keep from touching.

"Ask your question," she prompted, trying to remain as casually unaffected by his overwhelming sensual draw as possible. Her eyes fell to his crotch, where his very obvious erection bulged against the leather. She could not wait for that.

Patience is a virtue, she reminded her whimpering heart.

"I…" The cat had gotten his tongue. And Thomas wasn't anywhere nearby.

Pleased she'd challenged his sensual calm, Verity smiled. Looking down, she brushed her hair across her nipple, teasing him with the play.

Rook tongued the inside of his cheek. He rubbed his hands over his scalp. "Have you family?" came out quickly.

"Not much. A man who has lived for centuries can certainly understand that, yes? I've my grandmother Freesia, but she doesn't live in this realm. My mother and great-grandmother Bluebell are gone. No siblings or other family. I've never known my father. My mother never talked about him either. I used to dream he was a prince, but over the years I have grown to suspect he was probably a frog. Shirt, please."

He tore the T-shirt off over his head and dropped it near his feet. In a hurry? Verity dropped her mouth open at the sight of the ripped abs and pecs. Hard. As. Rock. And every movement eased the muscle in a sensual wave. There at his left shoulder was a raised mark a few shades darker than his light tan coloring. Looked like a scar, or— she couldn't determine, only that it was round. A bullet wound? She couldn't imagine it would be so wide.

But she didn't want to waste another question now that they were both down to one item of clothing. *If* he went commando. And the way the game was going, she would reveal all before he did. Which didn't seem fair. Where was the competition? The chance that one could win over the other?

"We need a challenge round," she said suddenly. "That is, if we're both down to the one bit of clothing. Are you going commando?"

"Is that another question?"

She blew out an exasperated breath. He wasn't going to let her win this one. "No."

"Then pose another question."

"Fine. I want to know what memories my fire magic stirred up in you."

"And if I refuse to answer?"

She grinned. "Then it's your turn to ask a question."

He tapped his chin with a forefinger, obviously weighing the question. It was a tough one, surely. And she expected he would not answer. Or at least, if she had strategized correctly, he would not.

"Why fire?" he challenged. "Tell me why a witch chose to study fire."

"So you're refusing to answer my question?"

"I am. I…can't get into that now. I hope you can understand."

"Very well. Why fire?"

This one hit her hard and stirred up a batch of memories. But she wasn't about to refuse his defiant dare. She was strong, and she'd learned to overcome and use the bad times to enforce the good.

Striding past him to her spell table, she looked among the accoutrements, found the glass vial about the size of her thumb and displayed it for him.

"My mother was burned at the stake late in the nineteenth century," she offered. "She had fallen in love with a man who, unbeknownst to her, was a witch hunter. You can guess that he tricked her and soon led her to the flames. I witnessed it. My soul compelled me to the gallows on that day. These are her ashes." She shook the vial. "And after watching such an atrocity, I was determined to never fall victim to something I could control. So I focused all my studies on fire."

"I'm sorry about your mother."

With some difficulty she swallowed the rising hollow that threatened tears. But she was strong because of her mother's death, and she didn't need to cry over it anymore. Besides, this night was going to end the way she desired.

"Pants," she ordered with a flick of her fingers.

The man fingered the metal button at his waist, popped it open, then slowly drew down the zipper.

Anticipation quickening her core, Verity realized her skin was warm and shivering and her loins were wet. She shifted her hips, pressing her thighs together. So ready for him. And they hadn't even touched.

He got the zipper halfway down, paused, put up a finger and turned away from her to shrug down the fitted, armored pants to reveal a very sexy backside. Sans Skivvies.

He stood upright and, arms out to his side, turned toward her. "Happy?"

"You've nothing else to take off," she said, not caring that her argument was moot. Because, oh mercy, his shaft sprang up tight against his stomach, long and hard, the head of it gorgeously thick and red. Her fingers ached to take him in hand and command him. "Yes, very happy."

Verity slipped off her panties and dropped them about her feet. "I concede. It's a tie. What next?"

Chapter 8

Rook plunged to his knees beside Verity and kissed her thigh, inhaling the sweet herbal odor of the cream she had explained protected her from the flames. He almost went down the route of *what if*—what if Marianne had known about the flame retardant?—but stopped himself. He knelt before a goddess, and he would not step toward the heart-wrenching lure of his past now.

Now was for warm skin and luxurious smells and violet hair spilling between his fingers and fluttering lashes dusting the air and the flex of her stomach muscles and the tempting curves of her breasts as seen from his position below them.

He kissed her hip, tonguing the skin and nipping it gently. Her fingers drove through his hair, igniting shivers across his scalp. He bit gently and she cooed, arching her back as his palm fit against her lower spine, his thumb gliding into the divot of one Venus dimple.

She tilted out her leg and fit it against his torso, a lift of her toes touching his heavy testicles. The skin around them tightened, hugging them up to his groin in anticipation. He gripped her firmly, sandwiching her stomach and back with both hands as he glided his tongue up her rib cage, following the herbal scent to the sweet, heated valley beneath her breast. Nuzzling up into a heavy globe, he nipped at the underside, wanting to tease himself by prolonging the treat. His face against her breast. Heaven.

Verity rubbed her mons against his abdomen. She was hot and wet. *Mon Dieu,* he should touch her there—but not yet. And there was that foot again, her toes tenderly testing at his tightened testicles, attempting to stroke up higher, but they were not positioned correctly. He'd let her continue to try; his focus was on devouring her moans, her wanting squirms, her gasps of pleasure.

"Oh, Rook." She bent forward, and he slashed his tongue along the divine center between her breasts. She wanted him to suckle her, but he continued to tease with lashes and testing licks. "Please."

Now that was what he liked to hear. And that quiver in her tone? Nice.

Rising to stand, he clasped her derriere and lifted her. She was light as a bird, and she wrapped her legs around his torso. And right there at his chest, those gorgeous breasts settled, full and round. The areolas were dusted a deep pink and the nipples so tight they peaked up in offering.

"Suck me," she begged on a gasp.

He opened his mouth over the curve of her breast and let her feel his teeth. Never so dangerous as one with fangs. He had taken a vampire bite a dozen times over the centuries and knew that piercing was erotic as could be. But her reaction to his tease pleased him. Shudders coursed through her body, raising Braille dots across her skin. He let his fingers wander over them, reading them, quickly deciphering before they disappeared. What he read was want.

Rook danced his tongue around the ruched peak of her nipple. Her fingernails drove down the back of his scalp and to his neck, prickling up his flesh. As he suckled her, her body shifted against his, her mons pressing hard to his stomach, demanding, grinding the core of her against him to heighten her pleasure. She was unfettered and took as she pleased. An armful of heat and want and desire, this witch.

The bed right at his side, he turned and laid her across the quilt, replacing his tongue with his fingers to squeeze her nipple while he tended the other wanting bud of flesh with his mouth. She slid a hand over his and encouraged his rough squeeze, and that was all it took to turn his rigid cock into a pulsing, demanding column of steel.

Swearing, he pulled her leg down to slap against her other leg, imprisoning his cock between her thighs. Hot and moist there, he pumped within the loose prison. Mercy, but he had to maintain control. It hurt so damn good to not let loose and come.

Sucking in her nipple deeply, lingering and holding it until he thought it must pain her, he then lashed quick tastes across her breasts. At her sides, her hands clutched the quilt, and he took a moment to watch those long, graceful fingers in an involuntary act of seeking. Needing to grasp on to something, to anchor to the pleasure.

Still he thrust his penis hard between her thighs. She had tucked an ankle under the other to tighten the clasp. He could come right now, but he would not when he was so close to entering this intriguing woman he was beginning to believe had been led to him by destiny.

Rook's every touch permeated her skin. Verity felt him rush through her system. Every lash of heated tongue, every demanding clasp of fingers, owned her. Embedded deep within her soul.

She couldn't stop herself from thinking that, indeed, her soul felt Rook enter her skin, her mouth, her thoughts and her desires. And it welcomed him, wanted him to stay, sighed at his presence. Perhaps even recognized him.

He kissed down from her well-suckled breasts to her panting stomach, lashing his tongue into her naval. Verity tilted up her hips but sighed as his penis slipped out from between her thighs. That thick, hot part of him she wanted to grip, yet it eluded her grasping fingers as he moved down the bed. Tufts of his hair tickled her below the naval—so sensitive there. Now his kisses grew lighter, merely dusting her instead of the intense, biting kisses he'd given her breasts.

Breathless, her fingers grasping at air, Verity could only close her eyes and take in whatever sensations he next gave her because she had lost control and didn't want it back. She was ready to step over the edge, yet when her toes touched air he would alter his pace, and the weight of his touch granted her a reprieve for moments of gasping delight.

"One final question," her lover murmured. He looked up from where he hovered so close to her wanting, quivering core.

"Anything."

"We've begun something," he said. His hand glided down her outer thigh and hooked under her knee. "Do you really want this?"

He was asking something beyond whether she wanted him to bury his tongue deep within her and bring her to orgasm. And although she didn't want to stretch her thoughts too far from the pleasure, Verity knew what he implied. Did she want to step into a relationship with a hunter? A man whose job must always come before her. A man who was inexplicably tied up in a hunt for her ex-lover.

A man she wanted to trust.

Who said it had to become a relationship? She was determined to keep it to three dates—make that three romps in bed. Tonight was only the first.

"Oh, mercy yes," she answered. Shoving her fingers through his hair, she clutched, and as he lowered his head to her, she moaned and let him put her leg up over his shoulder.

The heat of his tongue seared her wetness, stroking along her folds and mapping her out slowly, intently. Verity gasped, tilting up her hips. "Deeper," she cried.

Her lover's fingers glided inside her while his tongue tickled higher, aimed for her apex. He bent forward two fingers and skimmed the ripples of her G-spot. Verity released the sheets she'd clutched tightly. Her head tilted into the pillow, her mouth gaping open, but no sound touched the night. And as his tongue touched her clit and his fingers gently curled against her sensitive insides, she launched into an indulgent free fall into bliss.

Lost within the utter abandon of orgasm, Verity sighed softly. Her body shivered, her muscles tightening. She felt Rook wrap his arms around her legs and tongue her deeply, tasting her, drinking her., He worshipped her like a goddess.

She needed him to feel her ecstasy, and she tugged at his hair. "Inside me. Please. Quickly."

And then he filled her with his molten hard shaft, thrusting into her bliss, pushing her farther, his hardness dragging at her swollen clitoris and playing her to another orgasm that hitched a ride on the fading tail of the previous. Her muscles tightened about his cock. Rook groaned, and his palm slapped the bed beside her head.

"So good," he muttered. "Yes!"

The man above her matched her frenzied shudders, his hands clasping her arms tightly. His abdomen muscles clenched against her belly, and in that moment she owned him. He surrendered to her, coming deep inside her and releasing a part of him to her.

* * *

They lingered in the glow cast by the pale moon.

If the victim does not drink blood before the next full moon, the vampire taint will pass through their system.

Verity frowned and turned away from the light. Nuzzling her nose into Rook's hair made her forget the annoying thought she'd had about vampirism. She didn't doubt that her spell had worked.

Okay, so she had doubted it a little when Lyric and Vail had questioned her about it.

No. You're fine.

She slid a palm over her lover's chest, the dark hairs soft against her skin. His eyes were closed, but he wasn't sleeping; he'd just come and his body still panted as he lounged in the delicious reverie of after-orgasm.

"I wish my necklace hadn't been stolen that night. You were so close to your soul," she whispered.

He clasped a hand over hers. "I marvel that you've had it for so long and felt the need to keep it safe."

"Just doing what my soul demanded of me. Weird, eh? I've never thought about soul mates much, but do you think?"

He shrugged. "I've never given it thought either. I'm just thankful that I found you and recognized my soul. Oz is too."

"You'll find it. I'll help you."

"I didn't find it tonight. Sundays are always slow, for reasons beyond my comprehension. I should be knocking on every vampire's door. But instead, I was compelled toward you."

"Kind of how I was compelled toward your soul all those years ago. The necklace has been a sort of companion over the years, if you can believe that. You lose everyone you care about when you live a long time."

"I understand. All too well. I've been fortunate to have one good friend through the ages."

"Is he in the Order also?"

"Yes, we founded it together. And that's all I will say about that."

"You don't need to give me Order details, but I think it's wondrous you've had a friend for so long."

"We grew up in the late sixteenth century. We have been through everything together. He knows me better than Oz, even."

"And what about Oz?" Verity propped her head on the heel of her hand. He looked at her now, and she traced his mouth. The curves of him were firm and masculine. Devastating. "If Oz is inside you, can he…? Well, does he, uh…"

Rook chuckled. "You're asking if he's aware of everything I do. Including making love to a woman?"

She nodded, but inside she winced.

"He can and he does. To an extent."

The idea of a demon having been aware of what they'd shared—she wasn't sure what to think of it.

"As I am aware of his actions and emotions when I give him free rein once a month."

"You can set him free from you? How does that work?"

"He becomes me, or rather, himself within my body. Which isn't my body when he's out, but yet, it is. It's complicated. I do it on the night of the full moon. When Oz is out I remain within him, knowing, experiencing, as he is within me."

"Is he aware of our conversation right now?"

"He's probably sleeping. But then again, he could be. I don't think about it much. It is simply what I have been for centuries. It doesn't seem strange to me. Does it bother you?"

Verity tilted her head to his chest. "It is a little weird. Did I just have sex with two men?"

"No, you had sex with me. With…an audience."

Yikes. Really? That was too much to take in. So she would take a cue from Rook and not think about it too much. Or at least try not to.

Still. "Do you and Oz discuss your conquests?"

His smirk answered that question.

Verity rolled to her back to stare up at the crystals overhead. She'd had sex with a hunter. And quite possibly a demon. This whole trust thing was going to prove more challenging than she could have ever anticipated.

Good thing she intended to dump him sooner rather than later.

Rook noticed the flashing light on his cell phone, which he'd left on the spell table. He planted a kiss on Verity's forehead, then slipped out of bed and padded over to the table. Dawn stretched an orange dash across the horizon.

A text message from King told him Aaron had been ambushed by Zmaj last night and was in the Hôtel-Dieu, the city hospital.

"Hell."

King never texted unless it was important. He was probably wondering why Rook hadn't been out with Aaron. He'd made the first rounds and then…had gotten distracted.

Pulling up his pants, he shoved his feet into his boots and tugged on his shirt and coat, then stuffed his weapons back in the pockets.

"That eager to get away from me this morning?"

Verity lay on her side, the sheet covering her from hip down. Pale morning light glittered in her hair and on her eyelids. Rook wanted nothing more than to slide next to her warmth, bury his face in her hair and press his hands against her skin.

"Sorry. Bit of an emergency."

She pushed up on an elbow. "With the Order? What's up?"

"A knight was attacked by vampires and is in the hospital." He shoved the last stake into one of the loops at his hip. "I have to go. I don't want to leave you like this—"

"I understand," she said. "Someone's been hurt. You need to go to him."

Rook hadn't intended to go to the hospital—he'd thought to go after Zmaj—but she was right. He should debrief Aaron.

He took the first step down from the attic room and paused. Every part of his body was dressed and pumped to go out and stake some vampires. And every part of his heart wanted to rush back to Verity.

So he did. He stepped over to the bedside. Pulling her up in his arms, he kissed her, finding the slow, lingering rhythm they'd learned last night, and only reluctantly pulled away.

"Give me a call later?" she asked.

"I will."

"Get that vampire," she whispered.

"Oh, I will," he muttered as he marched down the stairs and into the morning.

Aaron Langdon had been out in the field a month. Only twenty-six, the young man had impressed Rook with his martial arts skills and his sensible reasoning. He hadn't joined the Order to repay vengeance for a wrong done against him or his family, and he was not a vigilante who sought the thrill of taking out vampires. He'd joined to protect humans. And his truth was apparent.

Now he lay in a hospital bed, his face swollen and bruised, his front teeth knocked out and his arm in a sling.

He winced and nodded when Rook walked in. "Sorry," he managed through what had to be a painful mouth. "I tried, but there were too many."

"You should have called for backup."

"I thought you were off for the night. Didn't want to bother you."

Yes, and he would have probably answered the call with an attitude until he'd heard the reason for the call.

"Did you identify them as Zmaj?"

"Yes, but not because I recognized any of them."

"Then how?"

"They said they wouldn't kill me because they wanted me to give you a message from Slater."

Rook curled his fingers into fists at his sides. "Go on."

"Slater knows the Order is after him. He's not going down without a fight. You asked for it, so now you've got a war."

Not what the Order, or the city of Paris, needed. Curse his complacency last night. What had he been thinking leaving the rookie alone so he could trip off to meet a woman?

Rook nodded. "Can you describe the vamps who attacked you? Sketch them?"

Aaron lifted the arm in a sling. "My drawing hand. Sorry, boss."

"I'll send in an artist to help you. We need identification because most of Zmaj hasn't been identified with their rapidly increasing numbers. Was there a bald one in the group?"

"I seem to remember…yes. I know because you told me to keep an eye out for him. Wish I could have taken him into custody, as requested. I've failed you."

"No, you have not. You survived an ambush. Not many knights can do as much. Rest. Heal. I'll see you in the gym next week, yes?"

"Before then," Aaron said. "It's just my arm that'll hold me back, but I still have one good arm and two legs."

"I would expect nothing less from you, Langdon." After clasping the man's good hand, he left the room.

Swinging by reception, Rook made sure Aaron's bills were sent to the accountant who handled the Order's finances. Then he decided that before heading home to shower and change, he'd stop by the office.

Verity lingered in the bathtub, lifting a leg from the thick, rose-scented bubbles to glide her fingers down her water-bejeweled skin. It was difficult not to imagine Rook's fingers doing the same, and so she did. Mmm…she wished he could have lingered in bed with her this morning, but she understood the emergency.

She hoped he didn't blame himself for not being there to protect the other knight. Rook was such a leader; he probably would shoulder the blame.

Sinking deeper into the water, she replayed watching him tear away his clothes last night, piece by piece. She'd marveled over his playful side. She'd expected quick and perhaps forceful sex, not such an intimate, intense connection. A few times he had been rough and demanding, twined with his gentler touches; she had loved it all.

Something about Rook was different from other men she had known. It was their connection. But why? Were they soul mates? Was such a thing even possible? How could two souls seek one another? And what if one's soul mate had been born in another time? It didn't make sense that true soul mates should be fortunate enough to be born at the same time, be close in age and eventually find one another out of all the souls in the world.

Curiosity would have her leaning over the family grimoire after breakfast to read up on souls.

Until then, she was happy to soak until the water turned lukewarm and the bubbles melted away.

Chapter 9

Rook shrugged off his coat and tossed it across the desk. Now he stared at the inside of his locker door, eyes not focusing on the item he'd hung there decades earlier after installing the locker. A reminder of why he hunted year after year, century after century.

His heart always stuttered to look at the object. Even Oz seemed to sigh within him, his exhale rippling through Rook's muscles until it reached his fingertips, and he had to shake his hands loosely as if shaking off the agonizing memory.

After a few moments, he dragged his thoughts back to the present. He sorted through the silver bullets. Tonight he would carry a pistol. The handmade bullets sported a wood core, which straightened their trajectory. They wouldn't kill a vamp, but they would slow one down so he could get close enough to stake them.

The office door slammed open, and King marched inside. Wrist resting on the top of the locker door, Rook turned to judge his friend's mood. He didn't have to look too long to read King's anger. It was rare but always sharp.

"Explain," King demanded.

"I sent Langdon on a job I felt sure he could handle. We'd been out half the night with no sight of a longtooth, so I felt he could manage the last stop alone. As he's done many times before. I had no clue Slater had sent out an ambush."

"Isn't that your job? To have a clue? Why aren't you the one in the hospital right now?"

Rook crossed his arms over his chest. "That's the way you think this should have gone down?"

"Is there some scenario I'm missing? Please, enlighten me."

"First of all, I'd never end up in the hospital, and you know that."

King agreed with a tilt of his head. "Touché."

"I'd been hunting all night. I assigned Aaron the last check over a nest location, as I would normally do had I not been on the case."

"But this is your case!"

"We'll never come to terms on this."

"Of course not because you're always the one who has to be right." King paced between the desk and the door on the opposite wall that led to the attached chapel.

Rook exhaled. He did like to be right. And he usually was. But he didn't always have to be right with King. Because if anyone needed to be right, it was King. They'd come to terms with that over the centuries. It had never affected their relationship, and it would not this time. But he could admit to himself he should have stayed with Aaron last night.

"It's that witch," King suddenly said. "She's distracting you."

"I do not distract easily."

"I know that. And I know a man needs a lover. I would never insist you abandon your personal life."

Rook lifted his chin. Where was the man going with this? He seemed upset, almost jealous.

"But she's something more, isn't she?" King swung an accusing look at him. "She's digging up all your old stuff."

"My—what? You're making a bold supposition."

"Yes, your stuff," King insisted.

"What stuff?"

King approached, and when he looked to stab Rook in the shoulder with a finger, instead he landed the finger on the small pentacle crafted from dried willow branches that hung inside the locker door. "This stuff!"

Rook grabbed King by his suit lapels. He wasn't about to read his truth by placing a palm over his chest. He knew it. It was bold, commanding and deeply secretive. But how dare the man suggest he was being controlled by—his truth.

"You can't deny it," King defied him.

The man did know him better than Oz did, and over the years that had become both a blessing and a curse to Rook.

He shoved King away and closed the locker door behind him, effectively hiding the telling bit of *stuff.* Marianne had fashioned the pentacle. She'd called it a safe hex, designed to protect the inhabitants wherever it was hung. It was the only thing he'd had the heart to save before burning their house to the ground. Some safety those little twigs had offered.

"And what if she is dredging up things I'd—"

"Rather not face? I'm surprised you'd confess, Rook. You're letting the Von Velde witch tear down your walls?" King implored. "It's been forever, man. Why does this have to come up now?"

"Is the timing so inconvenient for you?"

"You have your work—"

"Yes, yes! So we have Zmaj to deal with. If it wasn't that tribe, it would be another. There is always another.

You didn't think I'd be able to keep this stuff, as you call it, buried forever, did you?"

"No, but—hell." King stepped back, dropping his shoulders.

Conceding the battle?

"Since when have you started to believe I can't divide my time between two tasks?" Rook insisted. "I am a knight of the Order. The original knight, if you'll remember. I know my job, and I do it well. And if I choose to have a relationship—"

King swung toward him. "It's become a relationship?"

"I don't—maybe. Yes! I enjoy the witch's company, and I'm not going to stop seeing her because some badass vampire has set his sights on waging war with the Order. The longtooths are a bunch of blowhards—"

"War? I hadn't realized it had escalated to a war."

Rook blew out his breath, seeking calm in his center before continuing. Was it war, or had that merely been a means to tease him out into the light to face his enemy?

"Langdon delivered that message from Slater. The Zmaj leader has called war. But it's nothing I can't handle."

"Are you listening to yourself?"

King took a step closer, putting himself face to face with Rook. They held each other's stare too long. Rook read so much in his friend's eyes, which had witnessed centuries. But nothing he didn't already know.

"You want to be king of the world and fuck the girl, too," King said calmly. "It doesn't happen that way, and you know it. You cannot divide your focus like this. People get hurt."

Was the man listening to himself? Truly, if anyone wanted to rule the world—no. The argument wasn't going to win him ground, nor did he need to prove his superiority to a man he respected.

Rook exhaled again and spoke calmly. "Aaron is new. He was outnumbered six to one."

"Numbers you could have handled expertly."

"Because I've been doing this for centuries. This argument is moot. You're jealous I've found someone and you—"

The punch was not unexpected. Rook dodged King's fist, catching it in his palm with a smack. Rook would not retaliate, but King did not relent. The two struggled as they had not done for decades.

It wasn't like they'd walked through the years without their battles. But they also had been close. He loved King, and the love was returned. And he knew King was only concerned for his mental well-being now.

"She *is* bringing up stuff about Marianne," Rook confessed.

King pushed away. The man knew well how deeply he had loved Marianne.

"Verity is a fire witch." Rook rasped out his confession.

"Ah, hell."

"And she needs protection. Someone from Zmaj bit her. And I've learned she used to date Slater. He may be stalking her. She's entwined in this investigation, and I can use her knowledge."

"Rook. Fire? Why subject yourself to such torture?"

The man's warning tone did not sway him from giving all the details. "She could be in danger one way or another. I have to stay close to her. And I will."

"If she was bitten, was the wound sealed?"

"She performed a spell. She's fine. But safe? I'm not so sure."

King stepped back, giving Rook the space he needed. But he could read the man's disappointment, or rather, his worry, in his slumped shoulders. Only two people in this world knew of the torture King had mentioned. And the other was also in the room, just not present in corporeal form.

King twisted a look to Rook. "Do you want me to join you on this one?"

Did he? He wasn't any closer to Slater than he had been two days ago. And he still didn't have a location for any in Zmaj. He didn't want to assign more knights to the task—they weren't necessary—but one more wrong move and he risked putting all knights in the Order on high alert. He needed to focus.

You know you will not stay away from her. Like she said, something is drawing her soul and yours together. And if you abandon her now, you will never find that soul.

Oz's argument could not be ignored. Why shouldn't he be allowed this tryst? Wasn't he due some happiness? Fuck, the timing had been bad, but he wasn't going to give up this exciting new woman simply because some idiot longtooth wanted to play war games.

"What does Oz think about all this?" King asked.

"He wants the soul," Rook stated. "My soul."

King lifted a brow. Hell, he hadn't told him that part yet.

"The witch—" Rook began.

"Your lover?"

"Verity," Rook said firmly, "has been carrying my soul with her for a century. It's trapped in a piece of wood that grew up through the soul where Himself buried it long ago. She carved the wood into a heart and has worn it around her neck. I knew it was mine the night I saved her from a Zmaj attack and laid my hand over the thing. But it was stolen from her that night. Find the vamp who bit Verity, and I find my soul. And—an entrance to tribe Zmaj."

"That's…"

"Incredible. Unbelievable."

"Destiny," King provided.

Rook nodded. "And I don't intend to question it. She is in my life for a reason, my friend."

"It seems so. What if you use her as bait?"

King's suggestion infuriated him—but only for a second. Switching to knight mode, Rook realized it was a promising idea. If the vampire discovered his victim was still alive, he might return to finish the task. Rook could capture the vamp and force him to lead him right to Slater.

But she hadn't wanted to look at a few mug shots. What sort of bribe would be required to get her to actually play bait?

"I'll get on it," Rook said. "And you're right. My focus needs some readjustment. By nightfall I'll have a plan. I'll be in touch."

"Excellent. You know I am concerned about you, right?"

"You should not be. But yes, I know that you are. We have been through a lot together." Rook held out his hand, and King slapped his hand into the firm clasp. "Live to serve," Rook said softly.

"Die fighting. But you had better not die before I do, my friend. I'd never forgive you for it." With a smirk, King strode out.

And Rook opened the locker door and traced the outer curve of the symbol his wife had fashioned so many years ago.

"I can never atone for what I did to you," he said.

That is why he had not sought his soul through all the centuries. Because to take it back would mean he was over what he'd done to Marianne so long ago. Unrepentant.

"Someone else needs my soul more than I do now. I hope you can understand."

The night was cool and stunningly quiet as he raced toward the vampire standing fifty yards away.

Rook's rules for hunting vampires were thus:

If possible, always hunt alone. The hunter was responsible for his safety only and no others. And as a recent addendum: When hunting with another, do not presume the other man can handle any interaction with the enemy on his own.

The most important weapon is the brain, then the stake.

Anger (aroused in the vampire) reduces awareness.

Blood scent distracts the opponent. A good hunter will use his own blood as a weapon.

Vampires are supernaturally fast. Hunters use agility.

Without an invitation, vampires can only enter public buildings. If in a dire situation, entering a private domicile will give the hunter time to recover and concoct a plan. However, the risk of putting innocents in danger is great.

Vampires are not stupid. (Most of them.) Always expect the unexpected.

The old ones are not necessarily stronger, but they have greater determination to fight for survival.

Each rule had been developed through trial and error over the centuries. Vampire comes at you spitting blood and flailing some crazy wild talons? The knight had better compensate for that flimsy column of ashwood he carved the night before and had pridefully thought would save his ass.

King had tested a few disposal methods. He was always willing to make sure the tools and defense skills Rook invented were worthy—to a degree. Even King drew the line on occasion. The man had his pride.

Once Rook had traversed the French countryside with an arsenal tucked into a large wooden traveling trunk and strapped to the back of a wobbly carriage; he'd since streamlined the tools of the trade.

The Order coat was designed to protect as much of the

knight's body as possible without impeding movement. It was lightweight leather, reinforced with Kevlar where it laid over main arteries. Originally, chain mail had been sown into the leather, making it bulky and quite heavy. Thank the gods for modern technology.

Over the years, Rook had refined the trunk of tools. The fragile vial of holy water had become a small syringe, hidden within the palm and spring-loaded to eject the contents with one click.

A large wooden cross, inlaid with a brass figure of Jesus, had evolved into a streamlined silver weapon, again hand-sized and pointed at each of the four armatures. Gone was the holy figure; vampires laughed at the Christian symbol of hope. Silver did not harm vampires, but it was handy when werewolves were on the scene. Also, religious objects were only effective if the vampire had been baptized. But a holy wound would burn into a baptized vamp and never heal, slowly eating away at flesh, bone and organs until finally death arrived. The process could take days or even weeks.

The handsaw Rook had used on more than a few occasions to remove a vampire's head (when it was once believed removal of the head necessary for the final death) had been discarded and replaced with a thin gauged cable garrote that rolled up nicely, like a household tape measure. Again, it did not behead the vampire, but it hurt like a bitch, and not many of his opponents struggled for long when the cable chewed into flesh and bone.

A small leather-bound Bible had been weeded from his arsenal sometime in the nineteenth century. Again, vampires tended to laugh at the holy word.

Finally, the classic wooden stake, originally carved from ashwood and sometimes tipped in silver, had graduated into the titanium column he'd developed only a few decades earlier. Spring-loaded and tension controlled, it was ~~capable of piercing skin, muscle and bones. Anyone could~~ use it, even an unskilled human with little strength. Once the vampire's heart burst, true death followed.

Not all vampires ashed. The newest ones generally did not. As for clothing, it depended on how hot the ash burned. It varied from kill to kill.

What he'd learned over the years was to know your enemy. Know what works. Know what doesn't work. Never fear. Fear was a creation of the mind. And always take the first step toward the enemy before he lunged toward you.

And when things went wrong? Fuck all the rules and go with instinct.

Slamming his fist against a vampire's chest, Rook held the stake there, the deadly point of it as yet unreleased. A squeeze of the paddles was all it took, then—ash. Even Oz got off on this part. Defiant sneers and cocky confidence were innate to the longtooth. Yet no vamp had ever survived if he allowed Rook to get in this position with him.

"Namaste," Rook growled to the Mohawked vamp with heavy carbonite rings stretching his earlobes and black eyeshadow smeared over his eyelids. "You know where I can find tribe Zmaj. You wear their mark."

A red painted handprint decorated the vamp's leather coat. Rook was guessing the tribe had adopted that as an identifying mark.

"The handprint? It's old. I'm unaligned right now, dude. Chill with the stake, will you?"

With his fist pressed to the vamp's chest, Rook could read his fear. And his desperate hope. The idiot thought he could talk his way out of this one. He could also read the darkness that crusted about his soul, flake by flake, as he took yet another life in his quest to drain the victim to the point where their heart burst.

"You like the *danse macabre?*" he asked the vampire, referring to the never-ending nightmares the vampire lived—stolen from the victim on their death.

The creep licked his lips and winked at him. "You know it."

Wanting to compress the paddles and be done with the asshole, he calmed the urge with an exhale through his nose. "You give me Zmaj, I let you go."

"Those idiots don't know how to do it right. Slater is a control freak. Asks too much of his tribe. There's no freedom."

"Apparently you've been cast out by Zmaj."

"What of it?"

"Just give me an address."

"So you can slay them all? Hell no. I won't narc on my breed. Never."

Rook slammed the stake up against the vamp's shoulder and compressed the paddles. The tip pinioned out, piercing muscle and bone. The vampire yowled, and Rook slapped his free hand over his mouth. He yanked the stake from the bone, an abrupt tilt upward, surely cracking the fragile collarbone and making the vamp squirm under his hand.

"Where next?" he asked. "The neck? It won't kill you, but it'll hurt like a mother." And it would heal too fast for the vampire to remember the pain unless he worked quickly.

So he did.

Rook slammed the stake against the throat and delivered the punch. He could feel the stake's tip crush through spine and tap the brick wall behind him. Blood spattered his face. The vampire clawed at him.

"Uncle!"

Keeping the stake in the vampire's throat, Rook studied his teared-up eyes. Ready to squeal. He gracelessly unscrewed the stake from his throat. The vamp gurgled up blood and spat to the side. Rook allowed him to bend over so the majority of the blood would not again be spattered onto his face.

But time was of the essence. He yanked up the vamp by his hair and slammed his head against the wall. This time he pressed the stake over his heart. "Where?"

"It's in the eighth." The vampire rambled off an address in the 8th arrondissement near the city park. "It's not Slater's lair. Not sure where he hides."

"But Zmaj makes its home there?"

"It's sort of a club where they hang out from time to time."

"Excellent. You've done well. I'll make this easy on you."

"Easy on—"

The stake tip plunged into the vampire's heart, freezing the bastard in a silent scream of dismay to realize that had been his last second of life. Skin, hair and bones ashed. Clothing melted and shredded as the ash cloud fell in a heap at Rook's boots.

He wiped the stake across his pants leg and replaced it inside his coat.

On to the Zmaj hideout.

The abandoned nightclub sported windows boarded over and spider webs aplenty aboveground. Rook had entered the narrow building from the street and, sensing the place was empty, had quickly discovered the stairway that led to an underground passage. Half the buildings in Paris had a back door that led down into the cold depths beneath the city where the walls were dirt and limestone, some strung with useless nineteenth century electrical wires and plumbing pipes, and others marked with ancient writing or gang signs.

The world beneath Paris was not so secret, quiet or even evil as rumors would whisper. Cataphiles spent days and nights navigating the twisting labyrinths to achieve status among their own. Raves were often held in secret locations, only found by knowing the right password or following the right glow-in-the-dark symbols. The homeless marked the caves and passages with a language of their own. And the unlucky few who sought a thrill were sometimes never seen again.

The room below the nightclub was small but long, and it reeked of blood. Rook guessed the tribe must bring mortals down here to feed on them. Yet he found no bones, no signs of death. Did they bury their victims? Or had they another means to dispose of their travesties? A smart tribe would employ a cleanup crew for their victims.

Just thinking about the midnight cleanup ritual lifted the bile in Rook's throat.

He ascended the dirt and wood staircase and rushed out into the night, scanning his surroundings as he did but certain that this night tribe Zmaj was far from their lair.

Chapter 10

Instead of waiting for Rook to call, Verity decided to walk over to his place today and surprise him. She wore a pretty blue dress, her gray sweater coat and ankle boots with big black ribbons that tied up the heel instead of laces down the front. After purchasing a bouquet of daisies from a seller by the river, she strolled toward the Ile St.-Louis nestled behind Notre Dame.

She loved what she had with Rook. It was new and exciting, and he was a man like no other. He appealed to her in ways she'd never imagined possible. Certainly she was sexually attracted to him, yet he was also smart and strong and had that extra spice of humor she adored.

Their souls belonged together. She knew it. And perhaps it was time to abandon the three-strikes-you're-out rule. They'd seen each other three times, but if she was counting the sex, it had only been once. Keeping tabs was starting to feel like…keeping tabs. Unnecessary and a little foolish.

Could Rook possibly be the man grandmother Freesia had entreated her to seek?

She knocked once at his door, then turned the knob, finding the door unlocked.

She wandered into the kitchen, flowers dangling by her side. "Rook, you home?"

"In here! Just finishing up."

She strode through the living room and paused at the open bedroom door. Peeking inside, she spied Rook by the window, coming out of a backbend yoga pose and spreading his arms high above his head. He returned his palms to namaste position, pressed together in front of his chest. Eyes closed, he was in some kind of Zen moment that she didn't want to disturb.

He wore body-hugging gray boxer briefs, and the afternoon sun fell upon his hard, sinewy form as if he were a deity to inspire worship. Discipline stretched through his muscles. Control. And an innate coolness that made him more like the statue in the other room than a living, breathing human.

Yet he was so real when in her arms.

"Wait," she said when he started toward her. "Stay there."

He paused, shoulders back and straight, lungs expanding from the exertion. Hips squared, he mastered the room. A warrior. An athlete. A hunter.

A lover.

Rationally, Verity knew nobody was perfect. It was a ridiculous ideal. Yet this man was as close as she could imagine to touching perfection.

"You." She strolled toward him, tossing the flowers to the end of the bed. "Are." Closer, she could smell the rich spiciness of him mingled with perspiration, peaches and tobacco. "Fine."

She spilled her fingertips down his cool, moist chest. Steel muscle expanded and contracted with his breaths. He watched her explore him, and she liked that he didn't move to touch her. She wanted this man to herself. He was hers. She just had to decide if she had the courage to keep him.

Down to his abs, she traced the ridged muscle, feeling his strength shiver through her system like steam rising from hot asphalt. His skin warmed beneath her touch. "Yoga does all this?"

"It keeps me in shape. Quiets me. Grounds me. Makes me flexible."

"I like flexible."

She drew in a deep breath and curved her fingers to his side to follow the extreme cut of the Adonis arches that veed down toward his crotch.

Rook sucked in a breath. Beneath the boxer briefs, his erection pulsed against the tight cotton. "It's Oz's thing," he muttered through a tight jaw. "The yoga. I just follow along."

"Interesting. The demon knows what's good for the both of you. I think I like Oz. Hope you don't mind me stopping by this morning. If you have Order business…?"

"Don't worry about it, Verity. I don't have to work until later. And please, you can walk into my place whenever you desire."

"I'll remember that. I have a show later, so I can't stay too long. I usually practice in the afternoon. But I needed to see you again. To…touch you."

She skated a fingertip along the waistband of his briefs, drawing an invisible line that her tongue might like to follow. "Is everything okay with the knight who was attacked?"

"He's tough. Mmm…keep doing that. Touch me."

She stepped back but kept the tips of her fingers on his skin, gliding them along the demarcation between fabric and flesh. "Touch you where, lover boy?"

"Anywhere, anyway you want," he said. "Just don't stop."

"Hmm…" She took her time, looking him up and down from the flex of his abdomen to the hard pulse of that telling muscle in his jaw that always drew her attention. "How about this?"

Verity knelt at the edge of the yoga mat, the toes of her patent leather boots tapping the hardwood floor. Leaning forward, she blew a hushing breath upon his concealed erection, and it bobbed beneath the fabric. Drawing her fingernails up his toned thighs, she felt his skin shiver, and with a hiss, he grasped her hair.

He didn't force her to do anything, only tangled into her hair as if an anchor. Another breath against the gray cotton drew up a wanting moan from her lover. Verity walked her fingers up to the waistband and tugged. Slowly, as if opening a gift, she lingered on the unwrapping. This part was always the best. The head of his bold cock was revealed, the foreskin stretched around the thick neck of it. She kissed the smooth crown of him softly and dashed out her tongue to lick. Just once. Salt and man. A tease to challenge his patience.

And hers.

Gliding her fingers around the waistband and behind his hips, she slid it lower over his taut buttocks and squeezed the hard smoothness of him, his firm muscles pulsing in response. She pressed his hips toward her until his cock rested against her mouth.

Looking up, she met Rook's eyes. An intense pleading look asked her to continue, but he wasn't going to speak it out loud. That wasn't his style. He liked it when *she* begged. He was too calm and cool to take that role. And that would require he forfeit control.

Touching the tip of her tongue to his shaft, she didn't move it, only savored his salty, slick texture. He tilted his hips, indicating his need.

"Ask me," she whispered. A kiss to the pulsing thick vein that stretched along his erection. "What do you want, Rook?"

He tilted his head, raking his hands through her hair,

and eased his hips forward, pressing his hardness against her mouth. "Fuck."

"Tell me," she cooed. "I need to hear you say what you want."

"Suck me," he said tightly. "Please."

The win pleased her. A portion of control sacrificed. And so he would be rewarded with the spoils.

Verity lashed her tongue along his length, gliding up to nibble ever so gently at the reddened, wide head of him. Drawing her hands down his thighs, she dropped his briefs to the floor. She then gripped his shaft firmly and guided him into her mouth. Back and forth, she licked and savored and milked him of moans and read his desires from the subtle clues as his hands in her hair pressed lightly, then tugged for her to prolong her torture. When his fingers began to shake against her scalp and his shaft was engorged, she squeezed tightly under the head and cupped his testicles to stop him from coming.

Rook groaned with frustration. "Yes," he managed through his teeth. "Make me wait."

Oh, she would. And she'd take wicked delight in doing so.

A sticky sweet droplet pearled at his tip, and she licked it off and then sucked him hard and steadily. His hips shook, and his abdomen tightened against her palm. Yoga had nothing over her mouth. The man was a god, forged from muscle and determination. And he was at her mercy.

Teasing her teeth along the thick vein that lined his length summoned a hissing curse from him. She hadn't hurt him. He was enjoying this too much, and in proof, he pulled her in more firmly.

"Wicked witch," he hissed.

She squeezed him again, sensing his imminent explosion, and chastised, "Patience, lover."

"Fuck, Verity."

"You want to come?"

"Yes. No. More."

Smiling against his hot rod, she licked up and down, tasting every hard inch of him and memorizing the map of veins and pulsing scents that alchemized into a heady perfume that seduced her into his realm. On her knees before him she offered what she could to become his.

She had complete control over this man who lived his life regimented and restrained. He could not utter more than a word. His bones shivered inside his skin. He had grown so hard and thick within her mouth she could barely encompass the head of him, but she did so, sucking him as if a tasty dessert.

"Ver…" he gasped.

He dropped her hair. His hands slapped the wall behind him. The man's torso arced forward, his hips seeking her heaven, his head tilting back as his body curved in an exquisite bend. Sunlight melted across his stretched abdomen. His body begged for release.

Verity closed her mouth over the head, and with her hand she jacked him off into a forceful climax that spilled down her throat. He cried out and straightened his arms, coming forward in a stretch. Bowing forward over her to glide his hands down through her hair, he pressed his forehead to the crown of her head. His body shuddered, hips jerking subtly as he rode the wave.

She clasped his cock, slick with his seed, and held it until he sank to his knees to collapse up against her, spent and well used.

"Mine," Verity whispered as she cradled him into her arms and he settled against her chest, turning to stretch out his legs.

"Yes, yours, witch."

She smiled at his growling agreement. Captured then,

and perhaps surprised that he had been. But willing, most certainly.

"I love your cock," she said. "That's mine, too."

"You can have all of me, Verity, if you want me."

She buried her face in his soft, curly hair. "I do."

Rook strode to the ottoman in front of the floor-to-ceiling window. Clouds shadowed the room, and raindrops spattered the glass. He sat, back straight and palms up and open on his knees. She had mastered him with an ease that he would not argue with. And without removing a single piece of her clothing.

Verity tugged down her skirt, straightening it neatly, and flipped her hair over a shoulder as she licked his salty taste from her lips. Vixen. She wore a silky blouse and, he suspected, no bra beneath, because her dark areolas showed through the light violet fabric.

"Your tits are so hard," he said in a throaty tone. "Take your shirt off and come over here and put one of those in my mouth."

"You think so?"

"Don't displease me, witch."

Maintaining his command was difficult with the rich warmth from orgasm still flooding his system. Even as his cock grew soft, he felt the stirrings of desire in his root and knew he'd be hard again in minutes.

She unbuttoned the silk shirt with long, graceful fingers. Pale violet nail polish caught the sunlight in glints of mica. She liked violet and purple, and he wondered if she dressed to match her hair.

She dressed for herself, and for others to admire. And he liked that just fine.

"Slowly," he added.

Prolonging the pleasure was his favorite kind of torture.

* * *

Fingers falling down the purple silk, Verity turned and strolled to the window, where she leaned forward, catching her hands on the sill and jutting out her hips to give them a sexy wiggle. Peering at Rook through a fall of her hair, she parted her lips and slowly undid another button.

The man's cock was already hard again, and it jutted up proudly from his lap. His eyes narrowed on her, focused, content, pleased.

When all buttons were undone, she turned and put her hands against the rain-spattered window, thrusting up her breasts. The silk fabric draped them, and the sensual slide of it over her nipples sent delicious shivers across her skin. Standing upright, she posed there before the window, easily embracing her inner sex kitten. She drew a hand down the shirt and pulled it taut over her breasts. The nipples poked high and proud.

Stepping forward, she performed her sexiest sashay, heel before toe, hips shifting. The man's eyes fell to her hips and down her legs to her patent-leather boots, then rushed back up to her breasts. The intensity of his regard made her even wetter than she already was. Her thighs were quivering. But more so, her breasts craved the heat of his tongue. He had commanded her to put them in his mouth. It was all she could do to walk slowly, pacing herself as she neared her hungry lover.

She understood the incredible control it took to be patient. She hadn't mastered his control earlier; she'd only fortified it. Now she was the one in control—and she wanted to give it all up, to lie before him and let him do as he wished to her.

Soon enough.

Verity stopped three feet from the ottoman where he sat and planted her feet, her legs spread. Confidently, she splayed open her shirt to reveal her breasts. No bra today.

She'd been in a rush when leaving the house earlier, and her head had been out of sorts, thinking about seeing him again. So easily did she fall into the crazy good muddle of All That Was Rook.

Cupping her breasts, she eased her palms along the heavy fullness of them, pursing her lips as the pleasurable sensation shimmered over her skin and drilled into her core. Dashing out her tongue, she wet her lips and cooed from the depths of her desire.

Rook shifted and leaned forward.

She bit her lower lip and held his stare as she pinched her nipples.

"In my mouth," he repeated. And with a bow of his head and a dash of tongue over his teeth, his smoldering look invited her forward.

She took a step, bending at the waist. Her hair tumbled over her breasts and she purred at the sweet, silken glide of it over her skin. She pushed him backward. Rook caught his palms against the ottoman and she straddled his legs, heels tapping the floor. *Click. Click.*

Drawing a finger up his chest and neck and tracing the shadow of stubble under his lower lip, she teased his mouth open and lowered her mouth to it—but didn't touch. His breath hushed over her lips. He didn't move to touch her with his hands. Her breasts were so close to his chest, but she restrained herself from hugging against him.

Her nipples ached for touch, and she tilted her head to feel the skim of her hair over them. Delirious skitters raced through her body and congregated at her core. She needed his touch, wanted it desperately.

Grasping the hair at his crown, she jerked his head back and tapped his mouth with a finger. "You hungry?"

He bit down on her finger and sucked it in. She craved that feeling at her breast. The man teased his tongue along the inside of her finger, a place that was surprisingly erogenous and that stirred up a throaty moan from her.

Bracketing his face with both hands, she lowered her breast to his mouth and pressed it to his lips. First contact of hot, wet tongue to her hard nipple bubbled up a cry of joy from Verity. "Yes!"

He suckled roughly and drew her in deep, teasing all sensation to her breast. Then it dashed out through her system and scurried into every inch of her being. She crushed him closer, guiding his rough attentions.

He did not disappoint, laving her nipple and then drawing his tongue around her breast, high upon its mound where she was so sensitive and in between them and beneath where he sucked hard at the skin and she suspected he'd brought the blood to the surface in a hickey.

"The other," she gasped, head back and breasts thrust out. "Now."

He bit, lips over his teeth, at her other breast while his fingers squeezed and massaged the wet nipple.

Breathing rapidly, Verity grasped at the air, landing her fingers in his hair and curling them behind his ears, where she followed the tickle of curls down to his neck.

Suddenly he grasped her and turned her to lie on her back across the ottoman. Wrapping her legs around his hips, she pulled him onto her. His cock, hard and hungry, pressed against her while his mouth paid her breasts due worship.

He kissed down the side of her breast, and there she caught her breath because the pressure of his lips, punctuated with an insistent sucking at her skin, drove her mad with desire.

So wet now, she rocked her hips, seeking to position his cock between her folds and rub against her clit. He sensed her endeavor, and—damn him—he tilted his hips away from hers.

Rook smirked against her breast and chuckled softly. "What happened to being patient?"

"Fuck that. I need you here." She tugged his hand down to her crotch, and his finger slipped inside her. "Oh yes, and higher. Deeper."

His mouth at her nipple, he grabbed his cock and rubbed it against her clit slowly, harder, then softer and faster. Perfect. He felt like iron hot from the forge, and Verity greedily pulled him down with her legs.

"Inside me," she demanded. "All of you."

He pushed up onto his hands above her and studied her face.

"What are you waiting for?" she pouted. "Now."

"Please?"

"No, never please. Immediately. Roughly. Without permission, without asking, just—" She chuckled because she realized she was begging. "Fuck me."

"Just wanted to hear you beg for it, sweetie."

"I'm not your sweetie."

"You sure as hell are not. You're my wicked witch."

And he plunged his staff inside her, filling her with his thickness and length and slamming his hips in rapid thrusts that fed them both hungry sexneedlove.

Verity dug her fingers into the tufted velvet beneath her. She was right there, close to oblivion, and Rook's body shuddered above her, cluing her in that he was just as close to surrender.

He lunged and bit her breast softly, then sucked in the nipple, hard and deep, so wanting, as if to take all she had. And that pushed her to the peak.

Verity shouted a throaty cry of joy as Rook's thrusts slammed hard and forcefully against her. His shudders increased. He met the orgasm seconds after she had touched it. He let out an abbreviated growl. His arms that supported him above her shook, and the veins were thick and tight. Their bellies hugged, slick with sweat, and his cock pulsed inside her as she squeezed and worked him as the orgasm tightened then released their muscles in exquisite harmony.

"Thatwassofuckinggood," he muttered and collapsed beside her.

Their separation tugged up one last twinge of orgasm as Verity's breasts and mons were exposed to the whispers of cool air. She reached down beside her and grasped his penis, gliding her palm over it, not wanting to completely lose the connection.

Rolling up against her and onto his side, Rook nuzzled into her neck and kissed her throat. "Love you, witch."

Chapter 11

"I know I asked once before, but this still is kind of weird for me. Oz knows about and/or is aware during sex?"

"He knows all," Rook answered. Verity didn't want to hear that, but he was unwilling to lie about it. "He's present and not. It's hard to explain."

"I didn't just engage in a *ménage a trois,* did I?"

"No." He winced. "Kind of."

I will refrain from comment.

Rook smirked. Oz always commented on the woman's sexual prowess after a session of lovemaking. Some were too loud, others too weepy. And the demon hated the screamers.

You usually always have something to say, Oz, he thought.

This time I got nothing. I...like her.

So did Rook.

So it was best to let her think it had been only the two of them. "He's oblivious right now," Rook offered.

"Great." No belief in that statement.

Hell, a man who harbored a demon within him gave new meaning to the term *voyeur.* Even he tried to zone out when Oz was with his wife, Winter.

Verity asked, "What time is it?"

"Nearing five. You have a show tonight?"

"Yes, I have to get to rehearsal. I should have left an hour ago." She retrieved her clothing, spilled about the ottoman, and put it back on. "Can I return when I'm done performing?"

"I'll be out on the hunt."

"Right. Then tomorrow?"

"I'd love to make breakfast for you."

"You could spoil me, and I would let you. I do have to rush off. You see what you do to me? One look at you, and I fall to my knees."

"I like you on your knees."

"Anytime, lover."

She hopped on one foot as she slid on a boot and then the other. She wobbled, and he caught her in his arms.

His cock was hard and ready to go, but much as he wanted to make love to her all evening, they both had work to do. And, to be honest, he needed some distance from the witch. He couldn't forget what he'd said as he'd fallen into the bliss of orgasm. *Love you, witch.*

Had she heard him say that? She hadn't brought it up. Most women would latch on to those words and never let them go.

Had he meant what he'd said? How could he? It had been uttered in a mindless moment.

"This guy is always willing and able," she said, turning and grinding her derriere against his penis. "You may have some talent that the Demon Arts Troupe could utilize."

"What, an endlessly hard cock?"

"We feature erotic acts on Sundays."

"I don't think so." He hugged her from behind, pressing his erection against the soft sweater skirt until he fit between her buttocks. "Mmm…" He kissed her below the earlobe. "I'll miss you tonight."

"I suppose you'll be working all night?"

"I have to. I won't return home until I have a solid lead on Slater."

"I wish I could help you with that. That vampire moves often. I don't have a clue where he could be hiding out."

"I don't want you to get more involved than you already are. Besides, I've found a hideout for Zmaj. I'm staking it out tonight."

He'd considered the bait notion King had mentioned. Then he'd dismissed it because he hadn't thought she'd agree. He didn't want to unnecessarily endanger Verity. But…

"If I could find the vampire who bit you, then he could lead me to Slater."

"How to do that?"

"He would recognize you from the bite. Vamps can usually sense when one they've bitten is near. The bite bonds the victim to the vamp, in a way."

"Yes, I know that. But the spell has removed the taint, so there is that."

He kissed her again, unwilling to mention the idea of her as bait. If it occurred to her and she approved, she would have caught his little lure.

"You should get going," he said. "Talk to you sooner rather than later."

The lair harbored vampires, yet he saw no sign of the bald one. But as soon as Rook landed in the dark cave beneath the club, the vampires lunged for him—all at once.

He took out one immediately. Stake swinging, he slashed the air and on the return stroke took out another longtooth. Two grabbed him from behind, pinning his shoulders to the limestone walls. Another went for his neck—yet pulled back, his mouth bleeding from the blades.

Rook kicked him off and struggled with the others. He took a steel toe to his thigh. Bones shifted beneath his skin, but he didn't suspect a break. Still, the sudden pain brought him to his knees.

Time to fight or die.

After the show, Verity walked home as usual. The Metro was far enough away to make the walk about the same distance as catching a train. And although she should have at least taken a cab after her harrowing night being attacked by vampires, she hated sitting in the back of those smelly vehicles.

She was a big girl. She would not be forced to cower and shudder each time she went out into the world.

Unfortunately, now she felt as if she were being followed. It was a weird prickling heat that curled down the back of her neck and at her wrists—something she'd neglected to notice the night she'd been attacked. Because then she'd stupidly walked right into a pack of vamps, not even thinking as she turned the corner, "Hey, I should avoid that group of nasty-looking sneering men."

Now she wasn't going to think twice and vacillate on whether or not she was making things up. Her home was still a long walk away, so she dashed inside a late-night bistro and took a chair by the window. Scanning the streets, she didn't see anyone who looked like a vampire or who may have been following her, but then again, it could be anyone.

Or she could be imagining things.

Tugging out her cell phone, she started to dial Rook's number, then paused. "Shoot. I need to get his number."

Number or not, she didn't need to bother him every time the hairs on the back of her neck prickled. He was busy, hopefully stalking the vampires who could be following her. And a ringing phone could give him away to the enemy.

Her mother's voice rattled in her brain.

Don't trust any man. You can get yourself out of this bind.

Right. Bind getter-outer? Not so much lately. And she was beginning to trust Rook. Maybe a little?

It was time to take the next step. To move toward a future without fear. She wanted that. She just wasn't sure how to let go and simply allow it to come to her.

At the table next to her, the waitress delivered a steak and a bottle of wine to a rotund man. He cut into the bloody slab of meat and nodded his approval.

Verity usually gagged at the sight of such red meat oozing out pink juices, but now she sniffed the air. The scent was savory and strangely appealing, and as it grew stronger, it also grew less offensive. It smelled dark and—not horrible.

Clutching the fork from the place setting in front of her, she turned toward the man, and just as she almost brazenly stabbed at his plate, the waitress blocked her.

"Uh, *bonsoir,*" Verity said, trying to act nonchalant. She would order tea so they wouldn't rush her out. *"Thé noir, s'il vous plaît."*

The waitress nodded and strolled away. Unaware she'd almost tried to snag his meal, the man consuming the meat actually grunted with pleasure.

Now disgusted by the gourmand's gustatory habits, Verity turned toward the window and swallowed. Clasping a hand over her throat, she closed her eyes. Had she been thinking the bloody meat appealing? Still the smell reached her table, and it was so…appetizing.

The horror of it made her clutch her gut. This was insane. Finding appeal in something so horrible could only mean one thing. The spell hadn't worked. If it had, she certainly wouldn't find bloody meat appetizing.

She closed her eyes. *No. You can't transform to vampire. That would be...*

The worst. A terrible stigma among witches, not to mention unnatural and sickening. No witch would willingly welcome the vampire taint. It was everything the witches of the Light had protected themselves against for nearly a millennium.

Her spellcraft always succeeded. She used tried-and-true spells from the family grimoire. What could have possibly gone wrong?

No, she was overreacting. Maybe she was picking up on some kind of spice used in cooking the meat. She didn't find the blood appealing.

She glanced above the rooftop of the shop across the street. The moon was waxing but was five or six days from fullness. What little she knew about those bitten by vampires was that, as the moon neared fullness, the craving for blood became insurmountable. And those mortals who tried to withstand the hunger and make it past the full moon were known to go crazy. Literally. Fighting the incessant hunger took everything from them, including their sanity.

She wasn't a fighter; she was a performer. A lover. A witch who wanted to stay a witch. Nothing more. No fangs or unnatural cravings.

Smacking noises from the table next to her distracted her. A chunk of red meat speared on the fork looked like a delicious treat—

Verity swore under her breath.

She needed to perform the spell again.

Freddie Slater sat low in the driver's seat of the Mercedes just down the street from the bistro Verity had skipped into. He'd tracked her from the theater. She sat near a window, nervously tracing the street with her eyes. She couldn't see him through the darkened windows of the car.

He'd thought Clas had killed her. Idiot. That was the last time he put his trust in the burly bruiser. But the way Verity traced her neck with her fingertips did not go unnoticed. Had Clas's bite begun the transformation? How rich.

The witch he most loved to hate—and hated to love—would soon need blood to survive. Sweet revenge. And he hadn't even orchestrated it. He did like when the universe plopped surprises into his arms.

His cell phone rang, and after checking the screen, he decided to answer while keeping his focus on the bistro.

"What is it, Clas?"

"The hunter has found our lair beneath the club. He took out four of our tribe."

"And where were you when all this was going down?"

"I, uh—didn't want to take a stake to the heart, man."

"So you didn't attempt to help your fellow tribemates. What part of war don't you understand, Clas?"

"Uh, I've never really been in a war, boss."

Slater rapped his fingers on the dashboard. He'd stake the idiot himself. "Why didn't you tell me the witch didn't die?"

"What?"

"The witch I sent you to kill. She's alive."

"No, I bit her deep, man. Tore out her throat—"

Verity stepped outside the bistro, her head lifting as she took in the street up and down. Her long, pale neck was dusted by that impossible violet hair that he could still recall slipping over his skin.

"Her throat looks fine to me. We need to talk. Meet me at the mansion in an hour."

Clas's protests continued. Slater hung up. Reaching into

his pocket, he pulled out the wooden heart he hadn't been able to toss. It was always warm, and he liked to think it felt as warm as her skin. Also, it smelled like her. He'd licked it clean of blood.

"Bitch," he muttered, pressing the heart to his nose to inhale. "Wait until you know what it's like to crave blood. Then you'll know how I felt when you turned me down."

But he wouldn't go after her right now. He'd wait a few days, maybe even until the night of the full moon, so he could watch her fall, screaming and clawing, to the irresistible lure of vampirism.

Best to keep Clas safe until then. If the vamp took the stake before the full moon, the witch would not transform.

Rook returned to Order headquarters, stripped off his coat and the Kevlar vest and dropped them across his desk. The kick to his spine still ached, and he may have sprained a wrist. His leg bled, but with a few stitches he'd be fine. He had a surefire method to heal, but that would involve Verity's assistance. And right now, he was too wound up to consider seduction.

Catching the heels of his palms at his knees, he bent over and blew out a breath, shaking his head miserably.

"Where the hell is that bastard?"

How could one vampire be so slippery? He'd seen the bald vampire enter the lair with the other four. He'd been distracted by the others, but normally he could take on half a dozen or more if forced to it. Something was wrong with him. He wasn't up to par.

"Damn it!"

Stalking out of the office and down the hallway, he entered the gym and rushed the punching bag, beating it with his bare fists. Over and over he pounded his frustration into the sandbag until his knuckles bled, then he kicked it repeatedly until the leg wound began to bleed anew.

Pacing a wide circle around the room, he breathed in and out, seeking a tense calm and knowing he was only at his best when he reached a Zen state.

One bloody vampire kept giving him the slip.

"Fuck!"

He took out a stake from the hip holster and, compressing the paddles to release the tip, threw it toward the bamboo target set into the wall. It landed on the red center. He was still *en marque*. But he hadn't been out in the field.

Should he blame his failure on the fact that this was the first field job he'd taken in years? That would be too easy. He kept up with his training and worked out daily. He often went in the field with his trainees, so it wasn't as though he'd forgotten how to hunt. His reflexes were fine. His spirit was solid. His soul...

That is not what is distracting you, and you know it.

He hadn't heard from Oz for hours. Not even a snarky comment after he and Verity had made love all afternoon.

"Then what is it?" he asked, circling around and delivering a high kick to the punching bag.

You know who it is.

Indeed.

"Yet you insist I keep her close. She is the key to finding my soul."

So accept that tonight you were not in best form and move on.

"And what if I'm not in best form when Verity is again attacked? Keeping her close endangers her."

There is something about her that we are missing.

"I don't understand."

She is hiding something.

"You think? If I could read her, I would know if she was, but—hell, why can't I read her?"

Go home. Get some sleep. Tomorrow is a new day.

Rook shook his head at the demon's optimism.

You do not want to put her out of your life. You did tell her you loved her.

"I—right."

Had he meant it?

No.

You did.

What the hell was going on with him? In four centuries he'd not fallen in love. Not since Marianne. He couldn't allow himself to know the luxury of love again.

Yes, you can.

"Shut up, Oz."

Rook marched out of the gym and toward the elevator. He'd drive home and meditate before going to bed. Anything to clear his mind of…her.

Posed before her spell table, her hair let down and her body skyclad to the moonlight, Verity traced her finger down the Latin words in the grimoire. This was the same spell she had attempted the evening she had been bitten.

Something hadn't worked that first time. It was difficult to admit to that, but she had no choice but to believe she had worked the spell incorrectly.

The dove in her hand squirmed, its talons scratching her wrist. She squeezed hard enough to settle it. The black candle near her left foot flashed its flame high, bending to reach for the flame of the red candle that sat near her right.

Grasping the hat pin that had once belonged to great-grandmother Bluebell, and with a fleeting glance toward the quilt on her bed—"Be with me," she whispered—she knelt before the candles and began to recite the words.

They must be repeated over and over, her voice finding a cadence, a resonance that matched the frequency of the dove's pounding heart.

With the final word, which she carried out in a long hum that vibrated in her chest and outward through her extremities, she stabbed the dove through the heart. Blood dripped onto the flood of red and black wax. The substance coiled and swirled, spinning the colors together.

Verity dropped both things she held and leaned over the swirling wax, panting, smelling…so much. The blood called to her as if a sweet treat. A macaron swirled in red and black, pleading for a taste. She lowered her head and dashed out her tongue but retracted it when it swept the congealed red wax.

"No." She shuffled backward until her shoulders hit the base of the bed. Tugging on the quilt, she pulled it down and the blanket wrapped around her in a hug. "It didn't work. The blood—I want it!"

Chapter 12

The brown calico alley cat that had been scratching at Verity's back door sidled inside when she opened it. He pussyfooted straight for the pewter bowl she kept on the floor before the stove.

"I have your food," she said, opening a can of something moist with chunks and gravy and forking it into the bowl.

The cat devoured the meal while Verity did a little straightening in the cupboards. The maid who stopped in every Monday always rearranged the goblets beside the bowls, and she preferred them above by the other glasses. She'd been jittery all morning. No way to know if last night's spell had been effective. And she wasn't particularly motivated to go in search of raw meat to test the efficacy.

Peering outside, she eyed the flowers growing in the backyard. "Poppies and thyme," she said. "I'll have to cut those under the moonlight for my spells."

And the thought of moonlight tugged at her gut. She clutched her stomach and winced at the sudden surprising pain. It squeezed like a hunger pang, and the feeling strafed along her esophagus and up to her teeth. It was four times stronger than the mouthwatering pang she'd gotten last night when spying the bloody steak.

"Not the blood hunger," she whispered desperately. "Please."

That would mean the spell had not worked.

The full moon was five days away. She could manage the hunger pangs if they never got stronger than this one. But she suspected this was only a droplet compared to the smack she was going to be hit with soon enough. And just because she could manage them did not mean they would go away.

The inevitable was upon her.

A twisted *meow* preceded the snapping of bones and the weird leathery sound of stretching skin. The bar stool on the other side of the counter toppled but didn't hit the floor. Instead, the calico-haired naked man righted it as he stood.

"That moist gravy stuff rocks," he said. "Love the chicken flavor."

"Morning, Thomas. Robe's on the wall."

He claimed the blue terrycloth robe with the big gold T on the chest and threaded his arms through it, wrapping the tie tightly across his waist.

"I washed it for you."

"I can smell that. Lavender. Did *you* wash it or did the maid?" He slid onto a bar stool.

Verity dipped her head and avoided his gaze.

"Thought so."

The familiar was handsome. Average in height and with a head full of brown and golden tufts, he reminded her of a movie star with his big white teeth and sparkling green eyes. She'd almost swooned into his arms. The cat had a way about him she knew many women could not, and did not, resist. And that was good enough reason to leave him alone.

"So what's up, witchy chick? Haven't seen you for a few weeks, if you don't count your rude treatment of me the other night."

She had been rude when Thomas had stopped in the

other evening, but she'd had more important things in mind at the moment—namely, the sexy hunter.

"The usual. Shopping. Performing. Doing spellcraft. Getting chased by vampires. Meeting a sexy vampire hunter."

She ran her fingers over the love hickeys Rook had left on her breasts this morning. Mmm…marked by the hunter. But what would he think if he knew there was a possibility she could become the very creature he hunted?

"Is that the guy who was sucking on your tonsils the other day? The tall glass of salt and pepper?"

"His hair isn't that gray. And I thought you liked women."

"I do, but I can appreciate a handsome face. So, chased by vamps. Not good. Sexy vampire hunter. Good?"

"Very good," she said, leaning onto the counter. The sky-blue Ladurée box sat nearby, and she teased the corner of it with a fingernail. The sneaky hunter had known exactly how to get her on his side. "Extremely good."

Thomas toyed with the ends of her hair. It was a cat thing. "You sound like a well-fucked woman. And trust me, I know that sound."

"The man does have his talents."

"Meow."

"Yes, but Thomas, the vampire who chased me bit me."

"*Merde*. Did the hunter kill the bastard?"

"No, he got away."

"Double *merde*."

"But Rook is working on finding the vampire."

"Rook is the hunter's name? Cheesy yet masculine at the same time."

"I'm sure it's a code name. He's with the Order of the Stake."

"One of the secret knights, eh? But not so secret as they like to believe."

Thomas tugged aside her hair to inspect her neck where the bite wounds had healed, yet two red dots remained as if to insist she not forget her fate. "Does this mean what I think it means? The next full moon is in less than a week. Damn. Verity?"

"I tried a spell to stop the taint, but it didn't work. Twice. My magic is always effective. I don't know what's wrong with me. Thomas, I've been feeling hunger pangs. I had one just now when you were eating. Do you think the vampire taint is weakening my magic? Oh goddess, I can't let this happen. But I don't know what to do about it."

"I suspect you didn't tell your hunter lover about it? You and that never-trust-a-man thing, right?"

"I think I'm getting over that. I want to, at least. I intend to tell Rook. He can kill the vampire and no more worries. But what if he doesn't find him in time? If I transform, then he'll have to stake me."

"Exactly. You don't want the hunter to pencil you onto his list of most wanted."

"But Thomas, I think I could love him."

"Love? Wow. You're moving fast. Don't forget what happened last time you let a man into your heart."

"Slater was an asshole. Rook is true. He has his secrets, but I know he'll tell them to me when he's ready. And speaking of Slater…there's a nasty little complication."

"I thought you'd kicked that longtooth to the curb a long time ago. Hell, you moved across the city. Has he found your new home?"

"I'm not sure. I think he may have been the one to send the vamps after me in the first place. And now that he's aware Rook is after him, there's going to be a big mess."

"Don't worry about anything between the Order and Zmaj. You focus on you. And try the spell again. I don't want you vamping out anytime soon."

"I don't want that either. I nearly dove for some poor bastard's steak last night. It was bloody, Thomas. So horrible, but at the time I thought it smelled good."

"*Merde*. Maybe you do need to fess up to the hunter. Sounds like he's the only one who can help you. Do you trust him?"

"I want to, but you know what my mother told me."

"Yes, but I distinctly recall you telling me that your grandmother overruled your mother's entreaty not to trust any man."

Verity caught her cheek against a palm. "I'm so confused. I'm not sure what or who to trust. I care about him, but…he *is* a hunter. Do I or don't I ask for his help?"

"You can tell a lot about a man by the way he treats animals," Thomas announced and stretched back his shoulders. "I think I'll go have a sniff around this guy. See what he's made of."

The robe deflated to a pile on the chair. The cat extricated itself from the fabric and leaped to the floor, heading toward the still-open back door.

"Thomas, stay away from him!"

Verity raced to the door, but the cat was already halfway across the yard.

"I can never tell that cat what to do. I hope Rook doesn't have allergies."

Rook strolled out behind the cathedral the Order had retrofitted for headquarters and sat on the back step. Tucked within a populated area, the narrow alleyway hugged a row of four-and five-story walkups that also housed rental flats and tourist shops. The air always smelled like the Greek food from a restaurant on the other side of the block. He'd never admit it out loud, but he did like the shaved chicken gyros slathered with cucumber sauce and loaded with *pomme frites*.

He'd spent the afternoon going through computer records for local vamps, trying to place the face of the vamp who had bitten Verity. He'd gotten a good look at him last night and may have found a match. Clas Dreher. No location. But names carried weight, and he intended to go around asking after him tonight.

He needed to get to Clas before Slater brought the war to him. The only war he could imagine involved vamps coming at him in great numbers. Or vamps going after humans.

That was the war he did not want. This situation needed to be dealt with now.

Yet with thoughts of Verity dallying with his need to rush out and find the vamp, it had been difficult to concentrate on a plan of attack. Thus, the breath of fresh air.

"Meow."

"Bonjour, Monsieur le Chat."

The brown-and-gold-mottled tomcat sidled up to Rook's leg and rubbed a cheek across his leather pants. Rook scratched the cat between the ears, and the feline nuzzled up appreciatively.

"Aren't you a handsome fellow? I'd ask if you're hungry, but to judge that wide belly, you look well fed."

The cat sat beside him on the step, and Rook marveled at the ease with which the creature took up place. Normally felines were more skittish around humans, especially the strays that scampered in every alley, nook and rooftop in Paris. But he knew animals could sense when a human was trustworthy.

It had been a long time since he'd thought about Acteaon, the grey destrier that he had ridden while serving King Henri IV as a carbineer in the household cavalry. By the time Louis XIII had formed the musketeers from the carabin troops in the mid-seventeenth century, Rook had already been demon-inhabited and missed serving in the ranks. That horse had served in battle and peace time and had never flinched from rushing the vanguard.

"You look familiar," he said and wondered where he had seen this cat before. Could it be the same one who had so casually strolled into Verity's home as if he'd owned the place? "Are you—"

At that moment, a black Audi pulled up and King got out of the backseat. The man had never learned to drive, nor had he the desire to learn. It stymied Rook that anyone who had lived so long would not feel the call to learn all that he could about the modern world.

Of course, King still possessed the entitlement he'd been born with. Servants and drivers were *de rigueur* for him.

"Talking to strays?" King closed the car door. "Or recruiting for a secret four-legged tactical force?"

Rook scratched beneath the cat's chin. The feline stretched up his neck in delight. The car rolled down the alley to park but didn't drive away. "You have work here today?"

King approached but maintained his distance by about ten feet, hands in his pockets. "No, I saw you sitting out here and thought to stop and see when you're going to ask me for help."

He could use the help.

The cat suddenly hissed at King. Its back arched, and Rook could hear its claws scratch the cobblestones.

"I don't like you much either, cat," King spat.

"What is it about animals that they never like you?" Rook asked, though he knew the answer. "Remember the stallion in the eighteenth century?"

"Threw me thirty feet through the air to land in the Seine. Hated that damned horse. I should have had it bespelled."

"They can sense your nature."

"Get out of here, you mangy beast!" King hissed at the cat and sent it scrambling off with a hasty meow. "So what's up with the imminent war?"

Rook did not care for him referring to it as thus. "I got a name. Clas Dreher."

"Never heard it before, but that means little. He going to lead you to Slater?"

"I can hope."

"You want me to take the left bank and ask around?"

"And I'll do the right," Rook agreed.

"You heading straight to work or going to stop in to see the witch first?"

"Work," Rook said curtly, annoyed King assumed incorrectly.

"Good. That's the hunter I've known for more than four hundred years. Yet…"

Rook stood and splayed his hands in annoyance. "What?"

King squared his stance and shoved his hands in his pants pockets. He arrowed a serious summation over Rook. "What, exactly, does the witch mean to you?"

Rook shrugged, but he spoke the first word that came to mind. "Everything."

"That's the most interesting word I've heard you utter in a long time. You like this woman?" King sat next to Rook on the step.

"I do. She's, hell…everything might be stretching it, but—I don't know. Maybe I want her to be everything. It's been so long. I'm not even sure what that means anymore."

"Enough said. The occasional distraction is something you've earned. I've had a change of heart since our scuffle. You deserve this."

"Thanks, but I won't use her as bait. I can't put her in danger like that."

King sighed. Rook guessed that had been his reason for the sudden change of heart. A smart knight used any resource available to track his prey, including informants and friends. But Rook had never considered using someone he cared about.

"Does she know about Marianne?"

"No."

"Will she know?"

"Don't know. It's still new with us."

"Yet, new as it is, she has become everything to you."

Was that a trace of jealousy? King hadn't dated for the long term in decades. Both had settled into a hunter's lifestyle, seeking their pleasure in one-night stands or weekend flings.

"I want to keep her alive," Rook said.

"Another damsel in distress for you to rescue."

"Fuck you, man."

Truthfully, how many had he rescued over the centuries? A few, certainly. It polished a man's pride to help. Thus, much as he'd fought against pridefulness through Oz's yoga studies, he could never completely release himself from ego. Nor did he want to.

King shrugged. "Too bad you can't read your own truths. Oz would agree with me, I'm sure."

Oz did agree with King, and that was the kicker. Why couldn't Rook read Verity's truths? Had she cast a spell, some sort of glamour that hid something so deep and dark she couldn't reveal it to him? If so, it had to have been cast before he'd even met her.

I could read her truth.

That hadn't occurred to him. Should he let Oz read her? He wanted to know Verity. He should trust she would tell him what she wanted to tell him. Yet, he was keeping things from her. Could her secrets be keeping him from his soul?

I have already suspected she is hiding something. Let me at her. There is little time for dally. My wife will soon give birth. I must be there!

"Rook?"

"Huh?"

"Oz?" King guessed, familiar with Rook's occasional inward distractions.

"Sorry. Oz and I were discussing Verity's truths and why I can't read them."

"You can't? That sounds dangerous. I'm not going to step back into the role of warning you to be careful again, but—"

"I'll take care of it on my own time. Let's get to work. We each have half a city to cover. Check in with me on the hour."

"Will do."

Verity clipped the lemon thyme and laid the stiff stalks in a low-sided wicker basket with a wide handle that reminded her of the baskets the bunnies toted on the Christian Easter holiday. No chocolate eggs in hers, though, unfortunately.

She'd decided not to wait for moonlight, instead hoping she'd see Rook later. And who could bother with silly old herbs when a gorgeous man might show up to sweep her off her feet and into bed?

Well, she had to. She wanted to try another spell, something that would soften the hunger pangs, make them invisible to her. Tonight she would tell him. Time was running out. She would not fall to her knees again, enraptured by the utter sexiness of him. She must not.

She would not be stupid about this anymore.

When she heard the rustle in the nettle and the angry meow, she laughed. "Thomas, I've told you not to go

back there. That's where I grow the thorned and poisonous plants."

"Merde," blasted out from behind the shrubbery. "The
things I do for you, witchy chick. Ouch! Those things
sting."

"That's why they call it stinging nettle. What are you
doing shifting out in broad daylight? You want me to get
your robe?"

"No, I'll make this quick." A toe popped out from behind the thick foliage. "Besides, I'm bleeding. I don't want
you to see me like this."

"Poor Thomas."

"Do not condescend to me, Veritas Von Velde."

The scent of his blood carried to her, and Verity leaned
forward, catching her palms on the soil. "You are bleeding."

"You smell that? Sweetie, do not come any closer."

"I won't." But she did want to get a look at the blood.
Maybe inhale—*Verity!* She sat back on her heels. "Chill,"
she whispered to the annoying hunger.

"I've returned from a visit to your hunter," Thomas announced from within the greenery. "He was sitting outside
the Order's headquarters."

"You know where that is?"

"I know everything about everyone in this city. That's
what I do. I prowl and observe, prowl and observe."

And when he wasn't doing that, he was shagging human
women while in his human form. Such a player.

"And what did you observe about Rook?"

"Something troubling."

Verity set another clipping of thyme in the basket and
turned to the shrub. The solemn tone of Thomas's voice
worried her. "And?"

"Tell me why a vampire hunter would so casually wel-

come a vampire and sit and chat with him on the back
stoop of their headquarters, as if they were old friends?"

"A vampire? How do you know that?"

"I can smell a vamp a mile away. They can never erase
that minute metallic blood scent. And he was not too
pleased to have me near him."

"That's…" Verity slumped into a thoughtful pose. "…
weird. Rook hates vampires. It's his job to slay them."

"Exactly. I think you need to be cautious around him,
Verity. He is not the man your grandmother told you to
trust. And by all means, do not tell him about the bite.
Not if you value your safety and want to keep his stake
out of your heart."

Verity swallowed and clasped a hand over her chest.
She glanced skyward where the moon was already vis-
ible in the twilight sky, three-quarters round and quickly
growing more tumescent.

She had to stop this transformation from happening.
But how to do so if she did not tell Rook?

"He's my only option," she whispered.

Because she'd been going through the motions of cutting herbs for yet another spell to keep her hopes up, but
she knew the spell would not work. The vampire who had
bitten her needed to die. Either that, or she must make it
beyond the full moon without drinking blood. And that
wasn't looking very possible when she nearly stabbed
stranger's steaks off their plates.

"Find someone else to help you," Thomas said. "Or kill
the bloody vampire yourself."

"But if you said he was talking to a vampire, then perhaps…" Would Rook befriend her too if she transformed?

No! She couldn't think like that. The last thing she
wanted was to have to drink blood to survive.

"You're confusing me, Thomas. I don't know what to

do anymore. I shouldn't have let it go as long as it has. I should have told him immediately. But I had confidence in my magic. And then when I do want to talk to Rook, I can't think straight around him."

"Be careful around the hunter. He has secrets. I don't trust him with you."

The nettle rustled. Another crazy meow protested. Verity collected the basket and her pruning cutters and wandered back into the kitchen. If Rook did have a vampire friend, she needed to determine whether he was an ally or a future enemy.

"Tonight," Rook whispered as he strode across the bedroom floor.

As planned.

He toweled the sweat from his shoulders and abdomen. A long session of yoga had stretched his muscles nicely.

"You ready for this?"

What if she does not come?

"She will," he said to Oz. "She has to."

After her act, Verity rushed to the dressing room, seeking something to quench her thirst. The bottled water tasted awful, like salt to a dying man. She tossed it aside as Lyric entered.

"Whoa! You almost hit me." The vampiress brushed water droplets from her arm. "Verity? What's wrong? You're sweating."

"Uh…it's the fire."

"Your fire has never made you—you're also clammy." Lyric pressed her palm over Verity's forehead. "Are you coming down with something? I didn't think witches got sick."

"Oh, Lyric." Verity hugged her friend.

She needed to talk to someone, and she wasn't sure when she'd find a chance to tell Rook. She just needed a hug and an understanding ear.

"I have to tell you something."

Lyric nodded, and Verity confessed about the vampire attack, how it had brought her and Rook together and how she'd thought the spell had worked, until it had not.

"I'll sic Vail on the vampire. Clas is his name? What about the hunter?"

"I'm not sure."

"You have to tell him everything, Verity."

"I want to, but I just told you what Thomas learned. Can I trust Rook?"

"You have to. He may be your only hope. Go to him. Tell him the truth."

Chapter 13

Knowing that she was welcome to walk into Rook's home without knocking, Verity folded her sweater coat over the back of a kitchen chair, then strolled into the living room. Changing into her usual clothes after the performance, she'd dressed to seduce. It was her style to wear short skirts and silky fabrics. And the thigh-high stockings always made her feel sexy. She needed that confidence to be able to set aside her worries and confess all to her lover.

A man who may love her. A man she knew she could love. A man who may have his own secrets. Only when all their secrets were finally pushed out into the open could she truly surrender to her soul's desire to trust him.

The living room was empty. He must be in the bedroom. "Rook?"

No answer.

Feeling only a little sneaky, she wandered to the next room. He was home. The door would not have been unlocked otherwise. Entering the bedroom, her eyes took in the exotic blue fabric draped above the bed and—Verity stopped in her tracks. Her fingers clutched the air. Heartbeats speeded.

Standing before the window, shadowed by the hazy evening illumination from streetlights three stories below, was not Rook.

Her senses sorted the visual cues and determined it was demon.

The man—creature? demon?—turned toward her, his sleek black horns cutting the air in arcs and his snow white Mohawk jutting high and prideful as a stallion's tail down his back. Red eyes glowed. "Verity."

She pressed her back to the door frame as he approached on slow, agile, bare feet. He did not wear a shirt and his abdomen and chest were ripped with muscle, much like Rook's. He wore Rook's leather pants low on his hips. And he was about Rook's height and shape—but he was not Rook.

"Asatrú?" she tried.

"Call me Oz," he offered in a baritone that almost touched Rook's easy tone but was dipped in something murky and deep. Dangerous. "Do not be frightened."

"I'm not."

Maybe. She tried not to cower, pressing back a shoulder, but the stance felt too open and she clasped her arms across her chest. As a witch, she'd avoided conjuring demons simply because they were often malicious and hard to control.

"Okay, I am a little scared." She hadn't expected a demon to greet her today. "How are you out? I thought Rook said you only—"

"The full moon is my day. Rook hasn't completely untethered me, so I will only be able to stay out a short while." He stopped two feet in front of her, and she eyed his horns warily. Obsidian scythes cut the air. They were ridged along the spiral twist of their form, and the tips were pin-sharp. "We decided that I should have a talk with you."

"We? You and Rook? Is Rook in there? In you?"

"I am Rook. He is me."

The demon stretched back a shoulder, and his muscles

flexed. Verity watched the sinuous movement with admiration. And then she adjusted that thought. A demon stood in front of her. And he was also her lover. Maybe? His human-like face was not at all like Rook's, yet they had the same of angle of jaw and, yes, the high forehead. No scar at his eyebrow. Different hair and eye color. Cleanly shaven. But his mouth…hmm. Perhaps a bit like him.

How interesting that he was completely separate from Rook and…not.

"Rook cannot see your truths for some frustrating reason," Oz offered, "but I thought that I might be able to. I am a truth demon."

Verity crossed her arms tighter over the silk dress. "Why is Rook so worried about my truths? Does he think I'm hiding something? Maybe I think he is hiding something. Like, is he friends with a vampire? What do you think about that?"

The demon tilted a straight grin at her but offered no reply.

Verity stepped from foot to foot. She felt exposed. "Is Rook aware of our conversation?"

"He is always aware, as I am when he is in command. But I control this body for the moment. So."

A tilt of his head averted her attention to the horns that looked as if they belonged on a charging bull. She had never felt the urge to ward herself against demons. Until now.

The demon nodded. "You are part faery."

"Well, duh." Verity released her held breath and relaxed at the unsurprising revelation. "When Rook initially asked about my hair color, what part about my answer that it was natural didn't imply faery heritage?"

"Indeed." The demon grinned genuinely. "Sometimes Rook can be a little slow on the uptake."

"I have faery blood that traces back five generations," she explained. "It's dormant in the recent generations, but we still tend toward some physical anomaly associated with the sidhe. My great-grandmother's eyes were violet. And my grandmother is half faery. But that's not a truth Rook needs to worry about."

"Isn't it?" Oz stepped closer, and she shuffled against the wall, fearing the horns. "I will not hurt you, Verity. If either of us were capable of causing you harm, it would likely be Rook, not me."

"Rook would never hurt me."

"Not purposefully. He cares about you. I am impressed at his capability to love."

"Why?"

"Why not? The man is without a soul."

"Does lack of soul imply an inability to love?"

"It should. I give him the emotion and caring he requires to exist."

Interesting. As dangerous as it felt to have him stand so close to her, she was warming to the demon. He was handsome in a weird way because parts of him resembled Rook—she even picked up the tobacco-peach scent of her lover, albeit tangled within a slight sulfurous odor—yet Oz was his own entity.

"So about Rook being friends with a vamp—"

The demon put up an admonishing hand. "I will not play your silly game of twenty questions. If you have something to ask of him, you will do so directly."

Oz had been there when they'd played strip twenty questions. Verity wanted to hide her face until she recalled that the demon knew many more intimate things about her than how she answered questions.

"Now. There is more within that you hide."

The demon leaned forward, sniffing at her skin, moving his face so close she worried again about the horns. And when he glided down to sniff at her neck, she felt her nipples grow hard and hated herself for that reaction.

"Watch it, buddy. I'm Rook's girl."

"Do not flatter yourself, witch." The demon's eyes glowed red at her. "I am not interested. I am a married man with a baby on the way."

"You're a—how is that possible?"

"I make good use of my twenty-four hours of freedom a month."

"That's why Rook wants his soul," she guessed. "If he gets it back, you get freedom. And what could be more important than you having the freedom to be with your family?"

"Exactly. I must be there for the birth of my child. It is any day now. I will not be denied that joy. Rook and I have been companions for centuries. I have never disputed our connection or tried to force him to seek his soul, until now, when I have a purpose to freedom. You had the soul."

"It was stolen. But Rook knows that."

"Ah!" Oz reared from her, his body stiffening and his fingers arching into claws at his thighs. He stood with knees bent, as if ready to charge or perhaps in defense. "Now that was interesting."

"What?" Verity couldn't imagine what he may have seen in her, but his reaction frightened her.

The demon dodged to the bedside table for the notebook and pen Rook kept there. Oz scribbled a word on the paper and turned it to show her. When she almost spoke it out loud, he put up a finger to stop her.

He didn't want Rook to hear their conversation?

The word he'd written was *vampire.* So he wanted to talk about what he'd admonished her not to discuss—no. He'd seen that *inside* her? Hell.

Verity nodded to confirm his suspicion.

He wrote something else. *The spell did not work?*

She shook her head no.

"Four days until the full moon. You had better find that soul, witch, and let Rook take out the vampire who stole it or—" The demon opened his mouth wide to reveal fangs.

Verity stumbled backward, but Oz came at her with his mouth wide, as if a vampire lunging in for her neck. The demon stopped with his mouth only inches from her throat and chuckled out deep and syrupy laughter.

"Get away from me!" She shoved at his chest, but he did not move. Hard and as solid as the statue she had once compared her lover to. "Bring Rook back."

"I'm not finished with you yet." He grabbed her wrist and placed his palm against her chest as Rook had done that first night he'd found her huddled by the wall after the attack. "Something is blocking Rook from seeing your truths, and I will find that—" The demon hissed and swore, "Bloody Beneath and all the demons in Daemonia."

Oz exploded away from her and snarled as if defending himself against an aggressor.

"What?" Verity pleaded. She pressed both her palms to her chest, only feeling her rapid heartbeats. "Tell me!"

Oz stretched back his shoulders, flexing the insane muscles that wrapped his torso. Her lover's torso. Oh, she wanted Rook back!

"You have an old soul," the demon said.

"Well, yes, but—why does that freak you out? Reincarnated souls are nothing new. I've told Rook about it."

"But yours is…familiar."

"How so?"

"Describe it. What do you know about it? Tell me, witch!"

"My—my mother," Verity hastened out, "she always

said I was gifted the soul of a witch who died two deaths. That can't possibly—"

The demon shook his head and lashed out at nothing before him. He growled and beat at his chest, fighting… himself?

"Rook?" Verity called. "Is he trying to return?"

Oz stumbled across the room and slammed his back against the window frame. A horn clacked the window, cracking it. With one last growl, he fell to his knees and bowed his head. Horns receded into his skull. His hair shifted and changed to Rook's brown with gray salting above the ears. His body changed minutely, claws retracting and muscles rippling to encompass the slightly altered body shape.

And then he was simply Rook. A man, panting and huffing, hands to the floor before him.

He looked up at Verity and cried, "Marianne?"

Coming back from Oz always disoriented him. Rook could never manage to stay on his feet while the demon receded into him, the subtle shifts in the demon's body conforming to Rook's physicality. His mouth went dry. His ears rang. And the horns—it hurt like hell when those things spiraled back and screwed into his brain.

He collapsed against the wall, catching his palms against the ancient flocked paper. Inertia forced him to land in a sprawl. But what he'd heard Verity confess may have been the greatest reason for his inability to stand.

She was the reincarnated soul of a witch who had died twice?

In his lifetime he'd known one witch who had fit that description.

"Rook?" Heels clicking across the parquet, Verity knelt before him. She touched his shoulder gently. He shivered and winced against the last biting twists in his brain. "What is it?"

He clasped her hands, anchoring himself. Staring into her eyes, he hated that he still could not read her and that Oz had achieved such an intimate connection with her.

But he also came to a strange realization: If she were the reincarnation of Marianne, had his former wife somehow protected him from seeing Verity's truths?

"For what reason?" he asked aloud.

"Rook? Are you okay? You said a name."

He bracketed her face, studying the details of her warm, rosy skin, her narrow, deep violet eyebrows, her perfect nose and open mouth. Scented like sugar and roses. Nothing similar to what he remembered of Marianne. His wife had been fair and seemingly frail but strong, so strong. Her eyes had been pale blue, her lips barely pink. Freckles had dotted her nose and high on her cheeks.

Everything about Verity was bold and lushly tinted with rose and violet. Yet…could she truly be a reincarnation of Marianne?

"Who *are* you?" he pleaded.

"You're scaring me, Rook. I don't know what to say to you."

"Oz saw your truth."

"Yes. But I didn't think it was anything remarkable. My hair—I told you it was natural."

"Yes, part faery. That's not it."

"The vampire bite." She looked down, her face still in his hands. "I didn't want to tell you because—"

Yes, he recalled that strange exchange now. Oz had attempted to hide it from him, but he'd seen the demon write on the paper. "You should have told me, Verity. You think you'll transform to vampire?"

"I don't know. I thought everything was fine until it became obvious it was not. The spell didn't work. I'm frightened. I didn't know how to ask for your help. My mother said to never trust any man, and yet my grandmother—oh. That's not important right now. But you are intent on finding the vampire who attacked me, so I have to leave my fate in your hands." She stroked the hair over his ear, her blue-violet eyes glinting with worry. "That's not what's troubling you, is it?"

He released her and pressed his bare shoulders against the wall, looking aside. If Oz were still out it would have made this easier. Oz spoke the truth always and with such ease. The demon had been right; he was the one who gave Rook his emotion. Oz handled emotion with skill and élan, never angering or blowing his cool, as Rook often did.

"We will discuss you and the bite," he said.

"Yes, we should."

"I cannot abide you becoming vampire," he hissed.

"Of course not." She bowed her head and studied her fingers, entwined in a nervous twist. "I don't want that either. I'd sooner die."

Eyeing her sternly, he wished the fact that she had been bitten and feared transformation was the only thing he had to worry about. Hell. If he didn't kill the vamp who had bitten her before the full moon, she could change to vampire. They had, what, three or four days until the full moon? How could she have let it go so long?

"Who is Marianne?" she asked.

Tilting his head back and closing his eyes, Rook thought about pushing Verity away. Telling her to get out, to leave him in his newly dredged-up misery. How dare she bring this back to him?

But she couldn't know the events that had pushed him toward the Order so many centuries in his past.

He offered quietly, "She is the witch I told you I had

watched burn at the stake. She was…" he lifted his head to look directly into her tearing eyes "…a witch who died twice."

Fingers flying to her mouth, Verity gasped. The tears spilled down her cheeks, and Rook thumbed a hot droplet away. He pressed his thumb to his finger and squeezed the salty drop. When had he ever shed a tear for Marianne?

You have never had the ability to show your pain in such a manner. It is not a weakness.

Sometimes he hated that Oz was there.

"But that can't be," she started.

"How do you know you are the reincarnation of such a witch?" he asked.

"My mother always said it. She knew things like that. Same as when I told you I knew about people and their place in the world."

"Still never fathered a child," he offered but couldn't find the lightness that should have accompanied that comment.

"Yes, well, my mother always thought it was strange. I mean, a witch who died twice? How can you die twice? But that's why she knew it to be true because no one could make up a thing like that. And she never doubted her intuition."

He nodded. It was a damned insane thing to die twice. But possible. He knew it as he knew the blood that coursed through his veins was tainted with demon blood. Marianne had died twice.

Because of him.

Chapter 14

"Who was this witch?"

Pressing his hands over his face, Rook inhaled, taking a moment to calm himself. To let his breath spill out unfettered. Because he must. He must tell someone. He had chained the agony within his heart for too long.

"My wife," he said on an achy gasp.

"Oh, my goddess," Verity whispered. Kneeling between his legs, because he still sat on the floor, she touched his knee. "When were you married to her?"

"Fifteen eighty six. When I was young and mortal. I served King Henri IV in the light horseback cavalry. They called us carbineers. We were married only five years. I didn't believe in witchcraft back then. And Marianne was a witch."

"Did she convince you?"

"Yes. But only after summoning demons as a boastful answer to my constant insistence that she was nothing more than a product of her own beliefs."

"Witches are real," Verity whispered.

"I know that. But in the sixteenth century, most tended to believe that women who thought they had powers were either in league with the devil or had created the scenario in their own troubled minds."

"What of witch hunters? Didn't they have them back then?"

"Yes, but they also believed more in the mental state of the women than that they could possess actual supernatural powers. Or else, that they were demon possessed because of their alliance with the devil Himself."

He caught his head in his hands. Did he want to get into this now? He had things to do, like find Slater and the vampire who had bitten Verity.

You tell her all now. Or you will never earn her trust. It is a difficult issue for her. Marianne needs you to do this.

"Get the fuck out," Rook muttered.

That is what I am trying to achieve. Freedom. With trust, the witch will act as bait for the vampire who took your soul. If you care about her, you must tell her everything.

"You talking to Oz?" she asked.

Rook nodded. "Sorry."

"That's all right. Was Oz one of the demons your wife summoned to prove to you she was a witch?"

"Good guess."

"Will you tell me about it? I want to know how Oz got stuck inside you and…how your wife died twice." The stroke of her fingers along his cheek felt too tender, yet it was all he wanted. "If you trust me?"

Did he trust her? She'd not told him about the spell not working against the bite. Had it been fear that kept her silent, or was it lack of trust? He was already in pursuit of Clas, but had he known Verity's condition, he would not have relented until the vamp was ash.

He had to get out there, find that bastard and shove titanium through the vampire's chest.

Not yet. You do trust her. She is all you have right now.

That wasn't correct. Always, he had King. But he and

King had not discussed Marianne in centuries. King knew it was Rook's cross to bear. And he'd dragged that burden through deep channels all his life.

He pulled Verity close and turned her to sit against his chest and between his legs. Wrapping his arms around her, he clasped her hands in front of them and kissed the side of her neck. She smelled like macarons. That made him smile briefly. If only the world could fade into violet hair and macaron kisses. Easier that way.

Get on with it!

Very well. He owed Oz this confession.

"Marianne had her sights set on controlling demons without the use of a familiar. It's difficult for any witch to accomplish, and few nowadays can do such a thing, as I'm sure you're aware."

"That is the familiar's principal task—to assist a witch in the summoning of a demon."

"Exactly. But Marianne loved animals so much she couldn't allow herself to use a familiar in such a manner, even though they are classified as shapeshifters and not true animals. One evening she managed the summoning on her own, though it quickly got out of hand. She had conjured a rage of demons from Daemonia, a great swirl of blackness that rose above our cottage situated on the outskirts of Paris, very near the Bois de Boulogne."

At mention of the park, she twisted to look at him.

"I'll get to that," he said.

It was going to hurt like hell to dredge up all this stuff from memory. Long ago buried, literally and mentally, Rook wanted to do this as much as Oz wanted to remain inside him.

Yet he also wanted Verity's trust. And perhaps even her love.

"Most of the demons escaped Marianne's control. Neither of us knew what happened with them. Some were corporeal, so we assumed they walked the mortal realm, whereas the incorporeal ones, well, they may have found a human host. One dashed through me and got stuck. Asatrú. A truth demon."

You see? You are finally embracing your truths. Good boy, Rook.

"An annoying truth demon," Rook felt inclined to add. "It was after witnessing that incredible display, and knowing a demon roiled within me, that I had no choice but to believe Marianne was a witch. She apologized for the magic gone wrong. She guessed it was because of the pregnancy—she was soon to give birth—that her magic had been so difficult to keep in hand. And the next few days would become the blackest days of my and her life."

Verity pulled his hands up and kissed them, holding him tightly. The heat of her tears spilled over his skin.

Succumbing to the cool wash of memory that flooded his thoughts, Rook whispered, "Some memories haunt me vividly…"

Paris, 1592

She had suffered quietly through the day, fingers clenching the bed clothes and only taking the water Giles offered from the pewter cup in small sips. They called it labor for a reason, she'd said at one point.

But now Giles was worried. Her skin and hair were soaked. The bedclothes were wet from her laborious exertions. A strong woman who would never show others her pain, she was barely holding on now. Her waters had gushed out early this morning. It was now twilight, and the babe had yet to even move. Or so Marianne had said after probing over her stomach with her fingers.

"He's stubborn," she whispered.

Always, she managed that small smile of reassurance. And she was sure the child was a boy and said he would grow up like his father, stubborn yet fierce.

She constantly went out of her way to show Giles that she was well and that she loved him. As if she needed to compensate for her supernatural truths. Because he had married a witch. He'd not known she was a witch when they'd exchanged vows under the ash tree at the edge of the Bois de Boulogne. Over the years, Marianne had attempted to make him understand that her potions and herbs were magical. He would laugh and say she had a way with healing, that was all.

Only recently she had found it necessary to convince him of her nature. He wished she had not tried when she was so large with child, but alas, Marianne was the most stubborn of them all.

The rage of demons that had invaded their two-room cottage and swirled out into the atmosphere had convinced him well and good. From that day forward Giles had walked the streets of Paris with a bit less confidence and a lot more wariness. A king's horseman, he was. A man who charged danger and showed it his teeth.

Now a man who harbored a demon within him.

Yet should anyone learn his wife was a witch, they would try to harm her, to take her away from him. He would not suffer any man to live should the bastard conceive of harming Marianne.

"Tell me what I can do," he pleaded. Marianne's hand, clasped in his, was limp and feverish. "It's gone on too long. The babe—"

"Needs help to come into this world," she uttered. "You must go for the midwife on Rue Vaugirard. Esmarelda is her name. She is a witch I have confided in on occasion.

She will know how to prepare the spells I am too weak to manage."

"I will go immediately. But—no, I cannot leave your side."

He kissed her hot brow and smoothed the hair from her face. Normally her reddish-brown locks were springy and wild, defiant of taming and ever Marianne's bane. Now they lay wet upon the goose down pillow, as exhausted as his wife.

"Go, my love. It shouldn't take you more than an hour. Bring me wine, too."

Their wine stores had depleted last week after Rook had taken to drinking to get his head around the idea that his wife was a witch and that a real demon poked and jounced about inside his body. An accident born of his wife's need to convince him of her truths. There hadn't been enough spirits to change that reality.

"Yes, more wine. And the midwife who is a witch. I'll run and make it in half that time."

He pressed a long, lingering kiss to her belly, hoping that it might stir the babe into motion. *Your father wants you to behave. Don't be so cruel to your mother.*

"I love you, Marianne."

The midwife greeted him with a knowing nod. She was old, and warts pocked her chin. She looked like Giles's idea of what a witch should resemble. Not young and pretty like his wife.

Giles hastily blurted out that he knew she was a witch, like his wife, and he would tell no one if only she would help him.

Giles thought she sneered when she spoke his wife's name, but he was too frantic to pay attention. The midwife deemed it about time he finally got on board with the belief in their breed. Giles had not before heard the term witch labeled as a breed. So much he did not know. Yet he did know the world was populated with real witches and demons. And Marianne had casually mentioned vampires and werewolves.

Mercy, but he wanted his wife and child to be safe. He'd wonder about those other *breeds* later.

"I have to purchase wine for Marianne," he said. "And something stronger for me."

Esmarelda handed him a bottle of raspberry wine and sent him off to the tavern to seek his own devil in a bottle. After both had gathered their tools for survival, Giles met the witch at the edge of the Tuileries. She carried a sack of mysterious goods and wore a smart felt hat pulled down over her eyes.

"Lead on, man," she offered to his wondering assessment. "There's no time to waste."

Back at the cottage they found Marianne unconscious, an arm dipping off the bed, her fingers touching the floor. The witch ordered Giles outside to make a bonfire and boil some water. He initially refused to leave his wife's side, but the witch snapped her fingers and something inside him sat up and shivered. It was the first time he'd felt the demon's attention align with his own.

"Out!"

Giles did as he was told. He knew it was a command designed to keep him from underfoot while the women labored to bring a child into this world. He felt helpless. This was not something he could rush with sword held *en guarde* and musket primed.

If only he could be allowed to sit beside Marianne, to hold her hand.

He paced near the blazing fire he'd stoked outside the

horse shed, whiskey spilling down his jaw as he quickly consumed the bottle beneath the wicked red harvest moon. He rarely drank so much as to get soused. For some reason the demon within made him twice as capable of handling his drink as he once could.

"Demon-infested idiot soldier," he muttered, standing transfixed by the flames. "Married to a witch."

It felt like an epitaph, a derogatory slur against all the choices he had made in life. Yet it was real. It was his life. And he would not change it for the world. He loved Marianne with all his heart. His soul was not complete without her.

Hours later, he could no longer stand by helpless and uninvolved. His wife's soul called to his. And for a flicker in time it was as though there was another. Theirs. A new creation.

Giles turned toward the cottage. "My child?"

He rushed across the dirt yard that Marianne always tried to coax into a garden. Unholy soil, she'd once commented. In need of a midsummer's cleansing.

As he neared the cottage, the door blew open of its own accord, as it had on the night she had called up the demons. Giles's racing steps thudded to a stuttering halt. His heart thundered, suddenly fearful.

In the doorway stood Esmarelda and in her arms was a bundle swaddled in the bright emerald skirt that Marianne kept tucked in her trousseau. It had belonged to her mother. The silk was her only treasure.

The witch shook her head and held forth the bundle. It was not wrapped to expose a tiny face but instead completely covered. Mummified.

Giles dropped to his knees. His heart threatened to punch through his chest. Even Asatrú lurched about, anxious.

"No," clambered from his soul in an achy, wrenching cry to the heavens.

"I'm sorry." The witch stopped in front of him. "It was born dead. We both believe it has not taken a breath for hours. She tried…so valiantly. Some souls are simply not prepared for this realm."

"Don't tell me that!" Giles argued.

He beat the ground with his fists, but seeing the witch's tattered leather shoes brought him into focus. He stood. The bundle was held forth.

He couldn't touch it. Not yet. Not ready to touch death. To feel it darken his soul.

"How is she? I must go to her!"

"Monsieur!"

He ignored the witch's cry. He didn't want to hear her voice. Didn't want that tiny…being anywhere near him until he'd looked into his wife's eyes and knew their souls were still one.

Bloody bed clothes and linens littered the floor in wet islands. Giles stumbled over to his wife's side. She looked serene, and her skin was dotted with perspiration. Alive. Yes, so alive.

He kissed her forehead and pressed his to hers, sliding his palm along her cheek. Her skin was cool, but not alarmingly so.

"I'm so sorry," she whispered.

"We'll have another," he reassured. "I'm only thankful you survived."

She nodded, not a tear in her eyes, and fell asleep in his arms.

The old witch wandered toward town, leaving the grieving couple to their pain. The husband had not given a care to see why she had called out to him as he'd entered his home.

He should have.

Marianne had found herself a fine man, she had. The younger witch was too pretty. She'd never given a kind word to Esmarelda when she'd been in town and had once threatened to report her to the inquisition when she'd refused to help her deal with the foul bargain she had made with the devil Himself.

Giving it a squeeze, suddenly the bundle squirmed in Esmarelda's arms. She peeled away the wrap to expose the tiny face. The mouth miraculously gasped for breath.

Hmm, she had no use for a child herself. Save for in pieces to use in spells.

The idea of returning to Marianne's home and handing it over did not flicker in her twisted thoughts. She hated the young witch.

Yet if the babe remained in her possession, the devil would surely find it because she knew it had been marked.

Holding the swaddled bundle against her chest, Esmarelda made her way through the dark alleys and toward the nearest monastery. It would be safe and unseen by the dark prince there, protected by the holy walls. Also, she might manage a few sous for leaving the babe.

She'd never liked Marianne Rochfeaux and her fancy soldier husband. They would both get what was coming to them.

Chapter 15

Paris, 1592

Six days later, Giles Rochfeaux's world grew darker. He'd not thought such a thing possible.

It was.

Marianne had recovered from the taxing birth and busied herself cleaning the floorboards with a sweet lavender and rosemary wash. Neither of them had mentioned the babe, although one night over carrot and pheasant stew they had met eyes, and Giles had known his wife was thinking of the child.

The midwife had taken the babe away without another word to either of them, likely to bury it under a rowan tree deep in the forest. Giles's heart shivered to think he should have seen to having the babe baptized postmortem, but that soul was gone now. Out of their lives. If they were to move beyond this terrible loss, they must only look to the future.

It is what he told himself. And he must hold his head high and be the strong man Marianne needed to overcome this blow.

Dropping the scrub brush, Marianne stood stiffly and walked out the front door as if following a call only she could hear.

"What is it?" Giles asked.

"They're here."

Veins running cold, Giles sensed the secrets his wife held had not yet been completely revealed. Dread coiling about his heart, he rushed out behind his wife. Six men stood in front of her. He cringed at the sight of their drawn and dirty faces. Emaciated yet strapped with noticeable muscle. And at their mouths…fangs.

"What in God's creation…?"

"Vampires," Marianne whispered to him. "They won't come near me. My blood is poisonous to them. But you…"

"Vampires?"

Giles was only getting his head around being married to a witch and then being occupied by a demon who battered about inside him in an attempt to get free. He'd lost his child less than a week ago. And now this?

"Be gone! You are not welcome here."

Rushing back inside the cottage, he grabbed the pistol at the table, but it was not primed or loaded. He pulled the epée sword down from over the threshold and walked out with both weapons in hand.

"We have business with your witch," the leader said. He sneered at the ineffectual weapons Giles insisted on holding, as if they could protect him and his wife. "She owes Himself a life."

"What? Himself?"

"Do not say that name again!" Marianne hissed. "Or you will call him to this realm." She spat at the vampires, who stepped back from the offense.

Giles had no idea who she was talking about. Or why she was talking to vampires.

"Get me a knife," Marianne commanded over her shoulder. "Now."

"Stay right there, soldier!" The leader stepped forward. "She made a deal with the devil. We've come to collect."

"Marianne?" Giles moved up beside his wife. He wanted to clasp her hand, but it was more important he hold the weapons at the ready. His shoulder brushed hers. His blood ran cold when she shrugged away from his touch. And then she bit into her wrist, breaking the skin. Blood oozed out. Hell, what was—

Marianne thrust her arm out, sending blood droplets flying. "My blood will kill them," she cried. "Get me that knife! Or give me your sword."

Giles remained fixed, the vampire's words buzzing in his brain. The devil? His wife had...

"What for?" blurted the barely audible tones from his mouth. "What deal did you make?"

She turned to him, her face bloodless and drawn. "Does it matter?"

"I—no." It couldn't matter because he loved her, and it was likely a bargain she had made before they had met.

But what did matter? The sudden knowing that froze the blood in his veins.

"You promised our firstborn," he guessed. "You knew all this time that you would... That when you gave birth...?"

Giles's heart caught in his throat. He didn't want to consider it.

"No, my love, I would have never handed over my child to the devil. I would have figured out an escape."

"Witches," muttered the vampire, as if to console Giles's breaking heart. "Can't trust 'em. She did promise to hand over her firstborn, but I guess that was a failure, eh? Come on, gentlemen, this witch needs to pay."

The vampires flanking the leader took steps forward.

"No!" Giles raised the pistol.

A vampire lunged for him, and he dashed the epée

through its heart. The creature smiled as Giles drew the blade back. A drop of blood stained the vampire's tunic. He slapped his chest and chuckled.

Giles swore.

A fight ensued, but it didn't last long. He could take on a man or two with sword and fist, but defeating six vampires who possessed insurmountable strength was out of the question. And as he struggled madly with four of them, Giles saw the other two wrangle Marianne easily. She spat blood. She must have bitten her tongue. One of the vampires quickly bound her mouth and hands.

"No!" He took a punch to the jaw. They weren't trying to bite him. They merely wanted to detain him and keep him conscious.

Flames crackled. Marianne's muffled screams clutched Giles's heart.

An hour later the vampire who had contained his struggles dropped Giles, and he fell to the ground by the flames. Muscles exhausted from the agonizing struggles to not look and then to struggle free, he could only lie sprawled on the cold ground and pant. He had no more voice to cry out to the heavens.

Yet the demon inside of him gave him sound, and together they howled until the morning had extinguished the flames and wind sifted his wife's ashes across his face.

Verity clung to Rook, shivering as if she herself had stood at the flames witnessing the horror of his wife burning. The memory was familiar to her, and she could not hold back the pain of watching her mother burn. She had not cried out that evening; only the sound of fire ripping into the night had sounded like a scream to her. Tears spilled down her cheeks now.

Curse her knowing soul to have led her to the pyre. Why had she needed to witness such a horror? Hearing about it later would have sufficiently destroyed her. Her soul, that strange soul from the witch who had died twice—Rook's wife—had led her to her mother's burning.

Perhaps to know and to now be able to understand Rook's pain?

When they'd first met, she'd asked him the way to his heart, and he'd said that was a secret. But in fact his heart was gated, closed up and locked after the trials he had suffered. And the only way in was through compassion and simply listening.

Rook rubbed her back, comforting her. As if she were the one in need of support! She felt awful, and duplicitous, and sad, and so angry for him. For his wife, who may have had good reason for making such a deal with the devil. And for their child, who had never been given a chance to breathe.

And for her mother, Amandine Von Velde, may she rest in peace.

"That's why you became a hunter," she whispered through sniffles.

"I did go after the vampires. Weeks later. But my story isn't over yet. Marianne had only died once. She would die yet again the next day."

Verity pressed up against his chest, studying his eyes and finding no tears, not even a catch to his voice. Of course, if he allowed himself to become emotional he would go mad. Was it Oz who kept back his emotions? Controlled them to make Rook strong?

"You and Oz?" she prompted.

"After Marianne's death, he settled within me. And he began to communicate with me. He felt my pain because he had known the same pain. He'd watched his family die centuries earlier. Desperate, he too had sold his soul for riches and promised his firstborn. When he thought to renege on the payment, Himself was most cruel to him. Oz was made demon and condemned to Daemonia. A demon who could see the truth in others. It's not such a blessing as one would believe."

"Because his truth was so vile," Verity muttered.

Rook nodded. "Oz and I bonded that morning when I lay by Marianne's ashes, pleading to the world to take me instead. To reverse the hours and make the vampires tear me limb from limb, if only to save my beloved wife. She had suffered so much. She'd given birth to our stillborn child. I never did find out where the babe had been buried."

Now Rook's chest rose, and Verity felt his pain over the lost child.

"Your name was Giles?"

"It is my birth name. Giles Martin Rochfeaux. I took on Rook when I joined the Order. I shed…" He sighed. "All things that reminded me of that life."

"I can understand. You both went through so much."

"With much more to come. Sitting there by her ashes, I pleaded to Above and Beneath and any angel or demon who would listen to bring back my wife," he said.

"And someone was listening."

1592, One day after Marianne's death

The ground shook. Steam rose from the soil that surrounded the pit where the ashes twisted up. Giles tried to embrace the sooty swirl. He wanted to scoop it all up and bury Marianne's remains properly.

"Giles Martin Rochfeaux," came a voice so dark and empty that the chills tracing Giles's spine felt like ice, and he thought he felt something cold and hard crackle and fall away from his skin.

Spinning around, he cried out at the sight of the figure that towered over him. Cast in shadows, because the dawn had not yet arrived, its horns jutted into the sky, an arm span from tip to wicked tip. Shoulders of thick, rugged, black muscle flinched and twisted as it stepped forward on cloven hooves that dredged the dirt and ash up in dusty clouds.

"What are you?" Giles dared to ask.

"I am the one you summoned to bring back your wife."

"Oh, yes?"

Giles stood and reached out, but would not touch; he felt sure his fingers would singe upon touching the monster's black flesh. Monster? This thing was the devil, surely.

Himself, whispered inside Giles. Asatrú feared this one. *The Old Lad Himself. Do not do it, Giles!*

Ignoring the intrusive demon, Giles called, "She made a deal with you?"

"Upon which she reneged."

"You sent the vampires after her. How—"

"Dare I?" The devil inclined its head, and its eyes glowed red. "She agreed to the bargain to hand over her firstborn should I give her the magic she desired. Born of two witches, she had been sorely lacking in magical skill, an outcast."

Much as it pained Giles to learn that truth only after his wife's death, and to know it was something she had never dared tell him, he couldn't argue that now. "Marianne could not help that our child was born dead."

"As I could not prevent my fixers from seeking recompense for the broken bargain."

Giles rubbed his hands over his hair, wanting to shout at this demon, the most vile and lowest demon of them all, yet all he could do was shake his head. And fall to the aching needs of his heart.

"I want her back!" he shouted. "Can you do that?"

"I can do whatever pleases me. And it would please me to give you this boon in exchange for your soul."

"Take it!" Giles slapped his chest with a fist.

No! Asatrú shouted.

"Take all of me, if only to give her back the life she deserves. You want to take my life? It is yours."

"Only your soul, boy, only your soul."

"Then I give it freely. If you will return life to Marianne."

"Done." The devil stomped the ground with a hoof and stretched wide his grotesquely muscled arms. Inhaling, he sucked out the air from Giles's lungs. "Stand tall, soldier."

Unsure what was going to happen but only wanting to have Marianne back in his arms, Giles did as he was told.

You will regret this, the demon within whispered.

He was supposed to trust a demon? They were all mad, unreal, a bunch of faery tales. With Marianne back in his arms, Giles would take her to a new country, stop her from practicing witchcraft, of even speaking of bizarre breeds, and they would begin anew. A new life far from the atrocities he'd been shown only too recently.

The devil clapped his hands together and then curled the fingers of one hand into a fist. Pointing a finger at Giles, the demon lord crooked it toward him as if to invite his soul to flee his mortal bones.

Asatrú yowled as something was pulled out through Giles's flesh. A bold white ball of light coalesced and spun, much like the ashes that now spun in a tornado-like tunnel nearby. The soul light blinked and soared toward the monster. Himself caught it as if a ball. Tossing it up and down, Himself winked, then slammed it toward the ground that edged the forest, burying the soul deep and snuffing out its light.

Giles fell to his knees. Asatrú moaned and shivered within Giles's bones.

And Marianne's ashes soared skyward, forming into wings that flapped and moved over the cottage. With a clap of the devil's hands, the surrounding trees in the forest shook, the ground quavered and the ashes dropped through the air, dissolving as they landed on the cottage roof.

"It is done," the dark prince announced. "And do not beg for my return to fix this foul bargain. I have given you what you asked. You have paid for that gift with your soul. I buried it deep so you will never touch it again. Yet it will live on, knowing it was betrayed by you. With your soul absent, the truth demon is now trapped inside you. You should have listened to Asatrú, Giles Martin Rochfeaux."

Lifting his arms high above his head, the devil's eyes lighted bold and red and then he ashed into nothing, leaving the air colder than a winter's night.

Giles shivered, his breaths huffing out in foggy clouds. The wind creaked the old wooden door. He turned toward the cottage.

There in the doorway stood Marianne, alive, her clothing in tatters and her hair melted from the fire. Her skin hung loose on her bones. Her fingers were red, and he could see the white skull bone.

As she took a step forward, Giles realized the terrible mistake he had made.

Chapter 16

Giles had been over the moon to see his wife alive and standing there, arms held out, beckoning him—for about five seconds.

Now Rook inhaled and tried to push away the vision of Marianne, bedraggled and risen from the dead.

"Rook?" The voice of another precious soul whispering to him.

Thankful for her presence, which yanked him up from the past to the now, he pulled Verity to his chest and buried his face against her lush hair. Wrapping his arms around her, he finally surrendered to the pain and guilt and the ever-long agony he had carried with him through the centuries. His shoulders shook, and he squeezed her tighter. She was real, alive, and he would never harm her as he had Marianne. He must not.

"One should never bring back to life what was once dead," he managed and then released a sorrowful moan against her head.

He held her forever. When he'd started to cry he didn't know, but the tears came freely, and he couldn't stop them. Verity turned in his embrace and straddled his legs to hug him close, and now she cooed soft reassurance as she stroked his hair.

He wanted to climb into her and stay there. To fit himself against her soul as only a demon could and not have to answer to the world—and his mistakes. Because his truth was that he could never atone for what he had done to Marianne. And never again would he be deserving of his soul. A soul that Himself had buried and Verity had found.

Had Marianne been seeking him for the century Verity had worn the little wooden heart against her skin? Truly, had his dead wife led Verity to him?

"I'm so sorry for you," she said.

Finish the tale. Tell her!

"Oz is right. I have to tell it all."

"I'm listening," she whispered. "And I'm here for you."

With a nod, he resumed. "Standing in the cottage doorway…she knew what she was," he said against Verity's shoulder. "A revenant formed of lifeless sinew. A zombie. She pleaded with me to end her. She didn't blame me for bringing her back—or so she said—but she didn't want to exist. Her skin literally…"

He couldn't speak it. His stomach roiled at the memory of it. "It frightened her. And it destroyed her. So I had to end her life. Again."

He swallowed.

"All I had was an ax."

Verity pressed her chest against his. Rook pulled her in tightly. Oz seemed to stretch out his arms through Rook's and pull the witch in, too. They needed the anchor to this moment that only she could give them.

"You could not have known," she said softly. "What a tragedy to have to carry that with you for so long. If there was something I could do to make it better…"

"Is she really inside you?" he asked, sniffing back tears. "Do you think Marianne's soul…?"

She placed a palm over her heart. "Maybe. I don't know what reincarnation really means. Is it another person's soul that finds a new body, or do their thoughts, hopes and dreams enter and become their actions? I think I'm myself. I don't feel another person's thoughts like you do with Oz."

"But her soul was reborn in you?"

Verity could only shrug. "As I've told you, I was compelled toward your soul. It's been with me a few times in my life, the compulsion to do something. So maybe that was Marianne urging me forward."

Marianne has been protecting you. Perhaps she has kept you from reading this witch's truths until the right moment. A moment when you two trust one another enough to share the horrible burden of memory. Feel it, friend. Remember her. And own it.

"I do own it!" Rook pushed away from Verity and stood. He paced across the room, not to distance himself from his lover but—hell, he could never put himself away from Oz. "I've owned it all my life!"

That is a lie you tell yourself. You have never faced the pain like you have today.

Rook squatted in the middle of the room, catching the back of his head with his palms. "And now she's returned to haunt me in the form of this beautiful witch."

"I don't want to haunt you." Verity remained by the wall, a fragile, beautiful soul that had dallied with the darkness that was him. "I want you to know I can understand. And accept. All of it. Whatever part of your wife that resides within me is here right now because she needs to be. Do you believe she brought us together?"

Rook shook his head, unsure. "Sounds coincidental."

"There are no coincidences in life, only fate and destiny. And we must choose to believe and not dismiss it as mere coincidence. It was no coincidence that you touched me in the alley and felt your soul. And it's no coincidence now that I carry a part of your wife within me."

Rook stood and turned to her. He held out his arms and silently entreated her. Verity rushed to his embrace. Just as Marianne once had. And for a moment, he held not his new lover, but his long-lost wife whom he had selfishly tortured.

He buried his nose in the violet hair and breathed in… sweetness and light. Not smoke and death. He held Verity.

"Fate?" he whispered. "Or Marianne, knowingly leading you to me. But for what reason? You are not her."

"Maybe she needed you to confess your darkest secret to me so that you could finally rise above it and move on. Oz is right—you blame yourself."

"It was my fault. My confession to you changes nothing." He pushed her away and strode toward the window. Raking his fingers through his hair, he then fisted them and punched the air. "Why did you come here?"

"I, uh…" She scratched her head. They'd spent the entire afternoon entwined on the floor of his bedroom. "I had wanted to confess about the vampire bite and the spell not working."

"Right. I have to go out." Rook shucked off the emotion that threatened to bring him down if he did not cease right now and focus on work. "But three or four days until the full moon. I will not let you become vampire."

"Because if I do, then you'll have to stake me."

He swung about to stare into her tearstained eyes. Another of her truths revealed so innocently and with complete trust. But it was a truth that he had to face.

Rook nodded. "I won't let that happen."

He couldn't tell her he would not slay her if it came to that—because he would. It was what he did. And after hearing his tale about vampires burning Marianne, she had to now know to expect nothing less of him but fierce hatred for all bloodsuckers.

All but the one.

Rook ignored Oz. He could think only of the two women.

Marianne. Had she brought Verity to him so he could help her? He shook his head. No, she'd led Verity to his soul more than a hundred years ago. She could have no idea Verity would someday be bitten. Why had she led Verity to his soul? Was it simply because she had trusted the witch would care for the soul and someday find him?

He couldn't understand any of it, and he didn't have the time or the emotional energy to sort through it right now. He needed to get out on the street, to action. To rip out some vampire hearts. To prevent the woman he loved from suffering needlessly.

"Use me," Verity suddenly said. "As bait. It's the only way you're going to lure Clas and Slater to you."

Use her.

Both Oz and Verity pleaded. It was dangerous. He never wanted to endanger a woman again. But he could not conceive of loving Verity were she half vampire, one of the very creatures who had tortured and stolen his wife's life.

Rook nodded. "Come on then. Let's do this."

The man who waited for them on the back steps behind the ancient cathedral nodded in acknowledgment to Rook as they approached. He held Verity's hand tightly. Hadn't let go of her since they'd left his loft.

She never wanted to be more than a handhold away from him. But she sensed he had hardened during their drive here. He hadn't spoken. And she'd noticed his pulsing jaw more than a few times. The hunter was determined to rescue her, and she was cool with that. Even if he was doing it to atone for a past mistake, she could still stand beside him and allow him to use her in any way possible to accomplish it.

But that he'd so quickly fled after his tale of Marianne worried her. He was still running away from that pain. She wanted to help him with that. Perhaps getting his soul back would finally enable him to release the pain and stop blaming himself.

She didn't want him to stop loving his wife. She just wanted him to feel that her soul had moved on and was in a better place now. If Marianne's soul was now Verity's soul, what or where, exactly, was Marianne?

Did it matter? She wanted peace for the woman. That was all.

"This must be Verity Von Velde," the man standing in wait said in greeting. He held out his hand to shake.

Verity took it. The clasp was firm yet unthreatening, and his smile was warm. "I am."

"This is King," Rook said. "Verity is going along with us tonight. As bait."

She thought King's eyes twinkled at that revelation and decided that perhaps the twosome had already discussed this ploy. Didn't bother her. She needed to be in one hundred percent if she was going to survive to the full moon without developing a thirst for blood.

"She's been bitten," Rook said. "She attempted a spell to stop the transformation, but it didn't take."

King whistled. "You haven't much time, witch."

"That's why I've agreed to be bait. The Order gets Slater, and I get the vampire who attacked me."

"Both dead," Rook confirmed. "Come on. Let's head to the lair where I last saw Clas."

Nervous, Verity wandered in front of the nightclub that blasted out nerve-vibrating trance music. There was no line to get in; all patrons entered through the red metal door with the big W slashed in black paint. She tried to act as though she were waiting for someone. She noticed Rook, who stood down the street beside a black Audi. He slashed two fingers in front of his face, directing her toward the alley. A vampire must be nearby.

She strolled away from the lingering crowd and down the alleyway. Three vampires blocked her path. Turning, she saw two more stood behind her. Visions of the awful night she had been attacked threatened to stir up a scream, but she swallowed it.

One vampire dusted in a cloud shaped like a man. His cohorts hadn't seen the attack coming, nor had Verity. She held back a scream as King wrapped his arm around another vamp and plunged the stake through his chest.

Rook dodged a vamp, got to Verity's side and shoved her to safety. As she remained in the shadows, clinging to the brick wall, the knights quickly took out the vampires. She did not recognize her attacker among them. No Clas or Slater.

When all the vampire ash had settled, the knights had detained one survivor. Even with the nightclub just around the corner, they had worked efficiently, quietly. No human had been aware of the slaughter taking place so nearby.

They led the vampire toward the Audi, which was parked down the street in the darkness beneath a broken streetlamp. Verity assumed they had plans to torture the truth from him. Surely the Order must have a dungeon for such dirty deeds.

As they shoved the vampire toward the open back car door, the vampire suddenly flung out his arms and yelled in pain. Verity noted the wooden crossbow arrow stuck through his chest and then…ash.

King took off in the direction from which the arrow had come, yelling that he was going in pursuit.

"You okay?" Rook looked her over, touched her hand

and clasped it. She could feel his anxiety, the tension bouncing him on his feet.

"You can go after the shooter. I'll be okay."

"No, you won't. The last time I left you alone with vampires in the vicinity, you were bitten. King will get him. Get in the back of the car. Others could be around."

Verity was reluctant to slide in where they'd had intention to place a vampire, but she finally did. Rook slid in behind her. He kissed her brow and pressed a palm to her cheek, holding her there, their noses touching, eyes closed. His ability to find their intimacy with just a touch calmed her.

"Sorry. This was too dangerous to involve you."

"I'm a survivor," she offered. "And I'm fine."

"The arrow could have pierced your heart as easily. This is the last time I'm taking a civilian out on the hunt."

"You needed me."

"Yes, but still no Clas. Don't tremble so, lover."

She hadn't realized she was shaking until he'd said it. She shuffled closer to him, and he tugged back his coat lapels so the blades would not cut her and snuggled her beneath the leather coat.

"I just want it over," she said.

"So do I."

"So does she," Verity said, and she wasn't sure why, only that she'd been compelled to say those words.

And her lover's heart pounded beneath her hand. He knew exactly what she'd meant. Or rather, what his dead wife had meant.

Slater stopped Clas from rushing out for the hunter who pursued the shooter he'd positioned to ensure the loose ends were singed. He didn't want to take a chance losing Clas. Not yet. Not with the full moon looming.

He'd noted the other hunter touched Verity and helped her into the car.

"She is his lover," he guessed. "Did you see how he held her? What will he do when she wants to drink his blood?"

Clas snickered.

"I want that witch in hand. Before the full moon. Not only will she serve me a sweet treat, but she will also catch me some fine hunters. Follow them. But do not stop. I need to think over how to lure the witch to me."

Clas nodded and got out of the car.

Slater mused. "Thought you could cast me off by moving away, Verity? I don't scare off so easily. Most especially when it's a valuable fire witch I have my eye on. One more day. You will be mine."

Chapter 17

King nabbed the shooter, but the vampire clawed and snarled and spat blood at the Order founder. It was clear the creature wasn't going to talk. So when the vamp suddenly paused, his hand grasping one of King's biceps, his head tilting in wonder—the stake pierced his heart.

The hunter stepped away from the burst of ash and turned his back quickly to avoid the windy sweep of death. Wiping the blood from the stake across his thigh, he grinned.

He never tired of doing that.

When King returned, he informed Rook he'd had no choice but to stake the shooter. He wouldn't have gotten info from him in his wild state, and on his own he would have never been able to wrangle him and bring him in to Order headquarters. They planned to regroup tomorrow night.

It had been a long and emotional day. Rook sought a few hours of peace to sort his thoughts.

"I'm sorry," he offered a half hour later as he and Verity walked through his kitchen.

The purple-haired witch wandered into the living room, not replying to his apology. She was tired.

And he was frustrated. Both he and King had done their damnedest tonight. Where the hell was Slater hiding? And when had a mere vampire played such an elusive game of cat and mouse with the Order?

It was as though he had the vamp right under his thumb, yet he couldn't crush him. Certainly they were reducing tribe Zmaj's numbers, but the important ones, number one and two, remained elusive.

Moonlight shone across the parquet floor. Two more days until the full moon. No time for rest.

King had returned to headquarters to search the database for clues. Verity had insisted he take her here because she didn't want to be alone tonight.

Could he make love to her, tuck her in bed and leave her sleeping while he slipped out to go in search of Clas?

He must.

She turned to him, opening her mouth to speak, so Rook caught her words in a kiss. They should probably talk. There was a lot to say about vampires and imminent vampirism and…

They'd talked enough earlier in the day. He'd laid his heart out on the floor for her to inspect, and she had tendered it carefully beneath her touch. He couldn't conceive of another wrenching discussion right now.

Tonight was for action, for touch, for knowing. For the compelling need to connect with that which he had lost.

"You smell like blood," she whispered.

"I'll shower. Don't—"

She sat on his bed and toed off her shoes. "I'm not going anywhere."

After he'd showered, Rook laid his lover across the bed beneath the streams of blue silk that had been a payment to him centuries earlier after he'd helped a Romanian family flee from vicious vampires. They hadn't gold or riches but had not wanted him to leave without something offered in thanks. The simple fabric was like spun gold to him.

Verity pulled him on top of her and hooked her ankle around his. Their bodies crushed together, he naked and sprinkled with water droplets, and she still clothed. He pushed up her shirt and tugged down her bra, wanting to get to her skin, her nipple, the sensitive spot at the top of her breast where he knew a few lashes of his tongue would release her from anxiety and set her off into bliss. And then sleep.

The modena from his hickey blossomed at the side of her breast. "Pretty," he said.

"Means I'm yours," she said in a tired voice. "Mark me all you like, lover."

The world turned right when she was in his arms. Her kisses made him forget about the times he'd slammed a stake into a vampire's heart and had tasted ash for days after. Her dulcet moans made him forget the maddening death howls, a last protest at unavoidable death. Her skin made him forget how cool his skin was because he harbored a demon thanks to his inability to believe his wife's truths.

And her sigh sucked him out of the dark and into her bright, violet light that surrounded him with a hug as if it were her great-grandmother's quilt.

"Love you," he whispered against her breast. "I mean it. I love you, Verity. You are my everything."

Because she anchored him to the now.

Returning from the bathroom, Verity yawned and padded into the bedroom. She knelt at the corner of the bed. It wasn't on a frame, so the box spring sat directly on the floor. A skim of azure fabric dusted her shoulders. She liked it; it felt as if they were floating in the middle of the sea while making love with nothing to anchor them.

Rook sat up on the opposite corner of the bed, turning to face her and sitting with crossed legs, yoga style. Every sinew on the man flexed with movement. He wasn't bulked with muscles like a weight lifter, or even a werewolf; he was rather sleek and defined. Like a wildcat. A true hunter.

She was tired, but the sex had given her a second wind. She could never resist his sensual allure. Bending to crawl toward him, she stopped when he put up a palm. "Stay there."

She knelt to sit on her heels, mocking a pout. Both of them were still naked. It was after midnight, and the moon sat high in the sky. She would sleep…soon.

"Touch yourself the way you like me to touch you," he said. "I want to watch."

Dashing her tongue across her lips, she nodded. Anything he asked of her, she would do. Because she wanted to please him. Because in pleasing him, she was pleasing herself. And because she liked the idea of him set aside, a witness but also a participant.

And because that meant their thoughts would be on something other than the dire.

So she drew her palms up the sides of her torso to cup her breasts. Squeezing her nipples, she moaned softly, closing her eyes as she tightened the squeeze and then made it softer, gliding her palms over her nipples in a feathering brush.

She glided a hand down her stomach, circling her navel and catching Rook's intent gaze. Her hunter, his legs crossed and shoulders straight and back. And there in his lap, his cock jutted upward, intent, as if also watching. His jaw pulsed, and she knew he was participating in the touch.

Slipping a finger into her folds, she wet it and slicked it across her clit. Slowly, lingering, polishing. A hum giddied in her belly, and she closed her eyes to fall into the sensation.

"Look at me," he groaned on a lusty growl.

She met his gaze, yet flashed her look away to the window, then back to his. Could she look directly at his intense eyes while she pleasured herself? It was so intimate. More intimate than allowing him to sup between her legs. For he was the voyeur and she the performer. Yet this audience had come to see into her soul, be damned the flames she could manipulate for a thrill.

Then come take a look, she thought to that other voyeur, the one who watched with glowing red eyes.

Yes, a performer. *That's what I am.* And that made it easy to hold her lover's gaze. Her audience would not release her, and she wasn't about to flee. Rubbing her fingers faster, she neared the edge. Squeezing her thighs heightened the intensity of the need to release, to surrender to the perfect coil of pleasure.

Rook's mouth was parted. His breaths came quickly. Burnt peaches, tobacco, and male desire scented the air. Beneath the fall of azure, Verity found the truth in his eyes, and in that moment she released her breath and was finally able to accept him for all that he was, and—

—trust him.

The orgasm soared through her. She hushed out a giggly sigh and thrust back her shoulders, then curled forward, bending toward the exquisite thunder in her core. She fell to her side and rolled to her back, stretching out her arms and legs. Her hair spilled over the edge of the bed.

Rook leaned forward onto his elbows and played with her hair, rearranging it off her cheek and mouth as she breathed heavily through the after-orgasm. Mmm, her body was hot, lax and spent. And the flutter of his fingers along her hairline, across her cheek and there, at the join of her ear to her neck, stirred up tiny jolts of sensation.

Yes, she trusted this man. Completely.

His face moved over hers, his eyes tracing the contour of her head, meeting her gaze, smiling, then trailing to another point of her he wanted to explore. A delicate kiss touched her eyebrow. And another at the bridge of her nose.

"You are beautiful," he whispered.

His fingers floated down her arm, skimming the hairs. Propping his chin in his other hand, he lay there, his head near hers, watching her from the side. She didn't turn to look at him, only closed her eyes to better track his barely-there touch.

A butterfly danced over her stomach, touching down briefly, then lighting at the join of her thigh to her torso, where she was slick with perspiration. She arched her back, felt her nipples tighten, her core swirl.

Where had his touch gone? She needed it back.

And then it was right there, tapping, tapping at her clit. Not roughly, only so lightly that she quickly rushed forth to feel it, to own it, to surrender to it.

And at her ear, he whispered, "Encore."

With only two taps of his finger, she burst again, the endorphins of orgasm flooding her body in a warm rush that didn't flail her about in abandon, but instead hugged her in a full-body sigh that touched her very soul.

Her soul and Marianne's soul.

Verity tilted her head to the side. He kissed her mouth, his fingers at her mons curling into her to hold her, pressing into the humming sensation that would not cease.

Bliss.

She fell asleep under her lover's thumb.

Verity woke to the smell of copper pennies. It was strong. She felt it on her tongue and at the back of her throat. And in her gut she felt an intense and annoying hunger. She

needed sustenance. All it required was a drink of something warm and thick.

Sitting upright on Rook's bed, she looked about and
spied her lover's back. He stood in front of the steel cabinet on the far wall, unaware she had woken. Dressed in
full leathers and his long black coat, he sorted something
inside the cabinet. The room was light. Dawn seeped quietly through the cracked window.

When had he slipped from bed? Did he intend to go out
now during the day? Or had he returned from somewhere?

"Rook?"

He spun around, a stake in hand and a black cloth that
he'd been using to wipe the stake clean clutched in his fingers. "You're awake. I, uh, slipped out for a bit. Couldn't
sleep."

"More vampires?"

He nodded and turned away from her, placing the stake
in the cabinet. Cleaning the blood from his weapons. She
knew it because the smell was strong. He must have slayed
more vampires while she was sleeping.

The luscious aroma lured her to the end of the bed. She
wanted a taste. To dash her tongue along the cool titanium
column as if it were her lover's erection. To lick it clean and
savor the flavor of life.

"Goddess," she swore softly and grabbed her clothes.
Dressing quickly, she looked by the sides of the bed for
her shoes. "I need to leave."

He caught her at the bedroom door. Sunlight glinted on
the blades at his collar. "What's wrong? I will do anything
to find Clas. Are you mad that I left you alone? You were
perfectly safe here."

A ripple tensed her gut and squeezed inwardly. Verity
winced and shook her head.

"Verity? Do you feel okay?"

"I'm not sure. Just need to leave. Go home and shower. You have Order stuff to deal with."

"Not anymore. I'm home. I want to—hell, are you in pain?"

She tried to wrestle free from his grasp. He had blood on his coat. Somewhere. Perhaps in his hair? It smelled so good. Even better than his usual scent.

"Please, Rook, the blood." He let her go, and she stumbled backward to catch herself in the open doorway. "I can't be around the smell of it."

"Right. Sorry." He gripped her arms again and pulled her in for a kiss, but all she could concentrate on was the scent of vampire blood. "I'll see you home. Let me shower again, get the blood off me, then I'll drive you. I don't want you to risk walking home alone. It's dangerous out there."

She nodded and backed into the living room. As the shower turned on, Verity slipped into her shoes and took off. He was right about it being dangerous for her to walk home alone.

But she felt it was even more dangerous to remain and succumb to the scent of blood that lingered in the air.

Chapter 18

She is hungry for blood.

"Hell." Rook fisted the wall. "Are you sure?"

You have seen helpless humans in the throes of the irresistible blood hunger.

Indeed. One of the things that touched him most was witnessing a bitten human begging for blood as the wicked hunger took over. Either a victim, they begged, or their own death.

She needs distraction. Until you can kill Clas.

"Then I should go after Clas. I wish I could release you to look after Verity."

Clas will keep. She may not.

Rook nodded. Oz was right. If Verity so much as tasted blood, that was all that was required to begin the transformation to vampire. She did not want that. He did not want that for her. He wasn't sure he could continue to love a witch who was also a vampire.

Why not? Your best friend—

"Enough." Rook punched the wall again and marched toward the front door. "This is different."

Also, Slater was out there jonesing for witch blood. Verity had moved so the tribe leader could not find her, but what's to say the vamp hadn't discovered her home?

He'd go to her. Guard her against Slater. Distract her. But his mind would be distracted by the vampire he must kill to save Verity and to save his soul.

His best option? Call in another knight. Tugging out his cell phone, Rook sorted through the names of knights currently in the city.

Charging into her home, Verity aimed for the fridge. Hunger gnawed at her, forcing her to think things like "A sip of blood would hit the spot" and "I wonder if I have any raw meat?"

From the fridge she pulled out a jug of orange juice and drank the cold liquid until she had to gasp for breath. The sweetness did not appeal. She put it back and took out the blueberries, quickly popping the plump jewels into her mouth. Again, too sweet. Not at all satisfying.

"What am I doing? I'm not going to drink blood. I'm stronger than that. I can do this. I just have to make it past the full moon without tasting blood, and I'll be fine."

Squeezing her palms to her cheeks, she shut her eyes, mentally tallying the days and then the hours. Less than forty-eight. "I can do it. I have to."

Maybe a hot bath would put her thoughts away from hunger. Soaking always did relax her muscles and lure her mind toward peace.

Dashing up the stairs, she darted into the bathroom and turned on the water to fill the tub. Stripping off her clothes, she paced in the bedroom. Her spell table was cluttered with herbs, vials and accoutrements of the craft. She usually kept a live dove in a cage because they were always useful for spellwork. But the cage was empty now, taunting her with its lack of bird coos.

"Animal blood would not begin the change. Would it?" She shook her head and shuddered. "What am I thinking?"

Walking back into the bathroom, she sat at the tub's edge and bent forward, placing her head on her knees. Her hair spilled down her legs, and she touched the cool tile flooring with her fingertips. Maybe if she tried a few yoga moves like Rook did, she could avert the cravings.

She didn't know any yoga. And she was really hungry. The athame she used for the dove. Had she cleaned it properly?

As she shut off the water, she heard the knocks on the front door. Had someone been down there a while? She wasn't going to answer it. She was naked, and…

"Verity?"

He'd followed her? He'd told her to stay, to let him drive her home. She hadn't considered the danger while walking and—hell. She hadn't locked the door after returning home because she'd been so aggravated. And still was.

"You home?"

"I'm up here!" she called.

Considering dashing out for a robe, she stayed put. Rook had seen her naked. And—why was he here?

Pray to the goddess he'd showered.

"I'm in the bathroom," she called when she heard his footsteps top the stairs. She slipped into the water, reached back to coil her hair into a chignon, and then stabbed a wooden hair stick through it that she kept beside the tub for just such purpose. "You can come in."

The door opened a few inches, and Rook peeked in. Seeing her in the tub, surrounded by a cloud of bubbles, he entered. "I told you to wait for me. I worried."

"I made it home fine."

"I see that. Do you want me to leave?"

"Have you showered?"

"Yes."

"Then stay, please. I'm glad you're here." His hair was

wet, and she could only smell the luscious tobacco and peaches. Thank the goddess. "I was…just trying to—I need a—hell, I have to tell you. I want you to trust me."

"Is it the blood hunger?" He strode in and squatted before the tub.

Verity nodded. "That's why I left so quickly. I didn't want you to see me like that. And you had blood scent all over you."

"Sorry."

"You couldn't have known. I'm so hungry, but nothing I eat satisfies. And I keep thinking about how good blood would taste." She pressed wet hands over her face. "I don't want to think like that."

"I don't know how to make the cravings stop, beyond killing Clas or getting you past the full moon. Much as I want to stay here, not leave you alone, I need to get out on the streets to find Clas. So I've, uh…called in another knight to watch your house."

"You think that's necessary?"

"Very." He pressed his palms together in front of his nose. "Kaz won't get here for a few hours. He has an appointment he can't miss. But when he arrives I have to leave. Right now I can sit and talk to you. Distract you."

She nodded, catching her breath in a relieved sigh. "I'd like that. I like it whenever you're around. I like you."

"That's a good thing." He turned and sat, his shoulders against the tub wall, and rested his hands on his knees. "I like you too. A lot. You know when I said I love you—"

"Oh, don't worry about that. I know it's something that comes out during sex. It's like fuck, yeah or more baby, please. Sex words."

Rook scrubbed a hand over his hair, and it fell messily across his forehead. "That's the thing." He tilted his head back against the tub and eyed her. "I really do love you."

Verity didn't know what to say. His confession felt true. And it felt great. But it also felt ominous, especially when her gut lurched again, and she had to wince to keep from biting her lip to taste the blood. Instead, she busily spread the bubbles up her arm and neck.

"No comment?" he asked.

"I could love you, too. I might already. I want to love you, Rook. But I don't want to commit to that until I've beat this. You know?"

"I understand. You have my complete support." He clasped her bubble-laden hand. "I will do everything in my power to save you, Verity."

"And what of your soul? Don't you want to save yourself?"

"Will a soul save me? It'll give Oz freedom. But as for me? It'll return my mortality."

She hadn't thought about that. The man had existed four centuries. When finally his soul was placed within him and the demon was set free, he would become merely mortal. He would age. He would eventually die.

"How long have you lived?" he asked.

"About a century and a half. But I…well, I've always considered this my last century."

He lifted a brow.

"My great-grandmother Bluebell—"

"Of the magical quilt."

"Yes, that fabulous quilt. She used a source twice, then said enough. She had no desire to live forever. Felt she'd done what her soul had been born into this realm to do. So she died of old age. I think about that a lot, and I know I don't want to live forever. Two centuries will be a long time, and so far it's been great. To grow old naturally seems a gift. I might not take another source again."

"The centuries do wear on a person. When did you last take a source?"

They used the term so casually. A source was the unfortunate vampire a witch bespelled so she could then remove its heart and consume it while it still beat. That prolonged the witch's life another century. Not so much for the vampire. Vamps called sources ash.

"Thirty years ago?" she guessed. "About then. So I have another seventy years of immortality, and then if I don't take a source, well, whatever time should follow. I'd like to grow old with someone. Perhaps even a husband."

He smirked and laid his cheek against the side of the tub.

She traced the triangle of stubble beneath his lower lip. "Did you believe you were going to grow old with Marianne?"

He nodded. "We wanted half a dozen children and a big garden. That's all we desired, beyond each other. And love."

Verity's throat tightened. Such simple desires taken from him so cruelly. And he, forced to kill his zombie wife.

"Maybe the two of you have found one another again," she suggested.

"You mean with your soul?" He shrugged. "You are not Marianne. And that's a good thing. I miss her. I loved her. I will always love her. But now I love you. And it feels different and..."

"Wondrous."

He gave her a bright-eyed nod.

"Listen to us. Two souls with incredible odds stacked against them. We're both a bit fucked, don't you think?"

"That we are. Though I've been fucked for some time now. Your fuckery is a bit more immediate."

She laughed, and he did too.

He stroked his finger down her neck and under the water beside her breast. She tilted so her breasts were exposed, and he tapped the hickey. "I do good work."

"And you do like to sign your work. Your shirt is getting wet from the bubbles. Take it off."

"You trying to get me naked, witch?"

"As bare as I can manage."

He slipped off his shirt and turned to dangle his hands in the water. He glided his fingers over the hickey again, then down her stomach and between her legs.

"Your distraction is working, hunter."

"Now I know why you women are always cooing over bubble baths and those sparkly balls you like to drop in the water. It smells great, and the water is so soft."

His touch entered her, and Verity spread her legs to give him easy access. He lazily toyed with her, closing his eyes and resting his chin on the tub edge. She didn't need anything intense, just the gentle pressure lingering, teasing.

"And now I know what to get you for Christmas," she said. "Something sparkly to drop in your bathwater."

"You're all I need in my bathwater." He kissed the side of her neck, and his hand cupped her breast.

"So will you tell me how you met King? I assume it was soon after everything that happened with your wife's death."

His hand tightened against her mons, and she sensed his entire body tense.

"I'm sorry. If you don't want to talk about this anymore…"

"No, it's fine. King and I. That's all good. He sought me out after he'd witnessed me slaying the vampires who had killed Marianne. I had hunted them systematically, about a week after her death. I didn't know what a fixer was at the time—that they were a super-powered being due to their alliance with Himself—so the fact that I took out six blew King away."

"That's an odd name. King."

"His real name is Charles."

"Giles and Charles. I like Giles. You haven't used it since?"

"Never. I'm not that man anymore. Although King is certainly Charles. His full name is Charles-Maximilien de France, Duke of Angouleme, son of Henri II and Catherine de Medici."

Verity thought the long string of names familiar. She traced the French history she knew. "The former king of France? Back in the sixteenth century?"

Rook nodded. "You may know him best as Charles IX. But you didn't hear it from me. It is a persona he guards closely. I trust you with the knowledge."

"Thanks. So he is—was—a real king? Which makes him immortal. What *is* he, though?"

"Now that, I will never tell. It is his secret to own."

"Amazing. But I thought—wasn't he assassinated?"

"No, that was his brother Henri. Henri was named king after Charles, and not long after he was stabbed by a monk, of all people. Charles's death was…different. The history books have it wrong about the poisoning. In a fashion. And that's all I can say."

"Of course." Verity met the dancing twinkle in Rook's blue eyes. The man guarded an actual historic secret. His best friend was once king of France. "Wow. Should I bow to him next time we meet?"

"Certainly not. First, he'd love that too much. And second, I'm not telling you any of this, remember?"

"Right. So you impressed him with your slaying skills and he signed you on?"

"Yes, he'd been working on developing an organization

of hunters for a decade, but he hadn't had much luck. When the two of us put our heads together, everything clicked into place. We founded the Order and haven't looked back since."

So she assumed King had been touched by vampire violence in some manner. Oh, the wonders she could wonder. But she would give Rook the trust he asked of her.

"King and Rook and the knights. You two play chess much?"

"Never, actually. Though the rook is one of the king's most valued pieces. I liked the name, and so did he. It works for me."

"You two must be close, working together all these centuries."

"We are. We know everything about the other. We are brothers. Comrades in arms. Friends."

She captured his gaze and stroked a wet fingertip over his lips. "Have you ever been lovers?"

He tucked his nose against her neck to kiss her and said, "Yes."

Such information heated Verity's core, and a twinge of desire tightened her nipples. To imagine the two men entwined in a loving embrace tapped into a fantasy of hers.

"Then I'm jealous," she said. "But only a bit. You're mine now, hunter. For as long as we can work."

"Does that mean you've decided I am worthy of staying on beyond the three-date maximum?"

"Yes. At least until the full moon."

"Beyond the moon," he said. "I am yours beyond the moon."

His hand slipped high on her breast, and as his mouth moved over hers, he suddenly pulled away, splashing water over the side of the tub. The look in his eyes startled her.

"What?"

He pressed his hand firmly over her breast. "I can… read you. I can feel your trust for me and your—your love. Verity, I can read your truths now. It's there. The hunger. The fear. You're confused about it—and scared." He kissed her cheek. "Please don't be scared, lover. I will get you through this."

"I know you'll try. But really? You can read me? I wonder why now? Do you think it's Marianne?"

"If so, then she's kept me from reading you until now."

"Maybe she didn't want you to learn about her soul right away."

"Possible. Because she needed us to work together."

"Doesn't matter, does it? You can feel my love for you. You know I've given you all my truths."

"Yes, but you are—please don't be scared, Verity."

She sat up, bubbles dusting her chest. "When I'm with you, I'm not afraid. You've taken my thoughts away from *you know what*. You make me strong. When I'm with you I actually feel like I can make it past the moon. But…"

She glanced at the towel she'd set out to dry off with. She was cold now that she had sat up in the water.

"But what?"

The hunger pangs were still there, softer yet never gone. She needed to quench her thirst.

"I need to get out. I'm cold now."

She stood, and he coved her up against him and wrapped the big towel around them both. They stood there in the doorway between the bathroom and the bedroom, and he bowed his head to hers.

"Something is still bothering you. Tell me." He pressed a hand over her heart, and she wasn't so sure she liked that he could read her now. Because he must feel her reluctance.

"Verity?"

"It's just…if I do transform to vampire, you have to understand that is not something I can live with. And you've said as much."

He opened his mouth to reply, but she pressed her fingers to his lips.

"So if I change…will you slay me?"

He shoved away from her, striding out into the bedroom.

She'd said the wrong thing. But it was her truth. He would have known if she had lied. How could she live with herself if blood was what that life demanded?

Rook turned to her, jaw muscle pulsing. "Do you understand what you just asked me to do?"

Yes, to slay the woman he had confessed to loving. Oh, hell.

"Oh, no, I didn't mean it like that." He'd already been forced to kill a woman he loved. "I wasn't thinking about her. I'm sorry. So sorry. I just thought—"

"You didn't think."

"Rook, please." Verity lost her grasp on her towel. She shivered, pressing her hands over her breasts. "This isn't easy. I just…you felt it in me. I'm frightened."

"You said when you are with me, you are not scared."

"I'm not, but I am. It can't happen, okay? It just can't. And I need you right now. I know you're angry, and you have every right to be. And maybe I don't want a tender hug or kiss, I want…"

He tugged her from the doorway and into the bedroom, where he turned her against the wall, her shoulders hitting it roughly. He kissed her. Hard. Without mercy.

He gripped her thigh and lifted her. Shuffling at his zipper, he then shimmied down his leather pants, and without even asking, pushed inside her with his steely cock. And it burned so good. Verity slammed her palms against the wall behind her, taking his hot, angry need into her.

"Trust me, Verity."

"I want to."

"I won't let you fall."

He thrust deep, slowing his pace but not the intensity.

"I believe in you," he said. "You are a witch. You are powerful."

He was speaking to his past, to his dead wife's soul—to Verity. And she did trust him because he gave her everything he had without question.

Shouting as the orgasm shook his muscles, he crushed his body against hers. Verity wrapped her arms around his head as she held him there, his body shuddering. Their bodies joined in the truth.

But the real truth would be known in less than two days. Either she survived and surpassed the vampire taint or… her lover would be forced to end her life.

Chapter 19

"That mansion is where Slater holds court."

Rook pointed across the street and three buildings down from where he and King stood. Their location was on the outer side of the Peripherique road that circled Paris, within the outer edges of the Bois de Boulogne.

An anonymous note had been left on the windshield of Rook's car, which he'd parked in front of Verity's home. She did have vampire wards on her home, but Rook didn't trust that the tribe wouldn't find a way in. Certainly Slater had written the message, but perhaps a lackey delivered it. The tribe leader wanted to bring the war to his turf.

And he was using Verity as a pawn by luring Rook away from the one thing he most wanted to protect. So when Kaz Rothstein had arrived to post outside the witch's home, Rook had immediately left. He trusted Kaz. The knight was in love with his own witch—Zoë. He'd guard Verity's home as if it were his own.

"We get Clas," King said. "We've got Slater."

The war Slater had declared hadn't been the bloody battle Rook had expected. Instead, this more personal defensive move cut much deeper.

King slapped him on the back. "It all ends tonight. Who did you put on the witch's home?"

"Rothstein."

"He'll keep watch over her."

Rook knew that he would, yet the pinch of betrayal wouldn't allow him to accept that he'd left Verity in the hands of another man when he should be the one to stand guard over her.

King shrugged down against the wall to a squat. He was wearing full hunting gear, which surprised Rook. The last time they'd gone out, after a werewolf pack principal, King had worn dress slacks and a white shirt. He'd thought the man had forgotten how to hunt.

No. Hunting ran in their blood. They knew nothing else. It was simply easier for King to assume the different role aside from hunter.

Rook leaned against the wall, propping his feet out so he sat halfway down the wall, near King's shoulder.

"I'm not so sure about getting my soul back."

King met his gaze, and for a moment they spoke to one another. This was a true confession. Handle it with care.

"You should be unsure," King offered. "With a soul you'd become mortal. You'd age and die. Remember, you're not supposed to die before me. What would I do without my oldest and best friend?"

"I'd miss you, man. But don't you have days where you think it's been enough?"

"All the time. You know that. But what about your witch? If you become mortal, and she's immortal…"

"We'd still have many years together."

And she had said something about not taking another source. Interesting. Dare he dream that shattered dream about loving and living and growing old together? Wisest not to. But difficult not to want to.

"I have never heard you talk about a woman in terms of years," King said. "I couldn't imagine doing so. It's not normal. Not for us."

Neither he nor King indulged in long-term relationships, though King was more prone to check in with his lovers, both mortal and immortal alike, over the decades. Rook had learned long ago never to keep strings hanging. The heart made the hunter weaker.

So if a vampire literally held his soul within a semblance of his heart? Hell.

"Verity mentioned she may not look for a source when it comes time to do so."

"Interesting. So you two could, feasibly, grow old together."

Rook tilted his head against the brick wall. "What's it like to have a soul? I can't remember."

"Well, for one thing, you'd be much warmer than you are now." King mocked a shudder. "And, I don't know, I think your capacity toward emotion would increase."

"I can do emotion with the best of them."

"It's Oz who does that for you."

And do not forget it.

"Soon, Oz," Rook said.

"He getting anxious?"

"His baby is due within days. And you know how time is different in Faery."

"So I've heard," King commented. "I'd miss Oz, too."

"I won't set him free until he promises he'll visit."

I promise.

"He promises." Rook chuckled. It felt good to relax for a few seconds. But hunters never let down their guard.

He cast a glance around the corner, his eyes tracking the freshly paved narrow street to the opposite sidewalk clumped with overgrown weeds in need of clipping. The early nineteenth-century mansion they were watching was dark. And it was still before midnight. They didn't expect traffic until after the witching hour.

The moon was high and round but a sliver away from true fullness, which would come tomorrow night. He hated leaving Verity home with nothing to distract her from the blood hunger. It would only grow stronger. Which is why he was here right now. If she stayed at home, immersed in her spellbooks, as she had promised, that should keep her preoccupied.

He would not let the sun rise without staking Clas.

"I can't believe I missed this spell earlier."

Verity trailed her finger down the page that had been scrawled in unfamiliar handwriting. It wasn't her mother's or great-grandmother Bluebell's. It almost looked masculine, but who could know? The history of the Von Veldes generally passed the grimoire from maternal head of the family to the next maternal head.

No matter. The spell was a tracking spell to be used to find missing objects. Such as a soul pulsing within a wooden heart?

She had to give it a try because if the spell worked, it would lead her to the vampire who had bitten her. Worst scenario? The vampire had dumped the necklace but the spell would still lead her to it, thus resulting in Rook getting what he needed most.

"One way or another, one of us is going to be happy. And it's going to happen tonight."

Opening the little velvet-lined jewelry box she'd used to store the heart necklace in on occasion, she scraped the fine velvet weft off and onto the tinfoil she'd spread out on the spell table. She had already gathered comfrey, grave dirt, a newborn peahen's bone dust (she stocked up at the local witch's bazaar) and a fox's breath. She had everything that was required.

Now to make it work.

An hour later, the flames she set upon the emulsified ingredients flashed a sulfurous glow, then extinguished at her magical command.

Verity took the compass she'd dug out from the bottom of her mother's hope chest, which contained years of assorted treasures and collected ephemera, and pried off the back casing. The bespelled ashes fit nicely into the round brass cover. She packed them in with the tip of a spoon and then resealed the compass. The glass housing briefly glowed blue. If the spell worked, it would glow nonstop once she was near the intended object.

"Of course it will work. My magic…" Verity sighed. It would work. It had to.

She'd asked to find Rook's soul. The magnetic needle swung north.

"All right, then. I'm going out for a walk."

Slipping on a long sweater over her soft jersey dress, down in the foyer she stepped into some ballet flats. Turning off the lights and remembering Rook had asked her to stay put until he returned, she opened the front door.

A tall man with spiky brown hair and an easy smile turned to block her exit with his broad shoulders. He wore Order gear.

"Evening, mademoiselle. I'm Kaz. You're not going anywhere, are you?"

"Uh…" She shook her head. And she recognized the name because one of her friends was dating a Kaz, who was also a hunter. "Does Zoë know you're at some strange witch's house so late at night?"

"Now don't make it sound like that. I'm doing as Rook commanded. So get back inside. And—hey!"

He put up a hand when Verity lifted hers, intending to brew up some fire.

"No magic," he said firmly. He turned his wrist toward her to show the small pentacle tattooed there.

Verity pouted. "No fair." She slammed the door on him and marched down the hallway. "A tattoo against magic? Not a stupid hunter. I'm going to give Zoë hell for that one."

With a new tactic springing to mind, she scampered into the living room and stood before the window overlooking the back courtyard. It would be too easy to slip out the back way. But she would never question an easy option.

Kaz's head popped around the corner of the house. He waved at her. That sexy smile must have knocked Zoë off her feet the first time she'd met him. Again, no fair wielding the charm weapon.

Verity stuck out her tongue at him.

He was only one man. Albeit a skilled hunter who was warded against witch magic.

When she spied the calico tail snaking through the garden, Verity let out a whispered blurt of glee.

"Perfect timing, Thomas."

Cats pride themselves on their stealthy sneak. Thomas was a master at pussyfooting quietly through the night. He could follow a human for miles, always no farther than ten feet behind them, and they'd never be the wiser.

Verity had been too excited to see him at first. After showing him her fridge—empty—and dramatically pleading hunger, she'd then explained the hunter posted out on her front step was a precaution from the Order. She was under house arrest because she'd been seen on the Order's security cameras when Rook had clandestinely led her in to view some mug shots.

She wouldn't be long. But she was so hungry. And the hunter wasn't budging.

When Thomas had suggested she order pizza, she had pouted. Prettily. Damn, but he fell for the pout every time.

So he'd led the hunter into the back courtyard and all around until he'd lost his balance and landed in the stinging nettles. A five-minute distraction was all Verity had requested.

For some reason, he felt it best if he kept a close eye on Verity tonight. She'd been acting strange. The moon grew full tomorrow night. And that worried him. If she was going out to scam for blood, he'd have to bring out the big claws to stop her.

The compass led from her neighborhood, across the Seine on the Pont de Bir-Hakeim, and toward the city park. Beyond the Peripherique, Verity entered the massive forested park in an older neighborhood with grand mansions that had been built in the nineteenth century. Many were unoccupied, their dark windows either broken or boarded over.

The compass glass glowed, but not as bright as originally. She was close. Had to be.

Down a long street, a right turn and then another, she had the sneaking suspicion she was being followed. The hunter? Always that possibility. Thomas had managed to distract him long enough for her escape. And she'd worn flats so she could run those few minutes. Yet whenever she suddenly turned around, there was nobody.

"I'm creeping myself out," she muttered. "I need food to take the edge off. Something…"

A hunger pang clutched at her gut, bending her in half. Verity gripped an iron fence that gathered in overgrown climbing moon flowers before an ancient mansion. Her mouth was dry. She craved liquid.

She craved what she didn't want to crave.

Fingers shaking, she clenched the compass. The glass casing glowed brightly and the arrow pointed to her right, beyond the iron fence.

"This has to be the place."

A small yellow glow beamed from one of the long, tall windows, which she assumed must front a grand ballroom. If she knocked on the door and a friendly old human couple answered, then what?

Then my spellcraft needs practice.

Tucking the compass in her pocket, she turned and walked right into the tight embrace of a man she hadn't seen in months.

"Slater."

"The strays always return," he said. "And so close to the full moon. Hungry, sweetie?"

She struggled, but his grip pinched her arms painfully, and before she could scream, Slater's fist met her jaw and knocked her unconscious.

Around the corner and across the street, three houses down from the mansion, Rook stretched his legs and asked King if he was ready to go inside.

King checked the stake at his hip. "Ready to rock."

They turned, but both men dropped their jaws at the sight of the naked man rushing toward them.

Chapter 20

Verity woke in a standing position. Head bowed forward, her neck muscles twanged. Something was banded across her chest. Her arms were wrenched behind her, her wrists bound together. She wriggled but couldn't move much. The air around her was musty with a thick chemical smell.

Blinking completely awake, and wincing at the ache in her jaw, she realized she was tied to a wood column. Perhaps a structural beam similar to the others she saw here and there in the vast, hazy room.

She'd been tied to the post in what looked to have once been a grand ballroom. to judge by the elaborate flocked wallpaper, tattered velvet curtains and dusty chandeliers. Real candles were lit in the massive fixture just overhead and off to her side, casting a dull glow over her predicament.

The floorboards were dusty and scratched, and some kind of liquid had been poured before her in an arc. Looking as far as she could over her shoulder, she saw it formed a circle around her. And twenty feet beyond the inner circle traced another wet circle.

"Gas," she whispered.

Dreadful images of her mother standing within the blazing pyre churned her gut. A reedy moan stirred in her throat.

Slater was not stupid. No witch who could command

fire would purposefully use that magic when surrounded by a substance that promised her doom. If the gas caught, she'd be surrounded by flame. She was helpless.

"Mother," she whispered. "Blessed goddess, please help me."

Panicking, she wriggled at the ropes binding her wrists. The post she was tied to seemed solid, so she assumed it was a main load-bearing column that would not be moved. She had no weapons on her and no magic that could cut through the rope. Though she might try to loosen the knot with some focused concentration.

Closing her eyes, she searched her memory for a spell that would perform as she needed, but her heartbeats challenged her focus and she couldn't manage to come up with anything save a jittery stomach. Add to that the hunger pangs that clawed at her gut, and she almost screamed.

The measured click of a man's dress shoes echoed up beside her, distracting her from the pain. Verity would not give the bastard the pleasure of turning to look at him. Instead, she closed her eyes, but that only enhanced her sense of smell. The gasoline was strong, but she also picked up a foppish lavender scent, of which Slater was inordinately fond.

"This has been an interesting week," the vampire said. The footsteps stopped in front of her. He stood outside the inner ring of gasoline. "I'm losing tribe members left and right to a rather industrious knight of the Order, and then, when I had thought my ex-girlfriend dead and buried, I discover she's very much alive and quite possibly on the path to becoming vampire."

"You sent Clas to kill me, didn't you?" She opened her eyes. Slater's smug smirk was too familiar. He nodded at her. "Why? We broke up. We weren't compatible. Get over it. Go steal magic from some other witch."

"But I wanted your fire magic, lover."

"Don't call me that. It disgusts me to think I let you touch me."

"Fucked you well and good, if I recall correctly. And I do."

She wouldn't reply. He wanted to see her outrage, her begging protests. It fueled his malicious need for power. Frederick Slater corrupted control; Rook mastered it and made it his own.

Where was her knight? She should have never gone against his order to remain safe at home.

"You are rare, Verity. Not many witches—that I'd be willing to fuck—practice fire magic."

Asshole.

"So you've hooked up with a hunter? That should be interesting in oh, say…a day?"

She was so close to the soul. The compass had pointed her to this location. Clas must be in the building somewhere. If only she'd been smarter and called Rook to let him know she'd be going out to track the vampire. Kaz would catch hell for this. Thomas might never forgive her.

"I can't wait." Slater clapped his hands loudly and bent toward her. "Hungry yet?"

Yes, she was. Her insides twisted, seeking sustenance. But she'd never drink the bastard's blood, no matter how desperate she got. "Not for anything you could offer me."

"We'll see about that. You were tracking Clas, weren't you? Think you can stake him before the full moon and win your freedom from the inevitable?"

Slater reached into his inner jacket pocket and drew out a wooden stake. The weapon looked vulgar in the hands of a vampire. He tossed it onto the floor , and it rolled to a stop at the toe of her shoe. "Don't say I didn't give you opportunity. Clas!"

The bald vampire thunked into the ballroom on rubber-soled biker boots. Hands shoved in the pockets of his loose, baggy jeans, he stopped behind Verity, opposite from where Slater stood.

"This little witch wants to shove wood through your heart," Slater said.

At first Clas's laughter was a simple chuckle, then he let loose into a loud and roiling rumble.

"I need the heart necklace he stole from me!" Verity yelled. "There's a soul in it."

Slater tilted his head at her. She'd said too much. They would keep her tied here through the next twenty-four hours, most likely taunting her with blood, and eventually force her to transform. She could deal with that. But she mustn't let them keep Rook's soul.

"A soul? In a heart?" Slater paced before her. "Elaborate."

Verity shook her head.

"Wait, boss," Clas said from behind her. "The necklace I gave you. Wasn't that a heart?"

"Ah, yes." Slater snapped his fingers. "In my office desk. Run and fetch it, Clas."

Boot steps clomped out of the ballroom.

Slater dipped his head to study her gaze from below her line of sight.

"Whose soul would be in that little piece of wood, my fickle witch? Wait. You don't have to tell me. It must be someone you care about very much to risk going out on your own like this. Is the hunter *sans* soul?"

She shook her head furiously.

"You never were a good liar, Verity. Your chest flushes red, even when you don't speak a word. Yes, like that. So pretty."

Lavender choked the wanting hunger within her.

"Tonight is going to be special. Not only will I claim a hunter kill, but I'll also gain another tribe member. We'll take good care of you, lover. Real good care of my pretty vamp witch."

Rook peeled off his leather coat and thrust it toward the naked man, who stood in front of him and King, cupping his private parts with both hands. "What the hell, man?"

"I'm Thomas," he said, slipping on the coat and buttoning up.

"Be careful of the collar," Rook warned. "You're the cat that visits Verity?"

He nodded. "No time for chatter. She went out tonight—"

"What? She was supposed to stay put. Where was Kaz?" He tugged out his cell phone. Damn it. He shouldn't have turned it off so early.

"If you're asking about the hunter, erm, I may have distracted him," the cat offered.

A text message from Kaz told of Verity's escape. Rook clenched the phone, cursing both the witch and the hunter he'd trusted to keep her closely guarded.

"She told me you'd turned against her and she was under house arrest," Thomas offered.

"What?"

The familiar shrugged. "Sounded good to me. But also suspicious. That witch is not a very good liar. You ever notice how her chest flushes when she lies? No? Right. But now that I see you here, all suited up and ready for action—hell. I shouldn't have helped her."

The knight's look cut Thomas across his little cat heart.

"Anyway, I had a weird feeling about it, so I followed her. To around the corner."

Rook pushed past the familiar, but King reined him in. "I don't think she's standing around waiting for you."

"Well, she was," Thomas said. He preened a hand over his thick black and gold calico hair. "I'm all sweaty. All worked up."

"Thomas! What's going on? Where is Verity?"

"She was around the corner, standing in front of that mansion."

"The one we've staked out," King said.

Thomas gave him a long look and showed his teeth with a growl. King cast him a *what the hell* look.

"If you are both knights sworn to slay vampires, then I am confused," Thomas said, drawing his gaze sharply up and down King. "But that's for later. Verity was using a spell to track something. At least that's what I could figure."

"My soul," Rook said.

"Whatever she was tracking, it led her to the mansion. But she was taken."

"By whom?" King asked.

"Doesn't matter." Rook stepped out onto the sidewalk and studied the mansion's second floor, where the single light glowed. "They've got her. We go in now. You stay out here, Thomas."

"Right. But don't punish the knight who was supposed to guard her. I led him into the stinging nettles. He didn't stand a chance after that."

Then, behind Rook, a cat meowed and stepped out from the puddle of his leather coat. Rook grabbed it, and as he was pulling it on, he raced across the street and toward the mansion.

"I'll go around back," King called.

Rook rounded the corner cordoned off by a wrought-iron fence overgrown with white flowers that gave off an intense odor. Thomas careened past him and padded up

to the gate that Rook might not have noticed for the mass
of green vines that tumbled over it.

"Thanks," he muttered. "Now stay out—"

The cat dashed through the gate's iron bars, fitting its
not-so-sleek body easily through the greenery.

"—of the way," Rook finished his request. "Cats."

Perhaps the feline could prove useful. He did have the
skill to outwit an Order knight.

Rook pulled open the gate and slipped in, breaking off
leaves and stumbling over a low ground shrub but managing to step high and land on a cobblestone pathway that
he followed toward the side of the mansion. The night was
dark and sheltered amid the vines and overgrowth, but
the moon was too bright. If he stepped out into the open,
he'd be seen.

With a stake in one hand, Rook dashed aside a long,
hanging vine heavy with flowers and crept close to the
brick-sided house. If King entered through the back, they'd
find each other inside. Tilting his head, Rook listened, hon-
ing his senses toward the mansion and beyond the walls.

A meow alerted him. The cat sat on a windowsill, its
tail wagging and its ears back. Rook cast looks all about
in case the cat was signaling danger. He didn't see anyone, but vamps were like shadows and could still manage
to surprise him no matter how attuned his senses were to
sound and smell.

He crept closer to the window and saw the panes were
cracked open inward. The cat was good.

"I suppose I can't ask you to stay outside?" He stepped
over the hedge and then wedged a toe into the base of it
to lever himself up to the sill.

Using its head, the cat nudged the window open further
and leapt inside.

"Very well. But don't think this means you deserve an
honorary knighthood."

King would laugh at him for talking to a cat, even if it was a familiar. Could they understand human speech when in cat form?

No time to muddle over that one. He entered what looked like a boiler room for the old, rusting metal pipes that hugged the ceiling and floor. Brooms and buckets were piled against a wall, so he corrected that it had probably been a utility or servant's quarters. For the amount of dust, no one had likely been in here for years.

The cat went about his own way, and Rook was inclined to follow the paw prints. As he slunk down a dark narrow hallway, he noted the closed doors and ran his fingers over the knobs. All were dusty. No one behind those doors. Thomas darted left. Moonlight filled an open foyer tiled in black and white. The stairs leading upward in a grand spiral were not dusty.

Rook pressed his back to the wall and listened.

It is here.

Yes, but how many vampires lay in wait? he wondered. And where was Verity?

Oz hadn't the ability to determine things like that. He was only as sentient as Rook could be. The soul must be what allowed him to know it was here. Oz had once felt Rook's soul when he'd first gone into his body, so surely he would recognize it now.

Something swung around the corner, and Rook raised the stake in defense. King thrust up a staying palm. Rook signaled they take the stairs and took the lead on quiet steps that quickly brought him to the second floor. Foot trails through the dust verified that guess. They split up, Rook going right and King left.

Pressing an ear to the door, he heard something on the other side. Not footsteps, but low speech. When the doorknob turned beneath his fingers, he stepped back and to the side, stake at the ready.

A man walked through the doorway. Rook didn't pause to gauge threat level because moonlight glinted on the fang exposed with the man's yawn. He slammed his fist against the vampire's chest and compressed the paddles. The stake pinioned out, pulsing his fist with the force. It pierced hard bone. Muscle tore, and the heart burst. Before the vampire could scream, his body disintegrated into a cloud of man-shaped ash, the clothing burning slowly.

The ash dropped. Rook jumped over the dusty pile and entered the room the same time King appeared from the other door.

Assessing the situation, he was suddenly fisted in the gut. Not literally, but what he saw reduced him to a shaking, trembling man who had once owned a soul and who had stood before the pyre as he'd witnessed his wife burn. His mouth went dry. The stake slipped in his loosened grip.

Tied up below a grand chandelier that provided the only light stood Verity. The image was horribly similar to that night outside his cottage as he'd been forced to watch the vampires erect a pyre and string up his wife.

"Marianne," Rook murmured. "No. I can't stop it. I... tried."

Verity's arms were secured behind her back, yet her ankles were free. He could smell the gasoline. Candlelight glinted in the liquid.

The scent of burning flesh returned to Rook's senses, acrid and so horrible. Her long wavy reddish-brown hair had ignited so quickly, enflamed around her screams.

Rook's jaw dropped open. He sensed King enter the room, and his friend swore when he took in the sight.

"I was wondering how long it would take the Order to arrive!" the vampire who stood beside the trussed witch called. "Come in. Make yourselves comfortable. We have ~~an amazing show planned for one and all. The Demon Arts~~ Troupe will be so envious."

Exchanging glances with King, Rook assumed control, and King nodded confirmation. They would not rush them until they knew exactly what they were dealing with. Only two vampires in the room? If Slater had been waiting for them, he would have planned many more for defense.

But could he walk forward and stand before Verity when his soul had been blackened by his greedy desires?

He didn't have a soul. And he must never take it back. *No, please.*

I will handle this, Oz. Stay out of the way.

His eyes taking in the walls and the ceiling and noting the balcony on the opposite side of the massive ballroom, Rook stepped carefully forward. The balcony was dark, but he determined that others must hide behind the dusty velvet curtains, waiting for their tribe leader's command.

Verity struggled as he approached. She was not gagged, but she didn't call out.

The asshole vampire had poured gasoline around the fire witch in a wide circle. And yet, there, immediately around her feet and the column he'd tied her to, was another circle of gas, a replacement for the fagots that Rook had once watched burn his wife to cinders.

"Marianne," he whispered.

Stay in the present. Do not go back there. Not if you want to save the witch this time.

This time? It was happening again. Was he to witness another woman he loved burn?

"You looking for one of my tribe members?" Slater asked.

Rook lifted his head to meet Verity's eyes. She was frightened, and he didn't need to lay his palm over her chest to know that. But she was also worried. About him? She knew too much. And she knew all that she must to be a part of his world.

Stand strong, man.

Rook lifted his chin and exhaled. Tightening his fists and twisting his neck to stretch out the corded muscles, he nodded. No flames yet. He wouldn't allow that to happen.

If Rook could consider himself placed at the north point of the outer circle, just a few feet from the gasoline ring, King stood to the west, Slater to the east and another behemoth vampire at the south.

"Where is Clas Dehrer?" Rook asked calmly.

"Why him?" Slater asked, spreading his hands out in front of him. "What has my second in command done to attract the illustrious attention of the Order of the Stake?"

"All of Zmaj has been killing recklessly," Rook said. "You didn't think you could take innocent human lives without consequences, did you?"

"Consequences?" Slater mocked a shudder. "Are you going to punish me? Spank me for my transgressions?"

Rook's fist tightened around the stake. The longer he allowed a vampire to monologue, the more confident he grew and the more of his troops he could gather.

"I rather like Clas, idiot that he can be at times. I have another trade for you," Slater said. "Want to deal?"

Rook noted King took a step to the left. He kept his eye on the balcony and the behemoth.

"No deals."

"Not even if it returns her to you?"

"I'll walk out of here with Verity in hand and you in a pile of ash," Rook promised.

"Cocky hunter." Slater produced a Bic lighter and snapped the silver lid open. "The deal is, the Order looks away from Zmaj's philanderings and I'll let her live."

"I made a deal for a woman once," Rook said. His heart clenched with memory. The ax had been sharp, but he'd had to cut through her neck three times to finally behead her and give her peace. "I'll never do it again."

"Very well." Slater flicked the lighter's steel wheel. Flame shot up.

"You won't kill her. You want to watch her transform to vampire," Rook tried.

Slater's brow arched. The villainous vamp smirked. And he tossed the flaming lighter toward the outer ring of gasoline.

Chapter 21

Rook's heart stopped beating. Flames blurred his vision. Smoke tainted the air. The screams he'd once listened to for so long he'd thought surely he'd go mad echoed up from the past and raged at him.

After all Marianne had done to orchestrate bringing him to the witch and allowing them to share their sorrows, to know that only they two were meant for one another, would that all slip away in the flash of flame and gasoline?

His knees weakened. He saw himself—Giles Martin Rochfeaux—falling to his knees, struggling against the vampires who had held him before the pyre, forcing up his chin to make him witness his wife's gruesome death.

Yet Rook remained standing. The hardened knight who had abandoned emotion when he'd sacrificed his soul to the devil Himself no longer existed. The hunter would not allow the dark evils he had fought for centuries to destroy his happiness.

Rook felt a cool clench of terror climb up his spine. It was accompanied by the shuffle of feet as the creatures shrouded in shadow landed on the ballroom floor. Vampires jumped from the balcony, landing in a crouch or a walk. They crowded up behind Slater and the big one who had been acting as guard. Two dozen, he counted.

But no sign of Clas.

Rook sought his partner through the mire. King raised an eyebrow but also tossed him a wink. They could handle these odds. Been there, done that, ashed them all.

The flames were still far from Verity, but he mustn't delay. Rushing toward the circle, Rook saw a vampire come at him. A warrior's cry barreled up from his lungs, and he swung the stake through bone and muscle, his fist meeting resistance only so long as it took for the long-tooth to ash.

He spun, meeting two vampires with a high round-house kick, body twisting in midair and landing on his feet. Both vamps went down but only to allow their cohorts a chance at him. He flashed a look toward the center of the flaming circle.

Verity watched with pleading eyes.

He leaped over the flames and was slammed midair by a vampire who collided with his back. They went down within the flaming circle, wrestling for control. Pinching the nerve at the vampire's collarbone surprised his opponent, who swore and then dropped. Unconscious, but only for a few moments.

While King went at the vampires outside the circle, Rook crawled over to Verity. He wanted to embrace her, to kiss her, to whisper that it was all going to be all right. And it would be. But not with vampires running amuck.

He dug out a blade from his boot and sawed it through the ropes around her wrists.

"Rook, look out!"

Expecting a vampire to jump onto his back, Rook spun to see flame following the thin line of gasoline up to the second circle. It ignited the gasoline around Verity's feet. He stomped at it to no avail.

Verity screamed and stepped from foot to foot, but she

couldn't avoid the flames, which licked at her flat shoes. He managed to cut through the thick rope and free her hands. Rook pulled off his coat and placed it on her shoulders. He lifted her, feeling the flames lick his leather pants. Jumping and stomping at the flame, he rushed the outer circle and leaped over it.

He landed in a wobble and went to the floor, turning to hit with his hip and shoulder as he kept Verity safely to his chest to avoid the impact. He rolled over on top of her. A quick kiss was necessary. She tasted like fear and ash.

"Get out of here. Go downstairs. Stay away from the vamps."

"But Slater is hiding somewhere."

He'd forgotten about that bastard. "Over by the door then. Stay within my eyesight. I'll handle Slater."

A vampire gripped him by the back of the Kevlar vest and tugged him up to his feet. Verity scrambled away. A beefy arm wrapped around Rook's neck, jerking his head back painfully. He kicked and pushed them both to the floor.

Above and behind him, he saw the chandelier fall. Vampires yelped. King held the small crossbow he'd had fashioned centuries ago. Good shot. That would keep down the handful of vampires trapped beneath it in the flames for a while. Down, but not dead.

Elbowing his aggressor, Rook managed to free himself and twisted to stake the longtooth. He turned to see Verity—in Slater's grasp.

What caught Verity's attention was not her rescuing knight, but the slick lines of gasoline that glittered with reflected flame. The entire ballroom was crisscrossed with the fuel. As the fire circles blazed, slowly they began to feed into the lines radiating out from the center. It would be only moments before fire again threatened her.

With one arm banded across her chest, the vampire held her with ease. Reaching inside his pants pocket, Slater pulled out something.

"I've got one more trick in tonight's performance," Slater announced.

He gripped the back of Verity's hair and yanked her head up so she had no choice but to look at Rook. Her rescuing knight, who had fallen to his knees to see her tied in the center of the flames. She wished he had never seen such a thing. Twice.

Slater smelled…different. Some tangy note clanged at his unmanly sweet scent. Beside her cheek, he dangled the little wooden heart, which held Rook's soul and Oz's release.

"Choose," the vampire called.

Verity's vision was blocked by the wooden heart. She wanted to look into Rook's eyes and tell him it was okay. Choose the soul. For in doing so, he would save two people: him and Oz. She wasn't going to die. Slater wanted to keep her, to watch her transform. She would hate that, but she could escape from his clutches. Somehow.

"Such a dilemma," Slater said.

"Not really." Rook glanced again to King.

Verity knew the hunters communicated on a level they had forged over the centuries. They couldn't read each other's minds, but they had probably developed some nifty silent signals.

Rook announced, "I'm sorry, Oz. No deal!"

Slater squeezed the heart in his palm. "Then take him out, men."

The remaining tribe members rushed Rook from behind.

"No!" she shouted.

Yet she had the sense to fill her hands with flames. Slater held her at the shoulders and chest, and she couldn't move her arms around to touch him and ignite his clothing.

"You think I didn't have some of that flame retardant you used to rub on your skin before a show? I'm not stupid, witch."

Now she recognized the lemon thyme behind the obnoxious lavender.

Rook fought two vampires. He kicked high, clocking one on the jaw. The other grabbed his leg while it was still in the air and shoved, sending him to the floor and sliding close to Verity's feet. He twisted into a crouch and stabbed the stake into Slater's shoe.

The vampire yelped and softened his clasp on Verity enough so that she could slip free. Before she could move away from him, the vampire grabbed her by the hair, jerking it so she rebounded against his chest. He dragged her toward the fire.

Rook followed cautiously, stakes in both hands, his eyes darting from Verity to the melee that King handled alone.

All of a sudden Verity smelled blood. And felt the hot drip of it splatter her cheek. Slater had bitten into his wrist and held it to her face.

"Just one taste," Slater said, "and she's mine."

Goddess, it smelled so good. And she could feel the droplet sliding closer to the corner of her mouth. Verity released the fire from her hands and dropped them slack at her sides. Slater's arm around her neck banded her tightly to his chest. The blood glistened in the flickering glow of the fire.

Rook held out the stakes, then made a show of shoving them in the holsters at his hips. "Let her go."

Verity dashed her tongue out but couldn't quite taste the hot liquid.

"Give it up," Slater replied. "She's mine. What does a hunter want with a vampiress?"

"She has another twenty-four hours," Rook said. "I won't let her succumb."

Slater smeared his wrist across Verity's lips. "Time's up."

Verity compressed her lips in an attempt not to taste the blood. She wanted to—oh, but she needed to satisfy the relentless craving...

"Don't do it, Verity," Rook pleaded. "I promised you. Remember? I'll always stand by you, no matter what."

He'd promised he'd stay with her beyond the moon. Whether she was just a witch or a witch who was also a vampire. And she believed him. She loved him.

He was the man she had learned to trust.

Pressing her back into Slater's chest, she felt the hard, heart-shaped object in his pocket nudge her shoulder blade. The blood scent was sweet, thick. It would taste better than a Ladurée macaron nestled in a pretty pastel box.

"Open your mouth," Slater hissed. "Enough of the big sad eyes from the boyfriend. You're mine, witch."

The vampire shoved his wrist against her mouth. Her lips stretched over her teeth.

Verity felt Rook's hand slam into her chest and push her and Slater backward. They stumbled, and Slater's wrist slipped from her mouth. Her lips parted. She bit her tongue as she landed on the vampire in a sprawl on the floor near the flames.

A rough shove from two hands rolled her off her captor. Rook knelt over the vampire and plunged the stake into his chest. Ash dusted the air.

Heartbeats thundering in her ears, Verity blinked heavy

tears. They dropped to her cheeks and rolled downward. The vampire's blood pooled at the corner of her mouth.

Rook's body plunged onto hers. He roughly wiped at her lips, smearing her skin. "No," he said. "Not going to let you succumb. Keep your mouth closed, Verity."

She saw the vampire lunging at Rook from behind. Just when she wanted to yell in warning, instead, she stretched up an arm and blasted the vampire with fire. The fireball hit the longtooth in the chest and barreled him through the air to land as a pile of ash before King, who had wielded the stake that burst his chest.

"I can't get it all off," Rook said. He licked his fingers and smeared them around her mouth. And then he dashed his tongue across her lips. She didn't kiss him. He was cleaning away the vampire's blood, freeing her...

And when he did kiss her, it was quick and rough, yet she felt his need to keep her safe in that embrace. And—

—she tasted pennies on her tongue.

"I think you're good now. Only a few more left," he said. "Stay here. Don't move."

She nodded.

Beside her, a pile of ash and clothing made her smile. Slater was gone.

Yet in her mouth she tasted blood. Rook hadn't removed it all. When he'd kissed her, he had unknowingly impressed traces of Slater's blood. It tasted dusty, and a spark of satisfaction scurried within.

Great Hecate. She had consumed blood.

"There he is!" King pointed toward the open doorway.

A bald vampire dashed out of the room. Rook raced after him. The vampire trammeled down the curving stairs toward the foyer.

Rook ran toward the balcony railing and leaped over

and into a free fall. He couldn't see much in the darkened foyer below, but he did know the landing was going to hurt like hell. Unless he landed on something with cushioning.

Which he managed nicely. Colliding with Clas, they went down on the floor, the vampire swearing and Rook's bones jarring enough to make him reconsider flight ever again. His spine shifted, and his elbow popped, but the vampire who wrestled beneath him didn't care that his attacker was fighting excruciating pain.

Reaching for the stake at his hip—it wasn't there— Rook's hands reactively went to the vampire's throat. Choking wouldn't kill an immortal creature. And the beast was a brute, stronger than Rook, even with Oz inside him bolstering his strength. A boot heel hit him soundly in the spine, and he released the vamp long enough for it to scramble free.

Above them, King shouted down. "All dust in there!" His boots scrambled down the staircase. "And turning into a raging blaze."

Clas got free from Rook, and he swiped for his boot but couldn't catch him. Springing to his feet, Rook turned in time to see King wrangle the vamp's arms behind his back.

"He's yours," King said. "Take back the witch's life."

Stalking up to the struggling vampire, the creature calmed and sneered at him. He hadn't any stakes. And the garrote and holy water wouldn't get him far. But he didn't need either.

If a witch could do it, so could he.

"You thought she was dead?" he asked the longtooth.

Clas growled. "Stupid witch. You got in the way. Took something you wanted though, eh? Two somethings you want. The girl and the soul. Ha!"

"The girl is still mine," Rook said. "I don't care about the soul."

"Liar."

Yeah, well, he wasn't going to give the vampire the satisfaction.

"This is for Verity," Rook said, pressing his hands together before his chest. "Namaste, motherfucker."

He made a spade of his fingers and shoved them into the vampire's chest. It wasn't an easy task, but the force with which he thrust up his arms punctured skin and muscle and slid between ribs. The heart pulsed slippery against his squeezed fingertips. Gritting his teeth and shoving harder, he pierced the heart muscle and tore out whatever slippery chunks he could grasp through the rib cage.

Flicking his hand out to shed the vampire's tattered heart, Rook stepped back. King dropped the vampire, which spasmed and screamed. Dust clouded the air.

Rook fell to his knees. King backed up to sit on the bottom step of the spiraling staircase.

Thomas wandered across the black-and-white foyer floor, sniffed at the ash pile, then scampered up the stairs toward the smoking room as he meowed wildly.

Verity was up there. Alone. Among flames.

Chapter 22

Rook stepped back from the wall of heat that whipped before him. All the lines of gasoline had ignited. It was a virtual chessboard of flame, and the spaces of floor were spare. A wind of blaze flashed toward him. He dodged to avoid the orange death.

He shouted for Verity but couldn't hear anything over the crackle of fire. Floorboards creaked. The room would collapse soon.

Leaping over the line of flame, he dodged to the left and leaped over two more lines. The flames farthest from the center of the room were as high as his knees.

Verity's voice called out. He found her sitting beside a blazing circle of flames, sorting through Slater's ashes. To have witnessed the vampires go up in flames had lifted his spirits. Vampires had burned Marianne. And they had almost burned Verity.

Never again.

"We have to get out of here before the flames take over and burn this place down." He knelt beside her and took her hand. Ashes coated her fingers in a greasy mix. "King is calling the fire brigade. Verity, come on! It isn't safe."

"Not until I find the heart!"

"The—" Hell, he'd forgotten. He'd last seen the vampire tucking the wooden heart into his coat pocket. It had to have burned to cinders when he'd staked Slater. "It's a loss, Verity. We have to get out of here."

"Don't say that!" She coughed. "Oz needs you."

Yes, do not give up on me now!

Rook shucked off his vest and peeled his T-shirt off. He tore it down the front and then wrapped it around Verity's head and adjusted it to cover her nose and mouth. "Let's make this quick!"

He peeled away a burned portion of fabric and sorted through the ash alongside Verity. The heat of the flame was more apparent now that he'd removed his clothing. Verity was seemingly unaware of the danger. He pulled her closer, tugging her foot away from veering toward a line of flame.

"What the hell?" King called from the doorway.

"We'll be right there! Just have to find—"

A means to dismiss a friend he'd lived with for more than four centuries. And a final blow to his immortality.

So be it. He didn't need to live forever. Not if it meant Oz would not be there for his family. And not if it meant he might have a few decades to enjoy a family of his own.

A groaning creak preceded the splitting of wood. The floorboards were giving way not far from where they knelt.

Rook grabbed Verity's hand. "I'm getting you out of here."

"Got it!" She triumphantly displayed a piece of wood. She tugged away the shirt from her nose and mouth. "Oh, no. It's been broken in two."

His finger played across the other piece of the heart. It was scorched, but the fire hadn't eaten into the wood. "What does that mean? Do you think the soul is gone?"

She pressed her piece next to his and clasped his fingers over the piece. "What do you think? Can you feel it?"

He nodded. Oz stirred within him.

I feel it!

"Oz feels it."

"How do we put it back?" she wondered. "How was it removed?"

"Himself took it out."

"Right. Demonic magic. There has to be a way. A spell."

"We'll worry about that later. Come on!"

He grabbed Verity's hand and stopped abruptly as the flames flared wildly in front of them in a wall that stretched in an arch toward the collapsing floorboards and opposite toward the wall that would block their exit. They had to move forward.

He felt Verity crush up against his side, fearful.

"Can you control the flames?" he shouted.

She shook her head against his chest. Her body trembled.

He pulled her around in front of him and held her by the hips. Ashes in her hair dusted his face and melted from the heat that surrounded them.

"You can do this," he said. "You have to, lover. You are powerful."

"But I didn't create these flames!"

That was what he was afraid of. He could risk tossing her over his shoulder and rushing through the flames, but he didn't want her to burn. He was helpless. A man on his knees before the pyre—no.

"Concentrate," he said firmly over her shoulder. "Spread the flames, Verity. Make a path for us to get out of here. Will you try?"

She nodded. Flame licked at his ankles. He adjusted their stance to the left as Verity held up her arms and closed her eyes. Bowing her head, she thrust up her hands. She spoke no magic, but Rook sensed she was delving inward, mining whatever it was within that allowed her to control fire.

He bowed his head to the back of hers, closing his eyes and focusing prayer toward her. Oz joined in. *I honor the place in you that is the same in me. I honor the place in you of love, of light, of peace and truth. We are one...*

Together, they held the witch in front of the flames, not as a sacrifice but as an offering for the wrongs in their pasts. Neither were worthy of forgiveness.

With a bold cry, Verity swept her hands apart, and a force that billowed through the flames as if clear smoke roiled forward, pushing aside the roaring blaze and forming an aisle.

"Good girl!" Rook pushed her forward.

They ran toward the doorway where King waited. Rook gave her a good shove, and his partner caught her and whisked her out into the balcony hallway. Turning, Rook dodged the flames as the aisle closed. He stumbled against the door frame and out into the darkness.

Verity embraced him, and he crushed her against his heaving body. "You did it," he said on gasps. "I love you, witch."

"Come on, let's move outside," King directed.

Rook hastened behind his friend, Verity in arm. He lifted her and carried her down the spiraling staircase. Behind them the ballroom floor collapsed in a tremendous crash, and as they exited the front door and entered the fresh night air, the shrapnel of wood and marble and flame scattered out through the threshold.

Landing on the front yard, Rook pulled Verity to him and kissed her soundly, then stroked the ash-flaked hair from her face. "How do you feel?"

"Stupid for allowing this to happen and for having to depend on you to rescue me."

"You don't like being rescued?"

"Oh, I appreciate it." She kissed him quickly. "But if I hadn't gone out on my own, you might not have had to do it."

"I am always here for you."

"Beyond the moon?" And then she dropped the brave façade, and tears spilled down her ash-smeared cheeks.

"Verity? What is it?" He hugged her to him, and her sobs grew stronger. "Sweetie? It's over. I love you."

She shook her head, and when she pulled back, she tapped her mouth, which was smeared with ash and blood. "You tried to wipe it all off, but when you kissed me...I tasted blood, Rook. I'm going to transform."

He pressed another kiss to her mouth to silence her silly worry. "I staked Clas."

"You—you did?" She clasped her stomach. Checking for the raging hunger? Then with a nod, she said, "Goddess, I think it's gone. I don't feel the craving. You saved me again."

She plunged into his arms. The witch wrapped her legs about him, and he carried her toward the gate where King waited.

"You find it?" he asked as Rook passed through, Verity clinging to him.

"It's broken."

Outside the mansion, the trio made their way toward Rook's waiting car, followed by a curious cat.

They dropped King off at Order headquarters. Rook drove Verity to her home because that's where she kept all the items necessary for spellcraft. Much as he'd like to go home and shower off the ash, he wasn't about to get too far from the witch, who would now never become vampire.

Kaz, nursing some strange scratches on his face and hands, waited on the front stoop.

Rook put up a palm to dismiss any excuse he might try. "I know that cat."

"Yeah? But I was defeated by a cat."

"We'll talk in the morning. She's safe. That's all I care about."

Kaz offered another apology and then took off, promising he'd make it up to Rook somehow.

Verity sent him upstairs to shower while she rang Vika St. Charles. Vika was a witch who had a particular habit of attracting lost souls, so Verity thought she might have a clue how they could put Rook's soul back inside his body.

The tub had an ash ring around it when he was finished so he wiped it off with a towel, then realized he'd made a huge mess in her bathroom but didn't have the energy to try to fix it.

Towel wrapped around his hips, Rook wandered into the bedroom. Verity stood over her spell table. Barefoot, her skirt torn and blackened with ash, she looked like a bedraggled forest child with the moonlight dancing in her violet hair. Beautiful.

Sneaking up behind her, he wrapped his arms around her waist. Although she smelled like ash and smoke, he buried his face in her hair. He didn't ever want to let her go. She was that which he had been without for centuries.

And she was that witch.

"What did the St. Charles witch say?" he asked.

"Vika wasn't sure how, exactly, to put a soul back in a body. She's more about catching the ones wandering the atmosphere. The ones the soul bringer misses. But she's searching her grimoires."

Rook nodded and thumbed his chin. He'd had the opportunity and the displeasure to meet all kinds through the ages. Witches, vampires, soul bringers, werewolves. ~~He knew things that even some breeds did not know. But~~ he couldn't utilize magic. Only Oz gave him superior strength. And a determination.

"What about Ian Grim?" he suggested.

Verity turned a bright gaze on him. "The warlock? How do you know him?"

"Uh, he owes me one."

Recently Rook had been able to help the warlock come into a large number of vampires that he had needed for a spell. Grim had contacted him and given him weeks to consider the proposal. He'd discussed it with King. They'd decided having a warlock in their debt was not to be overlooked. And when was exterminating vampires ever a bad thing?

"Warlocks aren't tops on my list, though, that's for sure."

"Grim is kind."

"If you say so. I just don't like witches who take it into their hearts to practice malefic magic. He serves no good."

"But he owes you one? What have you done for him?"

"Can't tell you."

"Or you'd have to kill me?"

"Something like that." He brushed a ribbon of her ashy hair behind her ear. "Do you want me to give him a call?"

"He's our only option. And we don't have much time. What does Oz say?" Verity asked, turning around to study his petulant pose.

"I'm sure you can guess."

"He's in a hurry too. Tomorrow night is the full moon," Verity said. "Oz's day. Wouldn't it be great if you could release him for good? What if his wife is in labor as we speak? We can't waste any more time."

Call the warlock.

Never had Oz asked a thing of him. Four centuries he had existed within him, both of them accepting their fates as punishment for the cruel bargains made against the ones they had loved.

If you set me free, then you must also set her free, Giles. Give Marianne peace.

But he wasn't the one who harbored Marianne's soul.

You hold her memory captive.

Verity hugged him and said, "I can't wait to make love to you."

"We can make time right now."

"Nope. Later. Next time we have sex, I want it to be with only you. No offense, Oz."

None taken.

"He said—"

"I can guess." She winked. "I'm going to shower. You give Grim a call and then continue to page through the grimoire."

Rook shook his head. "Uh, sorry."

Verity paused by the bathroom door. "For what?"

"You'll see."

How one man could make such a mess was beyond her. But even as Verity picked up the dirty towels and wiped away the ash smudges from the tiled walls and sink, she had to smile. Rook was her messy man.

He'd rescued her. Saved her from becoming a vampire. And he loved her.

And she loved him. But more so, she had gotten beyond the ingrained need to follow her mother's tainted wisdom and now trusted him.

She lingered under the steaming hot shower stream, washing her hair of the ash and making sure there wasn't a spot of blood on her skin. She didn't feel the craving for blood, but she was still freaked about getting near it.

What if she could still transform? Was the hunger merely lying dormant, waiting to strike full force tomorrow night?

No, she had to believe she was safe. It would be maddening to think otherwise.

When she shut off the water and reached out, her lover handed her a towel and she stepped out into his embrace. He rubbed the terry cloth gently over her hair and her shoulders. He still wore only a towel, and she pressed her slick breasts against his chest and leaned into his coolness.

"I love you," he said.

"I love you, too. I'm sorry for going out on my own. If I hadn't…"

"We might never have gotten Slater and Clas and the rest of that damned tribe all together in one room."

"Bait?"

"Accidental bait. Thank you."

"You find anything in the grimoire?"

"Maybe. There's something about restoring souls. You'll have to take a look because most of it is in Latin, and I'm a bit rusty with that language. But first I need to hold you."

He tugged the towel across her hips and lured her closer, holding her there against his body and nuzzling his face into her wet hair. His cock hardened against her stomach, and she needed him inside her that instant.

And yet.

"I meant it when I said next time we made love it would be just the two of us."

"What if I don't agree to that condition?" He nudged his erection against her.

"Patience is a virtue, lover. Let's go set Oz free."

Rook held the two wooden heart pieces as he lounged at the head of the bed, naked, his ankles crossed. Verity had wrapped her great-grandmother Bluebell's quilt over his shoulders and had returned to look over the grimoire. The quilt actually did hug him, and he wanted to wear it always.

With moonlight flashing in the dozens of crystals hanging overhead, his mind was four hundred years away. He'd sacrificed so much and so foolishly. If he'd taken just a moment to consider what he'd asked Himself for, he would have never done so. And perhaps he also could have found a means to prevent Marianne from seeking her devilish bargain. He and Marianne would have lived happily ever after. They would have raised a brood of children and died of old age.

Or Marianne may have been proven a witch and burned at the stake while he, a king's soldier, would have been forced to watch and then be hung next for harboring a witch.

The future was not in a man's control. He could only live each day as best he could. Now he had the opportunity to share those days with the gorgeous witch crowned in faery tresses. It was a destiny he embraced, thanks, he believed, to Marianne, whose soul resided within the witch.

And this time around he would not screw it up. But did he deserve this second chance at love?

He hadn't noticed Verity climb onto the bed until her fingers clasped around the broken heart he joggled on his palms. "What is it?"

He sighed and tilted his forehead toward hers. She met him with a tender head butt and settled next to him. She'd slipped a loose white T-shirt on, and her hard nipple brushed his arm. He loved the easy comfort they'd developed with one another.

"This was my punishment," he said. "My soul, out of my body. It was the only way I could atone for what I did to Marianne."

She threaded her fingers through his, so their palms clasped the wood pieces. "You didn't do it to her. The devil Himself did it."

"I was the conduit to her destruction. Oz would agree. He's accepted his own punishment within me for the wrongs he committed against his family."

"How long must the two of you suffer to atone for something you did when you didn't know any better? Lover…" She brushed her lips against his earlobe. "You know better now. So you do better. Be strong and leave the past in the past."

"How do I do that? My past resides within your soul."

"You think if you take your soul it will mean you've forgotten about her?"

"I don't want to do that."

"And you shouldn't. Setting her free does not mean you will forget her. Your worry holds her in your heart. If you can release that, you must forever atone so she can finally be free to move on. Why else do you think she managed to bring us together? She was able to bring me to you because you hold her so strongly with your thoughts. And why do you think she did that? Marianne needs to move on."

"I never thought of it that way. You think she's trapped on this mortal plane? Within you?"

"A part of her soul must be."

He nodded as he studied the wood pieces. "She's waited a long time for us to come together."

He placed his palm over her heart. Closing his eyes, he focused on the rush of her blood beneath his hand, the beat of her heart and the subtle sigh of her soul. If a remnant of Marianne was attached to Verity's soul, he wanted to keep it.

But he knew he should not. Because Verity was right. Granting Marianne freedom would not take away her memory. And when he had most feared the dredging up of those horrid memories, now he could only be thankful he could still remember the good times they had shared. Those memories he would forever hold in his heart.

He nodded. "Let's set her free."

"Great! Did you get hold of Ian Grim?"

"I woke him up, but he's interested in helping with the spell. He told me to begin, and he'd be here soon. Guess that means I'd better put on some clothes."

"I tossed your shirt in the washer while you were showering. Your leather pants are in the laundry room. I'll gather the spell ingredients. Leave this."

She took the wood pieces from him and kissed them. With a wink, she scampered off the bed, and Rook said blessings for the serendipity that had allowed his long-dead wife to bring Verity into his life.

Chapter 23

Verity directed Rook to stand in the center of the salt circle she'd poured on the gray wood floorboards at the end of the bed. A good witch never let her salt supply get depleted.

"But if we intend to let Oz out…?" He pointed to the salt.

"It's how the spell is done, hunter."

Rook caught her intended admonishment. So he was the hunter and she the witch. He must trust she knew her craft. And he did.

"I'll open the circle if it works," she said. "Promise, Oz."

I do love your witch.

"He loves you."

"I love him too. He's taken care of you. You've both looked after each other. I can't wait to meet his wife," Verity said with a girlish shrug of excitement. "So step inside, and let's get this party started. I've left the front door unlocked so Grim can come in when he gets here. I have a lot of Latin to chant."

Clad in his reasonably clean leather pants, Rook padded barefoot across the room and stepped into the circle, which was wide enough to hold three grown men. But it would only have to contain two.

Was he ready for this? He'd lived four centuries with

Oz inside him. They were brothers beyond the kinship he and King claimed. What would he do on his own without Oz to comment on every relationship or direct him when his path veered the wrong way?

You will be the man she has fallen in love with.

He couldn't argue that.

"It's already the morning of the day of the full moon," Verity said over her shoulder as she drew her finger down a page in the grimoire. "Perfect for working spells. Oh, here!" She scampered over and handed him the two heart halves. "Hold them together. I'm not sure if it being broken is going to affect the spell, but let's hope for the best." She kissed him and dashed away.

Her enthusiasm boasted his confidence, and he surrendered to this whole wacky put-back-the-soul-release-the-demon-and-accept-mortality affair.

Rook fitted the pieces together and squeezed his fingers around them. "Did I mention how much I love you?"

"I love you too, hunter," she singsonged gaily.

God, he loved that witch.

"Now close your eyes and concentrate on the resonance of my voice and not so much on trying to understand the words. As my chanting becomes less words and more sounds, hold the tone in your throat."

That made little sense, but as Verity started to chant Latin, Rook closed his eyes and did his best. The tones danced in his head, undecipherable save for the warmth they stirred within him. Oz felt it too, and noticeably shivered.

Suddenly he heard a male voice twine within the tones of Verity's luxurious resonance. Rook didn't open his eyes. The warlock had arrived, walked up the stairs and quietly joined the spell.

What had the man done to bring the wrath of his breed

upon him? Witches only banished their own to warlock when a grave crime had been committed. And in terms of grave, Rook suspected the witches' definition went far beyond what an average human would consider grave.

Focus.

Sorry, Oz.

He focused on the sounds that, now that he thought of it, did vibrate at the back of his throat.

Suddenly a streak of heat rushed up his spine, flashing out each vertebra, then flowing out through his rib bones. His spine and ribs were on fire. But it didn't hurt. It felt…comforting, wide and expansive, a bit like a hug from great-grandmother Bluebell's quilt, yet more, as if his entire body had opened to take in whatever the universe should offer.

Shoulders thrust back, Rook spread out his arms, and his chest lifted. A brilliant burst filled him, softening his limbs and then tightening every muscle. And he knew what had once been his had been returned.

Rook fell to his knees, gasping. The broken heart lay on the floor before him. He clutched his chest. A smile filled him from head to toe to…his soul. The witch had done it!

"It's in him," he heard Verity whisper.

"I believe so," Grim said. "Now to cast out that demon."

My turn!

At a gesture from the warlock, the salt circle burst into flames. Rook shuffled back on his knees. He stood, seeing the tousle-haired warlock who controlled a small emerald ball of flame in his hands, tossing it back and forth as if a child's toy. Grim was short and seemingly young, and he didn't look so imposing. Or evil. Until the emerald flame glinted in his eyes. And with only a few words Rook recognized as holy, the warlock pushed the flames toward him.

Rook's arms flung outward as the green flames seemed

to eat his bare skin and enter his pores. Inside him Oz struggled, kicking and pulling at his tendons and the platelets and cells that formed this mortal body that had borne them both through the ages.

"It's hurting him!" he heard Verity cry.

"Don't go near him," Grim warned. "It's working."

Feeling as if something, some interior coating that had once surrounded his body, was being peeled away from the inside of his skin, Rook yowled and resisted beating a fist against his chest.

Thank you.

And the demon stepped out from him, one hoofed foot landing inside the salt circle, which no longer burned emerald. Oz's horns tugged at Rook's skin as they were freed, and finally the last of the demon emerged and stood beside Rook.

He'd never looked at the demon until now. Not even in the mirror. For he had not wanted to face his truth. Handsome fellow, in a punk-rock, horned kind of way.

Verity clapped gleefully. Ian Grim crossed his arms and gave a satisfied smirk. "Asatrú, I presume?" the warlock asked.

Oz clasped hands with Rook. "I've been waiting a long time to do this, my friend."

Rook held the demon's hand, noting its coolness, but even more so, he looked into Oz's red eyes and saw such joy that he felt it in his own heart. This was right. They'd come to the end of their journey.

"Live well," Rook offered.

"Only if you've set her free."

"Never from memory, but yes, it's time to forgive myself. We must both forgive ourselves. I forgive you your sins, Asatrú."

"And I forgive yours, Giles Martin Rochfeaux. They were committed when, as the witch said, we did not know better. And now we do."

Rook slapped the demon on the shoulder. "I'm going to miss you, man. Now go find your wife before you miss the birth of your child."

"I'm already out of here—but…" Oz turned to Verity, his horns sweeping the air proudly. "You'll take care of him now that he doesn't have me to look after him?"

"Of course I will." She grabbed a broom propped beside the spell table and swept it over the salt line a few times to clear an exit for the demon.

Oz stepped out, sniffed the air around Grim and made a face, and then took Verity's hand and kissed it. "*Adieu, mon amie* witch. I trust you with his heart."

"I will take good care of it. Promise."

Stretching his arms wide and calling out in a demonic language, suddenly Oz aported out of the room.

"He didn't like me much," Grim commented. "To be expected. Glad to finally be able to repay our debt, Rook." He held out a hand to shake.

Rook stepped from the salt circle and clasped the warlock's hand. A weird shimmer of knowing shot through his system. He'd never felt anything like it before, but he had to mark it off as residual magic and the amazing experience he'd just lived through.

"Thank you," he said to the warlock.

Verity placed her hand over their joined hands—and gasped. The smile she flashed Rook was as knowing as the feeling he'd experienced.

"Right." Grim tugged from the clasp. He studied his hand as if he'd felt something too. "You won't be needing me anymore. And I sense a reunion of souls coming on. You've an old soul, my dear witch. Died two deaths?"

"Yes," Verity answered. "You can sense that?"

"I get all sorts of weird feelings from the two of you. Familiarity. Shared history. A sexual heat that is off the scale." The warlock rubbed his jaw. "Indeed, the two of you were destined to find one another. I'm honored to have been a part of the final cleansing that will grant your souls peace. This is the first time I've shaken your hand with your soul intact, hunter."

"I feel different to you?"

"Yes. Disturbingly so."

"I'll count that as a good thing, considering the source."

"Thank you, Ian. I'll call you tomorrow." Verity kissed him on the cheek, and the warlock had the courtesy to blush. "You can let yourself out?"

"I will. *Au revoir…*" He studied Rook for a moment. "Rochfeaux?"

"Yes."

"We hail from the same century," Grim commented. "Maybe someday you can get beyond your disgust for me and we can chat. You fascinate me."

"You do not disgust me. Warlocks just aren't on the top of my list."

"I should hope not. Well." Grim clapped his hands abruptly. "I've overstayed as it is. Good morning to the two of you, and blessings to your future together. Oh, ah, and a warning—Rook, you are mortal now. You'll have to be extra agile when dodging vampire fangs from now on, hunter."

The warlock skipped down the stairs. Rook rubbed his arms of the strange sensation he had felt when holding Grim's hand. Familiar? That was the only way to describe it. And strange. Yet he wasn't about to ponder what sort of fastball destiny could toss him in the form of a warlock.

Verity hugged him tightly. "You're so warm! Your soul is back. And you're all mine."

"For as long as you'll have me."

"That long, eh? Then we'd better discuss living arrangements because I'm not going anywhere, hunter."

* * *

The demon stepped through the bright, viridescent Faery forest, his hooves taking the mossy land swiftly, his heart showing him the way to his wife. He'd made this trip monthly for years. It never took long, but it was always fraught with an urgency that he would lose it all if he were not quick enough.

When finally he landed on the snowy grounds that covered his wife's home, his hooves took the cool surface up to the portcullis. The doorman opened it and, recognizing him, rushed him along.

"She's in labor!" the hob-brownie called after him.

Oz quickened his pace. Was he too late? After all he'd been through to convince the hunter to finally accept his soul—no, he was just in time. He knew it as he turned into Winter's bed chambers and his beautiful wife of the long snowy hair and bright violet eyes beamed at him from her bed.

"The babe is coming! I wasn't sure you'd make it, my demon lover. Your mortal full moon day is nearly over. I wish you could stay longer."

"I am here forever, my love."

Winter's face lighted.

He nodded. "I'm free. I'm yours. Forever."

Epilogue

"Oz sends his love," Rook said as he strode into the bedroom.

Verity sat naked on the bed beneath the azure canopy. They'd made love all night. And now that it was morning, Rook carried in breakfast on a platter, which he set on the bed beside her.

"How did you speak to him?"

"He sent a messenger. A sprite, I believe. Oz is tied up with his new family and didn't want to leave them, but I sent return word asking him to promise to bring his wife and babe for a visit as soon as they feel up to traveling."

"So his wife gave birth in Faery?"

"That's where he plans to live with them. The message reports Winter had a girl with ten toes and ten fingers, two wings and two horns."

"Sounds like she'll be a real handful."

"They named her Azar. It means fire. I'll wager they named her after you." He kissed her. "My wild and fiery witch."

Verity smiled. "So how did Oz, the demon who has only ever been allowed to tread the earth twenty-four hours out of every month, ever manage to hook up with a woman from Faery and marry her *and* get her pregnant?"

"Easy." Rook poured her tea and settled beside her with a plate of crumpets spread with cinnamon honey. He took a bite, then offered her one. He loved to feed her, and she loved when he spoiled her.

"I actually dated Winter once about five years ago. She used to visit the mortal clubs, and one night we hooked up. Initially we hit it off, but it grew obvious as we tried to rush through what was lackluster sex for both of us that we just weren't meant for one another. Yet, all the while, Oz was bouncing up and down inside me. I took a chance and explained Oz to her and how much he wanted to meet her."

"That's the coolest meet story I've heard. On Oz's part, not yours. Lackluster sex? Really?"

"Sometimes the chemistry isn't there. Unlike us." He kissed her lips, licking off the smudge of honey. "Mmm, you're always tasty. So anyway, Oz and Winter hit if off immediately. And Oz, being a demon, has easy access to Faery. He'd always head there as soon as he took over my body."

"So, uh…" Verity teased a bit of honey from the crumpet he held and licked it off her finger. "I get that you were present when Oz was out, and vice versa. It was always your body, in a way, and he was just a passenger, and vice versa when he was out. Does that mean you might, if even partially, claim some parentage to this fiery new baby?"

Rook set down the crumpet and ran his fingers through his hair. "I never thought about that. Maybe? That might be the reason you thought you saw me as a father."

"No. I'm pretty sure that's not it. Besides, I saw you as a father *before* Azar was born. You sure you haven't fathered any children over the centuries?"

"I have always used a condom."

"You didn't with me."

"I…okay, so not always. Most of the time. Those things

were nasty in the earlier centuries. They tended to fall apart and get tears in them. No kids, Verity. I'd know. And the woman would tell me."

"Not if she didn't want you to know or couldn't find the man who very purposely made a point of only having one-night stands over the years."

"You have me there. I can say with ninety-five percent surety that the only child I have ever fathered was with Marianne."

"And you said the midwife took that baby away? It was swaddled. Did you look at it?"

Realizing she'd startled him with that question, Verity embraced her lover and tilted her head against his shoulder. "I shouldn't have put it that way."

"No, I'm glad you did. I never did lift the blanket to see the child. I was so concerned for Marianne. And we both assumed the witch had taken the child away to bury. I didn't seek her out after that. I was too heartbroken…and also battling vampires. Could it have been alive?"

"If so, then I wish that child had the best life." She kissed him and took the plate from him. "Can we go for a walk in the moonlight later?"

He nodded absently. She had put the thought about his child into his brain, and he'd muddle on it a while now, surely.

"Love you," he finally said and leaned in to kiss her.

The first snowflake of the season captured Verity's glee. Dropping his hand, she rushed ahead to chase the fluttering jewel down the cobbled sidewalk that edged the dark, bejeweled waters of the Seine.

Rook felt the life that stretched before him promised much happiness. Finally he was at peace with his past.

Once, he'd done what his heart had commanded. It had

not gone well. He'd been punished for that mistake for four centuries.

Now, he would move forward without fear. Mistakes would surely be made again, but he would face them with Verity by his side. And now, as a mortal man, he would have to adjust to the possibility that death could come easily. He'd have to step up his training and make sure that Kevlar covered all the important parts before he next went out on the hunt.

The witch's hand slipped into his, and her bright smile stole his heart. He would never tell her that he suspected Marianne's soul still shone from within her, that perhaps a piece of her soul had been imprinted forever. He was good with that, as he knew Verity would be.

And the question about his child would forever challenge his heart. Could the babe have been alive? He might drive himself mad with the wonder over it. Surely, had it been alive and the witch or some other couple had raised him, the child was now long dead.

Rook pressed a hand over his heart and wished blessings on the child who may have existed but he had never known. Had he been given opportunity to raise the boy, his life would have been fraught with vampires and demons and a strange conglomeration of wicked creatures that no child should have to endure. If he had indeed survived, Rook wished only that his life had been as normal and blessed as could be.

Verity tugged his hand up to kiss it. Her lips were cool, as was the tip of her nose as she brushed his wrist with her lips. "I love you."

"Beyond the moon," he replied. "Our love will last beyond the moon."

* * * * *

If you're interested in reading more about the knights in the Order of the Stake, check out Kaz's story,
THE VAMPIRE HUNTER,
and Lark's story,
BEAUTIFUL DANGER.
Lyric and Vail's story is
FOREVER VAMPIRE.
All are available at your favorite online retailer.

Also, Ian Grim has a habit of popping up in the stories I set in my world of Beautiful Creatures. If you're interested in learning more about the creatures and people who populate my world, stop by clubscarlet.michelehauf.com.

GHOST WOLF

Prologue

Two gray wolves loped across the fresh-fallen snow within a forest that edged acres of private Minnesota land. The wolves had a standing arrangement to run off their energy in the forest every weekend, a father and son get-together. A half-moon scythed the oddly clear black sky. Not a star dotted the atmosphere. Yet areas where snow had begun to tamp down the still-springy blades of grass twinkled from the cool luminescence.

The younger of the wolves always tromped ahead, challenging the elder to keep up. He was well aware he could never outrace his father, but he liked to goad him. Besides, he'd spotted a red fox and wanted to chase it until its heart gave out.

When an echoing retort shattered the calm night, the younger wolf stopped, ears shifting outward. It was a sound he had learned to fear since he could remember having fear. The sound of death. Whining, he flicked his gaze about, seeking his father. No sign of the old wolf.

Another gunshot sounded.

The wolf dashed into a race toward where he'd heard the sound. At the forest's edge the animal recognized artificial light from a mortal's vehicle. He quickened his tracks, his paws barely landing in the slushy snow until he reached the clearing where a man with a rifle approached a fallen wolf.

Snarling, the wolf leaped for the hunter, landing its front paws against his shoulders and toppling him to the wet ground. The rifle landed in slushy snow. The innate compulsion to sink his fangs into flesh and tear out anything he could manage was strong. He could break a human's bones with but a bite from his powerful jaws. Yet the wolf merely snarled and snapped at the hunter.

The hunter struggled with the wolf, slapping at its maw and crying for mercy. Fear and human urine scented the air. The wolf heard the fallen wolf's heart-wrenching whines. In pain. Dying?

In that moment of the wolf's disregard, the hunter managed to scramble out from under his aggressor.

"Damned wolves! Where's my gun?" Scrambling about in the snow, he gave up looking for the weapon when the wolf's snarls grew insistent. The hunter ran toward the lighted vehicle. "Wasn't what I needed. It didn't shift. God's blood, this trial will kill me!"

The vehicle's lights flashed across the tree trunks. Tires peeled through wet snow and soil, skidding until the rubber found traction. The car rumbled off, leaving the clearing tainted with the smell of gasoline and the echoes of the human's angry voice.

The younger wolf began to shift, its body elongating and forelegs growing into human-shaped arms. Fingers flexed out at the end of hands. Knees, bent upon the ground, sunk into the snow. Within seconds, he'd transformed from his wolf shape back to his human *were* form.

Beckett Severo scrambled over to the wolf lying in the slushy grass. Crimson stained the snow near the wolf's back.

"No. No, you can't die."

He found the entry wound over the wolf's heart. He felt the tiny beads of buckshot from the hunter's shell. One burned his fingertip. He hissed, pulling away. Liquid silver trickled within the bloody wound as if mercury.

The older wolf turned its head toward Beck and looked into his eyes.

"No, Dad, you can't…"

Beck laid his head upon his father's body and pushed his fingers through the thick winter fur. He cried out to the night until his lungs ached and the old wolf's heartbeat struggled to pulse.

The knock at the front door startled Bella Severo from her slumber in the big cozy armchair before a fading hearth fire. She'd dozed off while waiting for her husband to return home.

Heartbeat racing, she pulled the white chenille shawl around her shoulders and rushed to the door. It was well after midnight. She couldn't imagine who could be knocking now. Certainly her husband would walk right in. Her vampiric senses didn't pick up a scent, though she blamed it on the fact that she was still groggy from sleep.

Her husband, Stephan Severo, had left earlier with Beck, her son. The two always went out on weekends together. Severo generally returned early in the morning, while Beck drove to his home at the edge of town, where the woods at the back of his property framed the moon glimmering on a frozen pond. On occasion her son would stay here at the house. She loved being stirred awake in the morning to the smells of pancakes and bacon, made with love by her two favorite guys.

Tonight she'd stayed up because she had a surprise for Severo. He would be thrilled with her news.

As her hand wrapped about the front doorknob, a weird

feeling tracked up Bella's spine. The blood ran from her face and her fingers shook about the glass knob. Heartbeat suddenly stalling, she gasped, clutching her chest with a hand. With the other hand, she flung open the door.

Her son stood there in but blue jeans and winter pack boots. His wide shoulders and tall stance filled the open doorway. The whites surrounding his irises were red. Tears spilled down his cheeks as he shook his head miserably. Agony clawed his fingers against his bare chest.

And Bella instinctually knew she would never be able to give her husband the news that would have filled him with pride.

Bella's knees wobbled, her head falling forward. Beck lunged and wrapped her against his shivering chest. "I'm so sorry, Mom."

She didn't hear what he said after that. Her keening wails echoed through the foyer until dawn traced through the windows and forced Bella, a vampiress, into her dark bedroom, where she stayed for the next three weeks.

Chapter 1

Two months later...

Beck stumbled to the edge of the forest, tugging up his jeans as he did so. His breaths fogged before him. The mercury had topped out at ten degrees at noon; it had only fallen since then. He'd come out of the shift and retrieved his clothes from the hollowed-out oak stump where he always kept them. Wouldn't do for a werewolf to shift to human shape without clothing to cover his shivering mortal flesh. He didn't relish the idea of walking home naked, or trying to hitch a ride.

Though, to imagine hitching naked perked up his smile. If a carload of pretty women drove by? They'd pick him up for sure.

Nah. He'd keep his clothes on. The bitter January chill did not bother him while in wolf form, but his human skin wasn't so durable against the temperature changes. Good thing he had brought along his winter coat.

He zipped and buttoned his jeans. Shoving his feet into his pack boots, he wobbled. A swirl of dizziness spilled across his vision, and he had to put out his arms to stabilize his stance. Tree stalks blurred, and for a moment the sky switched places with the snowy ground.

"Weird," he muttered, and gave his head a good shake.

Shifting took a lot out of him. More so lately. But this was the first time he'd felt so odd. Like he wasn't right with the world. Must be because he'd eaten a light lunch. Earlier in the day, his date had suggested he try a salad instead of a steak. Why he'd succumbed was beyond him.

Ah hell, he knew why. He'd wanted to impress her. Guys did stuff like that. Stupid stuff like eating leaves instead of a juicy slab of steak. Never paid off. Later, the woman had giggled while standing before her door and told him she'd see him again sometime soon.

Sometime soon? Vague, much? For not having dated in months, the step back into the pool had resulted in a cold splash to his ego. He'd added her to his mental "don't bother again" list. A guy could only listen to a woman rave about the latest fashions or which movie stars were doing each other for so long.

Turning over the thick knit sweater and sticking his arms into it to find the sleeve holes, Beck raised his arms over his head to shuffle it down over his face when something rammed into his side, knocking him off balance.

Quick footwork prevented him from taking a fall. Beck whipped around to snarl at—a pretty woman. Out here in the middle of no-place-she-should-be.

Beck's odd meter zinged far to the right.

She was petite, the crown of her head leveled at Beck's shoulder. From under a black knit cap that sported cat ears, pink hair spilled over her shoulders and onto a bulky gray sweater, beneath which perky nipples poked against the fabric, luring his interest. She clutched a pair of knee-high riding boots—she was barefoot—and blew out an annoyed huff.

As if upset because he had been the one to bump into her. Really?

Beck instinctively knew what breed she was. It wasn't a sensation he got from touching his own breed—such as vampires were capable of—he just knew when he was around another of his kind.

"Out for a run in the woods? Did you forget your glasses at home?" He rubbed his elbow, drawing attention to where she had run right into him.

"Aren't you the funny one?" She bent to tug on a boot, followed by the other. Slender-fitted jeans wrapped her legs, and the oversize sweater fell past her hips. She looked cozy and sexy and so out of place. "I wasn't aware a big ole lug would be blocking my path."

"Trust me, the lug did not intend to get in your way. You just shift?" he asked.

"I, uh…"

Apparently she hadn't guessed the same thing about him, but quickly realization crossed her gaze as if sun flashing on metal. Pretty eyes that looked half gold and half violet and were framed by thick lashes. Her hair matched her plump lips, sort of a bleached raspberry shade. He liked it. Looked like some kind of dessert.

"Yes," she finally said. "I'm headed home. I've got a friend waiting in the car."

Beck glanced over a shoulder. He didn't recall seeing a car parked along the country road that was closest to where they stood. No vehicles out here for miles. Then he guessed she was leery, didn't want him to think she was out here alone. Yet he scented not so much caution as challenge from her. Interesting.

"I'm not going to hurt you," he felt compelled to say.

"Says the pervert before he kidnaps the girl and shoves her in his trunk." She pushed past him and walked quickly out of the forest and into the wheat field that boasted ankle-high dried stalks jutting up from the foot-deep snow-pack. "Don't follow me!"

Beck couldn't *not* follow her. The road edging the field led to town. And it had started to snow in tiny skin-pinging pellets. He wasn't going to wait for her to disappear from sight before he could take off.

He paralleled her rapid footsteps.

"Seriously, dude, would you stay away from me?"

"You think I'm going to shove you in my trunk? I think you'd scratch and give a good fight if I even looked at you the wrong way."

He noticed the curling corner of her smirk, though she maintained her speedy gait. She liked him; he knew it. But it didn't matter much. It was a rare pack female who would give a lone wolf like him the time of day.

"Do I know you?" he asked. "I'm not trying to be a creep. I promise. I just— I'm familiar with most of the wolves in the area packs. I think I'd remember a pink-haired wolf. Unless this is a new color for you? I like it, by the way. The cat ears, too."

She huffed and picked up into a jog. He was tired out from his run, but Beck could keep up with her if he had to. And he wanted to. But—hell, he was winded. What was up with that? Normally shifting invigorated him.

"Who are you?" she blurted angrily.

"I'm Beckett Severo."

The pretty pink wolf stopped abruptly, dropping her hands to her sides. Flipping back her hair with a jerk of her head, she eyed him up and down more carefully than he'd taken when looking her over. "Oh."

"Oh?" Beck slapped a palm to his chest, feeling as though she'd just seen parts of him he'd never reveal upon initially meeting someone. "That *oh* sounded like you must have heard of me?"

"Uh, yeah. Something about your father?"

"Right." Beck looked away. Shoved his hands in his back pockets. He didn't need this conversation. It was still too raw in his heart. He hadn't spoken to anyone about it yet. Not even his mother.

Didn't matter who this pretty wolf was. If she knew about his father, he didn't want to listen to the pity.

The walk into the closest town was fifteen minutes. His town was ten miles north by car. And the small bits of sleet were starting to stick to the back of his head and shoulders.

"You shouldn't run around in the forest by yourself," he said, changing the subject and keeping his back toward the brunt of the sleet. "The local hunters have developed a bloodlust for wolf pelts."

She shrugged and turned to walk, but slower now, unmindful of the icy pellets. Tugging a pair of black mittens out from a jeans pocket, she pulled them on. "I trust this neck of the woods."

"You shouldn't," he said with more authority than he wanted on the subject.

Beck was a werewolf. Like it or not, he made it a point to know what the hunters were up to. Because even though they didn't believe in his kind, and they hunted the mortal realm breed of *canis lupis*—the gray wolf—when in wolf form, his breed could easily be mistaken for the gray wolf. And thanks to the DNR delisting the wolf from the endangered species list, the hunt had become a free-for-all.

A fact he knew too painfully well.

"Didn't you hear the gunshots earlier?"

She shook her head.

"There are hunters in the vicinity."

"Maybe the ghost wolf warned them away from me?"

Beck chuckled. The ghost wolf was what the media had taken to calling the recent sightings of a tall, wolflike creature that seemed to glow white. Scared the shit out of hunters.

"You shouldn't put your faith in a story," he said to her. "You're not safe in the woods, plain and simple."

"Well, *you* were out alone."

"Yes, but I'm a guy."

"Do not play the guy card with me. You think I can't handle myself?"

"No, I just said you could probably scratch—"

The petite wolf turned and, without warning, punched him in the gut. It was a good, solid hit that forced out Beck's breath and jarred his lower ribs. Picking up her dropped mitten, she turned and walked off while he clutched at his stomach, fighting his rising bile.

"Thanks for the chat!" she called. With that, she picked up into a run.

Beck was perfectly fine with letting her run off and leave him behind. He swallowed and winced as he fell to his knees amidst the wheat and snow.

"The guy card?" Swearing, he leaned back, stretching at his aching abdomen. "She's got a great right hook, I'll say that much."

And he was getting weaker with every shift he made to werewolf. That was not good.

Daisy Blu Saint-Pierre landed at the edge of town just as the headlights of a city snowplow barreled past her on the salt-whitened tarmac. She'd left her winter coat at home, not expecting it to snow tonight. She never took along more clothing than necessary when going out for a run. Chilled, but still riding the high from the shift that kept her muscles warm and flexible, she picked up into a run.

Her teeth were chattering by the time she reached her loft in the Tangle Lake city center. There were three other occupants in this remodeled warehouse that featured lofts on the second and third floors. She wandered up the inner iron staircase, cursing her need to not drive unless absolutely necessary. Blame it on her parents, who were uber-environmental-save-the-planet types. Her dad drove an old pickup that must have been manufactured in the Reagan era. She suspected it would be more environmentally friendly to put that rust heap out of its misery and off the road, but her father, an imposing werewolf who could silence any man with but a growl, wouldn't have it.

Once inside the loft, she stripped away her clothes, which were coated on the back with melting sleet. Leaving them in a trail of puddles behind her, she beelined toward the shower and turned it on as hot as she could stand.

The last thing she had expected while out on a run was to literally collide into another werewolf. Though, why not? should be the obvious question. The wolves in the Northern and Saint-Pierre packs used that forest all the time. Yet lately, with the hunters spreading out and some accidentally trespassing onto private land, even that forest had grown less safe.

She never ventured too near the forest's borders, and always kept an ear and nose out for mortal scent and tracks. The gunshot had been distant. She'd not smelled the hunter, and usually, when out in nature, she could sniff out a mortal scent two or three miles away.

Beckett Severo, eh? She'd heard about his father's tragic death not long ago. Killed by a hunter who must have assumed he was just another gray wolf. Must be awful for Beckett. She had also heard he had been there with his father when he'd been shot.

Daisy felt awful for punching him, but it had been impulsive. She didn't know the man, and couldn't trust him, and he'd been all in her face and trying to chum up to her.

She preferred to meet her men in public places, and preferably with an advance review from a friend so she knew what she was getting into.

So maybe she wasn't an expert on meeting people. Her defenses tended to go up for no reason other than that she was uncomfortable making small talk.

Because really? That man had been one fine hunk of wolf. He'd towered over her, and looked down on her with ice-blue eyes. She'd never seen such clear, bright irises. His sun-bleached hair had been tousled this way and that. A scruff of beard had shadowed his chiseled jaw. He'd reeked of strength and—she could admit it—sensuality.

What a man. What a wolf. It was rare Daisy met a male werewolf who appealed to her on more than a simple friendship basis. It was much easier to be a guy's buddy than to flirt with him.

He hadn't known her? Probably because he wasn't in a pack. Yet she knew about his family. Severo, his father, had been a grizzled old wolf. Unaligned with any pack, but respected by many pack wolves for common sense and wisdom that had come from centuries of life. Surely Daisy's father had mentioned Severo reverently a time or two.

Maybe. Didn't matter. She didn't intend to bump into Beckett again soon, so she'd have to satisfy herself with a few fantasies about the sexy wolf.

With the way her shifting abilities had been testing her lately, she was more self-involved than she cared to be. Much as she preferred shifting to wolf, the faery half of her always vied for superiority. She wasn't sure what the deal was with that, but it was annoying. And embarrassing. She couldn't remember when she'd last shifted around a family member. So she spent much time in her human shape, which was all right by her, save for her lacking social skills.

She was trying to break free of her introvert's chains by competing for a freelance internship for the local newspaper. Every January the *Tangle Lake Tattler* offered an internship to a journalist who offered the winning story. Story competition was never fierce. She had two opponents. But that didn't mean Daisy wasn't giving it her all.

Researching the story got her out into the community and forced her to talk to others. She enjoyed it, and she was growing more at ease with introducing herself to strangers. Albeit, with a handshake. Not by charging into them while running out of the forest.

The story she knew would be the winner was the ghost wolf. Which is why she'd been out in the woods tonight. The great white wolf had been sighted twice in the last month. Daisy suspected the creature was werewolf due to the description the local hunters circulated on the rumor mill. Save for one odd detail. Hunters had noted the wolf glowed, as if a white specter. Thus, a ghost wolf.

If it was a werewolf, she wasn't sure how to handle the story. Her breed valued their secrecy.

She'd deal with that if and when she needed to. Should have asked Beck if he knew anything about the ghost wolf. Hmm…

Good reason to see him again.

Chapter 2

Tangle Lake's annual Winter Ice Festival parade was followed with a massive community picnic in the park. Since it was the second week in January, everyone bundled up in winter wear, pack boots, mittens, caps, scarves and face masks. It was hard to be cold with the festivities to lighten the mood. Hockey was played on the nearby football field (iced over for winter), ice sculptures were judged in the town square (which was more of an oval, really), and ice bowling, s'mores over bonfires and even a quilt-off were held throughout the day.

Daisy decided next year she'd try her hand at the ice sculpting. She had no skills, but she wouldn't let that stop her from learning how to use the chain saw. She loved a good competition.

Daisy's pack always attended the festival. In town they were not known as werewolves. The humans were oblivious. And the pack principal—who was also her father—was all about community and making nice with the humans. All packs existed amongst the mortals. Garnering friendships and fitting in was key to survival.

She recognized wolves from the Northern pack pushing a sled piled with ice blocks toward the sculpting platforms. Supposedly the Northern pack had been a pretty nasty bunch of wolves in the decades before Daisy had ~~been born.~~ Her grandmother, Blu, had been a member then, and Blu's father, Amandus Masterson, had been the principal. He'd died—but not before first torturing Blu's vampire husband, Creed. Since the Northern pack scion, Ridge Addison, had taken over the reins as principal, everything had changed, and the pack was now peaceable toward other packs, as well as vampires.

Daisy's father, Malakai Saint-Pierre, was somewhere in the crowd, probably testing the various hot dishes offered at the bake stands and flirting with the women. Her mother, Rissa, took it in stride because Kai was fiercely faithful to her. But with a former reputation about town as a Casanova, he had no problem soaking up the female attention.

Her mother had stayed at home today in favor of an afternoon to herself. She was uncomfortable in large crowds. It wasn't because she was one-hundred-percent faery; Rissa was just quiet and didn't much understand socializing.

Daisy could relate. Her mother had bequeathed her the scarlet letter of introversion. Her four brothers had inherited their father's extroversion. They could all be somewhere in the area, though she suspected Blade had stayed away. He wasn't much for crowds simply because he was secretive.

A familiar face smiled through a bustle of winter caps. Stryke was the second-youngest of Daisy's four brothers, and was full werewolf. Trouble was also full werewolf. Kelyn was faery. And Blade was a mix of vampire and faery (the vamp was thanks to their grandfather Creed's DNA).

"Hey, sis!"

Stryke pulled her into a generous hug. The guy was a

master hugger. When he hugged, he gave his all. The wise, more cerebral one of the bunch, he was the one his siblings went to when they had a problem and needed to talk.

"Why the long face?" he asked, turning to lean against the concrete bike rack where she had paused. "Not into the festivities?"

She shrugged. "I don't know. Just kinda melancholy, I guess."

"Yeah, this town isn't the most exciting. Hot dishes and lutefisk?" He shuddered comically.

"Tangle Lake." Daisy recited the town's name. "And not a tangle to it. This town is straighter than straight. The highway dashes a straight line beside it. All the streets are parallel and straight. Even the lake is square! I need a tangle, Stryke." She sighed, twisting the ends of her pink hair. "I'd even settle for a little twist."

"I hear you." Stryke's gaze traversed a nearby ice bowling match, where the participants bowled ice balls toward frozen autumn squash. "I can't wait for Aunt Kambriel's wedding this summer."

Kambriel, their aunt, who was their father's twin sister (and a vampire), had fallen in love with the vampire Johnny Santiago and planned to wed in Paris, where she currently lived.

"You might find yourself a European werewolf," Daisy said, knowing her brother's strong desire to find a woman and settle down. Yet for some reason Stryke was never compelled to put down roots with any of the women in the area. Not interesting enough, he'd often lament.

"That's the plan," he agreed. "A tangle, eh? I'm not sure you'll find the excitement you're looking for in Tangle Lake, Daisy. Most exciting thing lately— Well, hell, what about that ghost wolf? You think it's a werewolf?"

"Yes," she answered quickly. And then, "No. Maybe.

I don't know. I'm doing a story on it for the local paper. Or I'm trying to."

"Whatever it is, be careful."

"I will. Do *you* think it's a werewolf?"

"Yes," Stryke said. And then, "No. Maybe. I don't know. I'd have to see the thing up close. And I'm not sure I want to. Though I can promise Trouble would like to have a go at it."

The eldest brother of the siblings, Trouble (whose real name was Jack) had a thing for picking fights and pushing people to their breaking point. But he did it in a playful way. Unfortunately, most people did not get his confrontational humor.

"I have to go," Stryke said. He nodded toward a crowd of young women bundled up in bright ski pants and boots. Pom-poms bobbed on their heads and mittens, plus a few at their boot ties. A cavalcade of sex kittens. "Got a date."

"A tangle?"

"If I'm lucky." He winked. "You going to the fireworks?"

"Kelyn and I usually head out together. I'll see you later, Stryke."

He kissed her cheek, a cold smack that made her giggle, and strode off toward the pom-pom kittens.

Sighing, Daisy tugged out the paperback she always took along to public events and found the bookmarked page. She wore gloves with rubber tips on the fingers, designed for operating touch devices. Books were the ultimate touch device. Immersing herself in the fiction, she strolled slowly along the packed snow embankment that edged the hockey rink where makeshift teams had gathered to play. Should have brought her skates. What she wouldn't give to slap sticks for a while...

All of a sudden, someone charged into her. Daisy

dropped her book and made to shove away the annoying guy, but she paused when she saw who it was. The sexy wolf she'd run into the other night at the edge of the forest.

"What is it with you and the need to ram into me every chance you get?" she asked.

"Uh, sorry. I had my eye on the puck." He tossed the hockey puck he picked up from the snow toward the guys outfitted in knee pads and skates waiting on the ice. "Besides, this is the first time I've rammed into you. If you'll remember correctly—"

"Yes, yes, I recall. So you're playing with the mortals?"

"Exclusivity to one's breed is not wise in this small town." He swept a hand toward the players who had continued the game without him. "They're a great bunch of guys. I love hockey. There you go."

"I like hockey, too, but I don't think the boys would like a woman joining them."

"Probably not. All the girls are over at the food booths making cocoa and serving us men."

Daisy's jaw tightened. "I don't serve any man."

Beck swerved his gaze toward her. "Huh? Oh. Right. Sorry, that was—"

"An asshole thing to say."

"Whoa. This is fast going down an icy slope I don't want to slip on. Let's start over." Tugging off a leather glove, he then bent to pick up her book and handed it to her. "Sorry. The pages got snow on them. Don't you have one of those fancy e-readers like I see everyone carrying nowadays?"

"I have a few of them," Daisy said proudly. "Sometimes I prefer the touch, feel and smell of a real book."

She pressed the closed book to her nose and inhaled. Snow had dampened a few of the pages, but she couldn't be upset because she also owned the digital copy of this book.

"It's so personal to hold a book in my hand. I can open

it to any place I like with a few flutters of the page. I can trace my fingers down the words, rereading phrases that speak to me. The stories make my heart race and my skin flush. My toes curl when I've read a well-crafted sentence. Mmm…"

"Uh…"

She glanced at Beck, whose mouth hung open. Oh, those eyes could attract wise men on a clear winter night beneath a velvet star-filled sky.

He scratched his head. "You just made reading sound sexual."

So she had. "Books turn me on." Daisy resumed her stroll along the snowbank shoveled up around the rink.

The wolf in hockey skates followed, blades sinking into the packed snow. "Really? They turn you on?"

She nodded. She wasn't sure she'd ever find a man equal to the heroes she read about in her stories, but she held out hope. Of course, the stories *were* fiction. She knew that. But it was okay to dream. And besides, when she finally did find a hero of her own, she felt sure she'd recognize him immediately for his gleaming honor and smoldering sensuality.

"So it's one of those sex books?" he asked.

Daisy stopped and toed her boot into a chunk of snow. Oh, she pitied the poorly read. "Just what implies a sex book in your mind?" She waved her book between the two of them. "Anything with a pink cover?"

"Anything with sex in it, I guess."

He was out of his league, and he knew it. Daisy smiled triumphantly. Points to the women's team.

"Says the wolf who's probably never read more than fast-food menus and car manuals."

"Don't forget *The Iliad*. I may have been homeschooled, but I don't think there's a way for any breathing teenager to avoid that snorefest."

Daisy rolled her eyes. She wasn't much for mythology, but wouldn't admit to him that she agreed with his assessment of the classic tome. That would be too much like flirting. Of which she did not partake.

"I have read a lot of car manuals," he added. "I own a shop at the edge of Burnham."

"Hockey, cars and tromping through the forest without a shirt on. Such a guy you are."

He stabbed the hockey stick into the snow and propped both wrists on the end of it. "I can't tell if you're admonishing me or trying to flirt awkwardly."

"I—" Stymied, Daisy turned her gaze away. She did not flirt. Because if she did, it would be exactly as he'd implied—awkward.

One of the men guiding the puck across the ice with the mortal crowd called to Beck to return. He waved and said he'd be right there.

Shoving up the sleeve of his jersey to reveal the long thermal sleeve beneath, he winked at her. "If you're in the mood to test your flirtation skills later, come find me."

"I, er—"

Without waiting for what would surely be the awkward reply of the century, Beck tromped off, blades cutting hashed tracks toward the ice.

Daisy couldn't help but notice the flex of his quadriceps with each stride. Clad in jeans and a fitted long shirt, over which he wore a big loose hockey jersey, the attire highlighted his awesome physique.

"Nothing new," she said to herself. All the wolves in the local packs were ripped. It was the very nature of a werewolf to be so muscular.

Unless of course he was Kelyn, her youngest brother.

Who wasn't actually a werewolf at all, but rather, had in-herited their mother's faery DNA. He was lean and lithe, yet her father deemed him the most deadly of all his boys. Faeries were swift and malicious, Malakai would often say.

Daisy hated to think of Kelyn as malicious. And he was not. She hoped he wouldn't develop a complex because of her father's words.

No longer interested in the book, she stuffed it in her coat pocket and wandered under a massive willow tree where a half dozen tween girls were sipping hot chocolate and cider from thermoses and texting on their cell phones, fingertips bared by half gloves.

"Why is your hair pink?" one of them asked as Daisy walked by.

"Because my mom dropped a can of paint on it when I was born," she offered, smirking. "Why is yours red?"

The befreckled girl shrugged. "Yours is pretty. I wish mine wasn't so ugly."

"Yours is gorgeous," Daisy offered. "Don't ever let any-one tell you differently. It's good to be unique, not like everyone else."

The girl sat up a little straighter. The friend beside her, sporting a hot-chocolate mustache, nodded in agreement.

"What's the best food to get today?" Daisy asked the group. "I'm in the mood for something sweet."

"Try my grandma's chocolate peanut butter brownies. Over there." One of them pointed toward a table draped in red, around which dozens loomed. "She's selling them cheap."

"Thanks." Daisy waved them off and wandered toward the food tables, her boots crunching across the snowpack.

Unique, eh? She smirked at her encouraging words. But not so unique that a woman's body couldn't make up its mind whether or not to be werewolf or faery. That wasn't unique; that was just pitiful. She had to get it figured out. But she had no clue how to do so.

When she reached the table, she had to wait in line, and when only halfway to the front, a tall, blond man approached her and offered her a treat. "These are awesome. I figured you'd like to try one."

"Are you following me?" she asked as she accepted a brownie as heavy as a small kitten. She got out of line. "You were just on the ice."

"And then I was not. I always answer the call of my stomach. Even if it sets me back a cool ten bucks for two brownies."

"What? These cost five dollars apiece?" The girl had said they were cheap. Shady sales tactics at that.

Daisy bit into the thick, moist chunk of chocolate and peanut butter and sighed one of those after-orgasm kind of sighs.

"Right?" Beck agreed. "Well worth the expense. I may never eat my mother's brownies again. Ah, that's not true. I'll chow a brownie any day. Even the five-dollar kind. Now I need something hot to wash this down with."

"Over there." She pointed to a refreshment stand. He grabbed her by the free hand and led her toward where she had pointed. "Did I say I wanted something to drink? Dude, we are not on a date."

"I know, but I figured the brownie should earn me some chat time with you. I'll get us some cider, and there's a tree over there that's calling our names."

"Do you even know my name?"

He paused from digging out his wallet from a back pocket. "Uh…I guess not."

"Bring cider," Daisy said.

With a wink that surprised her probably more than it did him, she wandered over to the tree.

* * *

With the brownie gently clutched between his jaws, Beck headed toward the tree where the gorgeous pink-haired wolf sat. Reading while others partook of the festivities? She was a curiosity to him, and he liked that he couldn't figure her out.

He bit off a bite as he sat, catching the brownie in his palm. She snagged the foam cup of cider before he'd even settled against the trunk.

"I should have gotten two," he said.

"That's okay, I only want a sip." She handed him the cup.

Beck peered into the cup. It was half-empty. "A sip?"

She shrugged and finished off her brownie. He wanted to tweak those cat ears on top of her hat, but instead he wolfed another bite.

"So who do I have the pleasure of sitting with under the maple tree this chilled and frosty January afternoon?"

"Daisy Blu," she said, and offered a hand to shake.

Beck gripped the cup lip with his teeth, and with brownie in one hand, shook with his free hand.

"Saint-Pierre," she then said.

He dropped the cup and it almost spilled in his lap, but he made a fast-reflex save. "Uh, Malakai Saint-Pierre's daughter? The pack principal who makes swords for a living?"

She nodded, licking her fingers clean of chocolate crumbs.

"I thought he only had the boys."

Beck scanned the picnic area, filled with mortals and paranormal breeds of all sorts and sizes. Living in the next town ten miles north, he didn't know a lot of people in Tangle Lake. He kept to himself far too much. But everyone knew about Malakai Saint-Pierre.

"Four boys," Daisy said. "But I was here first. Who you

looking for? Don't worry, my dad's not around. At least, I don't think he is."

Beck stood and nodded that she follow him around the trunk. "Let's sit on the other side of the tree, okay?"

She settled next to him with a laugh. "Are you afraid of my father?"

"I wouldn't say afraid, more like leery with an edge of self-preservation. Dude's not the sweetest wolf in the pack."

"Yeah, he's not too keen on unaligned wolves. Which is what you are, am I right? You being Severo's son?"

"Not for lack of your father trying to get me to join your pack."

"Really? My dad has invited you to join us? Why haven't you done so?"

"I have nothing against the Saint-Pierres. Or any of the local packs, for that matter. Joining a pack doesn't feel right to me. My father was always adamant that a man didn't need a pack to stand up for what was right within the werewolf community."

"I've heard about your father. Severo was a good man. But I have to point out the serious flaw in your sneaky attempt to hide out."

"What's that?"

"Now we won't be able to see my father coming."

"Shit. Maybe we should—"

Daisy placed a hand on his knee just as Beck attempted to stand. The woman's hand was warm, even in this weather, and her heat crept quickly through the jeans and to his skin. Nice. He settled against the snow-encrusted tree trunk.

"I'd scent him before he got too close," she said. "I'll give you advance warning if you need to run." Then she smiled and tucked a swath of hair over her ear. "I shouldn't be talking to you, either. But I like a little risk in my life now and then."

"Don't get enough from your books?"

"Not exactly."

"Is that why you think it's a good idea to run in the forest all alone? You really should take someone with you."

"I'm a big girl. I'll be fine. You going to eat that last piece of brownie?"

Beck held up the piece, and Daisy made a remarkable snatch with her teeth. She giggled, pressed her fingers over her mouth, then snagged the cup of cider from him, as well.

Licking his fingers clean, he could but shake his head. This one, as much as he should stay the hell away from her, he wanted to learn more about. Because getting close to Malakai Saint-Pierre's daughter could prove a lesson in Stupid Things Guys Do. But at the same time: kitty ears, pink hair and an irrepressible giggle. How to resist that?

She looked at him now with such curiosity that he matched her gaze with an intense stare. "What?" he implored.

"I was just thinking there are probably icebergs in the Arctic the same color as your eyes."

"Wow. Look who just got their flirt on."

"I wasn't—uh…"

He waited for her to realize that she had indeed been flirting. Didn't take her long. She busied herself with the ends of her hair. Ha! She liked him.

"So what do you do, Daisy Blu with the kitty ears who wanders about with her nose in a book?"

"You mean like work? I am a budding journalist."

"Is that so?"

"I'm competing for a freelance position with the *Tangle Lake Tattler*. I've always wanted to be a writer, but I'm not so good at making up stories. I like digging for facts, learning the truth."

"A noble pursuit. So what truths have you dug up lately?"

"Well, Mrs. Olafson, who lives at the corner across from the courthouse? She's growing marijuana in her backyard shed."

Beck faked a shocked openmouthed gape. Could he touch that pink hair? Just a careful slide of his fingers over it without her noticing? Because if she wanted to flirt...

"Thing is, she has no clue what it is. I couldn't bring myself to actually write about it. Besides, I've got a bigger, better story I'm working on that I know will win me the job."

"Much luck to you. Isn't often you hear of pack princesses working."

"No one calls me princess unless they want a black eye."

"Duly noted. So you're the modern working-class prin— er, wolf chick, eh?"

"I'm half faery."

"Is that why your hair is pink?"

"No one will ever pull one over your eyes."

"A faery wolf. I like it."

"So what do you do? You said you're not from Tangle Lake?"

"No, I'm up in Burnham. I have a garage just off the highway. It's not open to the public yet. I'm working on some friends' cars right now. Want everything to be perfect and have a career plan in place before I put up signs. I get a lot of business just by word of mouth anyway."

"If I drove more than once every few weeks, I'd bring my car to you just because you were so nice to share your last sip of cider." She handed him the cup, empty, and served him a wide grin that teased him for a kiss.

But that would be too risky. Her father was a pack

leader. And princess or not, Beck knew she wore a flashing *no touch* sign as a tiara.

"I should have bought two cups." He snickered and leaned his head back against the trunk. "So journalism is a full-time job?"

"Hardly. Only a few hours here and there. When I'm not pursuing a career, I'm also a sculptor."

"That's cool. You enter the ice sculpture contest?"

"Next year. That'll give me the winter to learn how to use a chain saw."

It wasn't difficult to imagine her wielding a chain saw. Not after that powerful right hook she'd served him in the field. She was petite but packed a punch. "What do you sculpt?"

"Anything with recycled metal. My dad's a blacksmith. I used to watch him forge swords when I was a little girl. Always wanted to be able to manipulate metal the way he did. One day when he was welding on his old truck, I asked to help, and I've been welding my designs ever since."

"Welding? That sounds macho."

"Yeah?" Daisy bent up her arm, making a fist. An impressive bicep bulged beneath the sleek white winter coat. "I grew up with four brothers. I don't think I could do feminine if I tried."

"You're doing it right now." Beck traced a strand of her hair back over her ear. Score! It felt as soft as it looked. She flinched and gave him the curious eye. "Sorry, just wanted to touch it."

"It's hair, dude."

"And you're kind of defensive, you know that? Is it because of the 'you shouldn't talk to an unaligned wolf' thing? Or is it that I just don't appeal to you?"

"You appeal to me," she said quickly. She sat up, tilting her head down and closing her eyes. Shaking her head, she said, "I didn't mean to say that. It just came out."

"You like me," Beck teased. He dipped his head to catch

her straying gaze. "It's because I seduced you with brownies, right?"

She punched him playfully on the biceps. Beck winced. It hadn't been quite as gentle as she may have intended it to be. So he fell over to his side and moaned.

"Yeah, and don't you forget it," Daisy said.

The sass that ran through her veins just needed a little prodding to rise above what he suspected was a bit of a shy streak. He hadn't seen her talking to anyone here at the festival. And if she had a boyfriend, she wouldn't be talking to him right now.

"So what do you sculpt?" he asked, moving closer so their shoulders touched.

"Anything that I'm feeling at the moment. I'm working on a project for the wolf sanctuary up north. I use lots of abandoned scrap metal. Right now I'm into recycling bicycle chains."

"Really? I have a whole box of bicycle chains at the shop. They're yours if you can use them."

"Of course I can."

"Stop by anytime and pick them up. I'm at the shop most of the day, and if not, I'll let Sunday know they're yours."

"Sunday? You mean Dean Maverick's wife?"

"Yep. Sunday used to have a shop when she lived in North Dakota. She's a gearhead like me. My shop is the only place she's got to get her grease on."

"And her husband doesn't mind?"

"Dean's a cool guy. We chat when he stops by to pick up Sunday. Not all in the packs are against the lone wolves like me, you know."

"I'm not against you. I just don't understand why you don't feel the need for family that a pack offers."

"I have family with my mom and my—" He hung his

head. Now was no time to step into that bleak memory. "You want another brownie?"

"No, thank you. I should get going. I promised my mom I'd stop by with some treats from the picnic."

"You going to the fireworks later?" he asked.

"Possibly. Will you be at your shop this afternoon? Maybe I could stop by for the bike chains?"

"I'll be there in a few hours. But this is the deal—I'll give you the chains if you'll watch the fireworks with me tonight."

She crossed her arms and made a show of considering it. Her lips were the same shade as her hair. Beck bet if they kissed, she'd taste cool like ice but would warm him up faster than s'mores melting over a bonfire. Would she really turn down his offer? She seemed independent, yet certainly she was shy.

"I might have a brother along with me. Kelyn and I always watch the fireworks together. We usually find a quiet spot at the top of a hill."

"Oh. Well, I wouldn't want to intrude." Nor did he want to bring the wrath of the Saint-Pierre family upon him for talking to their precious daughter.

"We'll play it by ear. I'll stop by your shop later, and then we can decide, yes?"

"Sure. I'm north on 35."

"I've seen the shop. I know where it is."

She took off, tugging the book out of her back pocket as she skipped across the snowy field that hugged the rink where the men slapped the hockey puck back and forth.

Beck stood and brushed the snow from his jeans. "First date with one of the brothers as chaperone? I don't know about that."

Chapter 3

Beck's shop was about ten miles out of city limits. The next town, Burnham, was four miles beyond his shop. Daisy knew the Darkwood was in the vicinity. Her brother Blade lived at the edge of the haunted forest that locals told tales about. Even the paranormal breeds avoided it for its fearsome reputation.

Though the road was hugged by tall birch trees interspersed with thick pines, Daisy found Beck's shop easily and pulled in her Smart car before the shop's opened garage doors. While most fix-it garages in the area featured random junkers parked here and there, tires stacked against walls and general disorder, this area was well-tended. The snow had been plowed and banked, and there was an orderly parking area with cars tagged on the license plates, likely for pickup.

Stepping out into the brisk air, Daisy's breath fogged before her. She'd bundled up in cap, mittens and winter coat. Striding toward the opened doors, she scanned for signs of life inside and called out Beck's name. Instead of a handsome werewolf popping his head up from behind the raised hood of a truck, the blond dreads of a very familiar familiar swung around the front quarter panel of a red F-150.

Sunday winked at Daisy. "Hey there, sweetie!"

"Sunday! Beck told me you worked here, but I didn't expect to run into you." Daisy looked about the neat shop that featured four car bays. Tools hung neatly along the walls, and tires were stacked in a corner. There were even red-and-white-checked curtains on the door window that must lead to the office. "Does Dean mind that you work here?"

The self-confessed grease monkey laid a wrench on the engine and wandered around the side of the vehicle. Grease smeared Sunday's pale check. Daisy had known her since she'd been born because of the cat-shifting familiar's friendship with her grandmother. She considered her an aunt, even. Of all the women in the family, she got along with Sunday best. Probably because they were a couple of tomboys.

"Why should Dean mind?" Sunday asked. "I don't let my man tell me what to do. Unless it's in bed." She winked.

Daisy fought against rolling her eyes.

"So why are *you* here?" Sunday asked. "Shouldn't you be more respectful of your father and his very obvious dislike for an unaligned wolf?"

"My dad doesn't know I'm here. And you won't say anything to him."

Sunday quirked a brow, but her easy smile held the kind of knowing that all women shared when a man was the topic. "There's nothing to tell. Beck's a good guy. Just because he doesn't feel comfortable joining a whole group of wolves after living in a small family his entire life shouldn't make him a pariah."

"Exactly," Daisy said, relieved that Sunday had put into words what she should have said.

Behind the car bays, a big-screen TV flashed a news report that featured area gray wolves scampering across the screen.

Sunday noticed Daisy's interest and turned up the volume with a remote she tugged out of her pocket. The report was on the local wolf hunt. It had only been a few years since the DNR had passed legislation to allow hunters free rein on the gray wolves that had been removed from the endangered species list.

Thing was, the mortals didn't care what happened to the environment when they reduced the wolf population. Not to mention the devastation to the wolf packs. They were killing wolves that belonged to families. Fathers, mothers and pups. And the loss to the pack was no less heartfelt than a loss to a mortal family. Of course, the hunters never looked at it that way.

It made Daisy think of Beck's loss again. Poor guy.

"So, having car trouble?" Sunday prompted. "I wouldn't be caught dead in one of those clown cars. I can't imagine it has traction on an icy road."

"I try not to drive too much in the winter. But no trouble, as far as I know. I wish I was mechanically inclined like you. None of my brothers are, either."

"Not like they need it," Sunday said. "Those Saint-Pierre boys are too fine to get all greasy fixing engines."

"Whatever. I'm just here to pick something up," Daisy said, trying to ignore the news. Though she shouldn't. This was her story. But she was distracted by the obvious. "I'm not here for, you know, a date or anything."

"What's that about this not being a date?" Beck rounded a yellow sports car (sans windshield) at the end of the shop. A large cardboard box was hoisted on top of his shoulder. "I thought we were going to the iceworks tonight?"

Sunday tilted another eyebrow quirk at Daisy, and it was accompanied by a knowing smile. So much said. Daisy's neck flushed warmly.

"We hadn't confirmed that. Are those the bicycle chains?" she asked, to change the subject.

Beck set the box on the floor before the pickup, and both Daisy and Sunday bent to inspect the contents. Dozens of chains slicked with grease snaked within the box.

"This is awesome," Daisy said. "I can use these."

"Best way to get the grease off is with Simple Green," Sunday said.

"I know. I've done it before."

"How's your art stuff coming anyway?" the familiar asked.

"My work in progress is turning out a lot cooler than I'd hoped. I plan to donate the finished piece to the wolf sanctuary up in Ely."

"Cool."

"And now with these, I'll be able to finish it sooner than expected. Thanks, Beck."

Daisy swung around toward Beck, arms out as if to hug him—her family hugged a lot—then she paused, and dropped her arms. Right. Not ready for that kind of contact. At least, not in front of the familiar.

"Uh, how much do you want for them?"

"I've already stated my price." Beck crossed his arms and peered down at her with his arctic-ice eyes.

He meant accompanying him to the fireworks tonight.

Daisy blew out a breath that fogged before her, even standing within the garage. Attending the midnight iceworks near the ice castle on the lake was a family tradition. And the only way to really enjoy it was to bundle up, snuggle next to another warm body and sip hot chocolate from a thermos. She could completely imagine doing that with Beck.

She glanced to Sunday, who put up her palms and strode around the front of the hood, disappearing from view. "Not listening," the familiar called out. "But check out the news."

Both swung their heads toward the TV, where the female newscaster was talking about the ghost wolf that had been scaring hunters witless. A pair of hunters had sworn off hunting for wolves and anything else, including deer.

"The thing was big and nasty," one of the hunters said to the camera. He gestured widely with his red flannel-coated arms. "And white and filmy like a freakin' ghost."

Beck chuckled. "Ghost wolf. That's a good one."

Daisy wished she could have been the one to interview the hunters.

"But it was solid!" the other hunter chimed in on a shaky voice. "It slapped the shotgun right out of my hand. I ain't never hunting again."

Beck's smile captured Daisy's attention. He was proud of what the ghost wolf was doing. Either that or he was amused by the redneck hunters getting their justice and repenting. Both were good reasons to smile, in Daisy's opinion.

"Whoever or whatever the ghost wolf is," she said, "it's doing all the wolves in the area a big favor by chasing away the hunters. I hope he keeps it up."

"He?" Beck asked as he picked up the box and started toward her car. "You called it an it first. How do you know it's a he?"

Daisy ran up to unlock the trunk. Surprisingly, the tiny car held a lot in the back end. "I don't know if it's a he, or an it, or a ghost. But this whole story has superhero undertones, don't you think?"

"Superhero?" Beck winced. "I don't know about that."

"The underdogs, which are the wolves *and us* in this case," Daisy explained, "need a defender to protect them. And suddenly from out of nowhere comes a hero on a quest to set things right. I love it!"

"Yeah, but I'm guessing the ghost wolf doesn't have a cape."

"You don't need a cape to be a superhero. Just a focus and a desire to do good. That is my new angle."

"Your angle?"

"I did tell you I'm trying to win an internship for the local paper."

"You're doing a story on the ghost wolf?" His expression changed so suddenly Daisy wondered what she'd said to offend him. "I renew my warning for you to be careful and stay out of the woods unless you bring someone along with you."

"And I renew my assertion to being able to take care of myself. You are *such* a guy."

Beck sighed and shook his head. He did appear genuinely concerned, but Daisy was trying to prove herself here, so she disregarded his anguish. She could do anything the boys could do. Oftentimes better.

"So can I pick you up later?" he asked.

"Um, I guess I could call my brother and cancel with him."

"Really? So it's a choice between your brother, whom you've gone to this event with before, or the lone wolf?" Beck winced. "You should probably go with the safer bet."

"Yeah, but that'll never get me the tangle I want."

"The tangle?"

Oops. Where had that confession come from? Deep inside, where the yearning part of her ignored her armor of introversion and just wanted to get tangled, that was where. If she didn't stop blurting her secrets out to Beck, she'd tell him about her shifting troubles, too. No way. That was mortifying.

Daisy nodded toward the trunk, indicating he set the box inside. "I gotta go. I have some research to do online before tonight."

He settled the box into the trunk and stood back to look over the box. "I cannot believe that fit."

"Thanks, Beck. I appreciate it."

"Where do you live? I'll pick you up around ten."

The man would not take maybe as an answer. So she'd let it happen. Beck would make a much better date than Kelyn. She gave him her address, which he entered into his phone.

Walking around to the door, Daisy paused and turned to find Beck standing right before her. His breath fogged out. Ice eyes took her in. The moment felt as if he should kiss her. And then it did not. It wasn't right. Sunday wasn't far away, and even if she said she couldn't hear anything, Daisy knew that cats had as excellent hearing as wolves did.

She held out her hand, and Beck stared at it awhile before conceding and shaking. "Later. Uh, will there be brothers at this event tonight?"

"Probably. You scared?"

"Should I be? What's the one's name? Trouble? I should probably keep a good distance from anyone with a name like that."

"Trouble is all bark and no bite. Blade is the one you won't see coming until it's too late."

Daisy slid inside the car and turned the key to fire up the engine. As she backed out, she smiled and waved. Sometimes brothers came in handy. Couldn't let him think it was going to be easy courting her, could she?

But really? The guy was courting her. How cool was that?

Beck went over the brothers' names in his head as he pulled up before Daisy's building. Kelyn. Had she mentioned he was faery? Faeries were no problem. And Trouble was not the one he was supposed to worry about? But Blade was? There was another brother, as well. He didn't know his name.

But he did know the father's name. Malakai Saint-Pierre. The man's name was as much a mouthful as he was a menace. The wolf was big, and he made swords for a living. Freakin' swords. He'd asked Beck on two occasions to join the pack, once a few years ago, and then only a month ago when he'd seen him in town at the local hardware store. Both times Beck had felt disdain in the man's growl.

He couldn't do it. Severo had lived free and alone, but he had been the best wolf Beck had ever known. His father hadn't needed the approval of a pack. He'd lived life on his own terms and had thrived, earned respect from his fellow breed and married the woman he loved and had a son—

With another child on the way.

Beck squeezed his fingers about the steering wheel. His father should have been here for the birth of his second child. The hunter needed to pay.

The stir of his werewolf twisted inside. It straightened his spine, prodding his skin to form goose bumps. Beck growled. Now was no time to shift, so he redirected his thoughts.

He shut off the engine and stretched out his legs. Focusing on the pull at his hamstrings diverted the werewolf's urge to run free. He normally experienced a twinge of the werewolf when upset or angry. But lately? It was growing stronger. More insistent.

Concentrate on Daisy. Glancing over the brick building's facade and arrowing his gaze up toward the third floor, Beck muttered, "What am I getting myself into?"

Did he need to mess around with Malakai Saint-Pierre's daughter? He'd never let a pretty face distract him so eas-

ily. And then again, he'd always let a pretty face distract
him. Anytime he went out into the world, whether walking
through the grocery store or standing in line (even with a
date) at the movie theater, he appreciated a pretty woman.
If a guy didn't notice the beauty walking around him, then
there was something wrong with him.

But he hadn't dated seriously in months. Not since his
father's death. The salad chick last week had been a fruit-
less attempt at jumping back into the social game.

He'd gone through the grief process rather quickly. Or
so he felt. Lately, he was more concerned about his mother.
Didn't have time to worry about himself. He was fine. He
missed Dad dearly. But he had to move on. For his mother's sake.

So getting back into the groove with this date tonight
felt right. Like he was moving forward.

As long as Daisy didn't learn about the other thing
he'd been involved with lately, then everything would be
golden. Hell, he'd have a tough enough time acting ac-
cordingly if any of the brothers were wandering around
the fireworks, so he didn't have to worry about the other
thing coming up.

Jumping out of the truck, he landed on the compacted
snow. He wore his Arctic Cat overalls and a warm matching coat, plus gloves, pack boots and a knit ski cap. It was
already bitter cold tonight. And he intended to test the
whole *touch not the princess* theory. He looked forward
to holding Daisy close to keep her warm.

Grabbing the flowers he'd worried over for a full five
minutes at the grocery store, he headed inside and up the
stairs to the top floor, just as she'd directed him to do. It
was an old warehouse that was slowly being retrofitted
for apartments, and so far Daisy and a few other residents
were the only ones in the building.

"Nice," he muttered as he topped the stairs and took in the open framework that exposed the original ironwork and ducts. Not what he'd expect a woman to choose.

Daisy was the opposite of the usual sexy, soft, slinky woman he preferred. She punched, too. Entirely unexpected, but she had warned him he'd get a black eye for calling her princess. And the pink hair? He liked it. It looked like cotton candy.

Unzipping his jacket because it was hot up here, Beck knocked on the door, then whipped the flowers around behind his back. He waited a few seconds, listening. All wolves could hear well, and if she had been in the shower, he'd hear the running water and start to imagine that water slicking over her skin—

"Those for me?"

He spun around to find a pink-haired pixy wolf standing behind him, a smudge of black across her cheek. She wiped her hands down an old gray T-shirt, imbuing it with more grease.

"Uh, yes?"

He held out the fluorescent blue daisies. The color was god-awful, but they had made him think of her. "For Daisy Blu, blue daisies."

"That's so…" She wrinkled her lips into a moue as she accepted the horrible bouquet. Sporting wilted leaves, with one of the flower heads chopped off, it had been the best of the bunch. A guy couldn't find any better in the middle of January in a Midwestern Minnesota town.

"Thank you," she breathed, in a more impressed tone than he had expected or deserved. "It's sweet that you got them because of my name."

"You don't have to act all happy about it. They're an ugly bunch, but—"

"No, I love them. Come inside." She opened her door

and he followed her in, but stayed on the rubber mat inside the doorway. "I'll put them in water, then get ready," she called as she disappeared around a corner.

The vast loft ceiling was two, maybe even three, stories high. He loved the wide-open space. Immediately before him lay the living area with couch, TV and armchairs. To his right must be the kitchen that he couldn't see from his position. Off to the left and behind the living area, he saw something big covered with a sheet. Tools and a workbench stood nearby.

"I'm sorry." Daisy appeared before him, twisting her hair about a finger. "I completely lost track of time. I was over at my neighbor's. Her old stove is trying to kick the bucket, and she won't invest in a new one. I had to pull out the heating coil and give it a good talking-to."

"That works with appliances? A good talking-to?"

She shrugged. Such a pretty pink little pixy wolf. He could kiss her right now. Run his fingers through her hair, pull her close and taste her mouth until he forgot his name. But she probably read about that kind of stuff in her books all the time.

How to win over this particular woman, who was like no woman he had ever dated before? The flowers had been stupid. Should have gone for one of those paperback romances he'd noticed in the checkout line.

"Give me ten minutes," she said. "I'll go wash my face and change quick. You can sit on the couch."

He lifted a foot. "Uh, I should stay here. My boots are wet."

"Suit yourself. In that case, I'll make it five."

She scampered off to the back of the loft. A king-size bed sat against the wall, and near that an iron bar suspended from the high ceiling served as a clothes rack. She pulled a few items from it then disappeared into the bathroom, which appeared to be the only room that was actually walled and private.

Beck squatted down and took in the place. The window at the end of the bedroom was curved to a peak at the top, sort of cathedral-like. Cool. And probably romantic as hell to lay snuggled in bed together watching the moonlight.

He smiled and rubbed a hand over his grin, but realized he didn't need to hide his reaction to the sexy thought.

Beyond the window, the rest of the place was clean and industrial. It was the ultimate bachelor's pad. Big, spacious, minimal decoration. Nothing froufrou. And there was a welder's torch on the bench over by what he assumed was the covered artwork.

He'd like to see how she was using the bicycle chains. Hell, he'd like to see anything she wanted to show him, so long as that meant they got to spend some time together.

"What about the brother?" he called when she stepped out of the bathroom five minutes later, pulling her hair back and twisting it into a ponytail.

"Brother? Oh, right. Kelyn is going to look for me there. He's got a date tonight, too. So we're on our own." She scampered up before him, dressed in snug gray jeans and an oversize black sweater that looked softer than a kitten. "You okay with that?"

"With having you all to myself? I think I can deal."

"Great." She pulled on some snow pants, a coat and a black knit hat with the cat ears on the top and long strings that hung down over her coat and ended in big black pompoms. "What's wrong? You're staring."

"You're just so cute," Beck said.

Daisy punched him in the arm. Apparently this woman's way of dealing with compliments was with violence.

Good, he thought. She'd keep him on his toes. If not leave a permanent bruise on his biceps.

Grabbing a tote bag from the kitchen chair, Daisy led him through the doorway. Toggling a cat ear on her hat, he closed the door. "This way, kitten."

"Oh, do not kitten me," she said as she locked the door behind them.

"You prefer pixy wolf?"

"Pixy wolf?"

"Yeah, you look like a pixy."

"Apparently you have never seen an actual pixy. They're no bigger than six or seven inches and have pointy ears and a nasty manner."

"Then nix the pixy reference. How about faery wolf?"

"Why don't you try Daisy?" she suggested, and shuffled down the stairs.

Beck nodded. Hell, he was nervous. He felt like he'd never been on a date and he was doing everything wrong.

Chill, man. Relax and get to know the girl.

What was it Beck had heard about faeries and their wings? Something about touching them being a sexual turn-on.

"Nice," he muttered.

Chapter 4

They'd found the perfect perch on a hilltop and up against a rock, just behind the masses of people who had gathered at the park. The ice castle sat before the lake, its neon lights reflecting on the shoveled lake surface. The fireworks would begin when they turned off the multicolored spotlights on the castle, usually around eleven.

Daisy poured Beck a cup of hot chocolate that she had made before going to help her neighbor with her stove. The brew smelled so good, she took a sip before handing Beck his cup.

"Had to check," she said. "Make sure it's not too hot for you."

"Thank you, mother."

"Hey, I'm a chocolate freak, so you know. And I don't share my chocolate with just anyone."

"Then I'm honored. To sharing." He tilted his cup against hers, and they drank the toast.

"What?" Beck stared at the cup, mouth open in awe. "This is…" He took another sip, eyes closed and a satisfied murmur rising. "This is the most amazing stuff I've ever tasted."

Daisy bristled with pride. "Why thank you. It's a recipe from my aunt Kambriel."

"Did she steal it from the gods?"

Daisy chuckled. "Actually, one of her friends works at Angelina in Paris. It's a ritzy place known for its decadent hot chocolate. The recipe is a lot of work, but in the winter I make it at least once a month and freeze it for emergencies. It's necessary to me, like breathing."

"I love it. I love you. I love your aunt. Do you think she'd marry me?"

"She's getting married to a handsome vampire this summer."

"That's too bad for me. What about you?"

"A marriage proposal on our first date?"

Beck sipped again, his eyes closing in bliss. "Yes, please?"

"You stick with love for the hot chocolate for now. I'll reconsider your offer at a later date. Besides, love is so easy."

"You think so? I suppose I did confess love kind of quickly. But seriously, are there witches in your family? I think you've put some magic in this hot chocolate."

"No witchcraft. No even a smidge of faery magic. Just tender loving care. Love it all you like. You can even love me if you want to. Because the real challenge is in liking a person."

"How so?"

Daisy pulled up her knees to her chest and held the hot cup beneath her face. The scent was heady. "When you like someone," she explained, "you enjoy spending time with them. You can hold conversations and never get bored of what the other is saying. Or you can just be next to one another in silence and not feel the need to talk. You tolerate their bad habits, and admire their good. Trust me, like is hard work."

"I agree. To like!" Beck tilted his cup against Daisy's.

"So your aunt is marrying a vampire in Paris, eh? Fancy. And a werewolf pairing up with a vamp? Cool."

"Kam's a vampire. My grandpa Creed is vampire, so, well, you can figure things out."

"I can. My mom is a vampire. Though she was mortal until a nasty bitch of a vampire transformed her after she met my father."

"She's Belladonna, right? How is your mother doing?"

Beck took another sip, pausing for a while. She studied him from the side. The barely there stubble on his chin wanted a shave because his good clean looks demanded it. But she guessed he kept the stubble for that hint of danger, and it was probably warmer in the winter. He had the all-American tousled blond-and-brown hair, and that killer smile. And if she looked into his blue eyes long enough, she'd surely fall in *like* faster than a falling star.

She'd forgotten what she'd asked him, so when he finally answered she had to think back.

"Fine," he said.

"Fine?" His mother. "Oh, right. That's good. And you?"

"Me? Don't I look fine?"

"You look more than fine." The words came out in a dreamier tone than she'd intended.

"Is that so?" Beck wrapped an arm around her shoulders and pulled her against his side. "You look a little cold. Drink up."

She did, and the hot chocolate filled her gut with a warm explosion that loosened her nerves and coaxed her to settle against him a little snugger. They both wore cold-protective snow wear, so she'd never feel his body heat. But she could smell him now. A little bit of chocolate and a lot of sensual wildness. His aftershave wasn't too strong. She liked it. Woodsy and warm. Like an old leather book found in the hollowed-out trunk of a tree on a hot summer evening.

Mmm, she'd like to crack open his cover and delve deep into his pages. She bet his story was filled with adventure, action and some steamy sex scenes. She could hope.

"So where's this brother I need to worry about?" he asked.

With any luck, Kelyn would not find them tonight. Not that Daisy expected her brother to actually look for her if he was on a date. If they happened to see one another, then he'd probably wave across the crowd.

"Oh, I'm sure he's got an eye on us even as we speak," she said, then regretted that tease. "Kelyn's cool. If he sees us, just wave."

"Right. Why do I feel as if I have a target on my head, and there are four—five, including your dad—wolves who want to shoot holes through it?"

"I have no idea. You're the one getting all worked up over nothing. Haven't you dated a wolf from a pack before?"

"Nope. You did get the whole lone wolf part about me, right?"

"If you think it's such a bad decision, why are we here right now?"

"Because always making the right decision is boring. Sometimes the wrong one is a hell of a lot more fun. And not getting to learn more about you would be worse than losing my head to one of the Saint-Pierre boys," he said. "Besides, you've already forgotten. I love you."

"Right. A victim of my witch's brew. I can dig it. Love me all you want. Just don't expect me to fall head over heels in like with you too quickly. We don't even know one another."

"That is going to change. Let's talk."

"So what do you want to know about me?"

He toggled the kitty ears on her cap, then tugged the string hanging over her jacket. "What's a cute wolf like you doing without a boyfriend? I can't believe I didn't have to fight off a ton of wolves at the picnic to get near you."

Daisy shrugged. "I'm…" She sighed. The truth was she probably pushed men away simply by being who she was. And yet there were more days than most that she had no idea who she was. Wolf or faery? "I'm not so much shy as kind of content with my aloneness. If that makes any sense."

"Not really."

"I'm not like most women."

"You mean most women don't get excited over greasy bike parts and know how to fix the heating element in an old stove? Who would have guessed?"

"You tease, but next time your stove goes on the fritz…"

"I'll know who to call. So you like doing things with your hands. Nothing wrong with that."

It pleased her that he hadn't said boy things. She'd grown up with the tomboy label. Competing against her brothers for her father's attention had been as natural as breathing. And that had required a hard skin and masculine interests. The tomboy persona hadn't bothered her until her twenties when she'd noticed the women in their pretty dresses walking with their handsome lovers. Femininity was so easy for them. Walking in high heels? Daisy would rather jump in mud. (Which was always a blast.)

And really, dealing with the werewolf in her was always an issue when dating mortal men. But she loved being a wolf, so she wasn't about to complain. Though, her wolf was "one of the boys."

"My father taught me a lot about blacksmithing and

working with metals," Daisy felt the need to explain. "And if you grow up with brothers, well then."

Beck leaned into her a little more, just enough so she could relax against him without worrying about toppling over. "I think it would be awesome to have so many siblings."

"I can't imagine what it would be like to be an only child. I suppose your parents spoiled you?"

"I'm not sure doing chores every day, chopping wood and helping my dad tend our land could actually be labeled spoiled. Though I confess I am a momma's boy. She taught me how to cook. I can make a mean wild rice Tater Tot hot dish."

"Ohmygoddess, seriously?" Daisy twisted to fall against Beck's arm and curled her mitten-clad hand about his forearm. "I love hot dishes."

"Like I love your hot chocolate?"

She nodded. "I could marry it. So long as it doesn't have cream of mushroom soup in it."

"I'm not much for mushrooms."

"I knew there was a reason you appealed to me."

"I promise to protect you from any and all mushrooms we should ever encounter. And so you know? I would do anything for this hot chocolate." He held up the empty cup. "Tell me what you want and it's yours, oh pink-haired faery wolf."

Oh, she could think of a few things she'd like him to do for her—all of them involving privacy and snuggling before a warm fireplace. Daisy couldn't resist the lone wolf's allure any longer. "How about a kiss?"

Beck opened his mouth to reply, but at that moment the crowd erupted in an excited whoop. The lights on the ice castle blinked out. Immediately following, a multicolored firework dazzled in the sky, twinkling, lingering and spilling over the iced lake. More sparklers followed at a rapid pace, accompanied by the crowd's oohs and aahs.

Daisy snuggled against Beck's chest to watch. "I've come here every winter with my parents, and then with friends." She pointed to a particular small firework that spun like a Chinese whirligig. "But this time it feels more…magical."

"I like the sound of that." He slid down parallel to her so their faces were inches apart. "Now about that kiss."

Daisy tilted up her chin. Their breaths fogged in a mingled cloud. She closed her eyes, anticipation scurrying heat through her system. Beck's mouth touched hers. The cold night made the first touch icy but fun. She giggled, but didn't stop the kiss. He slid his hand behind her head as he deepened their connection. Warmth radiated through her system, and she forgot that it was colder than a deep freeze.

His stubble brushed her chin. When she breathed through her nose, the woodsy aura that surrounded him filled her senses and transferred her to that hot summer night she'd been thinking about.

Nothing had ever felt as good as Beck's mouth against hers. Not even winning a race against Kelyn, who was amazingly swift. This kiss was all hers. She hadn't needed to compete for it. It was a prize she'd not known she needed until now.

Above them the fireworks glittered up the sky. Beneath them the compacted snow crunched as their pack boots slid over the surface. Beside them, the thermos of hot chocolate rolled across the snowy ground and hit the booted toe of a man who had just arrived hilltop.

"Daisy Blu?"

She broke away from the delicious heat of Beck's mouth, wishing she hadn't heard her name and that she could kiss him again and again, but the voice was too familiar. And it wasn't a brother.

"Ah, shit," Beck said under his breath.

Daisy twisted to sit and looked up at the dark-haired man towering over them. "Hey, Dad."

Chapter 5

Daisy got a hand up from Beck. She noticed Beck did not stand tall before her father, but instead bowed his head, showing submission, as was expected when a lesser wolf stood before a pack alpha.

Most men might stand up to Malakai, to grandstand in an attempt to show him he couldn't be pushed around. Those men generally walked away limping or bleeding.

Much as her anger for her father tightened her muscles, Daisy appreciated that Beck showed her father respect.

"Hello, Mister Saint-Pierre," Beck said.

"What the hell are you doing here with my daughter?" Kai asked.

"Daddy, please."

"Quiet, Daisy. I'm talking to Beckett." The taller wolf was dressed in a leather jacket, his long curly dark hair pulled back behind his head to reveal his square jaw held in a tense frown. "Are you two on a date?"

"Uh…" Beck looked to her.

"Of course we are," she broke in. "And will you stop treating me like I'm a teenager? I'm a grown woman. I can see whomever—"

Kai's hand landed on Daisy's shoulder, a staying move that he'd employed as she'd grown up. A means to show her he was not to be trifled with, and must always be respected. It was his gentle way of showing authority.

And she quieted.

"You won't be seeing this lone wolf," Kai said, his gaze fixed to Beck's, who had trouble holding the alpha's stare. "Isn't that right, Beckett?"

"Uh, sir." Beck's shoulders rolled back. He tucked his thumbs in his pants pockets and looked Kai straight in the eye. "I don't want to cause any problems, but I think Daisy can choose whomever she wishes to date."

Daisy smiled inwardly. *Go, Beck!*

"Are you trying to tell me how to run my family, boy? My pack? Because it sure sounds like it."

"No, sir. I— It's our first time out together."

"And you thought it was okay to kiss my daughter?"

"Daddy," Daisy said under her breath. "Do not do this."

The fireworks had ceased. The night sky grew dark with few stars. The waxing moon hid beyond the tree line. While the humans tromped back to their cars, the trio of werewolves held position at the top of the hill. Daisy scented her father's anger, and yet, there was a tangible softness to it. Similar to how he reacted when she'd made a mistake when she was little. Like maybe he was puffing up to show aggression in display but didn't mean it as much as he showed it.

But she hadn't made a mistake this time. At least, she didn't want it to be a mistake. She could understand that her father wouldn't want her hanging around an unaligned wolf, but to approach her when they'd been kissing had been too much. She wanted to tuck tail and crawl off into the woods.

"I'll take Daisy home," Beck said.

"No, you won't. I'll drive her home," Kai asserted.

"I brought her here. I won't abandon her," Beck said, his shoulders tilting back a little farther.

"I said I'd take her home, boy."

"I want Beck to drive me, Daddy."

Malakai Saint-Pierre twisted his neck to look down at Daisy. The menace in his gaze could never be softened, and it did not fail to strike at her heart. She swallowed back her bravery and bowed her head. When would she be able to break free of her father's influence? Was it even possible?

"Get in the car, Daisy," her father said.

Beck bent to pick up the thermos and handed it to her. "I'm sorry about this."

"No, I am," she offered. "This isn't how things should have gone tonight." Inhaling a deep breath, she swept her gaze over her father's stare then wandered down the hill.

She hated leaving Beck at the hands of her father. And what had he done? He'd only wanted to get to know her better. Rare was it a guy actually asked her on a date to do something, as opposed to wanting to go straight to her house to make out on the couch. She craved the wooing process. And that kiss. It could have been amazing had her father not shown up.

Glancing up the hill, Daisy saw that her father was already on his way down. Whew. He hadn't given Beck a chewing-out. Her father was not a cruel man, but he was feared for the very reason that his physicality was remarkable. It was the rare wolf in this area who could stand against him, alpha or otherwise.

Daisy got into the old pickup truck and pulled the door shut with the duct-taped handle. As her father got in, she tucked her legs up to her chest and twisted to face the window. The engine rattled, and the truck took off.

"He's arrogant," Kai said after they'd driven a few miles.

"He's kind."

"I've invited him to join our pack too many times."

Daisy swung her head around and met her father's brief

glance. "How many is too many? Two? And the one time he was grieving his lost father."

"Two too many. He's refused both times. Says he doesn't need a pack. That's arrogance, if you ask me. Stay the hell away from him, Daisy Blu."

Beck had every right to refuse her father. Daisy could imagine that if he had grown up with a father who had been a lone wolf, then the idea of a pack must be odd to him. Overwhelming. Perhaps even threatening.

"You're not going to stay away from him, are you?" Kai asked softly.

Daisy bit her lower lip to fight the tears that threatened to spill down her cheek. She wanted to do the right thing in her father's eyes. But her right and his right weren't in alignment now. And she was a grown woman. Too old to still have her father tailing after her, approving or denying her choice in men.

"Daisy?"

"I don't know," she finally said.

Kai's sigh rippled through her skin and twanged at her heart.

The afternoon had been designated for research. Scanning the internet, Daisy tried various search words, starting with "ghost wolf," which brought up nothing. The data on werewolves provided for interesting reading, some laughs and a lot of head shaking. Eventually she typed in Fenrir, the name of a Norse god who was the son of Loki.

"The ghost wolf obviously isn't Fenrir," she said as she scanned the information. But there were some similarities. A monstrous wolf often depicted in paintings as white or ghostlike, he could not be restrained, save by a delicate ribbon named Gleipnir.

Though it was fascinating, it wasn't getting Daisy any

closer to results. The article needed facts, or in this case, some kind of legend to compare to the ghost wolf, at the very least. The creature was larger than life. She needed to communicate that on the page.

"I need a picture," she said. "That would be the ultimate scoop."

When her breed shifted to their werewolf shape, they could not be photographed. Well, they could be, but none had been that she knew of. They were fiercely protective of their secret. And should a hunter manage to snap a photograph? A quick slap of claws destroyed the camera.

What would ultimately show up on film, she wasn't sure. Nothing, much like a vampire? Or a ghost image of the werewolf? If the ghost wolf was already transparent or some kind of filmy state, the results on film were unimaginable.

She eyed her winter clothes hanging by the door. "I'll go out early in the evening."

The majority of hunters would be packing up and returning home for supper at that time, yet the ghost wolf sightings had been just after dusk.

Wishing she could give Beck a call and invite him along, Daisy waffled on the idea. Her father had been adamant about her staying away from him. Yet she'd been impressed by Beck standing up to her father. He'd cowered initially, to show respect, but hadn't been about to yield to Kai's demands without stating his own position.

"I could like him," she said to herself, remembering their conversation about love and like last night. Like was the goal. Love would simply be a happy bonus.

Beck had felt humiliated standing before Daisy's father last night. He should have stood up to the elder wolf, but it had been the right choice to show respect for the man, despite his intrusion on their date. He'd learned from his father that a man must never jump to hasty violence or make judgments of a man he did not know. If Saint-Pierre didn't want him to date his daughter...

"Hell." Beck wandered the edge of the forest a mile from where he'd parked. "He'll kill me if I see her again." Or at the very least, tear him a new one with a slash of claw.

But he kind of thought Daisy liked him. Make that love. Like was something even better than love, according to her. He agreed with her definition of it, too.

Man, did he like her hot chocolate.

Did she want to see him again? She hadn't called. But then, she didn't have his number, nor did he have hers. He'd thought about stopping by her place today, but didn't want to push it. Certainly, Malakai would scent him if he showed up anywhere near his daughter's home.

Was he going to let some big boisterous wolf scare him away from the girl? Was she worth the risk?

Beck nodded. The kiss hadn't left him. He could still feel her at his mouth, sighing into him. Clinging to his clothing and leaning in closer. Sweetly hungry. And her kisses had tasted like chocolate.

"I'm going for it," he muttered. Because he knew a good thing when it kissed him.

Now, with the sun tracing a vibrant orange line on the horizon, he shed his winter coat and boots and pulled off his sweater. Steam lifted off his hot skin as the cold assaulted his torso and arms. He stored a waterproof backpack in a hollowed-out oak trunk. The worst thing after shifting back from werewolf form was to find his clothes sitting in a puddle of snow that had melted from the lingering body heat.

Shoving down his jeans, he shuffled barefoot in the cold snow, and when he was naked he stretched back his arms and head, breathing in the crisp night air. The world was gorgeous, and he loved breathing it in. But the very reason he stood here was enough to make him want to punch something.

And then he knew he didn't have to. His shifted form would take care of matters nicely.

A gunshot in the distance alerted him. He judged it a few miles off. This time of day, most hunters were packing it in and heading home.

No time to waste.

Bending forward and narrowing his focus inward, Beck began to shift. His human skin stretched and prickled as fur grew in the pores and his bones lengthened. Claws grew out from his paws, and his hind legs formed into the powerful werewolf's legs. His maw grew long, and ears twisted into long, furred beacons that picked up every movement and sound from mouse to fox, to…hunter.

Beck's werewolf rose to an imposing height, sniffed the air and homed onto the scent of human.

Daisy kept the hunters in view, while hoping to stay out of their line of sight. She wore a vivid orange hunter's vest over her winter coat. She'd no plans to shift tonight—not with armed hunters in the forest. But she certainly didn't want to be so incognito that she invited a bullet.

Her camera wasn't the best at taking night shots. And now as she leaned against the base of an oak tree, fumbling with the settings, she wished she did have something more high-powered. She'd never win the internship by handing in grainy night shots.

Thinking it would have been awesome to have someone along to keep her company on this cold dark evening, her mind drifted to Beck's sweet smile and those entrancing blue eyes.

So maybe she was getting her flirt on with him. Felt kind of awesome.

He hadn't called her today. She didn't know what his number was. She thought he might have stopped by. Her father must have put fear in the handsome wolf.

Daisy decided if Beck never showed again, then that meant he wasn't deserving of her interest. Only a wolf who dared defy her father would be worthy of her time. At least, that was the romantic version she played in her head. In reality, she knew Beck was better off staying away from her and avoiding Kai's wrath.

Too bad. Beck's hasty confession to loving her because she had a talent with hot chocolate had won her over. The way to a man's heart was through food. And she wasn't beyond utilizing such tactics. But as well, his kiss was not to be overlooked. If she never felt his kiss again, the world might never again be as bright. Heck, she'd seen fireworks during that kiss. It didn't get any better than that.

She knew where his shop was. Nothing was stopping her from driving over to see him. "No," she muttered. "He needs to come to me."

A gunshot alerted her, and she whipped her head around, along with the camera. Set at its highest zoom, she peered through the lens and spotted movement. She'd turned the flash off.

There were two of them. Hunters. She saw the shotguns they held. Not aimed at anything because the wooden stocks were slung against their shoulders. And they were running for their lives.

Tilting the camera to the right, she caught a blur of white tracking through the birch trunks in the hunters' wake.

"The ghost wolf." Daisy tracked the blur, snapping shots repeatedly.

The frightened mortals ran within a hundred feet of

her. She recognized the hunter in the lead. He had bright red hair and was known in town simply as Red, a Scottish farmer transplanted from his country to Minnesota through love and marriage. She didn't recognize the man behind him, but he yelled for Red to hurry and get to the truck.

Then she scented the wolf. It was angry and feral, and so close she could hear its breathing. Steady, not taxed, and punctuated with vicious growls. Shaped like a werewolf, she estimated it grew two feet taller than even her father when he was shifted. It was indeed white, but a sort of filmy white, perhaps even transparent.

Remembering her mission, Daisy clicked a rapid succession of shots. When the hunters exited the forest and slammed the truck doors, the wolf paused at the tree line. It smashed out its fists to the sides, cracking the tall birch trunks, and howled. It was like no wolf howl Daisy had ever heard. The haunting noise climbed up her spine and prickled under her skin. She shivered, and sank down against the tree trunk in fear.

Her camera hand dropping to the snowy forest floor, she cast her gaze upward as the white werewolf stalked toward her.

The truck peeled away on the icy country road, its back end fishtailing until the chainless tires achieved traction.

And Daisy wished she had hitched a ride with the idiot hunters as she looked up into the ghost wolf's red eyes.

Chapter 6

Werewolf eyes always glowed golden when shifted. Daisy had never seen the likes of these before. This wolf's eyes were redder than a vampire's feast.

She swore under her breath. The camera slipped out of her hand and slid across the slippery snowpack. The werewolf must recognize her scent as wolf—she hoped. But was it even the same breed as she? It was like her, and yet not. Bigger and bulkier, its shoulders and biceps curved forward in impossible musculature and ended with talons coiled into fists.

And its coloring was surreal, not of this realm. Glowy and pale, but not see-through, as she had guessed. Iridescent. From Faery? Only Faery things glowed as this wolf did. Or maybe a god such as Fenrir? Couldn't be. According to the legend she had researched, that god had been chained until the end of time.

Its white leathery nostrils flaring, the wolf scented her, then whipped its head back and reared from her. Growling low in warning, the wolf stepped back and stretched out its arms. Emitting a long and rangy howl, it sent shivers throughout Daisy's body. She clutched her arms across her chest and tucked her head.

With a stomp of its massive foot, the ghost wolf took off into the forest, leaving its tracks imprinted deep in the snow near her feet.

Daisy breathed out. "Holy shit, that was close."

Holding a shaking hand before her, she assessed her heartbeat. Ready to bust out from her ribs. She shook her head. She'd take her father's wrath over another meeting with the ghost wolf any day.

And then she checked her fear. The wolf hadn't hurt her, hadn't even moved to touch her. For all she knew, it could be of her breed.

"I can't be afraid," she said. "Only girls cry."

By the time she arrived back in town, Daisy's heartbeat had settled. The fear had segued to an adventurous exhilaration during her walk. She'd stood face-to-face with the ghost wolf! Her brothers would be stunned.

With adrenaline tracing her veins, she wasn't content to go home and crawl into bed. Instead, she headed toward the west end of town where she knew Red lived. She marched up to the front door, passing the truck that hissed out steam from beneath the hood. Seeing a light on inside, she knocked.

Red answered immediately, frowned, then looked over her shoulder. As if she should have brought along an entourage?

"You it?" he asked.

"Uh, I'm Daisy Saint-Pierre, Mister Red. I heard about you seeing the ghost wolf," she tried.

"You bet I did."

"Would you mind answering a few questions for the *Tangle Lake Tattler?*" She whipped out her notepad to make it look official.

"Hell no. I ain't talking to no one but Karell News. I called 'em. I thought you were it, but apparently not." He pushed the door closed, but Daisy wedged a shoulder against it and shoved inward. "Nobody but the big news," he reiterated, and this time managed to shut the door completely.

Daisy stepped back and stared at the door. Karell was the most-watched news channel in Minneapolis.

"Shoot. I should have gotten here sooner. He must have called the station as they were driving back. Couldn't have been that scared if he was thinking about his fifteen minutes of fame."

Daisy wandered down the path back to her car just as the Karell News van pulled up. She recognized the blonde reporter who got out and directed her cameraman toward the house.

The woman rushed over to Daisy and shoved a microphone in her face. "Are you related to Red MacPherson?"

Daisy shook her head. "I'm with the *Tangle Lake Tattler*."

The reporter lowered the microphone. "Red didn't give you the scoop, did he? I told him this was my story."

"He didn't. But I had to try."

The woman sucked in a perfectly highlighted and blushed cheek and sneered. "Tough luck." She spun about and marched across the shoveled sidewalk in her high heels.

Who wore high heels and a business skirt at eleven o'clock at night in the middle of January? Daisy sighed. A reporter who was always prepared to get her story, she decided. There was a lot she had to learn about the business of journalism.

But she did have one thing that might scoop them all.

Rushing back to her car, Daisy pulled away with one hand on the wheel and the other clutching her camera.

The following afternoon, Daisy opened her front door to find Beckett Severo standing there, smiling sheepishly.

The frustration that had been building all day as she'd tried to understand the Photoshop program to enhance her photos slipped away. A more intriguing distraction had arrived.

And a sexy distraction, as well.

"Beck." She shoved a hand over her hair. Hadn't looked at it since stepping out of the shower this morning. Yeesh. "I wasn't sure I'd see you again after, well, you know."

"Do you want to see me?" He remained behind the threshold, hands shoved in his front pockets. "I mean, should I be here?"

"Yes." She took his hand and tugged him inside. "I didn't want to influence you one way or the other so I didn't make the first move. Also, I don't have your phone number."

He tugged out his cell phone and pressed a few buttons, then handed it to her. "Let's remedy that right now. Type in your number. If you give me yours, I'll do the same."

She grabbed her phone from the counter and handed it to him. Typing in her digits, she entered simply Daisy Blu, and not her last name. She didn't want anything in there to remind him of her father.

"I don't want to disrespect your father," he said, handing her back her phone and reclaiming his. "But I couldn't stay away."

"Why is that?"

"That I don't mean any disrespect to a pack principal?"

"No, I understand that completely. And I have to say I'm glad that humiliating episode did not keep you away. It must have been my hot chocolate that lured you back, right?"

"While I admit that wicked brew could certainly provide a strong lure toward you, that's not the reason. How can a guy walk away from pink hair and fluttery lashes like yours? And you're not like most women. You're smart, and you have interests in things beyond shoes and celebrities."

"I don't know what torture king expects us to walk in those wobbly high-heeled shoes."

"I like you in pack boots and your kitty hat. Can I, uh…" His eyes danced over her face nervously. Then he splayed out his hands. "We never got to finish that kiss before your father showed up."

Indeed not. The man had an excellent memory, and thank the goddess for that.

Daisy stepped up to him and tilted back her head because he was tall, and she wanted to stare into his eyes all day. Until such a view didn't matter, and she closed her eyes and tipped forward onto her tiptoes.

He met her mouth with his. A warm, sure kiss that belonged nowhere but now. She gripped the front of his sweater, beneath the open coat, and when he spread a hand up her back she leaned into him. He was so warm, and strong. The muscles beneath her hands were hard as rock, and she curled her fingers against the curve of his pecs. Yet at her mouth, everything was not hard but eager and searching. Inviting and exploratory.

He smelled like caramel and coffee. Whatever he'd had to drink before coming here, it was delicious. Beck moaned into her mouth and lifted her by the hips. Daisy wrapped her legs about his waist without breaking the kiss. He dipped his head to deepen their connection, dashing his tongue along hers. The taste of him ignited her desires. Her skin prickled, and her nipples tightened. She almost grinded her mons against his stomach but stopped herself. This was only their second kiss. And actually, it was just finishing the first kiss.

"You do that very well," she said against his mouth. "You said something about our kiss never ending?"

"I could keep this up for years." He kissed her eyelid, then tilted his forehead against hers. "You do things to me, Daisy Blu."

"Good things?"

"Good. Bewitching. You make the wolf inside me want to howl."

At that moment a wolf howled on the television turned to low volume before the couch.

Daisy laughed. "Appropriate timing."

"You watching a nature show?"

"No, I've had the news on while I've been trying to figure out how to make a computer program pair up with my camera."

Behind them the news anchor reported on last night's encounter between two hunters and the ghost wolf.

"Karell can suck it," Daisy said. She slid out of Beck's grasp and picked up the TV remote and clicked it off. "I almost had an interview with one of those hunters last night. I should have told him I was with Karell. He'd only speak to them. How's that for sucky?"

"Last night? You were out looking for interviews? How quickly does word get around when something like a white wolf stalking hunters happens?"

"Pretty fast. But even faster when it's witnessed first-hand. I was there." She spun, and her enthusiasm over what she'd witnessed last night made her bounce on her toes. "In the forest. I got a few shots of the hunters running in fear from the ghost wolf, and—you'll never believe this—I actually photographed the ghost wolf. They're too blurry, though. Nothing I can use unless I figure out the computer program. I'm so not tech savvy."

Beck's mouth hung open for so long, Daisy wondered if he'd slipped into a sort of catatonic state. When finally he swept a hand before him and clenched it into a fist, he blurted, "What the hell were you doing in the woods again? Alone? I thought I told you that was dangerous?"

"I'm fine. See?" She spun before him, not about to let the big tough male treat her like a helpless female. Been there, done that. Learned to punch the lug in the gut. "And you know what? The ghost wolf walked right up to me. Sniffed me, even."

"Daisy! It could have killed you."

"Oh, I don't think so. I'm ninety-five-percent sure it's a werewolf. Except bigger. And stronger. Its muscles were just so much…" she caressed the air in the shape of the wolf "…more. And you know, it really does kind of glow. It's white and transparent. Maybe iridescent—"

"I can't listen to this. Daisy, what would your father say? Does he know you go wandering in the woods alone at night where hunters are waiting to shoot their prey? You being just such prey."

"I'm no man's prey. I wore an orange vest. It's not the hunters I worry about. Besides, I went in human form because I needed to get the shots. Why are you getting so bent out of shape about this? I'm a reporter. Or I hope to be. I'm doing what is necessary to win the internship."

"Daisy, reporters don't risk their lives by standing before a wild animal."

"I think they do. At least, this reporter does. But I didn't fear the ghost wolf. Not for long, anyway. In fact, I know it wouldn't have harmed me. I felt that from it."

"Must have recognized your scent."

"What? How could it? Recognize it from when?"

Beck shook his head and wandered over to the long table before the windows. Her notes, books and various sketches were scattered beside the laptop and a digital camera.

He gripped his hair and paced. "I don't think it's wise. We don't know anything about this ghost wolf. And even if you think it's werewolf, it's not like us, Daisy."

"Yeah, I'm trying to figure that out. Let me show you."

She slipped around behind the table where half a dozen books on myth and even some volumes written by paranormal breeds listed a variety of the known and fantastical creatures that existed within this mortal realm.

"I haven't found anything exactly like what I saw. At first I thought it could be an incarnation of Fenrir, but I doubt that. This one comes close." She tapped a page in an open book that featured Chibiabos. "It's a Native American legend, and this area of the state is steeped in Indian traditions. There's a reservation not far from here. Or this one."

She pulled another book before her and Beck leaned over, though it didn't seem as if he were interested, but rather distracted. And not in a good way. She could sense his tension and smell not so much anger as concern.

"Here." She picked up the picture she'd printed out earlier. "This is the best shot I could get of it."

He took the photo and looked it over. It was a blurred image of something white. Could be the abominable snowman for the clarity. If she hadn't seen it with her own eyes, she'd never be able to look at the picture and say, *Yes, that's a werewolf.*

"What do you intend to prove by getting a picture?" he asked. "I know you want the internship, and that requires a winning article, but why this story?"

"It's what I know."

Beck frowned.

"Okay, I know I'm treading dangerous territory with our breed. We're all about secrecy."

"And for good reason."

"Right, and I get that. But the ghost wolf is already out there. The humans are making it out to be some evil creature. But I think of the ghost wolf as more of a superhero."

"Right, your hero in a cape theory. It's nonsense, Daisy."

"I didn't say he wore a cape." But that he'd dismissed it as nonsense hurt. Daisy lifted her chin. "And I want to make sure it's not hunted as a monster, but rather honored as something that made the hunters take a pause to rethink their motives toward mindless killing. The ghost wolf is helping the wolves."

"A noble goal, but…" Beck sighed and turned to sit against the table, facing her. He clutched the table edge and leaned forward, entreating, "What if one of these nights a hunter's bullet goes astray and you get hit? Daisy, this story is not worth the risk."

"So long as it's not a silver bullet, I'm good."

"Silver—Daisy. Wait." Beck stood, his hands pressed together, going to his face. "Silver."

"Right. That's the only thing that can kill us."

"Yes, but…fuck."

"Beck? What's wrong?"

She could sense his increased heartbeats. As well, her heartbeat sped up. What had she said? His mood had shifted from concern to something like angst. He must be thinking about his father. She had heard he had been with him when he'd been murdered.

"I don't know why I haven't been pursuing this all along."

"Pursuing what?" she asked.

"The shotgun shell that killed my father had silver in it."

"That's odd. Aren't most shells filled with lead shot?"

"Exactly. So the hunter had to have made it special. And to use silver…he had to have known what he was hunting. Who would do something like that?"

"You think it wasn't a human?" Daisy asked. "Vampire?"

"Huh?" He found her gaze, as if coming up from the depths, his eyes focusing on hers. "No, it wasn't a vampire. I jumped on him that night, held him down. He was human, and though I was in wolf shape at the time, I felt his fright."

"That's to be expected if a wolf attacks you."

"I didn't attack him. I just…kept him away from my father's body."

Daisy sucked in her lip. They were moving into intimate territory, and she felt the need for caution. It hurt Beck to retell this information, but that he trusted her to reveal a few details was immense.

"I have to go check on something," he said. "This is big." He started toward the door. "I'm sorry. I had come here to spend some time with you. But this is important."

"I understand. I have your digits now." She rushed to beat him to the door and pressed her shoulders to it as he arrived before the threshold. "I want to help you, Beck."

"I don't need any help. And I don't want you getting shot in your quest for a picture of a creature that could very likely kill you. Will you promise me to stay out of the forests? Please, Daisy?"

That wasn't something she could promise. And she was smart; she knew when she was in danger, and she hadn't felt it yet. Not even when the ghost wolf had walked right up to her.

She touched Beck's cheek and traced his stubble-darkened jaw. His thoughts were miles away, back at his father's side as he'd died in the forest. She didn't know how to deal with grief. It hadn't touched her life. And it had only been a few months since he'd lost his father. He seemed normal and stoic on the outside, but could he be a bundle of agony on the inside?

"Have you spoken to anyone about this? Losing your father?"

"Why? I'm not a weepy girl, Daisy. Something bad happened. I'm dealing. If anyone needs help, it's my mother. She's— Hell. I've got to go. I'm sorry about this."

"Don't apologize. I just… Can we make another date? Tomorrow night? I'll cook if you come over."

"I'd like that. You like wine?"

"Sounds good. Bring red. I'll make meat and potatoes."

He bracketed her head with his palms and bent his forehead to hers again. "You could win my heart, you know that, Daisy Blu?"

"I'll give it a try."

"You don't need to try, just…be you."

He kissed her again, this time holding still at her mouth. She thought she felt his heartbeat in that touch. And in the seconds that her heart stood still, Daisy knew she would try for that win, whether or not he wanted her to.

Chapter 7

Beck found his mother in the kitchen cleaning the copper-tiled backsplash behind the stove. Why she cooked was beyond him, but he was glad to see her not sulking in the big easy chair where she and Dad had always snuggled. She looked good, actually had color in her cheeks, and greeted him with a genuine hug and a kiss.

"How you feeling?" he asked.

"I'm well." She patted her growing belly. "I have a doctor's appointment tomorrow."

"Do you want me to come along with you?"

"No, you don't have to. But you're a sweetie to offer. Did you go to the iceworks the other night?"

"I did."

"By yourself?" she asked in a tone that implied she had already deduced the answer.

"Why do you ask?"

"I haven't been a complete hermit since your father's death. I talk to Blu on the phone once in a while. She said her son Malakai was all in a huff because he saw his daughter with my son. I only have one son—at the moment—so…"

"I've told you Malakai asked me to join his pack, and that I refused."

"You can join, Beck. You don't have to be like Severo."

"I don't feel a strong need to do so. Can we just drop it, Mom? What matters is that I think I like Daisy."

"Daisy?"

"Malakai's daughter. I was with her at the iceworks. But I don't want to piss off her father, so the whole thing is kind of sticky."

"Well, you already have pissed off Malakai. So what's to lose, eh?"

Beck caught the sparkle in his mother's green eyes. "Are you suggesting I see her without her father's approval?"

"I'm suggesting you do what makes you happy." Bella rubbed her belly. She was about four or five months along. "Life is so precious. You should enjoy it while you can." Sucking in a breath, his mother looked away so quickly, Beck knew it was to hide tears. "I was just on my way back to do laundry," she said softly. "I'm going to fold the load before the clothes get wrinkled."

"That's cool, Mom. I stopped by to get a few things from Dad's shop, if you don't mind?"

"Take anything you like." Her voice wobbled as she headed down the hallway.

Beck wished it could be easier for his mother. He considered giving Ivan Drake a call. The vampire had been the one to finish his mom's transformation after she'd been attacked and bitten by Evie, his father's nemesis. Drake had taught Bella the ways of his kind, and they'd been friends ever since. Severo had admired the vampire for his kindness to his wife.

Bowing his head at the lingering scent of sadness in his mother's wake, Beck sighed. Yeah, he'd give Ivan a call today. Maybe Ivan could lift his mother's spirits. At the very least, the vampire could make sure she was getting enough blood so the baby could develop. A doctor's appointment? He hoped she was going to the doctor who had delivered him. A werewolf M.D. who treated all breeds except humans.

Wandering down the marble-floored hallway that hugged the foyer, he arrived at the steel door that opened to Severo's shop. Inside was an arsenal that the old werewolf had kept for sentimental reasons. Severo hadn't used a weapon in ages, but was ever ready for those werewolves or vampires who thought they could tussle with him.

Beck's father had suffered in his lifetime. Severo had watched hunters murder his parents when he was a child, and had been caught in a hunter's trap himself. He'd limped because of that injury. Those hunters had been vampires. Vampires who had hunted werewolves for the sadistic thrill of it, not for their pelts or the bounty offered by the state.

Similar to the idiot human hunters who currently tracked the Minnesota wolves. The DNR claimed they were harvesting the breed, keeping their numbers down.

Harvesting. Beck hated that word.

Thing is, nature had a way of doing that just fine on her own. The harvesting was murder, plain and simple. And if any hunter dared to be honest, he was going after the wolves for sport, a new hunting experience and a unique trophy for his case.

And Beck would do what he could to stop it.

As he entered the shop and flicked on the light, a chill swept over his shoulders. Last time he'd been in here, he'd held his dead father in his arms. Beck had laid Severo's human body on the steel worktable and had plucked out the bits of shot that had pierced his heart. The silver had run through his veins. Impossible to clean away. All while listening to his mother's wails not far off down the hallway.

Beck's heart was racing with every step he took toward the steel table. The images of that night grew clearer and bold in his thoughts. His father had gasped once or twice as he'd driven him home. Still alive, struggling for breath. He'd been dead when Beck had gently lifted him into his arms to carry into his mother's house.

Falling to his knees before the table, Beck gripped the edge and pressed his forehead to it. He squeezed his eyelids shut and gritted his jaws. Why had it happened? He and his father had always played it safe, keeping to the private land Severo owned, and where they knew hunters were not allowed.

Someone had stepped out of bounds and onto private property. And that someone had used silver to make the kill shot. He hadn't given it a second thought that night. But then, Beck had only been trying to hold it together while he'd made his father's body presentable for his mother to look over.

When one of his breed was killed in wolf or werewolf form, it shifted back to its *were,* or human form, just before the heart pulsed one last time. To watch that shift had torn Beck's heart out as surely as the hunter's shell had pierced his father's heart.

A hunter who must know more than Beck had initially imagined.

Finding clarity through determination, Beck scanned the tabletop. It was clean. He'd wiped it down after wrapping his father's body in sheets in preparation for the funeral the following night. Dozens of wolves had arrived to witness the burning of Severo's body at the pond's edge at the back of their property, including many from various local packs. Beck hadn't known all of them. But he appreciated that his father had so many friends. Or rather, had earned the respect of so many, despite his lone wolf status.

He couldn't recall seeing Malakai Saint-Pierre there. But then, he hadn't looked for him, either.

Now he brushed his arm across the cold steel worktable. Then he bent and searched the floor and spied three tiny beads—shotgun pellets—that must have rolled to the floor. He picked up the pellets. They looked rusted—no, that was dried blood.

A teardrop splashed his hand, but he sniffed back more. He had to be analytical about this and keep emotion stuffed deep. Laying the pieces on the table, he reached up to click on the overhead lamp. Inspecting both, he saw that they were silver, but most shotgun pellets were that color. The third bead was larger and looked clear, almost like glass. Yet there was something inside it, as if encased in a delicate womb.

Beck grabbed a bowie knife from the shelf above the counter and gently crushed the hilt of it onto the bead. Glass cracked, and beneath the hilt a tiny droplet of silver oozed out.

He was careful not to touch it. Once silver entered a werewolf's bloodstream, it was only a matter of minutes before it infected his entire system. Death could result in a nasty inner explosion, or a slow, painful smothering from within.

Hell, to think about it wrenched his heart so painfully, Beck clutched his chest. His father had suffered in those long minutes as he'd driven him home. If only he could have done something for him.

He would do something now. He had to find a hunter in the area who used silver in his shotgun shells. These odd glass-encased pellets had been specially made. They didn't look like something that even an expert could manufacture. If he let his mind wander they looked…futuristic. Where to find such a thing?

If he asked around at the local shops, he might get lucky

and find the person who had ordered in glass-encased pellets.

It was a start. To a revenge his father deserved.

Hours after her son had left, Bella answered the front door. At the sight of the tall, dark-haired man who stood there, she broke down in tears.

"Bella, I should have come sooner." Ivan Drake stepped across the threshold because he'd been welcomed into her home a long time ago, and wrapped her in his arms.

Pressed against his comforting body heat and enclosed within his strong arms, Bella let her body go weak. She trusted this man, this vampire who was also a phoenix and witch. He had been the one Severo had trusted to complete her transformation after she had been viciously attacked by vampires. He had taught her how to be what she was. She loved him as a mentor and friend.

He lifted her in his arms and carried her into the living room, avoiding the easy chair where she and Severo had often snuggled and watched movies together. Setting her on the couch and kneeling before her on the floor, he grasped her hands and pressed her fingers to his mouth. He held her in his eyes, their silence so easy.

Beck must have called him. She was glad her son had done so.

"I'm here to talk. Or not talk," he offered. "Whatever you need from me. Dez sends her love."

Ivan's wife was a beautiful, centuries-old witch whom Bella also called friend.

"Ivan," Bella gasped. Though it had been months, the smothering clench on her heart never ceased to choke her up. "I miss him so much."

"I know. I've never lost someone close, so I won't lie and say I can understand. That's why I want to be here for you. Whenever you're ready to talk, to let it all spill out, I'll hold you and catch your tears."

"It's not me I worry about," she said through sniffles. "Beckett hasn't had anyone to talk to."

"I'll find someone for him to talk to. But I know you, Bella. You worry about everyone but yourself. You look too pale. When's the last time you drank blood?"

She dipped her head.

"That's what I thought." He slid up to sit next to her, and clasping her hand in his, he turned up his wrist and bit into the soft underside. "Drink, Bella."

And she did until her heart began to feel the tiniest flutter of life. It would never beat so bold and bright as it once had when Severo was alive. But she knew she needed to take care of herself, and the baby.

Wine bottle in hand, Beck paused before knocking on Daisy's door. He'd vacillated about coming here, and then his heart had pushed him out the door faster than his good sense could argue the worse points of that decision. Because...

Because he was an idiot. Because he wanted some pretty werewolf to kiss him again? No. And yes. And no. It was more than a visceral attraction to a sexy woman that stirred his desires. It was what he'd told her. She was different. And something about Daisy Blu pulled him toward her when all he wanted to do was put up his fists and fend off the softer emotions that vied against the tangle of red and violent emotions that stirred in him lately.

And if all those reasons did not exist, he wanted to keep her safe from her pursuits regarding the ghost wolf.

Shaking out his arms as if after a round of punching the boxing bag out back of his house, he nodded and then knocked. "This is good," he pep-talked. "I can do this."

When the door opened, Beck was hit by a cavalcade of sensual notes. The savory rosemary and sage of roasted chicken. The soft melody of some pop song dialed to low volume. The warmth of the air beckoning him forward. And the visual that so didn't mesh with what he had expected.

Daisy's hair was unbound and spilled over her shoulders in soft pink waves. A sparkle of rhinestones glinted at the crown of her head. A thin strand befitting the werewolf princess she claimed not to be. The usual bulky sweater hung past her hips, and black leggings led to toenails that flashed bright purple polish.

"Daisy?"

She punched him gently on the bicep. "Don't say anything. I found this in a drawer. Do not use the *P* word."

"Uh, okay." *Pretty? Pixy? Princess?* All of the above. "I love it."

"Love is easy, wolf."

"Well, I can't commit to like just yet. So what's with the sparkles?"

"You don't love it."

"I do, I just—" Had expected his usual pink faery wolf, sans any glint of feminine sparkle.

"It's not a tiara, it's just—"

And he leaned down to kiss her, because if he let her continue she might come up with another ridiculous excuse for him not to like her. *Love* her, that is.

He spread a hand through her hair and crushed it in his fingers. It smelled sweet as candy. Combine that with the roasting chicken, and he was hungry.

She ended the kiss and blinked at him. "Why are you so cool?"

"I'm not cool. I just don't live my life based on other people's opinions of what that life should be."

"Like joining a pack?"

"Exactly. And even though I know this is going to hurt, I have to say it. You look like a princess."

He caught her punch in his palm with a smack, and quickly kissed her again. "I win that one."

"I hate losing."

"I suspect that about you. Okay." He spread his arms, exposing his torso to danger. "Take your best shot."

Daisy wound up, and he winced in expectation, but she dropped her fist. "No." She took the wine bottle from him. "I'm not feeling it anymore."

He stroked his thumb across her cheek, as if he could feel the warmth brightening there. "I'm sure the feeling will strike again."

She smirked.

"The whole place smells amazing." He wandered into the kitchen, where two places had been set at the counter and the blue daisies had wilted. "Okay, that's just pitiful." He grabbed the vase and turned around. "Where's the garbage?"

She pointed over her shoulder. Beck plucked out the dead flowers and tossed them in a closet that hid a garbage can. "I'll bring you new ones next time I see you. A natural color, even. Promise."

"I'll look forward to it. Now, sit. Let me test out my culinary skills on you. I don't cook as often as I'd like to. My dad taught me, so I do have some talent."

"Your dad? Doesn't your mother cook?"

"Only bakes. She's into sweets big-time. Dad does all the hunting, so he insists on cooking, as well. Sweet potatoes with a pomegranate glaze," she said, spooning the side dish onto his plate. "I hope you're hungry. I think I made enough for four."

"I'll eat the whole chicken if you need me to."

"We are going to get along just fine," she announced, swinging around the end of the counter to sit beside him.

The meal was amazing. Beck wasn't sure if it was Daisy's culinary skill or just that a home-cooked meal always won over his heart and stomach. He ate everything she put on his plate. And she kept filling his empty plate with more.

As Daisy chattered about how she liked living in town because everything was but a walk away, but really wanted a place out in the country like her father owned, Beck's mind drifted. Standing in his father's shop this morning had worked a number on him. He couldn't erase the image of having to carry Severo home and show his mother.

And then he thought about the ghost wolf. Would the creature ever be able to completely stop human hunters from pursuing the natural wolves and his breed?

He wondered if Ivan had gotten around to his mother's house. She was thin, and needed care. Should he move in with her? Make sure she ate and took care of the baby? He wondered which of her friends might be willing to move in for a month or so, just until she got back on her feet.

There was so much to consider. And now, this beautiful woman sat beside him, oblivious to the torment in his head. She was sweet, and kind, and pretty, and he wanted to kiss her and then push her up against the wall and tug down her leggings and thrust into her, losing himself within her. Finding a solace that could comfort him, if only for a moment in time. Without a care in the world…

"Beck?"

"Huh?"

"You seem distracted. I'm sorry. I shouldn't talk about my work so much."

"It's not that, Daisy." He set down his fork and pressed the heels of his hands against his eyes. "I don't think this can work."

"This? You mean…?"

"Us." Hell, he shouldn't have said it. But better to say it now than to string her along. What an asshole. Taking advantage of her kindness and her cooking.

"There's so much going on right now." His thoughts blabbered out quickly. "You're so good, Daisy. And I'm a fucked-up mess. And my mom…" He stood abruptly. "I don't want to drag you through my drama."

"Beck, I don't want you to leave."

"I think I should."

"It's my dad, isn't it?"

"Your dad? No. Yes. I don't know. I wanted this to work out. You're such a pretty faery wolf. And your chicken is the best I've ever eaten. You sparkle. Your conversation is interesting. But right now things are so crazy in my life."

Could he just grab her and kiss her until all the crazy thoughts slipped away?

"You've been through a lot," she said, fumbling with the ends of her hair. "But I'd like to be here for you. Beck, I really want to spend time with you."

"And that's dangerous for you. At least, right now it is. I have to go. I'm sorry. The meal was so good. I don't want to be the kind of guy who walks out on a girl, but…"

He tugged on his coat and marched out the door. "So sorry," he muttered. "I'm the wrong wolf for you," he added, knowing she could hear him, but not sure how to face her.

Chapter 8

Denton Marx looked over the various ingredients he'd gathered over the past few months for the allbeast spell. Each was contained in a small glass jar capped with a screwable tin lid. Marvelous technology, that lid. He needed something like that in his own time.

Alas, to think of his own time—and the woman whom he had lived with in that time—never ceased to raise his ire. Too much time had passed. Sencha must believe he had stopped trying to rescue her from that horrible nonplace where she had become trapped.

She had once told him about the Edge. Witches feared it only if they traveled through dimensions and time. And as a wandersoul, Sencha traveled through time quite often. She was possessed of a soul that wandered the worlds and times, ever searching, until it found that one other soul it felt comfortable enough to remain with, and cease the wandering.

His soul.

Yet even after finding him, she had continued to travel through time because it pleased her. And she had taught him how to do it. He had drank her blood in a ritual that allowed him to actually travel through time on his own, but only once or twice before the magic was depleted. He'd used it to obtain the weapon he must now use to get the final ingredient to the spell.

He would kill a werewolf, and then he and Sencha could be together again.

Daisy pulled on her snow pants and zipped up her coat. She slipped the orange hunter's vest over that. It was dark out, but if a hunter's flashlight beamed over her while walking amidst the thick foliage, she wanted to be seen.

Sighing as she locked the front door behind her, she wished tonight's supper hadn't gone over so horribly. Beck had practically pushed her out of the way to leave. Something must have set him off, because he'd sat and eaten and talked with her for almost an hour before deciding it wasn't going to work.

Had she talked too much? That wasn't like her. She rarely gabbed anyone's head off. It was easy to let loose and be comfortable with Beck. She'd probably let her hair down too far. She'd freaked him out by wearing the crystal headpiece. It had once been her mother's. Finding it in a drawer had made her smile, and she'd felt the urge to pretty up for the guy. She should try to tap into her feminine side more often. It may be necessary to win the guy.

And she wanted to win him.

"So I don't have feminine wiles," she muttered. "Screw it."

Stepping outside, she gasped at the below zero weather and sucked the permafreeze into her lungs. Rushing to her car, she set her camera on the passenger seat and fired up the engine. Thank the goddess for heated seats that warmed quickly. In no time she was snug as a bug. Pulling away, she wondered if she should drive by Beck's shop on the way out of town.

She shook her head.

As much as she had wanted to grab him, pull him close
and offer him the comfort she sensed he needed, she'd also
felt the distance he'd asked for was the better bet. He was
struggling with loss.

Maybe this distance was best for the both of them?

Daisy sighed. Seriously? She was hot for Beck, and
she'd thought he was for her. She'd been hoping their kisses
would advance to something more tonight. What did a girl
have to do to get a little between-the-sheets action from a
handsome man? Was a skirt a requirement?

"Can't be. Just give him space," she said, turning onto
the country road where she usually parked.

Fifteen minutes later, she stalked through the forest,
camera in hand. The scent of humans was strong. They
were nearing her, but perhaps still a quarter of a mile
away. And then the other scent rose, and Daisy flicked
her head around to home in on it. The feral scent was familiar and strong.

"The ghost wolf. It has to be."

Finding a wide oak tree trunk, Daisy positioned herself
against the rough bark and waited. If another pair of hunters dashed past her tonight, she'd be ready.

The hunters did run by, fifty yards off. The luminous
ghost wolf pursued them. Daisy's camera snapped repeatedly, and the zoom was set high. As well, she'd adjusted
the f-stop and ISO according to an article she'd read online for better night photography. She really should use a
tripod, but she'd be thrilled if these shots showed more
than a white blur.

As long as she tried, she may come up with at least one
or two good pictures out of the dozens she was taking.

Headlights popped on, beaming through the woods,
but not lighting where Daisy stood. She scampered from
tree trunk to tree trunk, positioning herself for a better

shot. The hunters pulled away in a cloud of snow spit up by tire chains. Rock music blared through the closed truck windows.

The ghost wolf had struck again. Its howls echoed in the air, pricking up the hairs on Daisy's skin.

Where was it?

Daisy noticed the feral scent had risen. It was moving closer to her. She maintained her position against the tree trunk, unwilling to risk spooking the wolf. When she heard its huffing breaths, she sensed it was less than thirty feet away. Over near the massive copse of white birch whose trunks had been marked at her head level by moose antlers.

She dared a peek around the tree where she stood. The big white werewolf had slowed to a walk but wasn't coming toward her. Was it possible it wasn't aware of her presence? Bending its muscular body forward, it dropped onto all fours. It looked as if it would begin to shift.

The ghost wolf was a shapeshifter?

Well, of course, if it was a werewolf. Daisy just hadn't put two and two together. So the wolf could be a man. Who was it?

Clinging to the bark with one hand, she readied the camera with her other.

The ghost wolf howled, thrusting back its massive head as its body contorted into the shift. It was never painful, unless the wolf resisted the shift—but it did appear to others an agonizing experience. Within seconds the body had changed, losing fur and claw and taking on skin and the features of its *were,* or man shape.

"Holy crap," Daisy whispered.

She couldn't force herself to take a picture of the naked man lying there on the snowy ground before the tree trunk. He heaved in a breath as if exhausted, then crawled to the tree and pulled out a backpack from the hollowed-out trunk. When he turned around to sit and dress, he suddenly lifted his head, sniffing. He'd scented her.

What to do? Reveal her presence and risk his anger? Or attempt to run, only to be surely caught if he pursued?

Either way, he wouldn't be pleased.

Daisy stepped around the tree trunk, putting herself into his view.

The wolf swore.

"Beck," Daisy said.

Chapter 9

She'd watched him change.

The remarkable, luminescent creature who instilled fear in the hearts of many hunters was really a man. Daisy dropped the camera in the snow. Slowly, she approached the naked man sitting before the birch trunk.

Beck put up a hand. "Daisy, wait. Let me get my pants on."

She nodded and stayed her position.

"Turn around?" he asked.

"Oh. Right." She turned and listened as he pulled up his jeans.

He was still breathing heavily. Huffing, as if exerted. Normally coming out of a shift from werewolf was exhilarating. At least, it was for her. It stretched her muscles nicely and worked out any kinks that may have developed over the days since the last shift. Much more fulfilling than if she brought out her faery wings.

"Okay."

She turned at his voice and saw Beck stumble backward, catching his palms against the papery birch trunk and collapsing into a sitting position again. He tilted his head back against the tree and closed his eyes.

"Beck? Are you okay?"

"I'm fine. Just…it takes a lot out of me. Give me a few minutes to catch my breath. Come back to this form completely."

She crept closer and knelt beside him. His eyes still closed, he breathed in deeply, his chest expanding and stretching the gorgeous muscles. His biceps were tight, the veins cording them in graceful curves and ropes. He perspired, even sitting in zero-degree weather. His face was beaded with sweat, and his hair stood up at all angles.

When he opened his eyes and met her curious gaze, he shook his head. "I didn't want you to see this."

Daisy's held breath released in an exhilarated sigh. "But I did."

He nodded, closing his eyes again. "That you did."

"You're the ghost wolf," she added enthusiastically.

How cool was that? She'd discovered the secret behind the ghost wolf. He really was a werewolf, as she'd suspected, and—he was the man she wanted more than anything right now.

"How is this possible?" she asked. "Are you like me? A werewolf?"

He nodded. "It's a long story."

"I want to hear it."

"So you can write an article and print it for the humans to read? I don't think so. Daisy, I didn't want to drag you into my mess."

"You didn't do any dragging. I stepped into it. And grant me the right to make my own choices and speak to whom I wish, and date whom I want."

"I'm not your dad, Daisy. I'm just a guy who wants to protect you from the dangers of…" he spread his arms and let them drop at his sides "…this."

"How are you a danger to me? I saw the ghost wolf—you—the other night. You scented me. I think you recognized me."

Because in werewolf state they hadn't complete control over the human mind. Smell was the key sense. They were more animal in that shape, and they sometimes recognized friends, but sometimes did not. It was a good thing, because once back in human form, to remember having pursued and killed a rabbit, or even a deer, would not be cool.

"You would never hurt me," she said. "But why haven't you done something to the hunters yet? You've only been scaring them."

"I don't want to hurt anyone, Daisy. I want to scare the living crap out of them and hopefully, in the process, change their minds about ever killing wolves again. If I were to harm one, that would bring me down to their level."

"Beck, you're so right. I'm sorry. I shouldn't have insinuated that you could be so cruel. I can't believe it's you. I'm so glad it's you."

She lunged into his arms and hugged him, nuzzling her face against his bare shoulder. He was hot and smelled of musk and salt and the fresh tinge of snow and ice. Delicious. And sensual. "I won't tell anyone. I promise. But you have to tell me how you are able to do this."

"I will. Soon."

"Right. I won't push. And I won't take notes. Promise."

"Daisy, what are you doing to me? I walked away from your place today, thinking that was it. Much as I wanted you in my life, I knew it was better to keep you out. Safer for you. But now…"

"It's hard to get rid of me."

"You think?"

"Beck, now more than ever, I understand you're in a tough spot with everything going on in your life. I'd love for us to have a relationship. But if you're more comfortable with us just being friends, I can do that. I just don't want you out of my life."

"Your father will have an argument for that."

"Yeah, well, he's not here right now."

"Are you sure? Because he seems to turn up when we least expect him."

"Very sure." She leaned up and kissed him.

Moving to straddle him, she deepened the kiss and he moaned against her mouth. The ridiculous heat of him compelled her closer, and she wished she weren't all bundled in winter clothes so she could share his body heat. Then she corrected her lusty thoughts because she shouldn't push. If this was what he was willing to give her right now, she had to accept that.

"So we can be friends?" she asked.

His eyes traveled back and forth between hers. He smirked and tugged the end of one of her cap strings. "From you I need more than friends. If that's okay."

She nodded eagerly.

"Good, because I don't kiss my friends. And don't forget, I love you." And he kissed her again, pulling her into the exhilaration of the unknown.

Beck pushed his hands through her hair, and her cap fell off and tumbled down her back. There beneath the tree-filtered moonlight, they kissed like tomorrow was to bring the end of days. And it felt exciting. Daring. Dangerous. She was kissing the ghost wolf! And he wanted to be more than just friends.

Daisy could deal with that. But she knew she had only brushed the surface of Beckett Severo. The man was complicated. And that didn't begin to define the ghostly werewolf that he was able to shift into. She would learn him. But she'd be careful, and respectful of his need to guard his privacy and protect himself.

Honestly? She'd try hard to respect his barriers. But this touching, kissing and tasting one another was fast plundering all barriers.

"I want you to touch me," she gasped as he licked her lower lip. "I'm wearing too many things."

"I want to touch you, too. I want to put my hands all over your skin and read you with my touch."

"Mmm, I like the sound of that."

"See? I like to read, too," he offered with a wink. "But not here in the woods with me sitting in a pile of wet slush. Want to come home with me? You can open your cover for me and let me do a little reading."

"Keep talking."

"Yeah, talk. We need to do that, too. I think talking should be at the top of the list."

"Then let's go."

They stood, and Beck shoved his feet into his boots. Daisy handed him his sweater and coat, regretting his need to cover those awesome abs.

"Did you see which way the hunters went?" he asked.

"They ran out toward the east access road. I didn't recognize them." And she knew, as werewolf, he wouldn't be able to recognize their faces while in human shape, but their scents he should know if he encountered them again. "Was it the one…?"

He shook his head. "I don't think so."

How weird was it that Beck had the ability to become the ghost wolf to stalk the very hunter responsible for his father's death? Had he always been this way? Or had his father's death changed him so drastically that he had literally become a monster?

"Did you check on the silver? You said you were going to do that."

"Yes, the shell that killed my dad was handmade, laced with tiny glass pellets filled with liquid silver. I've never seen anything like it. It looked technologically advanced. Which means whoever killed my dad was purposely hunting werewolves."

"That's insane. You think a human knows about us?"

"Lots of humans know about the things they shouldn't know, Daisy." He grasped her hand. "Where did you park?"

"That way." She pointed over her shoulder. "Should I follow you to your house?"

"Or I could bring you back to pick up your car later."

"Good plan."

And she didn't want to let go of his big, wide hand. Not now that she'd gained some of his trust. And now that he was leading her to his home, where she would learn the truth about the ghost wolf.

Beck's first thought as he drove toward home with the pink-haired faery wolf sitting beside him was a feeling of relief. Now she knew. Someone knew. He didn't have to carry that burden alone anymore.

But he should. It was his burden. He'd asked for it. It could endanger anyone he got close to.

Yet his brain battled to keep the relief, along with the gratefulness that swept through him when Daisy clasped his hand and smiled quietly at him as they cruised down his street. He lived ten miles from where he'd been stalking the hunters. The land out here was selling too rapidly. He'd have to move soon if his neighbors got closer than the three-mile distance they were at now. He valued his peace and privacy. All wolves did.

Behind the house he'd built a few years ago, a four-acre pond had frozen over for the winter. The beavers were hibernating as well as the bears. He did not shift and hunt on his meager twelve acres. Because again, the neighbors were too close. And in this neck of the woods, seven out of ten humans owned guns and felt it was their right to shoot at anything they feared or didn't understand.

Which was pretty much anything on four legs. Two legs, if it glowed.

Someday he'd move up north into the Boundary Waters,

where a wolf had more freedom because the vast acreage offered privacy. But to move so far from his mother, especially now when she was so fragile, felt wrong.

"I like this area," Daisy said. The truck's headlights beamed across the thick woods that surrounded his house. "Quiet?"

"Very. You ice skate?"

"I, uh, yes?"

He chuckled at her reluctance. Parking, he swung around and raced to Daisy's door. She'd opened it by the time he got there, but she did take his hand to get out of the truck. Baby steps, he decided, would endear him into her trust.

"You can skate on the pond behind my house," he said. "It freezes thick. And I'm guessing you might be into hockey."

"I am a pond hockey champion. There's not a Saint-Pierre in the county who can beat me."

"An accolade I'm sure your brothers keep to themselves, eh?"

"You know it."

As they approached the house, a rabbit scurried across the snow cover, stitching tracks in the snow. Beck opened the door, and Daisy stopped inside on the rug and stomped the snow from her boots. He kicked his boots off beside hers.

"I'll get a fire going." He strolled into the living room and opened the hearth. A stack of wood he'd refilled this morning offered dry pine. He started a log on fire and closed the screen.

Daisy had shed her outerwear and stood in socks, tight gray leggings and a cozy purple sweater that looked two sizes too big for her, yet compelled Beck to pull her in for a snuggle.

"You always look like you need a cuddle," he said. "You and your pink hair and soft clothes. And these lips."

She turned up that raspberry sherbet mouth to him. "What was it you said about my lips?"

"They fit mine nicely." He kissed her quickly, because his brain was beginning to spin again. Sure, he'd invited her here to make out. But he'd also invited her to talk. And the talk, while necessary, would take a lot out of him. "Hot chocolate?"

"You know the way to my heart." She followed him into the kitchen and slid onto a bar stool.

Beck sorted through the cupboard, pulled out two small plastic cups and displayed them to her. "It'll never rival your magical elixir. Just Keurig."

"My brother Blade likes that coffee," she said. "I didn't know you could make hot chocolate with the machine."

"I can make cider, too, if that floats your boat."

"Chocolate, please."

It took but minutes to warm up the coffeemaker and brew the first cup, then the second.

Daisy cast her gaze over the kitchen's inner timber walls. "This house is cozy."

The furnishings were all clear-stained timbers with bright, patchwork cushions. The coffee table had been hewn from a single oak trunk. The hardwood floors had been made from reclaimed redwood. All natural or recycled.

It truly felt like home to Beck. His father had loved to sprawl on the couch and listen to Lynyrd Skynyrd while Beck had worked on taking apart a carburetor in order to learn how it worked.

"It's a home," he offered. He slid a cup toward Daisy. "Give me your rating."

She took a couple sips. "Not bad for powder. I'll give it a six."

"I'll take the six. But that makes yours a twelve, hands down. Let's go sit on the couch."

He put another log on the fire and joined Daisy, who had curled her legs up and settled onto the couch. She touched his cheek as he sat and turned her finger to show him the ash she'd wiped off his skin.

He rubbed a thumb over his cheek.

"Let me," she said. Licking her thumb, she then rubbed his cheek until she pronounced, "Gone." She leaned in, eyes closed, and scented him. "You smell so good."

Beck's skin tingled. It was difficult not to go straight to horny around her. Hell, why not?

Because they needed to talk. And talk would lead to trust. Trust was important before they could take this relationship further.

Setting her mug on the coffee table, Daisy then took his and set it aside. She climbed onto his lap and kissed him. Chocolate and winter, that was her flavor. She was sinuous and warm and so soft under his roaming hands. Beck glided his hands up her back and around to cup under her breasts. She didn't balk at that touch, so he spread his fingers over the small curves. He wanted to lick them.

Too fast.

But he sensed if she moved a little bit closer, she'd feel his need because he now had an erection that wouldn't stop.

Pressing his palms to her cheeks, he stopped her deep kiss. "We have to go slower," he said. "Just until…"

"I get it. You're the ghost wolf. I have a lot of questions."

He nodded. "Hand me my mug."

Chapter 10

An hour later they sat beside one another on the floor before the fire, their backs to the couch, their feet tangled together. Beck hadn't let go of Daisy's hand the whole time. She didn't ever want him to let her go.

He'd explained it all. It was fantastical. And that was saying a lot, considering Daisy's heritage. She thought she'd seen and heard it all.

In the immediate days following his father's murder, a streak of revenge had coursed through Beck. And yet, he was not the sort to commit retaliatory violence. Sure, he sought the hunter who had killed his father. But to kill him? Never. There had to be a way to prevent him from killing other wolves. He'd wanted to instill fear into the hunter—all hunters—and perhaps even save a few gray wolves in the process.

But he hadn't known how to do that. So he'd gone to a faery.

Faeries were not the first choice a person should go to for help. Daisy knew that too well. She'd grown up listening to her parents tell the tale of how they had met. How Malakai had been cursed by a malicious faery, and how her mother had been cursed as a leenan sidhe—a faery who fed on the vita of others until they literally died—because she'd broken off an affair with the Unseelie king, Malrick.

One should never dabble with faery magic without certain knowledge that it could never end well.

Daisy believed that Beck had not known what he was getting into when the faery had offered to give him supernatural ability to shift into something that would frighten mortal men.

"What did she ask in return?" she asked now that Beck had laid it all out.

"I'm not sure."

Clasping his hand against her chest, she nuzzled her head against his shoulder. "Beck, faeries never give away their boons. There is always a return favor in exchange."

"I know that. She wants a favor, but she didn't specify. She doesn't want repayment until I've accomplished my task."

"Which is?"

He quieted and looked down at their clasped hands. "You know. I…wanted revenge for my father. A life for a life."

"You said you couldn't imagine killing another."

"I can say that to you now. But in the days after my father's death?"

She nodded. That he'd confessed such a thing was immense. Awful, but trusting. She wouldn't question him for having murderous thoughts at a time when grief had surely overwhelmed.

"I did it when I was grieving," he explained. "I could never harm another person. Even the man who killed my father. It would make me as evil as him."

She kissed his knuckles and smoothed her thumb over his warm skin. That he was able to think like that now, with his father only dead a few months, was remarkable. She wagered whether any of her brothers would hold a death wish infinitely if someone took Malakai Saint-Pierre's life.

"Will you ever forgive the hunter?"

"Forgive him?"

"Seems the thing to do to close the grieving process. Maybe. I don't know."

"You don't know. And I have grieved. So let's drop it, okay?"

"Sorry." Who was she to suggest proper ways to grieve? Though she suspected Beck had not gone through the grieving process because his claim to have done so had been defensive.

"You didn't seem right after you'd shifted to *were* form in the forest," she said. "You stumbled."

"Lately I'm totally racked after a shift. It's weird. Usually I feel more alive and vital after a shift."

"As you should."

"Shifting to the ghost wolf drains me."

"There's always a price to pay for magic. Beck, what if continuing to shift to the ghost wolf kills you?"

"I'm fine, Daisy." He pounded his chest with a fist. "Feel better than ever now that I've rested."

"Exactly. You shouldn't have to rest after shifting from werewolf. That's not normal."

Brushing off her concern, he stood, picked up the empty mugs and padded into the kitchen. "You don't need to worry about me. I'm not exactly a normal werewolf, if you hadn't already noticed."

He'd tossed up an emotional barricade. But Daisy allowed it. She wanted to tender his trust with care. And really, she was no expert on compassion. She was most comfortable hanging with the men and practicing duels with Kelyn. Emotional support? That was out of her skill set. But even so, she wanted to be there for Beck because it didn't seem like he had anyone else to confide in.

"So you're going to keep scaring the hunters?" she called toward the kitchen.

He paused from placing the mugs in the dishwasher, glancing toward the window over the sink, darkened by the night. He didn't answer her.

Daisy wasn't sure she wanted to hear his answer. Did he believe his own words that he could never kill? She prayed that he did. But that wasn't the problem, was it? Maybe the ghost wolf had plans of its own?

"It's almost midnight," he offered, returning to stand over her. He gave her a hand, and she stood. "Probably should be getting you back to your car."

She nodded. He'd hit a limit on sharing. She was cool with that.

"If I invite you over for supper again," she asked, "will you stay for dessert?"

"I promise I will. I'm sorry for the quick escape the other day."

"It's cool. It's gotta be kind of freaky dating me."

"Because of the big bad wolf who is your dad?"

"I know you respect him. But you have to also understand if I don't push back at my dad now, he may never let me go. I'm his only daughter. I'm sure it's tough to see me in the arms of an unfamiliar wolf."

"Who is not in a pack."

"You don't think you'll ever join a pack?"

"Maybe I'll start my own someday?"

She kissed him. "It doesn't bother me that you're a lone wolf. So don't let my dad's voice have any room in your head, okay?"

"Too many other voices in there right now as it is." He handed her her coat, and she hung her snow pants over an arm. Didn't need them for the ride home. As they strode outside to the truck, Beck said, "You promise you won't tell anyone I'm the ghost wolf?"

She nodded. "But I still need to do the story for the competition. This is a chance for me to get a job, Beck."

"Daisy."

"You can't understand what it would mean to me. My father believes I should never work. And I don't have to, thanks to the investments he's made in my name. But I'll always feel tied to him, like I owe him. Do you see now what making my own money would mean to me?"

"Sure, but isn't an internship an unpaid position?"

"Initially, but I plan to quickly prove my worth and earn a paying journalist position. Beck, I didn't go to college. I have no real-world job skills. This is the best I can do."

"So it's got to be the ghost wolf?"

"I've put a lot of time into it already. I need to do it in a manner in which the humans won't ever believe the wolf is a real, living creature. Maybe some figment drunk hunters are conjuring? Like Fenrir reimagined in their wildest nightmares?"

"That's an interesting angle."

"I promise no one will ever know it's you."

"Especially your family?"

"Deal." She slid into the truck, and when Beck leaned up she bent to meet his kiss. He hadn't pulled on a jacket. She pulled off a long strand of pink hair from his sweater.

He took it from her. "I'm fascinated about the faery in you. Promise you'll tell me about that next time we meet?"

She nodded. "Tomorrow night. I'll make steak."

"Woman, you spoil me."

"It's all part of my devious plan."

"To make me like you?"

She nodded and kissed him.

* * *

Dessert was chocolate cake drizzled with caramel. Beck ate all three pieces Daisy offered him. The mood felt much lighter this time around. He didn't plan to suddenly bolt for the door. Spending time with Daisy did distract him if he allowed it. So he did.

"Leave the dishes," she said, grabbing his hand and leading him to the couch. "So how is your shop coming?" she asked as he sat beside her. "Didn't you say you wanted to open it to the public?"

"For as many cars as I have to work on just by word of mouth, it'll be another year before I can consider opening to the public. It's nice work. Keeps me busy."

"When you're not chasing after hunters? How do you feel today? Still weak from the shift?"

"Nope, I'm at one hundred percent. It's only immediately after the shift that I'm weak."

"Well, I hope it doesn't get worse. Do you want me to ask my mom about faery bargains? It worries me that you didn't have to repay the faery who gave you this ability."

"I don't want you to worry about me, Daisy." He kissed her again because he didn't want to get into all that was wrong in his life. Seeking her heat, he pulled her onto his lap. "Let's talk about you," he suggested. "You said you'd tell me about your faery side. So can you shift to wolf or faery? Or is it a combination thing?"

"It's an either/or thing. Wolf shift, or faery shift. I prefer being wolf. But lately things have been complicated."

"Like how?"

Daisy shifted on the couch to sit with her knees drawn up to her chest. She wrapped her arms about her legs. He sensed her closing up, much like he had just done, so he slid closer and tilted his head onto her shoulder. She smelled warm and homey, like the chocolate cake she'd made for dessert. Sexy.

"Tell me?" he said and toyed with a curl of her hair.

She slid her hand up around his neck and pushed her fingers into his hair. This comfortable embrace felt like perfect Saturday afternoons and summer nights that he never wanted to end. And if she would confide in him, that would mean so much.

"It's all screwed up," she said. "My shifting. I should have control of it. Should be able to shift like my brother Blade does. He can shift to vampire with wings. It's the most incredible thing to see."

"A vampire with wings? Can he fly like that?"

Daisy nodded. "Add in the fangs, and he's a threat every man should take seriously."

"Not someone I want to mess with."

"For sure. I'd take on my father before Blade any day. Trust me on that one." She tightened her grip about her legs. "But me. Lately I try to shift to faery and I might get a wing out, but then—and this is so embarrassing—my wolf tail pops out. And I can't seem to control it. I go for were-wolf and it happens for a while, but then it's like the faery doesn't want the wolf out so it comes over me. And vice versa. If I'm flying around with wings, suddenly the wolf wants out. Have you ever dropped from in the air, shifting as you fell, to land in a sprawl on the ground as a wolf?"

"Ouch."

"Yes. And embarrassing. That's why I haven't told anyone in my family. You can't tell anyone this, Beck."

The desperation in her voice made him ache for her.

"I won't. But would it help if you could talk to someone in the know?"

"Who?"

"Your mother is faery."

"But not wolf. And since she's lived in the mortal realm for so long—since before my birth—she's not up on all stuff Faery."

"Isn't there something like faery witch doctors?"

"Faery healers? Sure, but I don't know of any in the area. Oh, Beck."

He put an arm around her shoulders, granting her a closeness he sensed she needed. "Maybe it's just growing pains?"

"I don't know. That should have happened a long time ago at puberty. I'm a grown woman. I should have this all figured out by now. I can't talk to my mom about it, or my dad."

"What about Blade? If he's the same as you…"

"I don't know. Blade and I are close. I am with all my brothers. But it feels kind of squicky to me to ask any of them about this problem."

"It's not like you're asking them about sex, right?"

She smiled. "No. And I don't know why I should feel this way. As a girl who grew up in a household full of men, I've seen more naked penis than I probably should have for a lifetime. My family is into the natural state."

"Interesting. Do you think there's any way I can help you?"

"You didn't want me to worry about you, and I certainly don't want you to worry about me. I have to figure this out on my own. But thanks for asking. It means a lot. I'm glad I told you this. Did you feel relieved when I saw you shift from the ghost wolf?"

"I did. So if I asked you to show me your wings, would that be a no-go?"

"That would involve me taking off my shirt."

"Ah." He slid his palm down her arm, the thick sweater loose and warm. Turning his head, he kissed her at the base of her ear and she squirmed closer. "And what is it I've heard about faeries and their wings?"

Daisy nuzzled in and kissed him. "They help us to fly, silly."

"Right, but I thought there was something about wings and sex?"

She took his hand and placed it over her chest. His fingers conformed over her small breast, and Daisy sucked in a breath. If he could just hold her like this forever…

"To touch a faery's wings," she whispered, "is a sexual invitation. It would feel as if you were running your fingers over my skin. But the more intimate areas of my skin, if you know what I mean."

Beck nudged his forehead against hers. He breathed against her lips. "Then when you feel the time is right to show me your wings, I will be honored. And probably horny."

He captured her laugh with a kiss, and they fell backward onto the couch. Daisy stretched out her legs and he fit his hips against hers, lying on top of her but not putting his full weight on her. He lingered in the kiss. She pushed her hands up under his sweater, finding the rigid abs, and walked her fingers over the landscape.

"What are you doing?" he whispered.

"Counting your six-pack."

"All there?"

"I think there could be eight."

Pushing up on one hand, he used his other hand to tug off the sweater and toss it to the table beside the couch. "How's that?"

"Oh, yeah." Daisy pressed her palms to his abdomen and traced the muscles from side to side, then followed the ridges that veed down toward his jeans. He sucked in a breath at the erotic sensation. "I like these ridges," she said. "They are so sexy. Leads my eye toward—"

"Mischief?" he finished.

She tucked a finger behind the waistband of his jeans. "Maybe."

He pushed up her sweater, and Daisy lifted her hips so it would slide up more easily. When the soft red yarn reached just below her breasts, he settled onto her again and followed his curious hands with kisses. Pressing a kiss to her ribs, he placed another higher, and again, a little higher.

Daisy closed her eyes and clutched at his hair. Her body felt taut and warm. She tilted back her shoulders, lifting her breasts higher. Seeking, silently pleading.

"No bra. You make it hard to go slow, Daisy."

"You're doing just fine." He painted his tongue along the underside of her breasts, and she sucked in a breath. "I like that."

Sliding his hands up under her sweater exposed her nipples to the air. The aureoles tightened. Beck sucked in one hard tip, lazily curling his tongue about it. She tasted like summer, winter and autumn all rolled into one. His knees bracketed her thighs, squeezing her snuggly. The eight-pack she'd counted rubbed her belly and mons, and his erection angled against her body.

She tucked her fingers into his jeans waistband, the tip of her finger skimming his cock head. Beck jerked up. "Whoa!"

"I'm sorry. Are my fingers cold?"

"No, I'm just… You're in a hurry."

"You think so? I just assumed… Well, you're a handsome guy. I'm sure you've had many girlfriends and lovers…"

"Yeah, but Daisy, that's all they've been—lovers. Not worth spending time with and getting to know. I don't put you in the same category as any of the women I've previously seen."

"I'm not sure how to take that."

"It's good. And because you're different, I want this to go slower, but fast enough that I don't injure myself trying to hold back." He slid a hand down her arm and to her wrist. She pulled her fingers from his waistband. "It's going to happen between us. Sooner rather than later. But let's play it cool for tonight. The moon *is* full in three nights."

"That means in two nights," she started, but didn't have to finish.

Beck knew exactly what she was thinking. The nights preceding and following the full moon, the werewolf wanted out. Most werewolves restricted themselves to just the one night of the full moon. When they lived so close to humans, it was dangerous to let their beast out more often than that. And in order to keep back the beast on those two nights, their bodies needed to be sexually sated. So sex was a given.

Beck dipped his head near hers, their cheeks brushing. "So, uh, how about Saturday night?"

He was asking for sex before the full moon. He couldn't bear a refusal, and he knew he was being forward. He adored Daisy. And he needed more of her kisses and her hands and tongue roaming over his skin.

And if he didn't satisfy his wolf's need for sex, the ghost would come out.

"You don't have to get all ghosty on Saturday night?"

He shook his head. "I'll save it for the full moon." He hoped. He kissed her breast, then nuzzled his cheek against her skin and between her breasts. "I'm not trying to push things, Daisy."

"I know that. I think I'm the one who is more eager."

"Trust me, I'm eager." He ground his hips against hers. "I thought you noticed that?"

"I did. Can we play it by ear until then?" she asked.

"Of course."

"I want to see you tomorrow night."

She hadn't refused him. Whew. "How about a little pond hockey?"

"Really? You think you can take me on?"

"It'll be worth the try."

"Then game on. I'll come to your place after supper. I've got a standing dinner with my grandmother."

"Your grandmother is the werewolf married to the vampire, right?"

"Yes, Blu and Creed. Is it all right if I get to your place around eight?"

"I'm not going to get any work done tomorrow because I'll be thinking about you all day."

His kiss was soft, lingering. A perfect end to a perfect evening.

Chapter 11

Moonlight shimmered on the ice-covered pond on which Beck skated back and forth with a shovel, pushing the light snow cover to the banks. Hockey sticks jutted from where he had jammed the handles into the snow.

Daisy settled onto a snowbank, wiggling her hips to form a seat in the moldable snow, and laced up her ice skates. Within minutes she landed on the ice, hockey sticks in hand.

"You got a puck?" she asked as Beck stabbed the shovel into a snowbank.

He pulled out a thick black rubber disk from his pocket and tossed it onto the ice. His grin curled deliciously. "I'll take it easy on you."

"If that's the way you want to play it. I sure as hell am not a duster," she said, using the term players called one who spent all his time on the bench. She tossed him a hockey stick; he caught it in a gloved hand. "I did grow up with four younger brothers. I would have worn my hockey skates, but they're in Dad's shop for a good sharpening. These will serve."

Her figure skates glinting with flashes of the moonlight, she performed a graceful spin on the rough surface. Growing up in Minnesota made it natural for a girl to take to the ice in the winter, no matter her breed. Daisy could probably skate better than she could fly. She preferred that method to travel, that was for sure.

"Where are the goals?" she asked.

Beck pointed to a nook he'd carved out of the snow in the bank just behind him, and then to a thicket of dried weeds at pond center, around which the ice had grown. Without warning, he took off, stick to the puck, blades shaving the ice.

"Boys," she muttered. "Gotta be careful, Daisy. Don't show him up. Too much."

Yet she could not allow him to win. Such benevolence would screw with the very fiber of her existence.

Going after the puck, Daisy easily stole it away with a sweep of her stick. She made a long shot and landed the goal.

"I let you have that one." Beck skated around her casually, his body leaning into the curve. He wore but a sweater, jeans and gloves. His muscled thighs swept him across the ice like a pro. Claiming the puck from the snowy goal, he shot it toward her.

Daisy returned it to him. They skated, zigzagging toward the goal in the center of the pond. When they neared the thicket of weeds, Daisy swerved in front of Beck, claiming the puck, and deftly backhanded another goal.

"Stop letting me win," she said over her shoulder as he retrieved the puck.

"Deal."

This time the steal was a little harder, but Daisy was not beyond some body checking to get the prize. Slamming her body against Beck's, she knocked him off balance, and his stick arm wavered. She made another shot, achieving the goal.

"Hat trick!" she announced.

Beck's smirk had disappeared. Daisy thought he might have even growled. About time. She craved a challenge.

Skates cutting the ice, they dashed across the surface jockeying for the puck. Daisy kept her body tight and her center low to increase her speed and make herself a smaller target. Beck's body nudged hers, but she sensed he still wasn't giving it his all. If he knew how many bruises she'd collected battling her brothers in a Saint-Pierre family game, he wouldn't be so gentle.

She liked that he respected her. But he was still going down.

"You've got the moves." Beck managed to finagle the puck away from her. "I'd hate to see you with the hockey skates."

She checked him again, but he swung his stick and slammed it onto the ice, cutting in on the puck. With a flick of his wrist, he made the goal in the weeds.

"Score!" He circled the goal with arms raised triumphantly.

Yeah, boys always liked to make sure everyone knew when they'd done something like make a goal. Or beat their sister at chess. Or managed to win a four-legged race through the forest. Yes, wolves could stand on their back legs and punch the air with a triumphant forepaw.

Daisy shook her head and chuckled. "I'm ahead by two."

"Yeah?" Beck skated beside her, guiding the puck with his stick. "Let's make it interesting."

"What do you have in mind?"

"Next one to score a goal gets a kiss from the other."

Sounded like a win-win situation to her. But when challenged, she took it seriously.

Dashing in for the steal, Daisy commandeered the puck momentarily. Beck shoved her hard, jockeying for the puck. He sliced it away from her. She kept on him, skates

spitting up ice in her wake and arms pumping to gain on
him. She checked him with a body slam, and he returned
the shove. Hard. But it didn't set her off balance.

Thrilled he was finally giving her his all, Daisy chased
him with her stick gliding near his. He slapped the puck
back and forth, and she slid in for the steal, and with a shift
of her hip, bumped his thigh. Racing toward the goal, she
felt him on her, his stick in her peripheral view.

Smiling at the brisk kiss of winter against her face, and
the thrill of the moment, Daisy flicked the stick. Beck slid
in and blocked the puck from what should have been a winning glide across the ice toward the goal.

He shifted position, facing her, their sticks to either
side of the puck. Heartbeat racing, Daisy growled defi-
antly yet playfully.

"Is that so?" he said on a light tone. "I don't think so,
Saint-Pierre. This goal's mine."

He slipped the curve of his stick against the puck, and
Daisy shoved him hard. His stick left the ice. Daisy commandeered the puck and made a long shot for the goal in
the snowbank. The puck slammed into the snow, wedg-
ing in deeply.

"Yes!" Time for the winner's dance. Daisy wiggled her
hips and skated backward, shifting her shoulders in a vic-
tory shimmy. "Oh, yeah, I am so good. I win. I win."

"Competitive much?"

"Always have been. Always will be."

"I think I like you better when you're flirting awkwardly with me."

"Sore loser."

Beck skated up to her, a darkness falling across his
eyes. He looked like one of those imposing goalies that any
player should fear and back down from. Standing straight
from her silly dance, Daisy's mouth fell open. She wasn't

sure what he was thinking, what to say to him. He didn't look too happy.

Just when an apology tickled her tongue, Beck slammed into her body, gripped the back of her kitty-eared cap and pressed his winter-iced lips against hers.

His breath hushed coolly against hers. Daisy's hockey stick clattered onto the ice. She moved up onto her ice skates' toe picks to stand a little taller and keep the exhilarating kiss.

Her arms falling slack she went with the *being held* feeling. Crushed against him by his powerful embrace, she wanted to take what he gave. And his kiss was delicious. Urgent and hot. His tongue traced her teeth, her lips, her tongue. It was a slow, sensual glide that stirred every portion of her being to a jittery spill of desire. Her nipples hardened beneath the thick knit sweater, and her fingers curled within the mittens she wore.

If every game ended in such a reward, she'd sign on with the NHL tomorrow.

"You win," he said against her mouth.

"I most certainly do. Screw the game. I want more."

She tugged him back down for another kiss. Picking her up, Beck glided toward the snowbank where he'd carved out the goal and, tilting forward, he deposited Daisy onto the shoveled heap. He went down with her, jamming his knees into the snowpack on either side of her legs. Biting off his gloves one by one, he dropped them onto the snow.

His warm hands bracketed her cool cheeks as he lifted her up for another kiss. This one wasn't going to let her win. She felt as if he were controlling her, and it felt…awesome.

"Wanna play another round?" he asked.

"Of pond hockey?" She tapped his mouth. His lips were burnished red from the chill and their kisses. "That's up to you. Would you rather slap sticks or swap spit?"

"Both sound appealing."

"Really?"

He waited for her to pout, and so she did. And then he tugged her upright and pulled her across the ice, collecting the sticks as he did. "Game over! I'm all for warming up inside with a pink puck bunny."

"Dude, I am no man's puck bunny. They're the silly bits of fluff who hang on the players in hopes of getting lucky."

"So you're saying you don't want to get lucky with me?"

She considered it. "Puck bunny it is."

Daisy raced through the living room and dodged the ottoman, where a patchwork quilt lay strewn. She giggled and headed toward the kitchen. But her plan of evasion was thwarted when Beck slipped around the opposite side of the kitchen and met her near the dining table.

She shrieked playfully as he swept her into his arms and carried her over to the couch. He dropped her onto the plush couch piled with pillows, and she landed on the softness but didn't expect the handsome wolf to follow so closely.

He crouched over her, hands near her shoulders and knees bracketing her legs. "I win."

She supposed he did deserve some small win after she had just kicked his ass at pond hockey. "Deal. You win one silly puck bunny." She scooched up to sit and brushed her hair aside from her face. "Well, not so vapid. Much smarter, I hope. But I suppose being a puck bunny is all about what's on the outside, isn't it?"

"No way. I don't want anyone looking at you."

"So you'll take the tomboy over the bunny?"

"I'll take Daisy Blu, the gorgeous wolf who is not afraid to be herself." He pulled her onto his lap, and she snuggled against his insane heat. "Wanna snuggle?"

"You are a man who knows how to please a woman."

Chapter 12

"The only place is town that sells custom-made shell cartridges is now closed," Sunday said as she strode around the side of the F-150, tugging up her overall straps on each shoulder.

"So whoever made the glass shot probably got it in the Twin Cities."

"Or could have ordered it online," she suggested. "What you're dealing with is custom-made. I'm guessing its origin is paranormal, not human-made. I mean, if the pellets were glass filled with silver?" Sunday shook her head.

Beck rubbed the grease smear on her cheek. "Thanks, Sunday. I appreciate you looking into that for me. You heading home?"

"Yep. It is the night before the full moon." She winked, and strode into the back room that was more a storage for everything Beck couldn't find a place for than a neat employee lounge.

Sunday, the familiar, and her husband, Dean Maverick, the werewolf. How those two ever got together was beyond Beck. But they'd been together a long time, so it proved that opposites really could attract.

And he certainly didn't need reminding that it was the night before the full moon. His breed, for reasons beyond him, needed sexual fulfillment the night before and after

the full moon. Well, they didn't *need* it. If they did not re-
~~spond to the carnal pull, their werewolf would come out.~~
Nothing wrong with that. Only, living so close to humans,
the werewolves tended to let their wild side out one day
a month—on the full moon. Otherwise they risked too
much if ever seen.

Perhaps mating with Daisy tonight would bring them
closer. He hoped to have sex with her, but he seriously did
not want to push. They both needed sex tonight, but just
because they did didn't mean they had to take it from one
another. He didn't want to do anything to screw up this
new relationship.

Nor did he want to bring the wrath of Malakai Saint-
Pierre knocking on his door.

Beck blew out a breath. "I'll take things as they want
to go tonight. Let her call the shots." He grinned to think
about the shots that woman had taken last night.

Playing hockey with Daisy had been a thrill and a surprise. The chick was competitive. And a great player. She
was no puck bunny, but he wondered if she'd be okay with
the term puck faery?

The idea of giving over some of his control to a woman
was novel, but it didn't feel entirely out of left field.

He headed into the garage office, where he kept a computer. He'd search for silver sales in Minneapolis and St.
Paul. He had no idea how to track down this hunter, but he
wasn't about to stop until he'd found him and made him
pay for tearing his family apart.

Daisy set aside the log she'd printed out from the paranormal forum. She'd had the idea to go in as someone
looking to hunt werewolves, and who was looking for the
best weapon. She'd gotten all sorts of replies, but no silver shot in glass capsules. Yet. Beck had thought it was
advanced technology. Maybe Stryke could help. He knew

enough about most things that he may have an idea regarding a lead.

She couldn't think about work right now. It was date night. With the one man she couldn't stop thinking about. Dreaming about. Wanting to kiss, touch and…

"Have sex with," she said, and rubbed her palms together in expectation. "I am so ready for you, Beck. I hope you're ready for me."

She sorted through the clothing on the steel bar suspended from the high ceiling. Her grandmother had offered to let her go through her closet yesterday during dinner, but Daisy had been in Blu's closet before. It looked like some kind of costume warehouse for every mood, color and emotion a woman could ever have. That chick had the clothes.

"Grandma is so spoiled." She trailed her fingers down her few pieces of clothing. Guess that was possible when Blu's husband was a nine-hundred-year-plus vampire who had acquired a vast fortune over his centuries.

Growing up in her family, Daisy had learned the value of taking care of one's things and not needing something just because a person wanted it. She had a few things she adored, and the rest were functional for when she worked on a sculpture or was out reporting. Sure, she was set for life thanks to her father's investments in her name, but…

"I have to show him I can take care of myself."

Her fingers trailed over the soft red sweater that featured a narrow black marabou tuft around the V collar. It was angora, and she loved wearing it without a bra, feeling the übersoft fabric caress her skin. It was the sexiest thing she owned.

"Perfect."

A pair of black leggings and some black riding boots with skull-studded metal buckles at the knees finished the look. Casual yet sensual.

Beck liked her this way? Not all dolled up like a puck bunny? She'd bought that mostly. But she still sensed he wouldn't mind if she showed him her softer side.

"Do I have a soft side?"

Panic rushed heat into her chest, but she quelled the sudden anxiety by pressing a palm over her heart.

"We'll find out tonight."

Already her inner wolf squirmed in anticipation. Her faery half could care less. This night before the full moon, the werewolf wanted release. So part of her pranced about in an attempt to ramp up her adrenaline, get her to answer the feral call, while another part looked forward to quelling the werewolf the only way it could—with touch, taste and erotic connection.

She needed sex until she was sated. If she'd had a boyfriend who did not know she was werewolf, then he'd always marveled at her incredible horniness and was raring to please her. If no boyfriend, she was not beyond a one-night stand, but she generally drove into the city to find someone she would never again see. It was her nature. She needed to answer this call.

And tonight was going to be perfect. Or she hoped, very close to something wonderful.

Beck assumed Daisy would have eaten by the time she arrived. He set out some wine but wasn't sure what else he should provide. He scanned his cupboards. Ripple chips or cheese crackers sounded wrong. And the tin of BBQ-coated almonds was so not romantic. He supposed cheese and fruit would have been appropriate to set the mood, but he wasn't that talented of a grocery shopper.

Cheese crackers it was.

A clench in his gut suddenly bent him before the kitchen sink. He gripped the stainless steel and closed his eyes, fighting the odd wave of what didn't feel painful, but what

was beyond the usual *let me out* pangs he got from his
werewolf.

He felt his bones shift slightly and shook his head. "No.
Not tonight." While normally he felt the urge to shift the
night preceding the full moon, he could always control it.
This was insistent. "What the hell?"

If he shifted against his will, that would be a new one.
And dangerous. He didn't want to shift to the ghost wolf
when Daisy was around.

The twinge of whatever it was subsided with a tug down
his spine. Beck straightened and flexed his fingers in and
out of fists. "Whew!" Exhaling, he prayed he could keep
it under control.

The doorbell rang. He slapped a palm to his bare chest.
He'd been in the middle of dressing when it had occurred
to him he might need to entertain the woman and had gone
in search of wine.

Halfway to the door, the werewolf again gripped his insides and demanded release. Beck slammed a palm to the
front door and yowled. He must fight the twist inside his
body. He dropped to his knees. His hand began to shift and
he frantically shook it, forcing it back into human form.

Again the doorbell rang, followed by a knock. "Beck?"

"Daisy." He gripped the doorknob. The wolf that wanted
release suddenly fought against the *were* that he was, the
man who needed sensual touch—hell, sex—to tame that
wolf. Drawing in a breath through his nose, he smelled the
sweet pink faery wolf on the other side of the door. He got
a hard-on like that. "Ah, shit."

The door opened against his back. He sat on the floor,
legs bent and toes digging into the rug. His senses were
dialed to ultraalert, and Daisy's sweetness spilled across
his skin like a summer breeze warming his flesh and stirring him to a moan. A wanting, needy moan.

What the hell? He couldn't act like this in front of her.

He did not want to scare her, or allow her to think he was some kind of freak. She had to leave.

He slapped his hand against the door, closing it. But she was already inside. Standing there in some thigh-hugging black pants. Metal skulls stared at him from the tops of her leather boots. And up over her winter coat, he eyed the pretty pink waves spilling to her elbows like a treat. Kitty ears capped her head. Those silly pom-poms at the ends of the strings looked like a toy he needed to bat at.

Yeah, to play with the kitty. Mmm…

"Beck, what's wrong?"

"Daisy, I'm sorry." He yelped as an insistent punch to his libido goaded him to jump up, grab her and push her against the wall. "I— This is not right. Something is happening. I'm not sure I can control it."

"Is it the ghost wolf?"

He shook his head. The last thing he wanted was to be in this position before a woman. Unsure, unstable and out of control.

"Do you feel the need to shift?"

He shook his head adamantly.

"Yes?"

"Yes. And no. It wants…you."

She pulled the kitty cap from her head and knelt before him. "*It* does?"

He closed his eyes, biting his lip. Not this way. He didn't want the first time with Daisy to be like this. It couldn't be. He'd never forgive himself.

She pressed a palm to his cheek. The sensation of her slightly cool skin to his heated face shocked an erotic zing from there directly to his cock. The main shaft tightened against his jeans.

"Sex?" she whispered.

Ah hell.

Chapter 13

He was suffering. Daisy had seen the same signs with her brothers at times on the night before the full moon when they'd been younger and had been trying to discern the whole *should I shift* or *should I seek a sex partner* thing.

Beck's skin was so hot. His chest glimmered with perspiration. He pushed her hand away and snarled at her. Was he fighting the shift, or fighting the urge to take her in a loveless quick means of satisfying his driving needs?

While the idea of sex without emotion did not appeal at all, Daisy had come here knowing it wasn't going to be a gushy love-filled event. Love wasn't even in the equation yet.

Okay, so it was. Like was the ultimate goal. And she was on a straight path to liking Beckett Severo.

But desire was the issue right now. And her wolf responded to his panting need to repress his desires with her own delicious tangle of desires. Ah, the tangle she had wanted. She wanted Beck. She wanted sex, plain and simple. She simply…wanted.

She pulled off her coat and pushed it aside.

"You can't stay," he said through a tight jaw. "It can't be this way, Daisy. It's not right."

"Beck, your wolf needs to be sated."

His mouth stretched taut. She smoothed a hand down

his chest, glancing over his tight pectorals and to his ridged abdomen. Inside, her wolf stirred, hungry yet patient, if only she would serve it the sensual treats it craved.

"Daisy, please."

She wanted to lean forward and lick his fevered skin, trace her tongue over the ridges of muscles that hardened his frame as if a suit of armor. She wanted to go on the wild ride this uncertain moment promised.

"I want you, Beck. I need this. Don't you desire me?"

"Ah, fuck."

She leaned in closer to his face. Musk and male aroused every nerve ending on her body. Her nipples hardened. Aware her soft sweater brushed against his skin, she leaned in closer and her breasts snugged his chest.

He gripped her hair, holding her back, yet with his other hand he pulled her forward by the hip.

"This excites me. You excite me," she whispered near his ear, then dashed her tongue along his lobe and sucked it into her mouth. "I'm a big girl. I can handle a horny werewolf. You want to try me?"

"Daisy—but it won't be right."

"Who's to say what is right or wrong? We both want something from the other. We do love each other. Do you love me?"

He nodded fervently. "The easy part, right?"

"Right. No like yet."

His hips bucked up against her as she squatted upon his thighs. He clutched her sweater. "So soft," he muttered. "And red. Oh, Daisy…"

"Let's do this," she said. "Fast, furious, and don't stop until we're both satisfied. Yes?"

"You're not going to go away, are you?" He pushed his hands up under her sweater and palmed her breasts. With a moan, he squeezed her nipples.

"Oh, hell no," she said. "And you don't want me to leave, either. Do you?"

He shook his head frantically.

"Let's make this right. There's no other man I'd rather be with right now than you."

"Same. I…I want you, Daisy. Beyond my werewolf's needs. I swear."

"I know that. So let's get it on."

Daisy thrust her breasts forward, giving him what he wanted, and greedily taking the exquisite pleasure of his touch. She tugged off her shirt, and Beck hissed at the sight of her bare skin. He braced an arm across her back as he pushed her down onto the rug before the door and bent his head to her breasts. Laving at her nipples, one and then the other, he slicked them with his hot tongue. Suckling them hard and then kissing and licking all over her breasts. She squirmed under his ministrations, and pulled him closer with fingers through his hair.

"Not on the floor," he suddenly said, and lifted her with one arm.

Daisy wrapped herself about Beck's torso and kissed him aside the neck as he marched down the hallway. He panted heavily. Still fighting the shift, surely. She wanted to tame him, yet at the same time, keep him wild.

The bedroom was dark, save a beam of moonlight that sifted through the sliding glass doors on the opposite end. A patchwork quilt and mounds of pillows lured them toward the king-size bed. It looked so inviting that Daisy jumped from his arms and sat on the edge of the bed, then fell backward against the pillows.

"Come here, wild one," she said, crooking a finger at him.

"You are…" He shook his head as he approached, unzipping his jeans. "Much wilder than me. Beneath your bookish exterior…"

"You did want me to flirt with you."

"That I did."

He dove for her, landing on all fours above her, which made her giggle. He cupped one of her breasts and gave it a quick lick before moving up to kiss her neck, and up under her chin until finally his mouth landed on hers, and he groaned into her as he ground his hips against hers.

His erection rubbed against her mons, and with a wiggle of her hips, Daisy positioned herself to feel the hard rod against her sensitive apex.

"Oh, yeah." Threading her fingers into his hair, she took his rough and wanting kiss. Everything about his urgency excited her, made her want to rush to the finish line right along with him. As if they tracked the forest on four paws, she would run with this wolf through the night. "Condom?" she suddenly thought to ask.

He nodded and from a drawer beside the bed pulled out a crinkly package and set it on the pillow.

"Now that's sexy." She slid a hand down his hard abs and farther, over his jeans to cup his erection. It was wide and so hard. "Another stick for this puck bunny to handle."

"Woman, you touch it, you can't put it back on the shelf and walk away."

"Oh, I won't."

Daisy toed off her boots, and they dropped to the hardwood floor with a double *clunk*. Beck reached for his fly, but she stopped him. "Let me."

He hovered above her, in a plank position, allowing her to shove the jeans down his hips. His penis sprang out and landed on her thigh, the hot, wide head of it flaming her skin. She gripped it firmly, and his moan played a wanting melody above her thundering heartbeats.

Hips rocking, he slid his cock up and down in her grasp.

"You're so hard, Beck," she said with admiration. "I can't wait to feel you inside me."

"Not until you're ready." He tugged down her leggings, and she shimmied to wiggle them off. Now they were both naked, and their skin put off intangible steam.

Beck bent to kiss her breasts, gently, pulling at the nipple and then letting it spring from his mouth to cool in the air that tightened the ruched tip to a diamond.

His explorations journeyed south, his kisses marking her belly and navel, and moving lower, licking and tasting and kissing until his nose tickled along her mons.

"Pink here, too," he said in amazement.

"My hair color *is* natural," she said, following with a giggle. "Mmm..." She gripped his hair loosely as he bowed to kiss along her folds. Head falling back against the pillows, she surrendered to whatever he wished to do. "Yes, do that, you big sexy werewolf."

Spreading out her arms across the pillows, she closed her eyes and fell into the giddy, tingly sensations that coiled up her spine and through her being with every lash of Beck's expertly placed tongue. He tended her on the outside for a bit, and then dove into her, thrusting his tongue as deeply as he could and challenging her need to lay back and experience when all she wanted to do was answer back with equal zeal.

He suckled her and teased at her clit, tendering it carefully even though they were both frenzied by the moon. The innate need to connect, to become one with another. To satisfy the carnal within that would otherwise set free their werewolves.

Shoulders pressing into the pillows, Daisy felt the orgasm swirl within her core. She didn't want to fight it, and wouldn't. "Oh, yes!"

Hips bucking as her lover kissed her deeply, Daisy

soared into the climax. Beck withdrew to allow her to ride the bliss. Yet he maintained contact, his forefinger gently tracing over her humming clit, while his kisses again moved up her belly and to her breasts. And when his tongue lashed her nipple, the subsiding orgasm swelled and she cried out at the bonus climax.

"Wild wolf," he murmured. "I love the sound of your pleasure. Let me hear it again." He teased a little firmer over her swollen clit, and Daisy's panting breaths increased. "Will you come for me again?"

"Of course I will. But…ohmygodess."

She wanted to ask *what about you?* But the climax hummed too close. And she knew he would get his rewards soon enough. Releasing her voice again, Daisy's body quivered beneath her masterful new lover, a willing recipient of all he wanted her to have.

Holding Daisy in his arms as her body shivered beneath him was amazing. Beck had forgotten about the inner pull to shift. The sex was working. He'd been unsure, had wanted to push her away because he wanted this to be right. But her suggestion that this crazy joining may be right had been on target.

Her sinuous body stretched out alongside his on the bed. Small breasts hugged his chest as she kissed his neck, placing snowflakes here, then there, then moving lower. If she went down on him, he'd lose it too quickly. Every atom in his body was ready to explode. He needed to take his time.

When her fingers wrapped around his cock and slid lower to squeeze at the base, he released a heavy breath. Just what he needed. The woman was well-informed about tending a man's hard-on. He wasn't going to question it, and in fact, he could only applaud. For the moment, the urgency to come had subsided. But not completely. He walked a line between flame and volcanic lava flow. He just had to balance a little longer…

Daisy slicked her fingers between her legs, wetting them, and then slid them in a coil up and down his rod. "You're nice and thick," she purred. "I want you inside me. But first I want to play with you. You like this?"

Her hand had moved up to squeeze under the crown of his cock, where it was supersensitive. Beck's ability to put two words together ceased. Instead he groaned and gripped her hair. When her tongue lashed the head of him, he thought he saw stars, but that was just because he'd squeezed his eyes so tightly he'd captured the moonlight against his irises.

"Daisy…"

She laved up and down his length, slowly, then a little faster, then licking again at that sensitive underside of his crown. She knew exactly how to ignite every pleasure receptor. His inner wolf danced, tamed and unwilling to shift.

He swore and gripped a pillow as her mouth encompassed him as deeply as she could manage. Hips wanting to thrust, he fought to sustain the crazyhummingwant vibes. Right there. Everything hummed just at the surface.

When she reached up and claimed the foil condom packet, he could only groan as he felt her expertly slip the tight sheath over his pulsing cock. Just one more squeeze…

Beck came forcefully. Even as he rode the pleasure, she mounted him.

"Yes," she whispered, and then she settled onto him, sheathing him deeply within the heat of her body, the exquisite, tight walls that hugged and squeezed him. "Again," she commanded.

And with but a few thrusts, she milked him to a shouting orgasm that bucked his hips up and bounced her upon his loins. She rode him until they both cried out with pleasure. His faery wolf collapsed to his side and, legs tangled together, they faced one another with a smile.

He nudged his toes over her ankle bone, teasing at the smoothness. So soft, her skin. "I like your feet."

"Should I be worried you have some weird fetish?"

"I don't know. I just like touching them."

"Works for me."

"I'm thirsty," she said.

"There's wine in the kitchen. I'll be right back." Beck rose and, his hard cock bobbing, wandered across the room. He pulled off the condom and veered toward the bathroom first.

"Nice ass," she commented.

Daisy scampered out to the kitchen and found her naked lover waiting with a glass of wine in hand. He was munching some orange-colored crackers that looked not at all appealing.

The sex had been great. It had fired her adrenaline and stirred up her wild need for more. And what an incredible specimen with whom to get her sex on. She dragged her clawed fingers up his thigh and pressed her belly against his hard, sweat-sheened abs.

Beck tilted the glass toward her lips. Crisp, cool wine slid down her throat. Her lover's hand tweaked her nipple. She grabbed the glass from him and finished the wine before setting it in the sink, then wrapping her legs about his hips and kissing him deeply.

"You taste like winter spiked with frozen grapes," she said to him. "You know winter is my favorite time of year?"

"Really?" He shifted to lean against the counter, and his erection bobbed against the underside of her thigh, teasing, yet it was just nice being held in his arms. "I grabbed another condom when I was in the bathroom. Want to wrestle in the snow?"

"Naked?"

"I'll keep you warm." He waggled his brows. "We can take a hot shower after."

Daisy dropped to her feet, grabbed his hand and headed for the sliding glass doors that opened to the backyard. The bite of cold January air chilled her skin, and the perspiration beading in her hair may have frozen instantly.

She whooped and danced from foot to foot on the snow-covered back porch. Beck whisked her into his arms and jumped, landing them in a soft snowbank on their sides. They sunk into the soft snow, and he tugged her up to sit on top of him.

"It really is cold out here," she said.

"You'll get used to it. Our wolves would love it."

"Yeah, but we're trying to keep the wolves away tonight, remember?" She circled his erection, which was still hard despite the cold. "Hand me that condom." He did, and she rolled it over the thick head of his cock and down the shaft. She didn't wait for his response as she slid onto his erection, hugging him deep within her.

"You feel so good," he crooned. "I could stay inside you forever."

"We'll end up in a puddle," she teased.

He gripped her hips and moved her up and down his cock. "You're the prettiest wolf in the woods. Faery, too."

"Leave the faery out of it," she gasped. "Or she might try to intrude."

"Really?"

"Beck, please." He could never understand how difficult it was for her when her sides constantly battled for the lead.

"Okay, no more talking because I gotta…" And instead of a cry of climax, as her lover achieved orgasm beneath her, he broke into an ecstatic howl.

* * *

Beck carried her inside, tracking snow and water across the living room floor. He didn't set her down until they'd hit the shower and the hot water thawed their icy skin. He kissed her until she thought the only way she could ever survive was through his breath.

Flicking off the water, Beck reached outside the stall and grabbed a big purple towel and handed it to Daisy.

"Wait." She spread the towel wide to reveal the Minnesota Vikings logo that sported a viking head replete with gold, braided locks and purple helmet. "I don't know about this. Seems blasphemous."

"What?"

"Dude, I'm Packers all the way."

"You're a cheesehead?" His abs tensed as he ran a palm over his wet hair. "That's just wrong. Seriously?"

"We so kicked the Vikings' asses this season."

"Oh, no, no, no. This changes everything." He crossed his arms, hair dripping down onto her as they stood in the shower. "If you're a Wisconsin fan, then I don't think I can love you anymore."

Daisy shrugged and handed him the towel. "Easy come, easy go." She stepped out, dripping wet, and performed a hip wiggle. "We're still going to kick your ass in play-offs."

She was grabbed from behind and tossed over his shoulder. "We'll see about that. Play-offs begin right now."

He headed into the bedroom and tossed her onto the bed, wet and giggling. An hour later, the twosome lay in a tangle of sheets. The score? A tie.

"I think I'm sated," she said against his mouth. He kissed her nose, her eyelids, her cheek, her earlobe. "What about you?"

"Oh, yeah. The werewolf will rest peacefully tonight. But I need to ask."

"Yeah?"

"Who's your favorite hockey team?"

"Minnesota Wild, of course."

He hugged her. "Whew. I think I can still love you."

Denton Marx strode the snow-packed yard back and forth, his eyes avoiding the figment that paced so close, yet was unaware of his presence. It had been months. He could not bear to know she was still trapped in the strange middlewhere of nothingness she had once told him about. The Edge. It was a place of unknown horrors inaccessible to him because it was in an entirely different dimension.

He had but one final ingredient he required to prepare the allbeast spell. And though he was not a witch, he knew he could concoct the spell. It simply required following the instructions he'd found in Sencha's grimoire.

He sighed and stopped pacing. She stood there, head bowed and long dark hair tangled about her face. He'd not looked into her eyes. Did not want to, for if he did her expression would eviscerate him.

She was lost. He must rescue her.

No matter the cost.

Chapter 14

They had agreed they would go to different locations tonight. Each werewolf had his or her turf. And as much as Daisy wanted to spend all her time with Beck, joining him in werewolf form could wait. Because as werewolves, they would be compelled to mate. And mating in that form would bond them. For life.

It was a big commitment to make, though the idea of bonding with Beck was appealing. That man was perfection. Daisy had only dated humans and one werewolf. And surprise! That one werewolf, Ryan Addison, had decided to come out to his pack as gay the day after their date.

She really knew how to pick them. Either that, or she turned men gay. Urg.

So she'd only had sex with humans. What Beck brought to the table that humans could not was stamina and a crazy sexy charm that oozed from his every pore. That smile of his! And a certain intimacy that she suspected only came when having sex with her breed. Their senses were heightened; every touch, smell and sound orchestrated their making love.

Not that they'd made love. Last night had been sex. Great sex. And she couldn't wait to do it with Beck again.

She was genuinely starting to like the guy.

"Daisy, you going out soon?"

She'd gone to her parents' house tonight. Theirs was the safest land for shifting. And if she happened upon another werewolf, Daisy knew they'd be family.

"Yes. You going to bed soon, Mom?"

Rissa looked over her shoulder as she strode up the stairs to the bedroom, her cotton-candy-white hair fluffed effortlessly. "You don't want me to answer that, sweetie." And she strode onward.

Daisy blushed.

The Saint-Pierre children had grown up knowing their parents were crazy for one another and had sex. A lot. They were never blatant, but it was obvious that their dad could never get enough of their mother. And on a night when Malakai Saint-Pierre shifted to werewolf? The sex must be interesting.

Daisy quickly erased that thought. She didn't want to know what it was like for her parents.

On the other hand, she had the wings and the faery dust like her mother. Whatever she could glean about a faery's sex habits with a werewolf could only prove helpful to her should she finally master her wings and want to get it on with Beck in that form.

Outside, a wolf howl perked up Daisy's ears. She'd seen Trouble and Stryke go out earlier. They'd been arguing even as they'd been pulling off their shirts. The fur would fly tonight, but in a playful, brotherly way.

Tugging off her shirt and wandering outside to the deck where years ago their father had built an outdoor clothes cubby for the family to leave their things, Daisy shivered. Her breath fogged before her.

"I wish Beck was here." She rubbed her arms, recalling the sexy heat from their rollicks in the snow.

"Tomorrow." She'd see him again.

* * *

Beck's massive ghost werewolf shifted painfully back to *were* form. When normally his muscles reveled in the luxurious stretch and return to human form, it felt as if the ghost wolf had torn his muscles beyond repair, and now they shrank to a ragged mass that pulsed weakly beneath his skin.

He slapped his biceps and thighs to get the blood flowing. His feet ached, and the bones felt as if they'd not aligned and reformed properly as he stepped awkwardly to the tree stump that housed his clothing. He grabbed the folded clothes and then noticed his fingers and nails were bloody.

"What the hell?" He sniffed the blood. It wasn't his own. And it didn't have the gamey feral scent of an animal. "What have I done?"

These modern snowshoes formed from ultra-lightweight metal and straps were far superior to the clunky wooden shoes Denton had used at home.

Home.

He paused in the forest, sighing. Home seemed so far away. Across an ocean, yes. But as well, across centuries. He preferred his time. It was simpler. Safer. A man could barter for things as opposed to being required to always carry a shard of plastic in his pocket. Money was hard to come by without a job, and he wasn't exactly employable. Nor could he devote time to a job.

His job was tracking the werewolf. And these tracks he followed, while large, were yet too small.

He wanted the big white one.

Slipping off her welding mask, Daisy then pulled off the leather apron and shook out her sweaty hair. The creative bug had bit hard after returning this morning from her parents' home. She'd figured a way to do the tail of the sculpture and had been going at it since. She glanced to the clock in the kitchen.

"Six already? I missed lunch. Supper time!"

Some leftover chicken sat in the fridge. But first a shower. Flicking on the TV on the way to the bathroom, Daisy paused by the bathroom door when she heard the news anchor talking about a wounded hunter. She rushed back to the living room, climbed over the back of the couch and grabbed the remote to turn up the volume.

The segment flashed to a reporter interviewing a man sitting in a hospital room. A doctor stood off to the side. The hunter's face had a slash across the cheek and had just been stitched up. Stunned, he didn't know what had hit him. They'd been wolf hunting when all of a sudden, a big white creature growled and he saw the claws and felt the blood. He ran like hell, initially thinking it had been a bear. Until he'd looked back and had seen the manlike wolf.

"The ghost wolf strikes again," the reporter announced with mock dramatics. "Only now it's getting deadly. Will the citizens of Tangle Lake continue to be frightened by the growing danger, or will they band together to hunt what has become an increased threat?"

Daisy gripped her throat, feeling a sickening bubble rise. "They're going to hunt the ghost wolf? Beck couldn't have hurt that hunter. Would he?"

Beck only wanted to scare the hunters. But he'd said the ghost wolf was hard to control. Getting stronger. She'd seen evidence of that the other night when he'd wanted her so desperately.

The phone rang, and she jumped. Another ring rushed her to the kitchen counter to answer the cell phone. "Yes?"

"Daisy, did you see the news?"

"Beck, what happened?"

"I don't know. I came out of the shift with blood on my hands. I've been sitting in the forest half the day. I didn't want to go home. I hurt that man, Daisy. I…"

"Come over here, Beck."

"Yes. I need…"

He needed to talk, and he needed her to hold him. But he couldn't verbalize it. He must be scared as hell that he had committed such an act.

"Come over, Beck. I'll make us something to eat and we can talk."

Chapter 15

Beck raised his hand to rap on Daisy's door, but paused.

"I shouldn't have come here." He turned his back to the door, then turned to face it again. "I need to see her."

He risked pulling her deeper into the weirdness of what he had become. And what had he become? Some kind of monster? Had he really hurt that hunter last night? Oftentimes he could remember snippets of things his werewolf had done. It was a form of self-preservation that he could not recall hunting small animals and eating them, wasn't it?

But last night? He could recall nothing.

And that scared him. And made him feel like he wasn't in control of the situation. He couldn't be weak now. He'd begun something that required follow through. He had to find the man who had killed his father.

But running into Daisy's arms wouldn't do that for him. It would only…

"Feel good."

He touched the door. Images of Daisy in his arms, kissing him, her bare skin against his, were so sweet. He needed sweet right now. Something soft and pink in his life to counter the dark and unsure.

The door opened to a bright smile and gorgeous pink hair. "I thought that was you. You are all kinds of sexy-smelling, you know that?"

She grabbed his hand and led him inside. Beck reluctantly closed the door. And when Daisy turned to kiss him, he kissed her back, but his body wouldn't completely surrender and allow him that treat. The ghost wolf yet hummed within him. And it wanted out. But since he'd sated his desire to run free last night, he was hoping it would be easier to control tonight.

"And you smell like…motor oil?" he tried.

"Sorry. Just got done working with the bike chains. Taking the grease off them. I haven't had time to shower since you called. I popped some enchiladas in the oven, and they should be done in ten minutes. Do you mind if I shower quickly?"

"I like you smelling like motor oil or Mexican food." He pulled her in for a hug. Her arms wrapping about his torso worked like some kind of therapy he hadn't known he needed. Beck buried his face in her pixy flame hair. Her body melding against his was insanely luxurious. It was everything the ghost wolf was not. Sweet, soft and so giving. Not dangerous. Loving.

"Tell me about last night?" Her bright violet eyes blinked up at him.

Raking his fingers through his hair, Beck walked over to the couch with Daisy attached to him, her legs about his hips. He never wanted to stop touching her. She kept his wolf tamed, and he desperately needed that right now.

Sitting, he curled her around to sit with her back against his chest and her bare feet propped on the coffee table. He wrapped his arms around her, bumping his fists together over her stomach.

"I don't remember anything," he confessed.

"Nothing?" She tilted a look back at him, her eyelashes dusting his cheek. "Is that weird for you? I mean, I can usually recall bits and pieces from my werewolf's adventures."

"I can, too. But since I've been shifting to the ghost wolf…nothing."

"I think you should give this gift back to the sidhe who granted it to you. It seems as though it's getting stronger." She turned on his lap and met his gaze. "More powerful?"

He hated to admit it, but he was losing control of it. He must be if he'd attacked a hunter.

"He was okay though, right?" he asked. "The guy on the news?"

"I think so. Looked like he'd had stitches. Do you always get that close to them?"

"I don't think so. I just scare them. They run. My werewolf feels some sort of triumph. Everything is good."

"Except not anymore."

He bowed his forehead to her shoulder. She stroked his cheek. The tenderness shamed his inner wolf, yet his *were* tilted closer to her.

"Daisy, you're so good to me. I feel safe with you. I know that sounds weird, coming from a guy."

"I understand. It's become something you hadn't expected. Bigger."

He nodded.

Turning on his lap, she dipped her forehead to his and bracketed his face with her warm palms. A few breaths. The touch of her mouth against his wasn't quite a kiss, but so much more. An understanding. The silence was comforting, because it was accompanied by the calm pulse of her heartbeats.

"Will you talk to the faery who did this to you?" she asked.

Beck sighed. "I can't. It's not finished yet."

"When will it be finished? When the ghost wolf has killed?"

"You know I don't want that."

"You obviously can't control it. Whether or not you want it isn't key here. Be smart, Beck."

"I will be. I have to be. But I can't give up looking for the man who killed my father. I won't. I refuse."

"No, you shouldn't. But maybe you need to make a new plan?"

"Yeah, I don't know." He stroked her hair. "Can we just be together tonight and not talk about the ghost wolf?"

"I thought you wanted to talk about this?"

"I do. We just did. I don't know, Daisy. This is tough for me. I feel like you're pushing me." He leaned forward, catching his elbows on his knees and his forehead against his palms.

"Do you know you can trust me to tell me anything?"

He nodded and sighed. "I don't trust easily, Daisy."

She nuzzled her nose along his jaw and up to his earlobe, and whispered, "Trust me."

"I do trust you. But I don't want you to get hurt by trusting me."

"That's up to me to decide whether or not I want to trust you. And you know that I do."

Something dinged in the kitchen, and Daisy jumped off his lap and skipped toward the oven. "Supper's ready!"

After supper Daisy excused herself to take a shower, because even if Beck didn't mind the motor oil that smelled as if she'd dipped the tips of her hair in it, she did. She was just rinsing off when the shower curtain slid on the metal bar and Beck stepped into the tub, naked.

He moaned near her ear and tugged her against his body, sliding his hand down her slick belly to land his fingers at the apex of her thighs. "Now you smell like candy. Makes me want to eat you up, but you fed me so much."

"I do like to cook. My one feminine grace."

"You are all woman, Daisy."

His fingers worked lazily at her clit, and she jutted back

her hips and shifted her feet wider to allow him access. She slapped her palms to the wet tile wall. His other hand cupped her breast, massaging, softly tweaking and squeezing. She wiggled against his hard cock, until it nuzzled between her thighs.

"That's nice," she said. "Slow like that."

"I want you facing me. Turn and sit on that ledge."

The ledge at the back of the tub where she usually propped her head when bathing was just wide enough to sit on comfortably without slipping on the slick surface. Daisy barely got situated when Beck knelt beneath the shower stream and bowed his head to her. He licked his way down to her folds and danced the tip of his hot tongue teasingly, then made his movements more promising, and finally, focused.

She slid a leg over his shoulder and gripped his wet hair. Sucking in her lower lip, she closed her eyes and took what he gave.

Beck rolled to his side and stroked his fingers down Daisy's back. She cooed a murmuring noise that sounded exactly how he felt. Satisfied. Exhausted. Extremely blissed out.

Pale morning light shimmered on her skin. The delicate hairs lifted in the wake of his strokes, then settled. Scents of the candy shampoo, remnants of the sugar cookies they'd eaten for dessert and the erotic aroma of her sex curled in his nostrils.

He had never been happier.

Yet he felt guilty for it. Had he a right to such happiness when his mother was alone and pregnant? When innocent wolves continued to be slaughtered for sport by idiot mortal hunters? When his father's death was yet unavenged?

No. But he wanted to steal a few more moments to himself. Be greedy and bask in Daisy Blu. He had to. He needed this quiet sanctity with her. Because it was a warm respite amidst the darkness that had haunted him lately.

He closed his eyes and held his hand millimeters above her skin. The heat from her rose, pleading him closer.

"You are like no other woman," he said.

She turned to face him. "I hope not."

He chuckled. "You have rammed into me, punched me and kicked my ass on the ice. You cook like freakin' Julia Child. You wear grease smears like some kind of Alexander McQueen fashion statement. Your hair always smells like my favorite childhood memory of candy binges on Halloween night. And…you kiss like you mean it."

She kissed him. Firmly. Intently. "I meant that." Another perfect kiss. "And that one, too."

"I like you, Daisy Blu," he whispered.

It was the truth. And it was real. He liked spending time with her, talking to her, listening to her, just being with her. Definitely stronger than love.

"I like you, too, Beckett Severo. And what are we going to do about that?"

"Do we have to do something about it?" He kissed the tip of her nose. "Let's just go with the like. Take it for what it is, and enjoy it."

"Goddess, but I like you." She nuzzled her head against his collarbone and spread an arm across his torso, finding her place, legs curled up to her stomach, against him. "Do you think it was just the whole moon thing? Us needing one another, and being there for one another, that makes us feel this way?"

This thing he felt for Daisy ran deep within him. And it had been brewing since the first time she'd bumped into him in the forest.

"Do *you* think it's that?" he asked.

She shook her head. "No. This is real. I want it to be real."

"It is, my pink faery wolf."

Closing her eyes, she landed a kiss on his mouth with precision. "One question."

"Shoot."

"Who is Alexander McQueen?"

Beck smirked. "He's some designer guy whom Sunday is always going on about."

"Sunday talks about fashion?"

"She has a serious fetish for all the fashion shows. Plays them all the time when she's working in the shop. She'll talk my head off about sparkly shoes."

"Seriously? Sunday, the one chick who may be more of a tomboy than me?"

"Oh, hell. I did not tell you this."

"Oh, yes, you did. I so have to tease her—"

He kissed her hard enough to steal her words. "You'll go to your grave with that info, or Sunday will never forgive me. Promise."

She sighed. "Fine. But only because I don't want you to get beat on by a girl."

"You're the only girl allowed to beat on me."

She punched his arm gently. He faked a wounded grimace.

Beck smoothed his hand over her back, tracing down the curve of her spine and the fall of her hair. "Show me your wings?"

Her lips parted. She exhaled.

"I mean, if you want to," he said. "What you told me about having trouble shifting… If it's a problem…"

"It could be. If I bring out my wings, the wolf might take over. But I want to show you. Now that we've declared mutual like for one another, you need to know all of me."

She sat up and scooched to the end of the bed, but turned as he leaned up on an elbow. "Promise you won't laugh if it goes wonky?"

"Daisy, the only thing that could ever make me laugh at you is the fact that you are a cheesehead."

"And I have the foam cheese hat to prove it," she said proudly, pointing to a shelf below the clothes rack where, indeed, a bright orange wedge of foam cheese had been tucked. "We are so going to a game together some time. My team will kick your team's ass."

"If that's the way you want to play it. Wings, lover. Stop stalling."

"I've never shown anyone but my family my wings."

"Really? Not even…?"

"Other lovers? Beck, I've only had human lovers. I would never reveal my true nature to them."

"No, that wouldn't be smart." He sat up against the pillows and scruffed fingers through his hair. "I suppose it's not like you can walk down Main Street with them out. Kind of like our werewolves."

"Exactly. I only use my wings when I'm in the forest on my parents' property and feel like flying. But then, I usually get small."

"You can get tiny?" He held up his fingers in a guesstimate of her size.

"About twice the length of your hand," she said. "You've never seen a faery small before?"

He shook his head. "Werewolves and vampires. That's it for my experience with the paranormal breeds. Oh, and a demon one time. My father pointed him out to me. I've led a sheltered life, Daisy. And it's not like Minnesota is spilling over with all sorts."

"You just need to know where to look. All breeds are everywhere."

"Maybe I've never wanted to look."

"Yeah. I get that about you. You've been protected by your family."

"Says the princess whose dad stalks her lovers."

"Touché."

* * *

Knees bent, Daisy sat back on her haunches and shimmied her shoulders. Dare she?

She wanted to share herself with Beck, but the wings thing was intimate—beyond getting naked and having sex. Never had she shown her human lovers her wings. They hadn't been aware she was anything but a chick with pink hair. And they had surely suspected the pink had come from a salon. It was never wise to bring up the fact that she was an entirely different breed than human. Secrecy was her best means to survival.

But secrets weren't necessary with Beck. Heck, he'd shown her his deepest secret with the ghost wolf, albeit accidentally. So she would give him this. Because she wanted to, and because she wanted to take their intimacy to the next level.

He liked her. And it felt wondrous.

Fingers crossed the wolf wouldn't horn in on the action and turn her into a freak show.

"All right." Daisy slid off the end of the bed and stood naked before Beck's ice-blue gaze. "Close your eyes."

He did so.

Daisy sucked in a breath and closed her eyes. Bringing out her wings was different than shifting to wolf. And she didn't do it often. When shifting to wolf, she pulled her focus inward, but her wings required she move part of her vita outward. Shoulders back and head down, she felt the tingle along the upper part of her spine. It tweaked painfully, and she winced. Her mother had commented that she didn't shift to faery often enough; that was the reason for the pain.

With an inhale and a hopeful wish that things went well, Daisy sent out her vita in the form of wings behind her shoulders. And they curled out from her body and unfurled, stretching out seven feet at their highest.

All faery's wings were different, some shaped as the insects she had seen in the mortal realm, such as the butterfly, cicada or dragonfly. But others were unique, like no insect or creature she had ever seen, and she could only imagine they were common in Faery.

Daisy had never been to Faery. She didn't have the compulsion to visit as her brother Kelyn did.

A sifting of faery dust sparkled in the air about her and landed on the end of the bed and Beck's legs. Another good thing about not shifting to faery often? No constant sweeping up of dust.

"Open your eyes," she whispered.

Beck sat forward, arms resting on his knees as he opened his eyes. He immediately said, "Wow."

Hands to her hips, she twisted side to side. When Beck motioned she spin about, she did so, pausing to look over her shoulder to gauge his reaction.

"Those are incredible. They look like something from a fantasy painting. Pink and silver. Gorgeous."

The filaments on the peaks of her wings curled in appreciation at his admiring tone. Daisy ran her fingers over the edge of one wing, which looked silver under certain lights, and then clear or iridescent in the sunlight. Sheened over in pink, the upper sections resembled an arabesque butterfly wing, and the lower sections were closer to cicada wings. She gave them a flutter, and they dusted Beck's face and arms.

"Mmm…smells like winter."

"You think so?"

"Yes, crisp and fresh. Like an ice-covered meadow I'd like to run through in wolf form. Is this faery dust?" He rubbed his fingers over his forearm to display glinting fingertips.

"If you were vampire," she said, "you'd be high right now."

"I am high on you, Daisy Blu." His grin burst off the scale. "Come here. Can I touch them?"

"At your own risk, lover boy."

"Right, because there's something about touching a faery's wings…"

She straddled his lap and curled one wing forward and around behind Beck's shoulder. He ran his fingers gently along the top of it, and the touch sent shivers through her wings. The veins flashed bright pink briefly before the erotic sensation entered Daisy's pores and scurried over her skin.

"Mmm…" She dipped her head against Beck's. "I can feel that as if you were stroking my skin."

He blew a hot breath over the sheer wing fabric. Again the veins brightened. Daisy moaned as that one moved lower. It was almost as if he'd blown on her loins. She felt his heat there. She'd never gotten intimate with a man while her wings were out. Could this be the start of something new and exciting?

Spreading his palm, he pressed it carefully against her wing, tracing tiny circles along the ridged cartilage that formed the structure.

Daisy pushed a hand over her mons and gasped. Putting pressure against her clit, she arched her back, and her breasts skimmed Beck's chest.

"That really turns you on."

"Oh, Beck, you have no idea. If I would have known, I would have done this sooner…"

"With a human man?"

"Oh, no, never."

She curled her wing along his back, and the heat of his skin permeated her wing. She felt it all over her body.

Beck lashed her breast with his tongue, sucking in the nipple. His hands carefully traced her wings as if he were

exploring her skin, and he mined a delicious deep pleasure that Daisy had not before felt. It focused on her core,
and yet sent out tendrils to her extremities. It was as if an
imminent orgasm wanted to explode at the end of every
nerve in her body.

Gripping his hair as he suckled one breast and then the
other, Daisy tilted back her head, unable to form words.
She surrendered to him. To the heady, overwhelming sensation and flame and cool and giddy and gasping, panting,
racing, thundering—

The orgasm struck with surprising force, capturing
her body in a glamorous shiver of pleasure. Faery dust
glittered out from her pores. Her muscles constricted and
danced and then loosened and again tightened. Beck held
her across the back as she soared in his arms, her wings
spreading wide behind her and shivering in joy.

"Oh, my God, Daisy, you're so gorgeous." A kiss there
at the base of her throat, and he laid his head against her
skin. "I can feel your pleasure vibrating in your body."
He slid his fingers between her legs, and the slip of one of
them glancing over her clitoris sparked the orgasm anew.
"Come again, faery lover. Mmm, I love to hold you close."

Her body grew liquid within Beck's embrace. The
room indeed smelled like winter. Though Daisy had never
thought to describe the scent of her dust like that before,
it fit. Riding the orgasm, she melted forward onto Beck's
strong arms and chest, nestling her head on his shoulder
and sighing. Wrapping her legs about his hips, she then
curled her wings around to hug them both.

"Thank you," she whispered.

"What for? I like to turn you on, Daisy. It turns me on.
That doesn't need any thanks."

"Thanks for being someone I could trust enough to do

this with. That meant a lot to me. I've never come like that before. It was amazing."

"I'll say."

All of a sudden, Daisy's body jerked without volition. Her gut clenched. The tips of her fingers tingled. And she knew what wanted to happen. "Oh, no."

"What is it?"

She ran toward the bathroom. "Don't follow me!" Closing the door, just as her wings folded down, a wolf tail popped out. "Damn it!"

"Daisy?"

She tilted her head against the door, sensing Beck stood just on the other side.

"Your wolf?" he asked carefully.

"Yes. Just uh, give me a minute."

"Take all the time you need. I'm not going anywhere."

She spread her fingers over the door and closed her eyes. Hearing Beck land on the bed and puff up a pillow, she couldn't help but smile. So the worst had happened. Before her lover. He hadn't freaked. And she hadn't freaked. Too much.

Everything was going to be okay with Beck. Whether or not she ever got her faery and wolf to play nice together.

Chapter 16

The phone on the nightstand vibrated. Beck grabbed it. Daisy's phone was encased in hand-tooled brown leather. Probably something her dad had made for her.

She was still in the bathroom. Poor girl. She'd been nervous about showing her wings to him and risking her wolf sneaking out—and it had.

He checked the incoming call info.

"Can't a guy get a break?" he said. "Seriously. The man is stalking me."

The bathroom door opened, and a naked faery wolf without a tail or wings wandered out to the edge of the bed.

"It rang while you were in there." He handed her the phone. "Still ringing."

She kissed him, then answered. "Hey, Daddy."

The dad. That man had impeccably discomforting timing.

Beck sat up, his feet hitting the hardwood floor. At least the old man hadn't intruded on their pairing last night. Or this morning.

"What?" Daisy's fingers flexed near her thigh. She paced beside the bed. "When? How is he? I'll be there as soon as I can get there."

She began collecting her clothing from the floor. Beck

sensed her urgency and scented her sudden fear. "Daisy, what is it?"

"It's my brother Stryke. He's been hurt by a hunter. Hit with a silver arrow."

"Ah hell." Beck joined in the clothing search and pulled up his jeans. "Is he okay?"

"Yes, he was just grazed. Mom called in a witch to help him get through the silver poisoning. But I've got to go to my parents' house right now."

She jumped on one foot as she pulled up her jeans and buttoned them. Beck tossed her the sweater he'd pulled off her last night. "Thanks. I'm sorry to leave like this."

"Don't be. Your family needs you. I'd go with you but—"

"But that's okay." They knew Beck would not be welcome in her father's home. "Will you lock up for me? I have to leave right now. But you can stay. Shower. Whatever."

He nodded. "Call me when you get a chance, okay?"

"I will!" she called as she ran for the front door and shoved her bare feet into the pack boots on the rubber tray. "Last night was great! We need to do it again. Er, without the wings and tail fiasco, I mean. Talk to you soon!"

The front door closed. Beck collapsed backward onto the bed and closed his eyes. Last night had been great.

But should he have been out looking for the hunter with the silver arrows instead of here? He might have prevented her brother's injury. Hell, the brother could have been killed.

Arrows? Was that another weapon in the hunter's arsenal, or was there more than one bloodthirsty human wandering the local woods in search of werewolves?

The family had gathered in the Saint-Pierre living room. The vast country cabin featured an open layout, the cathedral ceilings two and a half stories high. The south wall that looked out over the nearby stream was entirely windows. Daisy had spent many a sunny summer afternoon swimming in the stream that boasted a waterfall a half mile west. Now it was iced over until March, or even April.

Stryke lay on the comfy leather couch in wolf form. Daisy beelined for him and hugged her brother. "Oh, Stryke." She nuzzled her face into his brown variegated fur. He smelled like winter and blood. "I can't believe this happened to you. Is he going to be okay?"

Her mother sat beside her and pulled aside Daisy's hair from her face. "He will be. He just needs to rest. I sent Kelyn to the witch for more wolfsbane. Dez is the keeper of the Book of All Spells and is very wise. I trust her. She said we need to keep feeding it to Stryke to counteract the poison."

"Wolfsbane? Isn't that dangerous to us?"

"If used incorrectly. In the right dose," her mother explained, "it can heal. I don't want any of my children going into the forest anymore."

Daisy cast her eyes over Trouble and Blade, who sat on the other couch. Trouble's fist bounced on his jittering knee, contained anger tightened his jaw. Blade's silence was always stunningly chilling. Her father stood in the kitchen, arms crossed high upon his chest.

"That's an impossible request, Rissa," Malakai said. "If they stick to my land, they'll be safe. Why was Stryke out on public land anyway?"

Trouble tilted his head back against the couch, looking toward the ceiling. "He was wasted."

"Since when does Stryke drink?" Daisy asked. He was the cool, calm and collected brother. The wise one the other brothers always went to for advice. "Blade?"

The darkest of the family closed his eyes and shook his head.

"It's a woman," Trouble offered. "She was snarking about him to her friends. He's been really down."

"Idiot," Kai muttered. Then he looked directly at Daisy. "Daisy Blu. Outside. Now."

"But I want to sit with Stryke." She leaned across her brother's body and nuzzled her face against one of his soft tufted ears.

Kai strode toward the side door. "I won't repeat myself."

Feeling resentment at her father's command, Daisy reluctantly rose and wandered out behind him. Since she'd left the family home years ago, she'd expected more independence. It seemed her father would never grasp the concept that he could no longer tell his daughter how to live her life.

The formidable werewolf wore a flannel shirt and jeans. He'd strode out barefoot onto the heated concrete sidewalk that led from the house to his workshop. It was a great place to return to while still in wolf form to warm the chilled footpads.

Kai paced a few lengths, then turned on Daisy. "I thought I told you to stay the hell away from Beckett Severo?"

Daisy cringed from his tone.

"I can smell him all over you."

Shoot. Should have showered before she'd come here. Big mistake.

Her father stepped closer, using the intimidation tactic that he often used with his sons. She'd never garnered harsh words from him. Had always been his little girl. Could do anything and get away with it.

And she wasn't about to stop.

"You can't tell me who I can see, Daddy. I'm a grown

woman. I have relationships. I—" She wouldn't go so far as to say she had sex with men. He knew that. "I wish you'd respect my privacy and my need to make my own life."

"There is no privacy within the pack."

"There should be! How's a girl to ever find a boyfriend if she's always got her father breathing down her neck?"

"I don't do that!"

"Yeah? Well, you're doing it now. And besides, Beck is a good man."

"Who sneers at the idea of a pack. He may be good—hell, I respected his father. The boy came from good stock—but he's not right for you, Daisy."

"I'm not going to listen to this. You're spoiling everything. I came here to support Stryke, and now you're making this about me."

"I'm…" Kai blew out a breath, jammed his hands at his hips and looked aside. "You're right. We need to focus on Stryke and making sure he heals. We'll talk about this later."

"I'm not going to be here later."

Daisy marched back into the house. But once in the kitchen, her bravery waned. Tears spilled down her cheeks as she neared the hallway. From behind she felt Blade's arm slip around her shoulder, and he led her outside through the front door and pulled her into his embrace.

Blade was the second-oldest of the brothers, but so different from his siblings in his darkness and utter stillness. He moved like a shadow, and most paranormals feared him without even knowing him. His vampire was wild yet controlled, a fierce warrior. He'd suffered for his vampire's hunger. And he had the scars to prove it.

But he'd ever been gentle with her, his older sister. And she and him were close because they were each part faery.

Yet Blade had mastered his faery side beyond Daisy's expectations for her own faery.

"Why the tears?" he asked.

"Oh, Blade, sometimes Daddy can be such a hard-ass."

"It's because of the guy I smell all over you, isn't it?"

"Seriously? I should have showered before coming here."

She hugged her brother, who stood in a shirt and jeans, no shoes, despite the below-zero weather. His black hair, which was so black it gleamed blue in the pale daylight, spilled across her cheek.

"It's Beckett Severo," she confessed to him. "He's not in a pack, and that is driving Daddy crazy. Blade, I think I'm falling in love with him. Well, I'm already in love with him. But I just stumbled into serious like, too."

"Like," he muttered. Blade knew Daisy's definition of love and like were very different things. "Really?"

"Yes, I like everything about him. And while it should be fun and exciting and silly and sexy, Daddy is making it so not-fun, and he's ruining it."

Her brother kissed the top of her head. "I'm pretty sure that's what fathers are supposed to do. How about the men who believe they've the worth to woo their daughters? But did you ever think maybe Dad does it because he wants to challenge Beck?"

"I don't understand."

"If the Severo man can stand up to Malakai Saint-Pierre for you, then he'd be a worthy wolf. I'm guessing that's in Dad's thought process."

"Yeah? Well, he needs to stop it and let me have some fun. It's not like I'm picking a mate."

"You're not?"

"No. I don't know. No. I don't think Beck has that in mind, either."

"Then you should ask him. Because if you don't, Dad will. Or maybe your brothers need to ask him what his intentions are?"

"Blade, no. Stay out of my love life, will you? Why does this have to be so difficult? Just let me have this with Beck."

She pushed past him to head back into the house, but his final words reached her.

"Sometimes family can be a bitch, Daisy Blu."

Beck strolled into the small pawn shop off of Lake Street in Minneapolis. He'd begun to search for silver dealers, and after seeing just how many in the Twin Cities did sell, he decided to try a different tact.

A gruff, leather-clad, bandanna-wearing shop owner strode out from the back room. The beaded fringe before the door clattered and slid over his shoulders. He looked the classic bearded, motorcycle-riding bit of well-worn human who probably worshipped Lynyrd Skynyrd and never met a beer he didn't like.

Thinking about the band rushed a sudden and overwhelming heat to Beck's heart. He gripped his chest, so visceral the feeling was as it quivered the muscles in his jaws and tugged at the corners of his eyes.

His father had listened to the '70s rock band all the time. Severo had been what this man was before him now. Easy, laid-back, seasoned and worldly-wise.

"Help you, son?"

What Beck wouldn't give for one more moment standing before his father, waiting to hear whatever it was he wanted to say to him. Whether it was to suggest he buy land in the country instead of getting a house in town, or to tell him about the time when he'd had to escape a vampire tribe that had kept him and his parents captive, only to then witness the hunters slay his parents.

His father had been the strongest man Beck had ever known. Physically and mentally.

"Boy?"

"Uh." Beck shook off the memories that threatened to release tears. "I'm looking for some silver. The purest stuff you've got."

"All sold out. Don't get a lot of it lately. Silver is trading at a prime price."

"Actually, I'm trying to find someone who may have bought some from here and altered it for a shotgun shell or an arrow."

"Why? You a cop? You don't look like a cop."

Beck raked his fingers through his tousled hair. "I'm not a cop. I'm just trying to solve a puzzle. Do you get a lot of hunter types in here looking for silver?"

"What would a hunter do with silver? Unless he's hunting werewolves, eh?" The man chuckled, and shrugged off the joke as he walked around behind the glass counter and slid aside a velvet tray filled with gold rings. "You going werewolf hunting, boy?"

"I can't honestly tell if you're joshing me or if you're serious. Do you believe in werewolves, mister?"

"If you watch the news, you would. You hear about that big white wolf monster that's stalking the hunters?"

"The ghost wolf. I think it's the other way around. The hunters are going after the wolves. The ghost wolf is trying to protect his own."

"Aren't you all save-the-wolves?"

Beck's eyes landed a bumper sticker under the counter glass that touted *Will hunt for fur*. He realized that this man would probably shoot a wolf if he had the chance. His hackles tightened, but he gritted his jaw so he wouldn't growl.

The man shook his head. "I'm just having fun with you, boy. But no. No one looking to make silver bullets."

Beck pulled out the tissue he'd tucked into a pocket and spread it on the counter. "You ever see anything like this?"

The man bent to study the glass bead, then grabbed a jeweler's loop to give it a closer inspection. "Is that silver *inside* crystal?"

"Glass. The glass shatters on impact, and the silver leaks out."

The man straightened. Now his look grew hard, and Beck scented an edge of fear. "I think you should leave, boy."

"Does that mean you have seen it before?"

"It means I don't entertain idiots who think to hunt nonexistent creatures. I suppose you're packing a stake for Dracula, too?"

Beck swept up the tissue and backed away. "Thanks for the help. Sorry to have bothered you."

Denton proved a better aim with a bow and arrow than the modern rifle he'd attempted to use previously. Though the rifle had served him a kill, it hadn't been the breed of wolf the spell required. And that other wolf had been there. Snarled and snapped at him. He'd decided to let the dead one lie. He couldn't use it.

It had been the first time Denton had killed for a reason beyond to bring food to the table. And he wasn't much of a hunter, which explained his thin frame. But he'd made five kills in the months he'd been in this horrible time.

"Only one left."

He eyed the arrow, which had a glass point filled with silver. He'd gotten it one hundred years from now. But he only needed it to work once, in this year, and finally he could concoct the allbeast spell.

Chapter 17

Daisy finally cleaned up a photograph using Photoshop. The white wolf stood on powerful hind legs. Its head was ruffled with thick white fur. Ebony talons scythed the air. Its eyes glowed red.

She couldn't publish this photo. It exposed her lover for a monster.

But not publishing it would compromise her chances at winning the internship. This was truly a prize-winning photo. Dare she? Did she really need it? Maybe journalism wasn't her thing?

She needed this internship to finally prove her independence to her father.

The day had been long and cold. Icy rain slicked the tarmac. Yes, he lived in Minnesota. Cold was a natural state six months out of the year. Why hadn't his parents moved to Florida to raise him? He could seriously work the beach-bum vibe.

A stop for groceries on the way home was necessary, but Beck wasn't feeling motivated after the shop owner's rude treatment. Though he felt deserving of it. How to ask around about silver bullets without sounding like a complete wacko?

The blinking blue neon sign outside the Blue Bass bar—the last dive bar before Burnham—called to him. A shot of whiskey to warm his bones sounded more interesting than squeezing oranges in the produce section.

Inside the small bar paneled in wood timbers and blinking madly with various beer signs hung all over the walls, a few men played a game of pool under the watchful milky eye of the bar's mascot, a stuffed blue bass. One man sat at the bar, his head bowed and long black hair concealing his face.

An old-timer sporting a white beard to his belly and commandeering the table next to the men's room waved to him. Beck nodded in acknowledgment—the guy was here every time he stopped in—and ordered a whiskey. He asked the bartender to pour the old man another of whatever he was drinking. He'd never spoken to him, hadn't a clue who he was, what he did or where he lived. Didn't matter.

The first swallow of whiskey burned sweetly. Beck pressed the shot glass to his forehead and closed his eyes. The sounds of pool balls clacking battled with the cheesy country tune that proclaimed cowboys the best rides.

Beck laughed to himself, thinking that women should really give werewolves a try if they were looking for a wild ride. Then again, best keep all the wild goodness away from the mortal females. They wouldn't know how to handle him.

Hell, what was he thinking? He'd dated many a mortal woman. They could handle him in *were* shape just fine.

Daisy had been his first wolf. And it had been a risky pairing. Normally packs protected their females as if they were gold in Fort Knox. The only wolves allowed to sniff around them were fellow pack members, or wolves from neighboring packs. But if Beck knew correctly, Daisy's pack was just her family. So she would have to seek a wolf elsewhere to mate and marry. Naturally, her father, the pack principal, would insist she marry another pack wolf. It could prove a good alliance for the two packs. Hell, the whole lone wolf thing was a real stigma to packs.

One of the men at the pool table whooped triumphantly. He bounced back and forth on his feet as if a prize fighter. He was wearing—a leather skirt? With a plaid sweater that stretched across his physique. And combat boots. Yikes.

Beck shook his head and noticed the other two players shook off the winner's antics and approached the bar. One was tall, thin and had messy blond hair. His face was angular and alien. He looked down his nose at Beck.

The other revealed short hair shaved to his scalp when he pushed back a hoodie. Sleeves covered his hands to midfinger. He also glanced at Beck, while the other, the one still cheering his win, bounced around as he racked the balls.

"Trouble!" the one closest to Beck called. "We get it. You won."

The bouncing winner wandered up to the bar next to the one who had spoken. The twosome exchanged looks. The winner asked, affronted, "What, man?"

The one in the hoodie nodded toward Beck.

An uneasy creep tightened at the back of Beck's neck. Then he scented them.

Ah hell.

"This guy smell familiar to you?" the one in the hoodie asked his cohort.

Now the dark-haired one, who had been sitting at the bar, lifted his head, tilting it as he observed the one in the skirt walk up to Beck and make a show of sniffing the air.

"Well, I'll be," Trouble, the skirted one, said. "You Beckett?"

Yeah, this felt fifty ways of wrong. Beck pushed the empty shot glass toward the back of the bar and turned to offer his hand to the man, who stood about as tall as he did, yet his shoulders were a bit broader and his wild eyes gave him a menacing edge that Beck sensed he was going to learn a lot more about. Like it or not.

"Beckett Severo," he said.

Trouble didn't shake his hand. And then Beck realized who he was. Who all four men were. But before he could speak, Trouble's fist connected with his jaw, knocking him off the stool and grasping for hold on the brass rail edging the bar.

He'd felt the Saint-Pierre power punch before. Daisy's right hook had nothing on this guy.

"This is the one who has been nosing around Daisy Blu," the hooded one said. "I could smell you on her the other day when she came to see me."

Beck winced and shook his head. His jaw might have dislocated with that punch. "Visited you? Are you Stryke? The one who got hit by the silver arrow?"

"What the hell are you doing with my sister, eh?" Trouble punched him in the gut.

Beck caught his elbows against the bar. Now Stryke and the blond moved around to stand beside Trouble. Without looking over his shoulder, he sensed the dark one at the bar remained sitting.

"Take it outside," the bartender ordered. "Unless you're willing to pay for the damages. Could use some new decor."

Trouble gripped Beck by the scruff of his neck and shoved him toward the back door, which opened out to a small parking lot, glazed over from the icy rain that had stopped when Beck had entered the bar.

Beck eyed his truck, parked across the street. He was

grabbed from behind, an arm hooking around his neck. Punishing knuckles met his kidney in a bile-stirring introduction. They'd paired up, the sneaky Saint-Pierres. And he was going down. He staggered forward, swallowing his bile. Shit, they could punch.

But he wasn't in the mood for running with his tail between his legs. He had worse things with which to deal. And these boys had better learn he was not a wolf to mess with.

Righting, and turning to face the trio—the dark one with the long hair had leaned against the trunk of the bartender's black SUV, arms crossed over his chest—Beck thrust up his fists.

"Listen, guys, I don't want to start anything with Daisy's brothers. But I sure as hell am not going to stand here and let you beat me to a pulp."

He swung for Trouble, catching him on the jaw.

Shaking it off as if a nuisance, Trouble bounced back and forth on his combat boots as if a prize fighter. The ice gave him little challenge. "A love tap? Is that all you got, lone wolf?"

Beck swung again, this time pounding his fist into Trouble's gut. The wily wolf huffed out his breath, caught Beck at the nape of the neck and, with a twist, slammed the side of his head against a nearby car trunk.

Face to metal scoured pain through Beck's skull. His nose dripped out blood. He didn't want to do this. And oh, yes, the ghost wolf inside him wanted to do this.

Swinging around, he thought to punch the crazy wolf in the face, but instead one of the others caught his fist, smiled and delivered a high kick that doubled him at the gut. Bent over, he felt the new wolf's fist at his jaw.

"Good one, Stryke!" Trouble called. The wolf still bounced at the periphery of Beck's vision. "Hey, lone wolf, take it easy on Stryke. He's still healing from the hunter's arrow. Almost killed him, that asshole."

Turning, Beck gripped Stryke by the shirt and shoved him against a pickup cab. "You see the hunter who shot you?"

"Dude, I was on four legs at the time."

"Yeah, but you have his scent, right? I need to find that hunter."

"You talk too much." Stryke swung up a fist, which Beck blocked with his forearm.

The two tussled, throwing punches and dodging a few swings. The guy was fast on his feet, but his punches didn't pack the power that his brother Trouble's did. Just when Beck thought he had the guy, he swung high, and Stryke's boot caught him in the gut. Damn, he'd gone for the kidney again. These boys did not fight fair.

Spinning around, Beck's eyes fell across the crazy one who was clapping and cheering for his brother. Still, the tall dark one stood off by a pickup box. Beck decided to stay away from him. The less he had to face, the better. And the blond one? Where was—

An iron fist crushed Beck's jaw. His feet left the ground. His body soared high, and he landed on top of a Camaro hood. Blackness toyed with his consciousness.

"Kelyn, that is the only punch you get," Trouble reprimanded the blond one. "You'll waste the guy before we've had our fun."

As Beck's body slid from the hood, he matched gazes with the tall, lithe one who'd just punched his brains into next week. A violet eye winked at him. The faery of the bunch. Beck's boots slid on the ice, and he went down.

Trouble looked over Beck, sprawled in a prone position. "That's our bro, Kelyn. Feel like your brains are oozing out your nose right now?"

Beck swore. He'd never think faeries a bunch of pussies again.

"Yep, he's a one-punch deal," Trouble said. "But you're still conscious, so we'll give you points for that. Come on, lone wolf, we're just getting started."

Beck clasped the proffered hand, and Trouble tugged him up to his feet. He winced and stumbled forward, but knowing the enemies stood close, didn't focus on the pain. Instead, he just needed to survive this.

Whatever the hell *this* was. They were having too much fun working him over. Because he was screwing their sister?

Good reason. He couldn't argue that.

"If you think you're going to scare me away from Daisy—" Beck spat blood to the side "—you're going to have to try harder."

Trouble whistled and bounced high, stomping the ground in his macabre glee. "Oh, I'll bring it! Hold him, Stryke."

Beck swung at Stryke and managed a punishing blow to his gut. Stryke spat aside blood, grinned, then lunged, slipping an arm behind Beck's neck and his arms to get him in a shoulder pin. As he struggled against the wolf, he felt Trouble's boot hit his cheek. His skin broke. Blood spilled down his face.

"You think you have a right to move in on our sister?" Trouble asked. "Wolves who don't run with a pack shouldn't be so bold, don't you know that?"

Beck shoved Stryke backward against a truck. The wolf chuffed out a breath. Arms still wrenched back, and Beck rolled forward, flipping Stryke over his head. The two brothers collided and went down.

"Good one," Trouble groaned from the ground. He shoved his brother off him. "Kelyn, let's end this."

"Ah, shit." Beck turned but didn't have time to register more than a fist aimed between his eyes. Blackness won over the pain. Beck dropped to the icy pavement.

Trouble bounced up to his feet, but a groan struck from his aching side.

Blade, hands in his pockets, strolled over to the fallen wolf and knelt over him. "This wolf can certainly take some punishment."

"That he can." Trouble pounded a fist into his opposite palm. "I like him."

Blade stood, nodding agreement. With a whistle from Trouble, the brothers gathered. They performed a group fist bump over Beck's prone body.

"Let's get the hell out of here before the owner calls the cops," Kelyn suggested.

"Right." Trouble wandered off toward the parked vehicles. "Stryke, grab the loner."

"What? I thought I was the one recovering here?"

With some grumbling about always having to clean up the mess, Stryke bent and managed to hoist Beck's body over a shoulder. "Where's his car?"

Blade pointed down the street, and the brothers found the truck. It was unlocked, fortunately for Beck. Trouble would not have paused before smashing out the window with a fist.

Stryke laid him across the front seat, and Beck stirred from his blackout.

"He must really love her," Stryke muttered.

"Yeah, that's what I was thinking, too, when he stood up to us. Poor guy." Trouble toed Beck's foot out of the way so he could close the door. "We were just playing with you, lone wolf. It's the big guy you should be worried about. That would be our dad, Malakai Saint-Pierre."

"Bring it," Beck muttered. Then he passed out again.

Trouble and Stryke laughed. Kelyn shook his head, muttering about pussy wolves.

And Blade had already wandered off, blending into the night.

Beck woke shivering. He sat up on the front seat of his truck. The windows were iced over, but daylight glinted in the rearview mirror.

How had he—?

Opening his mouth to yawn, he winced and swore. Rubbing his hand carefully along his jaw, he wondered if it was broken. It should have healed from the beating he'd taken last night. If it hadn't been for—

"That damned faery."

The brothers must have scraped him off the ice and tossed him in his truck. A surprising courtesy. He shuffled in his front jeans pocket for the keys and turned on the ignition, flipping the heat onto high. Collapsing back across the seat, he pushed his hands over his scalp.

They'd been toying with him last night. Maybe. Probably. But those punches hadn't been a tease.

"Daisy's brothers."

And yet one of them had said something about watching out for the dad. And Beck had idiotically said something like "bring it." Oh, foolish lone wolf.

He groaned and sensed the pain shifting from his back to his side. Some well-aimed kidney kicks. He lifted his shirt and saw the mottled maroon-and-green bruising. When it took longer than six to eight hours for a werewolf to heal, then he'd really taken a beating.

He wondered if the dad wasn't on his way to finish the job right now. Maybe Malakai Saint-Pierre was standing outside the truck, waiting for Beck to wake up?

Sniffing the air, Beck didn't sense anyone in the vicinity. He was alone. Beaten. And freezing his ass off. It was going to take the heater a while to warm up.

Pulling himself upright, he let out a groan and shuffled behind the steering wheel. While good sense told him to drive home and sleep off the pain, all his heart wanted to do was turn toward town and knock on Daisy's door.

Chapter 18

"Come in," Daisy said to the sad-faced werewolf standing in her doorway. She winced. His jaw was bruised green with spots of violet, and he clutched his ribs. "I heard about what happened."

"Yeah? Did your brothers call to report the gory details as soon as they'd finished working me over?"

"Aw, they didn't mean it. They were just love taps." Daisy forced the words out even while she was torn apart inside. Damn, Trouble. Her brother could never let anything be.

"Love?" Beck paused in the living room as she coaxed him toward the bed. "If that was a love tap, I don't ever want your faery brother to love, adore or otherwise even like me. The man left a permanent impression of his knuckles on my kidney."

Indeed, her brother Kelyn may look like the weakest of the Saint-Pierre brothers, but he was the secret deadly weapon. Why had Trouble allowed him to participate? He knew Kelyn's strength was deadly. That was so wrong.

"Come here. Let me take a look at the damage. Sometimes Kelyn doesn't know his own strength."

"You think?" Beck dutifully followed and sat on the end of her bed. "They all had their go at me. Except the one." He lifted his arms as she pulled the blue sweater over his head. His ribs were mottled and green. He was healing, but still sore, for sure. "The tall dark one stood back and watched."

"Blade only raises his fists for one reason."

"What's that? To maim?"

"To kill."

She met his wondering brow with a shrug. She wasn't about to explain the dark stuff Blade had already experienced in his short lifetime. Gliding her fingers down his chest, she stopped when he winced. "That does not look good. Kelyn?"

He nodded as he lay back on the bed. "Got me twice." He slid a hand over hers as she unbuttoned his jeans. "Really?"

"I want to make you comfortable. Loosen your clothes a bit."

"You going to work some faery healing on me?"

The thought to try hadn't occurred to her. Though certainly if her faery were stronger, she could do it. And oh, did she want to make it all better for him right now. "Uh, I could try?"

"Anything that involves you putting your hands on me is okay by me."

"My mother has been trying to teach me healing since I was a little girl. If I can tap into my faery side, I can draw up my vita to heal yours. It's just—well, I explained how my faery and wolf battle. You've seen the results. And I haven't practiced much. Do you trust me?"

"Of course I do. And if it doesn't work, who am I to argue with a faery wolf putting her hands on me, eh?"

He stroked the ends of her hair that dangled over his chest. The man's arctic eyes tempted her forward to kiss him. Softly. She didn't want to put too much pressure where her brothers' fists had likely pummeled. She hated that her brothers had done this to Beck, but she understood it had been their means of checking him out. Beckett Severo had been weighed and measured and, thankfully, had not come up wanting in her brothers' opinions.

That was the real reason she wasn't railing at the Saint-Pierre boys' cruel treatment of her lover. Trouble had even said he liked the guy. Seriously. He'd said he respected Beck for standing up to them and taking his punches like a man. But none of them had thought their opinion would change their father's mind about Beck.

"That feels so good." He kissed her gently, then closed his eyes as she floated kisses down his chin and neck. "You know they had the courtesy to stick me in my truck and not leave me lying in the icy parking lot all night?"

"That's my brothers for you. Strange kindness." She dashed her tongue down the center of his chest, and he moaned.

"Is that how the healing works?"

"No, I'm just getting you warmed up."

"Ah. Well then, proceed as slowly as you like."

She straddled his thighs and spread out her arms. Much as she preferred her wolf half, her faery half did have some useful skills. For Beck's sake, she hoped to tap into them. Focusing inward, she summoned her wings. They unfurled with a whoosh of wintery chill and a flutter of faery dust that settled with a glint onto Beck's chest.

"I like your wings," he said. "You know a guy could have all kinds of fantasies involving them?"

"Keep a few in mind, big boy."

She clapped her hands together before her, rubbing her palms rapidly to warm her skin. Slowly she began to pull her palms apart, focusing her thoughts inward to the vita that raced through her system. Every molecule in her being and in the world responded to her thoughts. She felt the stirring between her palms.

A spark of violet faery magic grew within her hands and stranded in pink, blue and emerald that glittered with faery dust. Daisy knew it was her very life essence. As it manifested, it sputtered and disappeared, raining faery dust over Beck's abs.

"Give me a minute to warm up," she said. "I've got it in me. I can do this."

If she had spent more time nurturing her faery half this would be a breeze, but she'd never thought anything about being faery was useful. Or comfortable. What girl could slap a hockey stick and make the goal with the impediment of wings slowing her down? Or trying to keep the wings from getting singed while welding metal? Not going to happen.

Though she did like having her wings out for a good stretch. And to give it a moment's thought, wings made her feel…pretty. More womanly.

Hmm…maybe she needed to devote more focus to her faery.

Again the green and violet strands formed between her palms. Daisy rushed both palms to Beck's ribs, where Kelyn had gotten him in the kidneys with his iron fist.

Beck moaned and tilted his head to see what she was doing.

"Lay back. Take it in," she directed. "This may not last long."

"It feels cool, and I can feel it…inside. As if it's wrapping about my kidney. Wow." He closed his eyes and laid back. "Crazy."

Crazy, indeed. That she was even managing this giddied Daisy's hopes, and she got so excited she lost her concentration, and the healing vita poufed out again.

But with Beck's eyes closed, he didn't immediately notice. Curling forward a wing, she brushed it over her lover's face, drawing his smile widely.

Beck sucked in a breath. "Oh, yeah. I…I think you did it."

"Of course I did." She smiled and sighed. Well, he had been close to fully healed before she'd gotten to him. But she may have helped a bit.

She strolled her hands, now coated with faery dust, across his skin and up toward his collarbone where the bruise had receded. Gliding down his chest, she roamed over his hard curves, pausing when she felt the tenderness of damage beneath her delving touch. It was an intuitive feeling that her mother had taught her to utilize. She wanted to be able to kiss the pain away, to protect her lover from all hurts.

She wondered if faery healing could help a man's grief?

Hands gliding down his stomach, she curved them over his hip.

"Doesn't feel cool anymore," he murmured.

"That was all the healing vita I could manage. Now, for your lovely parting gift."

"My—wha?"

"Pants off," she whispered.

"I don't think they got me below the belt," he muttered.

"Really? You don't want me to even have a look?"

Beck quickly shimmied down his jeans and kicked off his shoes, and the whole tangle landed on the floor at the base of the bed.

"Thought so," she said.

She glided her hands down his hips and over his boxer shorts. Black with tiny white skulls on them. Cute. His erection bobbed against her palm. She gave it a firm squeeze.

"Please?" her werewolf lover asked.

* * *

Daisy's wings swept forward over Beck's chest and up along his face. It felt as though he was being touched by the wind and snow and summer all at the same time. The faery wolf settled onto his cock, welcoming him inside her depths and rocking a slow yet insistent rhythm. She felt so good. There were no words to describe being inside her. *Hot. Awesome. Wondrous. Sticky.* All insignificant.

He turned his face into one of her wings and breathed in deeply, then licked the delicate wing. She even tasted sweet. He'd fallen into some kind of wonderland, and he wanted that damned white rabbit to catch him. Here was home. She felt so right.

"Oh!"

Daisy's body jerked above him. Suddenly his cock slapped against his belly. She stumbled off him and dropped off the bed and to the floor. The wings disappeared.

"Shit," she muttered. "Not again."

"Daisy!"

Daisy's wolf whined and scampered out of the bedroom area, toenails clicking across the hardwood. She crept around to the other side of the couch. A few miserable whines struck Beck right in the heart.

He caught his palms against his forehead. "Poor girl. She's having as much trouble shifting as I…"

He blew out a breath. He couldn't speak it out loud, but he knew how Daisy felt. Because he was struggling with his own shifting troubles. Troubles he had brought upon himself. And now that the sidhe gift had begun to take its toll on him, he wasn't sure how to stop it, or change it, or make it drain him less.

He was destined to move forward, even if it killed him. And it likely would.

Maybe Daisy's suggestion that he talk to the faery who had given him the ghost wolf was worth a try. But could he stop being the ghost wolf before he'd finished what he set out to do?

What did he really intend for the ghost wolf to do? Scare the local hunters out of ever hunting wolves again? Kill the hunter who had killed his father?

He knew that answer, and while he hated claiming it, he knew he had to. He wanted the hunter dead. An eye for an eye. Wasn't that only fair?

Yet instinctually, Beck knew his father would never be proud of such an action.

"Beck?"

Sitting up, he spied Daisy's crop of pink hair pop up from behind the couch. He pulled on his jeans then padded over to the couch. Pulling his naked faery wolf into his arms, he sat with her wrapped up against his chest. Kissing her hair, he held her and didn't speak. Words weren't necessary. He'd just witnessed her greatest challenge, and he felt sure she was embarrassed, frustrated and probably even angry with herself for allowing him to see it.

He bent to whisper at her ear, "Nothing will ever make me stop liking you, Daisy Blu."

Beck held her on the couch for the longest time. Daisy was glad he didn't talk, save to whisper that he liked her. She liked him, too. This romance had developed into serious like. And she'd once again revealed the most devastating part of her life to him, and he had merely wrapped her in his arms and told her he liked her.

Like was so much better than love. Because they both knew love was a part of it. They'd fallen into each other and genuinely enjoyed being there. She just wished there was a way to figure out what the heck was up with her.

Beck wouldn't have answers, but it felt as if she'd released a heavy weight from her soul now that he was in on her secret.

"I'll get it figured out," she muttered, turning on his lap to sit forward and clasping his hands over her stomach. "Wolf or faery? Seems like I can't be both."

"If you had to choose," he asked softly, "which would it be?"

She shrugged. "My family is mostly wolves. Yet my mother is faery. I have always favored my wolf. To be honest, the faery half of me has always felt so…feminine."

"Your wings are crazy gorgeous. What's wrong with being feminine?"

"Nothing. But you should have noticed by now that it doesn't come naturally to me."

He stroked the side of her feet. She remembered he liked to touch them. "You're not a tomboy."

"You don't think so? Even after I kicked your ass at pond hockey?"

"You're a chick who happens to play hockey well. And who enjoys working with a welding torch. Why do pink bows and silly high shoes have to define you as feminine?"

She shrugged. "Never thought of it that way before. But I'm going to pick wolf, if I have a choice between the two."

"I'd miss your wings. And your healing. That is an incredible skill. Could you really give that up?"

"Don't fool yourself. I barely healed you. Your body was already well on its way to healing."

"You helped."

She turned and brushed at the faery dust on his biceps. "You feeling better?"

"One hundred percent."

"So tell me how it's going with your ghost wolf?"

"It's about as good as your shifting situation. Honestly?

I get weaker every time I shift, Daisy. I don't think I can do it for much longer."

"Then stop."

"I intend to. But I still haven't done what I set out to do. My search for the hunter with the silver bullets is turning up a dead end."

"Stryke was hit by a silver-tipped arrow. Do you think it could be the same hunter?"

"Possible. I can hope it's only one man we have to worry about. I'm not sure what to do, Daisy. What would you do, as a journalist?"

She tilted her head back against his shoulder. "I am an aspiring journalist. This story about the ghost wolf is my first big investigation."

"And look, you've discovered the truth behind it."

"Right, but I can't tell anyone. Do you know how that drives me bonkers?"

"You want to tell people about me?"

"As a journalist? Hell yes. I'm sure this story could win me the internship. But as your lover and fellow werewolf? Heck no. This is your secret, and a secret the whole werewolf community needs to guard."

"I'm sorry to have put you in this position."

"Don't be. Beck, what you're doing is awesome. You've scared the shit out of the hunters."

"Yeah, but for how long? The ghost wolf hurt someone, Daisy. I don't think it'll be long before they come after me with pitchforks and silver bullets. And after that, who's to say the gray wolf population won't again feel the threat? And what about Stryke? He was almost killed. I think I've screwed this up, big-time."

"No. Let's think about this." She stroked her hands along his thighs. "I agree that the ghost wolf needs to pull back for a while until things calm down."

"But what if I can't? Daisy, at night…"

"What is it?"

"It's like the ghost wolf pulls at me if I even see moonlight. I've drawn all the curtains in my house."

"That's weird."

"And you saw how I was the other night when you came over to my house."

"Horny as heck."

Beck sighed and hugged her to him. "I don't want to hurt anyone else. I can't. My father would have never wanted that."

She kissed his knuckles. "I think your father would be proud to see what you've accomplished."

"I'm not so sure he would approve of the means to what I've done."

"The faery bargain?"

He nodded.

"Yeah, that worries me still."

"That makes two of us. I'm worried about your faery situation. I'm worried about mine. When did life become so full of worries? I'm too young for this crap."

He stood and padded over to the bed to retrieve the rest of his clothes. Daisy popped up her head and leaned on the back of the couch, watching him dress.

"If you go to the faery to ask about giving the ghost wolf back," she said, "I'd go with you. Maybe…"

"Maybe the faery would know how to help you?"

She nodded, glanced aside.

"Sounds like a plan. But I've got some work to do before then. If you don't have any ideas on how to track the hunter, then I've got to rack my brain and come up with something. I wish your brother could help me, but I asked him last night if he recognized the hunter, and he was more interested in putting bruises on me."

"How could he know anything if he was in wolf shape?"

"Exactly. But he might remember his scent."

She followed him across the living room, naked. When he paused before the front door, she wrapped her arms around him from behind. She wanted to ask what he would do when he finally did find the hunter, but she wasn't sure she wanted to hear the answer.

"Should I tread carefully around town now in fear of your father?" he asked.

"I'll have a talk with him."

"You shouldn't have to, Daisy."

"Yeah, but we are a couple, right? I mean, I want us to be."

He turned and kissed her forehead. "You're my sexy faery wolf. But that goes against everything dear old dad wants for you. And you know I don't want to make trouble."

"Kind of late to consider the ramifications, don't you think? I don't want us to end, Beck."

"Neither do I. I guess I'll have to figure a way into your father's good graces."

"Let's just play it by ear for now. My dad is not part of this relationship."

"I don't want to sneak around. Your brothers have already given me a warning."

"It wasn't a warning so much as they weighed and measured you. And do you know? Trouble actually said he likes you."

"He did? Wait. That's like friend like. Not the kind of like we have?"

"Right. My brothers approved of you, but they don't get a vote where my dad is concerned." She kissed him.

"I've never had brothers, so I can't imagine. But maybe soon, eh?"

"What do you mean?"

"Uh…" He stroked her cheek and shrugged. "My mom is pregnant."

"Really? That's amazing."

"She was going to tell my dad on the night he died."

"Oh, my goddess. Beck, I'm so sorry. You two have been through so much."

"I'm a survivor."

"How is your mom doing?"

"She's much better lately." He kissed her again. "I'm hoping for a brother, but Mom said she wants a girl. Ivan Drake has been visiting her, and I think that's helping her a lot."

"I'm glad. It's got to be hard being alone and pregnant."

"Which reminds me, I think I'll stop by my mom's today and give her a hug."

Daisy wrapped her arms about Beck. "I hate to give you up."

"How about sharing me?"

"I can do that."

Chapter 19

"Hey, Mom."

Beck kissed his mother and noted she was wearing a soft floral perfume. Her long brown hair was pulled up into a neat bun with a few curly strands hanging down around her face. And her smile remained even after she'd acknowledged him.

"Feeling good?" he asked.

Bella led him into the kitchen, where it smelled like brownies. "I'm feeling great, Beck. I even guessed you'd be around today, so I made you brownies."

"Heloise's recipe?"

"You know it."

The former maid had died while serving his parents— killed by vamps—but Bella always made her brownie recipe in honor of the woman whom she and Severo had loved as if a family member.

Beck had to use a fork to dig into a brownie heaped with cream cheese frosting and served on a plate because it was cut so big. Man, this was heaven. And if his mom had brought these brownies to the ice festival, she would have had to charge double what the others had charged— and would have made a fortune.

"How's the baby? Have you been in to see the doctor?"

"Ivan is taking me next week."

Beck nodded, but kept a comment to himself. So how close were Ivan and his mother getting? Because Ivan was married to a witch, had been for decades. He didn't want to bring the two together that much.

"I know what you're thinking," Bella said.

The twinkle she'd always had in her eye had returned. That set down Beck's shoulders even more. His mom was doing much better.

"Ivan is a friend. And Dez stopped by yesterday to help me make these brownies. The two of them have been what I've needed to…you know, take a step toward the future, is the best way to describe it."

His mother's sigh was evidence that she would always hold Severo in her heart. Hell, it had only been three months since his father's death. It was going to take a while for them both to get over his loss. Did they even have to get over it? And really, who decided how long the grieving process should be, or what, exactly, it entailed? He'd grieved already and was moving on. And now that his mother seemed to be heading toward the future, he could relax and know she would be all right.

"How are you doing, sweetie? Is the shop ready for opening?"

"I'm in no rush to open it to the public."

"No rush, or no energy? Beck, now, I know I'm the last person to be telling you what to do—"

"You're my mom. You sort of have that right," he said through a mouthful of brownie.

"Right. But lately, I've been—you know."

He rubbed her arm. "Understandable."

"Thanks. But I'm surfacing from the depression. Every day feels brighter and more promising. Yet I wonder if you've gotten stuck lately?"

"Stuck? No, I'm just taking my time with the shop."

"I'm not talking about the shop. Have you talked to anyone about losing your dad? Beyond me?"

Beck's stomach clenched. He pushed the plate across the counter. "Dad's gone. There's nothing more to say."

"He'll never be gone, Beck. We both hold him in our hearts."

Beck lifted his chin. He had to stay strong for his mother. "Yeah. You're right. He's in my heart. So do you think I could get a couple of these brownies to take with me?"

Bella smoothed her palm over his forearm. "Have you visited his grave?"

They'd buried his father out at the back of their property beneath the willow tree Severo would often sit under when in wolf form. An escape from the world, he'd once explained to Beck about the spot. But as well, a connection to the earth, the very universe that grounded him and brought him peace.

"It's just ashes and bones in the ground, Mom. Dad's spirit is long gone from this realm."

Saying it released a tear down Beck's cheek, which he hastily swiped away. That was a lie. Severo's spirit remained within him. He hoped forever.

"It's getting late." He stood abruptly and turned toward the foyer. "I'm going to get some more things from Dad's shop."

"I'll cut up some treats to take home with you."

"Thanks!"

He rushed to the shop and closed the door behind him, leaning against the steel surface and sniffing away the tears. "Damn it."

He'd anticipated some random feelings when coming here, but he'd expected them to be over his mother and her sorrow. But Bella seemed to be improving. And here he stood, crying?

He hadn't cried at the funeral. He had shed copious tears as he'd knelt in the snowy forest over his father's dying wolf. So why now? Tears would not bring back the dead, nor could the dead know he was heartbroken without him.

Beck slapped a palm over his chest. Heartbroken?

No, he was— It certainly felt as if something inside him had been broken. Cracked open. But *heartbroken* was a stupid word. It was something lovers felt after breaking it off. The heart didn't really break. It just felt like that sometimes.

But if he admitted it to himself, his heart had been torn apart and pried wide open by his father's death. And it hurt in ways he couldn't explain.

New tears spilled down Beck's cheeks. He slid down against the door and squatted, catching his forehead against his palms. Angry with himself for such a weak display, he slammed a fist behind him, punching the steel door. He swore and punched the door again. Turning and standing, he pummeled the door with both fists, over and over, jaws gritted and muscles tense. He shouted, releasing foul oaths he'd never speak in front of others.

And then he pressed his forehead to the cool steel where his knuckles had carved in dents. An exhale climbed from his being, slowly, resolutely. Lungs panting and body shaking, he no longer shed tears. But his heart felt hot and heavy, oozing with something he had only felt that night of his father's death.

Very well. His heart was broken.

And within him stirred the ghost wolf. The part of him that knew how to manifest his pain. It howled and clawed. His biceps flexed, tingling with the urge to shift.

Beck twisted his head to eye the door at the back of the shop, placed there as an exit into the night for the werewolf. He pulled off his sweater, and even as his arms began to lengthen and shift, he toed off his boots and shuffled out of his pants.

The door swung open as the werewolf's howl greeted the cold, winter twilight.

Bella had listened to the sounds echoing out from behind the steel door of her late husband's shop. Her son hurt. And he didn't know how to let go of that pain.

Beck's howls brought tears to her eyes. And then she could only hope that perhaps by beating his anger out on something like a steel door, it could begin to help him heal.

Now she saw him dash across the yard in werewolf shape. Yet—that wasn't Beck. What was that creature?

She raced to the patio door and pressed a hand to the glass. The werewolf loping off behind the hedge was taller than usual and sleek. Less fur covered his body than a normal werewolf. He was pale, almost ghostlike.

"White?"

That wasn't Beck. When he shifted, he took on much the same fur color as his father's dark brown, yet with some blond shades mixed in.

As the werewolf howled and dropped to all fours to race across the vast meadow behind the house, Bella clutched a hand to her throat. She'd seen the news stories. Could it be? Her son? But how?

"Oh, my God, Beck, what have you done?"

Early morning woke Beck with a freezing clutch at his skin. He came alert abruptly and looked about. He was lying on his parents' snow-covered patio deck before the tarp-covered pool. Naked.

He immediately checked his hands. No blood.

He lashed his tongue around inside his mouth. Didn't taste any blood—a sure sign his werewolf had been successful on the hunt.

Glancing to the patio door, he looked for movement. His mother slept late. A vampire thing.

Stepping quickly toward the back door, he found a shop towel to wipe off the melting snow and dirt, and then dressed. He'd leave, and call his mom later. She shouldn't question his shifting and going out for a run. He did it often. They owned a vast parcel of land, and it was safe here. His werewolf always stayed on the property.

Opening the shop door, Beck was startled by his mother, standing in a long red velvet robe that caressed her swollen belly. Her hair was down, and her eyes were puffy. She hadn't slept.

"We need to talk," she said, and turned to stride into the living room.

Chapter 20

The morning was too bright. And oddly warm. Daisy dashed across the street in a long pink sweater and some brown leggings. Her rubber-soled riding boots splashed in the slush. Yes, slush in mid-January. The sun was bright and the weatherman had promised forties, if only for the day. Wonders did not cease.

The Panera restaurant was a favorite meeting spot for her and Stryke, who waved her to the table where he sat. The only one in the family who didn't do coffee, he sipped a huge cup of chai latte. He splayed his hand over the plates already sitting on the table.

"You ordered for me?" She sat and immediately forked into the egg-and-steak breakfast platter. It was hot, and the tomatoes tasted summer fresh. "Have I told you lately I love you, brother?"

"Not often enough. Beautiful day, isn't it?"

"Yep. But I suspect that is not the reason you called this morning meeting."

"I just wanted to see my big sister. Does everything have to have a reason?"

"Probably not. And most especially not with you. I'm sorry, Stryke. You're right. We haven't had a good talk in a while." She slid a hand over his and rubbed his wrist. "So how are you healing?"

"Truth? I feel great." He rubbed his shoulder where the arrow had skimmed him while in wolf shape. "That witch's spell herb stuff worked like a charm. There's not even a scar. Wolfsbane. Whoda thought? Almost believed I was going to bite the big one."

"You're tough. All the Saint-Pierre men are."

"As well as the women." He winked.

"You know it. Though the fact that there's a hunter out there with silver bullets and arrows disturbs the hell out of me and—" Daisy shoved in a fork loaded with egg to keep from finishing that sentence.

"You and Beckett?" Stryke prompted. He set down the chai and rapped his knuckles on the table. He wore a platinum ring on his thumb, fashioned by their father.

"I thought you guys approved of him," she defended.

"Trouble liking the lone wolf is not the mark of approval earned, Daisy Blu."

"Oh, please." She rolled her eyes at her brother's pompous assumptions about Beck. "He's the first decent wolf I've ever dated."

"He is also packless."

"He's kind and caring."

"I sure as hell hope you haven't bonded with him."

Eyes flashing wide, she met her brother's discerning brown gaze. "That's none of your business, Stryke."

"Daisy." He leaned across the table. His voice lowered, and his stare intensified. "Don't be stupid about this. Sure, you can date the guy and piss off Dad all you like. But you know bonding with another wolf is serious shit."

"I know." She set down her fork and leaned forward to clasp Stryke's hands. "Don't worry. We're just having fun. Dating and, you know, doing stuff like playing a little one-on-one pond hockey. I like the guy, okay?"

"Yeah, well, we all know what 'like' means to you."

"Because it means the same to you."

They'd shared their ideas of love and like a few summers ago, after Stryke's first devastating breakup with a human woman who had moved to New York for her career. How he had wanted to follow her, but family compelled him even more.

"And since you're in like," Stryke said sharply, "pretty soon you won't be able to resist the urge to bond."

"Like you would know. You've never bonded with anyone."

"And I don't intend to until I find the one. Someone in a pack, whom my family approves of, and who will give me children and—"

"Really? Stryke, you're not making an order. Bonding with someone you love is a real thing. You don't do it to please anyone but yourself and that person. You make it sound so clinical. Like it's been written down in some rule book, and you have to check off all the right boxes before it can happen."

"Maybe that's the way it's supposed to be. Daisy, the pack has rules."

"I know. But how's a lone wolf like Beckett Severo ever supposed to find someone to bond with if he isn't allowed to date within packs?"

"That's his problem, not yours."

Daisy stabbed her fork at the thinly sliced steak. "I can't believe you're being like this. You're always the one to see both sides and weigh things rationally."

He sat back and rubbed a palm over his close-cropped hair. Daisy liked that he kept it shaved a quarter inch to his scalp. His eyes were so bold and bright, so telling, and nothing should distract from her brother's appeal.

He was being anything but appealing right now.

"Much as you may not believe it," he said, "I am standing on middle ground. Good for you that you've found someone you enjoy spending time with. I mean, it's difficult for us—our breed—in the mortal realm. Much more so for us males." He lowered his voice, his eyes taking in the half-filled dining room. "It's not like the female werewolf population is vibrant up here in this neck of the woods."

"You need to go to Europe. I hear the werechicks are abundant over there."

"Is that so? Werechicks?" He winked and sipped his chai. "We are heading to Paris next summer for Kambriel's wedding." He shook his head and chuckled. "Can you imagine me falling in love with a fancy Parisian werewolf? That's never going to happen."

"Why not? You think the wolves in Paris are too good for you? I think you're too good for them. You're a wolf out of place, Stryke. A renaissance man stuck in the land of ten thousand flannel shirts. I know you'd fit in well in Europe."

"Just because I don't wear flannel like the rest of the population doesn't mean I don't fit in."

"Sure." But she really wanted to see her brother flourish, and to find that woman he dreamed about. "We'll leave it for the trip, eh?"

He tipped his latte to her, then sipped. Suddenly Stryke sat straight. His chin lifted as he sniffed the air. He set down the cup without a sound.

"What is it?" she asked.

Staying her curiosity with a subtle lift of his forefinger, he slowly turned about, taking in the patrons sitting nearby. The restaurant was peopled with all sorts, including a few hunters in flannel and orange vests who had stopped for a fuel break during the morning hunt.

"He's here," Stryke said. "Call your boyfriend."

"What? Who's here?"

"The hunter who almost killed me. The one with the silver arrows. I can smell him."

* * *

Beck got the call from Daisy just as he was trying to avoid talking to his mother about what she had seen last night. His cell phone jangled. Bella glared that motherly "don't you dare" look at him.

Beck put up his hands, signaling he'd let the call go to voice mail.

"Are you the ghost wolf?" Bella asked.

"Mom, I don't know what you think you saw, but it was definitely not that." He hated lying to her. But she didn't need that kind of angst right now. "The snow was blowing last night. I'm sure your vision was blurred."

"I have excellent vision," she snapped. "And I know what I saw. That werewolf was not you."

"So maybe there was another wolf around the house last night? I should go take a look around. Make sure everything is secure—"

"Beckett Severo, stop lying to me!"

Beck's phone rang again. He clenched a fist near his hip pocket.

"Answer it!" Bella entreated.

He dug out the phone, saw it was from Daisy and answered. "Hey, I'm at my mom's right now. Can I call you back?"

"I don't want to bother you, Beck, but I'm with Stryke, and he's one-hundred-percent sure we're sitting in the restaurant with the hunter who has been using the silver in his ammunition."

"Does your brother recognize his scent?"

"Yes. We're at Panera. Can you get here fast?"

"Yes. Uh…" Bella silently waited for his attention. "Yes. Ten minutes. Don't let him get away."

"He just sat down. You've got maybe twenty minutes at most."

"Thanks." He shoved his phone into a pocket and grabbed his coat from the rack by the door. "Mom, we're going to have to take a rain check on this conversation."

Shuffling around to block his path, Bella flattened her back against the front door. "What was that about?"

"It's Daisy. She's...." Beck exhaled. "She thinks she's found the hunter who killed Dad."

Bella's jaw dropped open. Her hand went instinctively to her belly, smoothing across the swollen signal of life beneath the red robe. In an instant, his mother was reduced from a confident woman to a frail, needy girl who just needed to be protected from all the bad things the world put before her.

He pulled her in for a hug. But if he didn't move now, he may lose this only chance. "I have to go."

She gripped his coat. "What are you going to do if it is him?"

Beck ground his jaw tightly.

"Don't you dare, Beckett Severo. Your father would never—"

"You know I would never hurt another man, Mom."

"Do I? Beck, if you are the ghost wolf—what I saw on the news the other night…"

He hugged her because he didn't know what else to do to quell her fears. Because her fears were real. And even he wasn't sure what the ghost wolf would do to the hunter.

"I can handle this," he said. He would have to handle it. "But I have to hurry. I'll call you later."

"No, I'll stop by your place," she called as he dashed outside into the daylight.

"Mom, don't do that! It could be dangerous."

He thought she said, "Danger doesn't frighten me."

Beck shook his head as he fired up the engine. His mother had been fearless when his father was alive. It was the vampire in her. It had emboldened a woman who had once been merely mortal, a website designer and dancer who hadn't asked to get involved in the realm of all she had once believed fantasy. Love had changed her life irrevocably.

He could completely understand that emotional power now.

"Too many people could get hurt," he muttered as the truck spun out of the driveway. "Have to stop this now."

Fifteen minutes later Beck spied Daisy in the Panera parking lot, walking alongside the brother with the short hair. Stryke, the one who had been hit with the hunter's arrow yet had recovered well enough to deliver him some punishing blows in the bar.

Beck touched his ribs over the kidney and muttered, "Damn faery."

Clad in a pink sweater darker than her hair, and knee-high brown riding boots, Daisy waved to him, pointing north with a mittened hand.

He drove up alongside the siblings, rolling down his window. Stryke ran around to the passenger side and hopped into the truck.

"He just left," Daisy said.

"Drive," Stryke said. "I've got his scent, but now that he's in a vehicle he'll be harder to track. Step on it!"

Beck leaned out the window and kissed Daisy. "Thanks. I'll be back for you."

"I'm good. I'll head home. You two do what you need to do."

"Right," Stryke directed as they pulled out of the parking lot. "He's headed south, out of town."

Beck followed directions, his fingers clenched about the steering wheel. His senses were so heightened, he couldn't get Daisy's smell out of his brain. And combined with Stryke's subtle aftershave, he had to lean his head out the window and suck in the brisk air.

"Chill," Stryke directed. "You're on edge, man. I can

feel your need to shift. Relax. We'll get him. We just need to follow him, discover where he lives."

Beck could indeed feel the shift. It stirred in his fingers and felt as if his gut muscles were being stretched up and down. The last thing he wanted to do was reveal what he was to Daisy's brother. That would end any possible relationship with the sister right there. And he didn't want to hurt the guy.

"I can't let him wander out to harm another wolf," Beck argued. "We've got to stop him now."

He stepped on the gas, tracking the hunter's car only four car lengths behind.

"I want to get the bastard as much as you do, but we have to think about this." Stryke rubbed his hands together.

"You called me. I have to assume you wanted to go after the man as much as I do."

"Yes, but to track him. Get a bead on him. There has to be a better way. A way that involves more than you leaping in to break his neck. You need numbers."

"Numbers?"

"More wolves."

"Why? To give that asshole more targets?"

"If you think some big white ghost wolf is scaring hunters, what do you think a whole pack would do?"

"Yeah well, I'm fresh out of a pack."

"I've noticed." Stryke rapped the car door with his knuckles. "My brothers will help."

Beck winced.

"Dude, you want to date my sister? You'd better get tight with her brothers."

Right. But getting tight might involve shifting, and that way was too dangerous. And if not that, Beck wasn't sure how many more beatings he could take from the quartet.

Once out of city limits, the hunter's truck pulled off the

road and drove up a private driveway. Beck pulled over to the side of the road and parked.

"I can do this myself." He pulled the key out of the ignition and grabbed the door handle.

Stryke's fist twisted his jaw sharply to the left. Beck shook his head. "What. The. Hell?"

"I've thought about it. We do this with my brothers or not at all."

Beck rubbed his jaw, unsure if the bone had cracked, but he wouldn't be surprised if it had. "Fuck."

"Look, that's the only option I'm giving you. Otherwise I knock out your lights, drive you back to town and leave you to sleep it off in the cold again."

"I can take you."

"You want to try?"

They were wasting time. Likely they'd parked before the hunter's land. Beck needed to track the hunter into the woods.

"Call them," Beck said. "But if they're not here in ten minutes, I'm going to track him down on my own."

"We've got time," Stryke said as he pulled out his phone. "Look."

Beck saw a single headlight zigzagging at the back part of the land.

"He's on a snowmobile," Stryke said. "I'm sure he's got traps to check and other shit. We'll find him. Hey, Trouble! Gather the troops. I found the hunter who sliced me."

Chapter 21

Daisy slowed on her walk toward home. A brown Mercedes seemed to be following her. She dared a look over her shoulder. The woman behind the wheel waved and pulled over to the curb. A smiling chestnut-haired woman got out, tucking a scarf about her neck. "Are you Daisy?"

"Uh, yeah?" She thought she recognized the woman, but with the scarf over her hair and the winter coat tugged up around her neck, she couldn't be sure.

"I couldn't let him leave like that. So quick. And without an explanation. I need to talk to you," she said, and held out a gloved hand to shake. "I think we can help one another."

Daisy tugged off her mitten and shook the woman's hand. "And you are?"

"I'm Belladonna. Beck's mom."

Beck drove around the posted private-property signs, heading south along the forest edge. He didn't want to have to deal with trespassing issues.

Thing was, he knew this land. Or knew about it. It was a mysterious piece of property that had oftentimes sat vacant over the years. Rumors in Burnham told that it had been owned for centuries by the same family. Family members came and went, some taking up residence, others living off-site, yet keeping the property tidy until the next willing family member decided to occupy the spot.

Beck hadn't heard that a new resident had moved in. In fact, his wolf had, on occasion, gone sniffing around the boarded-up house. But the smoke wafting from the chimney proved someone was living there now.

"There's Trouble," Stryke said, pointing out a black Ford pickup truck. "Blade and Kelyn are with him, too."

Beck pulled off the gravel road onto an old trail that hadn't been used for years, to judge from the tangled and rusted barbed-wire fencing. There were no private-property signs, so both guessed this would be a good spot.

"Still got him in your nose?" Beck asked as they got out to meet the brothers.

"Barely. We'll have Kelyn track him from the air. Kelyn!"

"The air?"

Beck shook his head, but followed Stryke over to the brothers, who got out of the truck. When he saw Trouble marching toward him with a focused look in his dark eyes, Beck flinched. And then he took the punch to his gut like a trooper.

"Good to see you again, lone wolf," Trouble said, retracting his fist. "Stryke says you've spotted the hunter who tried to take him out?"

Straightening from the less-than-friendly punch, Beck nodded. "Could be the same hunter who killed my father."

"Well then, we're on it." Trouble gathered the brothers around. No skirt today, just leather pants, a turtleneck and a vest that looked like real fur—but really? "What's the plan, Stryke?"

"Kelyn needs to fly high and track him from the air. I'm losing his scent," Stryke explained, "so we need to hurry. Let's walk in a ways in *were* form and shift far from the road. Beck, follow us. You cool with that?"

"So long as we're not standing around. Let's go." Beck strode forth.

Trouble wandered out to lead, along with Stryke.

The quiet dark one, Blade, took up the rear, and Kelyn was nowhere to be seen. Until Beck noticed the fall of faery dust on the trail ahead of him. He tilted his head back and saw the bird-size figure soaring through the treetops.

"Kelyn will find him," Stryke called back.

They tracked deep into the forest, where the thick pine trees brushed Beck's face with fragrant yet scratchy needles. The ground was packed with snow and layers of brown pine needles. He noted the lingering scent of rabbits, squirrels and deer.

The faery flew back and near Trouble's head where, Beck assumed, the brothers were somehow communicating. When Trouble pulled off his shirt and kicked off his boots, the others followed suit, save for Blade.

Time for the shift. Beck stripped down, tossing his clothes near the base of the same tree as the brothers had. That they'd not beaten him bloody yet was a good sign. But they had no stake in finding the hunter because of Severo's death. They were here because of Stryke.

The brothers shifted while Beck struggled to control his inner wolf's need to shift to werewolf. They weren't going werewolf right now. Wolves on four legs would serve this mission much better by providing stealth and a smaller target.

But the ghost wolf wanted out.

Trouble's wolf was black dusted with white around his maw. The cocky fighter howled as he dropped to all fours. Stryke, a brown wolf, wandered up beside the punch-happy brother. Blade—he didn't see him anywhere.

Snow began to sift down in thick white flakes. Beck

felt the coolness on his face and used that to concentrate on shifting to four legs.

The brothers had loped on ahead.

The faery buzzed about Beck's head. He swatted at it, then slammed a shifting palm against the birch trunk. "Fuck" was his last human utterance as the ghost wolf took control.

Daisy warmed up hot chocolate for Bella and was thrilled to find a few unbroken almond biscotti in the cupboard. The vampiress sat silently watching as Daisy went about the motions of preparing hospitality. Daisy had spent a lot of time with her grandfather Creed, so she wasn't leery around vampires, nor did she fear them. They were just another breed that occupied the vast and wonderful world.

Yet Bella had been a mortal until she was bitten in her twenties. Daisy couldn't imagine what it must be like to have known one life, then to be thrust into another life that was so different. Drinking and eating food one day, and then to survive on blood the next? It sounded almost as complicated as trying to balance one's wolf with one's faery.

As she set the steaming chocolate and a plate of cookies before Bella, Daisy realized her faux pas.

"I'm sorry. You probably don't eat."

Bella turned the mug around and gripped the handle. "I like to taste things." She sipped the hot chocolate. "Ohmy-goodness." Her eyes brightened, and her cheeks grew noticeably rosier. "This is mead."

"Beck likes it, too." Daisy sipped from a mug that declared her a bookworm.

"My son does love his sweets. This must be how you won his heart."

Daisy didn't know what to say to that. Because really?

"Oh, I'm sorry," Bella suddenly said. "I'm sure it was more than a sip of chocolate that turned Beckett's eyes onto you." She sighed and drew her gaze gently over Daisy's face. "You seem like a nice girl. Your hair is pink, though." Bella sipped again, quickly.

"It's natural. I'm half faery on my mom's side."

"Oh, that's right. She's so pretty, your mother. Married Casanova, eh?"

"I hadn't thought anyone called my father that anymore."

"Sorry. It's what I remember the women used to whisper about Malakai Saint-Pierre."

Indeed, her father had been the area's resident Casanova before her birth. But no more. Her mom and dad were solid.

"Are all your siblings like you?" Bella asked. "Half werewolf and half faery?"

Daisy laid out the details on the family genetics, and Bella consumed the whole mug of hot chocolate and a few nibbles of biscotti. "I like your son a lot, Mrs. Severo," Daisy offered. "He's kind and funny and, well, he is so honorable."

"He takes after his father," Bella said. She looked aside, catching her chin in hand. Her thoughts were probably on her late husband, Daisy decided, and she didn't know what to say. But after a few seconds, Bella returned with a smile. "I hope the next is a girl." She smoothed a hand over her belly.

"Beck told me he's going to be a big brother. If you ever need anything, you must let me know."

"Thank you, Daisy. What I need is to know if Beck has spoken to you about his father."

"Like how?"

Bella shook her head, bewildered. "I don't think he's

talked to anyone about Severo's death. He certainly hasn't with me. And I think he's holding it all inside. And now I've learned about… Uh, have you heard the news on TV about the ghost wolf?"

"He told you?"

"I figured it out. So you know that's what Beck is? Whew. I was pretty sure he had told you, but just now I had a moment where I wasn't sure if I should say anything."

"I saw him shift," Daisy offered. "I was in the woods one night he was out. So you've only seen the news reports?"

"Actually, I saw him last night. And he didn't look as his werewolf normally does. Has he talked to you about that? Daisy, I'm at a loss." The woman's eyes glossed, and her hands shook as she pushed the mug away. "I need to know my son is okay."

"He believes he has it under control, but I'm not so sure about that." She clasped Bella's hand. "I want him to stop being the ghost wolf."

"Me, too. But how does he do that?"

"Has he told you everything about what he's become?"

Bella shook her head. "I wanted him to talk to me this morning, but then he got a phone call from you and rushed off. Is he going after the hunter?"

"As far as I know, he's just tracking him. The same hunter nearly killed one of my brothers."

"Oh, no. Is he all right?"

"Stryke is great thanks to a little witch magic from Desideriel Merovech."

"Ah, she and her husband, Ivan Drake, are good friends of mine. Your brother is one lucky wolf to be under Dez's care. But tell me, Daisy, what do you know about this beast that my son has become?"

Beck wasn't a beast, but Daisy knew that the ghost wolf

looked like it to most. And if the ghost wolf had a mind of its own that could control Beck, then surely it was a beast that needed to be stopped before it went too far.

"He went to a faery for the gift of the ghost wolf. I think he needs to return to that same faery to get rid of it."

"Then why doesn't he do it? Oh." Bella dropped Daisy's hand and pressed her palms to her face. "I don't know why I didn't see the obvious until now. He wants to avenge his father's death."

Daisy nodded. "I think so."

"I don't want to lose another family member." Bella's voice trembled. "I can't. I don't know how I'd survive—"

Daisy clasped her hand. "We won't let that happen. It's going to be all right. I'll do anything I can to make it so."

"Can you get him to talk to the faery?" Bella asked.

Daisy nodded, though she wasn't sure she had such persuasive powers over Beck. She didn't want to trick him or force him to do something that she felt was best for him. He had to do whatever he felt was right for him. But revenge wouldn't be right for anyone.

"Do you love my son?" Bella asked.

"Love?" It was more on the lines of serious like. But Daisy thought to keep the explanation of her scale of emotional commitment to herself. So she simply nodded.

"Then for the sake of your futures," Bella said, "we need to stop the ghost wolf."

Chapter 22

Denton Marx stood in a snowy clearing, a leather-bound pair of binoculars dangling about his neck. At the sight of the wolf pack charging toward him, he turned to race back toward the snowmobile he'd parked near a ravine. Hasty bootsteps kicked up snow in his wake.

One wolf, the darkest in color, split off and headed toward the snowmobile, while the other herded him away from the escape vehicle.

Yet from out of the forest emerged a creature that surprised even the wolves. The black-and-white wolf, getting ready to lunge for Denton, suddenly startled. Tail curling down and between its legs, it lowered its head and looked around behind it. Its brother backed away, growling, showing its teeth to the ghost wolf.

Denton, scared but fiercely determined not to lose the opportunity he'd waited weeks for, hissed as the two wolves suddenly began to shift to larger forms.

"About time," he said. "I knew I'd see this sooner or later. Just one silver bullet should do the job nicely. And then, finally, I can free Sencha."

Overhead, a darting birdlike creature gave the hunter little worry. He didn't remark on the creature's wings or the sprinkling of dust that sifted down to blend into the snow's glinting surface. Yet higher flew a dark shadow with a vast wingspread.

What the hell?

Marx needed a weapon. He raced for the snowmobile, a fascinating contraption that he favored over a horse as conveyance in this deep snow. Behind him the shifted werewolves growled at the approaching white beast. It was two heads higher than them and did not slow its approach.

The black-and-white werewolf lunged for the white, ghostly wolf. Not slowing, the ghost wolf slapped the nuisance out of its path.

Shaking and determined, Denton eyed his bow and arrows strapped to the back of the snowmobile. The shotgun was tucked in a knapsack. Just twenty more strides…

Leaping, the ghost wolf passed him and landed on the snowpack before the snowmobile. The force of the creature's landing pushed the snowmobile over the ravine's edge, and it tumbled down forty feet to an iced-over stream edged with boulders frosted in thick snowfall.

Denton swore and turned to face the monstrous creature that loomed over him. He'd stood up to a vampire, a demon, a snake shifter and more. He would not back down now. He'd invested too much. Claws slashed the air before him and—

Suddenly the werewolves snarled into a tangle, attacking the ghost wolf. Crawling toward the ravine, Denton wanted to slip away from the danger. He wasn't armed. But he wouldn't miss this for the world. Real werewolves going at one another. If he could just kill one of them…

But it was over too quickly. One of the werewolves yelped, having taken a brutal slap of claws to its back. The ghost wolf stepped away, and then raced off toward the forest.

In but a blink the two remaining werewolves shifted to their wolf state and wandered over to the ravine's edge.

"No!" Denton cried. He clung to the edge, thankful he'd worn the rusted cleats he'd found in the shed on his boots, which kept him from falling.

The pack growled, showing him their teeth. One lunged for him, snapping warningly. Denton felt as if they were merely trying to scare him.

Stupid wolves.

They turned and raced off, leaving him dangling over the ravine even as the great winged creature circled overhead.

Beck arrived at the site where they'd shed their clothing and shifted, coming out of the ghost wolf with the agonizing twist at his spine and muscles that had accompanied the shift this past week. As if it wanted to cling to its werewolf shape and never release him.

He landed on the ground on all fours and grabbed his jeans. Behind him, he sensed the faery change shape, coming to full size. A glance over his shoulder revealed Kelyn, fully clothed—how did he manage that?—standing with hands to his hips.

"Don't say anything," Beck barked as he pulled up his jeans. A wave of dizziness wobbled him over the snowy surface.

"What's to say?" Kelyn offered with a chuff. "You…all right?"

"Of course!"

The brothers arrived as a pack and shifted up to *were* shape. Something dropped down from the treetops with a flap of wings. Without bothering to grab clothing, Trouble stalked up to Beck and slammed his hand beneath his jaw, shoving him against a birch tree. "What the hell?"

Beck eyed the bleeding cuts slashed into his shoulder. From the ghost wolf.

"Give him some room, Trouble," the faery insisted. He kicked the snow and turned to retrieve his brother's pants. He tossed them to Trouble. "Get dressed."

Trouble shoved Beck hard against the throat, but backed off, taking his brother's offering and pacing away. His back was marred with three long slashes. He slapped his shoulder. "Damn, that hurt!"

"You're the ghost wolf?" Stryke said as he pulled a sweater over his head. "Why didn't you say something, man? It would have been good to have some advance warning."

"I hadn't meant to shift like that," Beck defended. He stumbled on nothing more than the snow, but caught himself by balancing his arms out to his sides. He shook out his left foot until he felt the bones snap into place. Damn, that was just wrong. "It's getting out of control. But it doesn't matter right now. The hunter is on foot. We have to go after him."

"The hunter will keep," Stryke said. "But you are another issue. Who did this to you?"

"It's faery magic," Kelyn offered. The blond one drew his violet gaze across Beck's face. "I can sense it."

When Beck made to argue, he was stopped with a challenging lift of Kelyn's chin. If the faery could sense the origins of his ghost wolf, perhaps *he* could help him? No. He didn't know where he stood with the brothers. And wherever that had been, his stance had just gotten worse.

"Did Daisy do this for you?" Trouble asked, stomping back over as he pulled his fur vest on. "I didn't think she could do stuff like that."

"Daisy did not—"

"It takes great faery magic to accomplish something like the ghost wolf," Kelyn said. "And you can't control it?" The brother shook his head and wandered off to where

Blade, the dark, silent one—how had he gotten dressed so quickly?—ventured toward the parked vehicles.

"This is not good," Stryke said. "The hunter has seen us shift."

"He already knew," Kelyn called back.

"What?" both Stryke and Trouble asked. They rushed to catch up to Kelyn and Blade.

"I heard him say 'it's about time' while I was hovering overhead. The man knows what he's hunting," Kelyn said. "The question is, *how* does he know, and why the hunt?"

"To bag a werewolf," Trouble offered. "Idiot humans don't need any better reason than that. But now…" He glanced over a shoulder at Beck. "I bet that hunter's sights have been set higher. Fuck, man, you pack a punch as that creature. Excellent challenge, I must say. You got me good."

"I wasn't trying to get you, good or otherwise." Beck started down the trail toward the vehicles behind the brothers. "I wanted to get that bastard."

"You pushed his weapons out of the way," Kelyn said. "You saved my brothers."

Beck waved that suggestion off with a dismissive gesture. They'd fucked this one up, and now the hunter would not stop until he'd gotten his prey.

Back at the trucks, Beck jumped into his and fired up the engine.

"Where you headed?" Trouble asked.

He didn't reply. He'd had enough of the group approach.

"You can't do this on your own, man!" Trouble called.

The dark one shook his head and said, "Let him go."

And with that, Beck drove off. He avoided driving by the hunter's property again. The man wouldn't have returned home yet with his snowmobile a loss. He'd have to walk. Might make it back by nightfall.

And by nightfall Beck hoped to return.

* * *

Daisy had just arrived at Beck's house to find he wasn't home. She and Bella had decided the gentle approach to getting Beck to return to the faery might work.

Just when she thought to hop in her car and call a brother to see if they were still out hunting, or possibly had stopped for a drink afterward, Beck's truck pulled up the driveway.

She laughed at herself for thinking her brothers would have a drink with Beck. Beck would probably suspect they were greasing him up for the slaughter. Her brothers meant well. And the fact they'd gone to help Beck look for the hunter only proved that. They'd accepted him in their own way.

How to adjust her father's attitude about the lone wolf?

Beck charged out of his truck toward where she stood at the front door. Daisy sensed the anger wavering off him like steam after a shower. She stepped down onto the shoveled sidewalk because it felt wrong to stand on the step, higher than him. She wanted to show him respect, an innate wolf quality.

"What are you doing here, Daisy?" he asked as he walked by her and shoved the key into the door lock.

No hello kiss? No hug?

Though she wore a winter coat and her kitty-eared cap and gloves, Daisy rubbed her arms. She wasn't cold, just…

"What did I do?" she asked. "Beck, are you mad at me?"

Shoving the front door open, he turned and slid his eyes over her face. Just when she thought he would soften and pull her in for that hug and kiss, he gritted his jaws.

"Didn't it go well with my brothers?"

"They let the hunter go."

"What?"

"Your brothers…" He fisted the air. "I don't want to

talk about it. I'm…not in the best mood. I think you should leave."

"But, Beck—"

"Daisy." He grabbed her by her shoulders as a father would a child. "Don't you understand how dangerous it is for you to be around me? I don't want to hurt you."

"Yes, but—what happened with my brothers? Tell me."

Jaw tight, he finally blew out a breath and confessed, "They saw me shift to the ghost wolf."

"Shit."

"They took it well enough, but damn it, the hunter got away. They wouldn't let me go after him."

"Or were they protecting a human from a ghost wolf who might kill it?"

He squeezed her arms tightly. Grimaced. Then let her go. "Right. You would think that."

"Beck, they were saving you from yourself. You can't continue to shift to the ghost wolf—"

"Leave," he insisted.

His tone was curt. Final. So he was in a bad mood and didn't want to talk? She could stand up to a grumpy man any day.

But when he turned to show her his teeth, canines down, Daisy stumbled backward, stepping off the sidewalk onto the snowy bank. She almost toppled, but caught herself.

"Go!" he said. "Get the hell away from me!"

With no words to reply, Daisy rushed to her car and got inside. Heartbeat frantic, she fumbled to turn the key in the ignition. Beck stood on the steps watching as she backed out the driveway. And only when she turned onto the main road did she see his front door close.

"He may be a lone wolf, but he sure likes to work the alpha vibes," she muttered. "Stupid, angry wolf."

Intellectually she knew he probably needed time alone

to work off some steam, to come down from the weirdness she suspected the ghost wolf worked on him every time he shifted. He had a lot to deal with. The hunter who had killed his father was out there, and he had been close enough to…

Would he have killed the hunter had her brothers not been there to stop him?

Daisy shook her head, not wanting to believe Beck capable of murder.

But it wasn't Beck she had to worry about. It was the ghost wolf.

Malakai Saint-Pierre dialed up his son Stryke because he knew he had plans to meet Daisy this morning. It was evening, but she hadn't been at her place. "Stryke? Your mom wanted me to pick up some things at the store, so I stopped by to look in on Daisy. She's not home. You see her today?"

"Uh, this morning for breakfast?"

That was a strange kind of nonanswer that had ended on a questioning tone. What was the kid hiding? Stryke was the siblings' confidante, and he was damned good at keeping secrets. "So where is she now?"

"I uh…haven't any idea, Dad."

Evasive? Hmm…Kai could always tell when his children were hiding something, or trying to protect one another. Which they'd managed with flair while growing up. And just because they were adults now didn't mean they'd stopped the group protection ploys.

"You sure you haven't the tiniest guess at where your sister could be?"

"Nope."

"Fine. Talk to you later, Stryke."

Kai hung up and swung the car around at the corner. He had a damned good idea where to find his daughter.

He'd hated treating Daisy like that. The moment her car had reached the end of his driveway, Beck had wanted to rush out and chase after her, beg her to forgive him and give her a second chance.

But he wasn't stupid. The last thing he wanted was to hurt Daisy. And right now, he was so wound up in trying *not* to shift to the ghost wolf that it was all he could do to keep it back.

So Beck had gone out back, just off the snow-covered patio where he'd laid out stones last summer to form another patio around a fire pit. A punching bag hung from the oak tree, and he pummeled it with his fists. Stripped to the waist, he worked so furiously that the sweat didn't have time to freeze.

He beat the bag soundly, kicking it, imagining it as the hunter. So long as he kept physical, moving his body, engaging his muscles and mind, the ghost wolf kept back, seeming satisfied with this workout.

His father had helped him hang this punching bag. Severo had been the first to try it out, giving it a good kick and then remarking that he was getting too old for the physical stuff.

Beck had laughed and clapped his father across the back. He was stronger than his son, but Severo did like to spend most of his time hanging around Bella. He would have been proud to know his wife was carrying his second child.

Another punch set the chain jangling as the bag bounced in the air and fell heavily. The solid oak branch creaked.

What would he do with a little brother? Or sister? How would that child's life be affected, growing up without a father? It didn't seem fair. It wasn't fair. And Beck certainly had no idea how to lead someone younger, to show them a good example and raise them right.

Maybe his mom could find a new husband? No. He didn't want that for the family, or for Mom. She would mourn Severo for a long time, he suspected. As would he.

Because he did mourn. He felt his father's loss in his gut, and his head, and his broken heart.

"Not broken," he muttered as he delivered a punishing kick to the bag. "Can't be. I won't let it be!"

So maybe he hadn't moved through the grief as he'd convinced himself he had. Screw it. He was tough. He could handle this. Because he had to. He was the last standing Severo man.

He hadn't heard the approach, but now he smelled the intruder. Beck swung around and charged the man, who stood not ten feet away. He shoved his shoulders and pinned him against a wide oak trunk. Growling and showing his thick canines to the man, Beck didn't even blink when he realized who it was.

Malakai Saint-Pierre smirked, then narrowed his brows. His face changed from the surprise of the attack to a determined expression indicative of a deadly predator.

"Come at me, boy," Kai challenged. "Let's see what you've got."

Chapter 23

Shoving away from the older, stronger wolf, Beck did not stand down. Instead he put up his fists and growled. How dare the man show up at his home—on his private property—without an invite?

He swung a fist. Kai dodged it with a taunting chuckle.

So the alpha wolf would laugh at him? Wrong move.

Beck swung a left hook, knowing the man would dodge that, and so caught him in the kidney with a right uppercut.

Kai grunted at the connection. "Good one."

His opponent moved so quickly, Beck could but shuffle on the snow-and-ice-packed ground, his boots slipping, but he maintained stance. His adrenaline pumped as he took a fist to the jaw, and another to the gut. Still not as powerful as the faery's punches.

Daisy's father pushed him, and Beck lost footing on an ice slick, landing in a snowbank. He scrambled up, barreling into the other wolf. They both tumbled to the snowy ground, fists finding their mark against tender organs. The Saint-Pierres had admonished and ridiculed him for the last time. Beck's father would have never taken such treatment. He would show Malakai Saint-Pierre who he was dealing with.

They battled it out, crashing into the boxing bag, other times rolling across the snow as fists flew and kicks connected with ribs and shins. Grunts of exertion and huffs of breath leaving pummeled lungs marked the air in puffs of chilled pain.

Beck struggled inside. He didn't want to do this. He fought against the man he should try to impress in order to win a chance to love his daughter. Yet he had already stolen Daisy out from under her father's care, and Kai had every right to come at him with all he had. Which is what he was doing now.

Beck landed on the packed snowbank behind him, gripping his gut. Ab muscles tight and flexing, he pushed off from the low bank, yet couldn't quite stand, landing on his knees before the towering werewolf, who heaved and panted over him.

Depleted, his soul ached more than his muscles ever could. It was too much. He had suffered too much lately.

"I can't do this," Beck sputtered. Blood drooled from his mouth. His jaw had taken a bruising punishment. "Not right. But he would want me to…maybe. I don't know anything anymore. He shouldn't have…"

Beck heaved in a breath, and when he exhaled, he caught his palms on the boot-trampled snow before him. "He shouldn't have left me." His ribs ached with each inhale. But worse, his heart clenched. "I need him. I don't know what to do anymore. I…I can't…"

He was acting foolish before the other wolf. But he couldn't stop the fluid stream of emotion that coiled up from his broken ribs and squeezed about his heart before spilling from his mouth.

"I loved him. I…I want him back."

"Boy, your father was a good man."

Beck nodded, bowing his head, his focus on the man's rubber-soled biker boots. His father had worn the same, yet Severo's boots had been as tattered and worn as the man had been. Beck remembered trying to walk in his father's boots when he'd been a quarter his size, stumbling about in the heavy things until he'd toppled into a graceless sprawl. Severo would pick him up and hold him upside down from his ankles, swinging him until he begged to be tossed onto the sofa in a fit of giggles.

"He was my family," Beck muttered, his bloodied fingers clawing into the snow. "I've known nothing else. I can't accept another family just like that. It wouldn't feel right. Please understand…"

Beck felt Kai slip his fingers through his hair. The man jerked his head back to meet his eyes. "You're like your father, Beckett Severo. And that's something you should be proud of."

And when the wolf should have delivered the final punishing blow to knock Beck out and put him out of him misery, Kai did something strange. He pulled Beck up to his feet and wrapped his arms around him, crushing Beck's face to his chest in a hug.

Beck struggled, but only initially. It was too difficult to fight now. He was exhausted. Emotionally, he was broken. *Heartbroken*. He had only wanted one final hug from his father. And now, he clung to Malakai Saint-Pierre and buried his face against his shirt. He didn't cry. Tears had long left him. But his body shuddered with the pent-up pain and grief that he'd held within for too long.

It flowed out now, shaking his bones in the frigid air and against the man's brawny frame. He couldn't think to push away because this was stupid or nonsensical. He needed this release. So he surrendered to it.

Kai gave the back of Beck's head a firm pat. "Give it time. You'll come through this. I know your father was proud of you, and you won't let him down, will you, boy?"

But he already had.

Pierced through his heart by an intangible silver-tipped arrow, Beck disengaged from Kai. "I think I have let my father down. I've done something terrible."

Beck shoved away and shuffled back to fall against the snowbank that had been beaten down by repeatedly catching his sorry body during the fight. "Mister Saint-Pierre, I have to tell you something."

"Is it about my daughter? I know you're fucking her, boy."

Beck winced.

"Just let me say one thing." Kai leaned in so close that Beck wasn't sure if the man would bite him, punch him or hug him again. "If you marry my daughter, then you'll have no choice but to join our pack."

"I…I…" What? "I don't know what to say to that."

"Just putting it out there." Kai straightened and smacked a bloody fist in his palm. His grin wasn't so much menacing as playful, much like Trouble's teasing I-like-to-beat-you-bloody smile. Like father like son. Or vice versa?

"I've harmed a human," Beck confessed. "I'm sure of it. It was on the news." Sitting there, he caught his head in his palms and pulled at his hair. He looked up suddenly. The urge to spill all was irresistible. "I'm the ghost wolf."

Kai cast him a disbelieving tilt of the head. A what-the-hell look. And then he whistled in appreciation. "Is that so? You've been up to some stuff. How the hell is that possible? What *are* you? I thought you were full-blooded werewolf?"

"I am. I…went to a faery after my father's death. All I could think about was avenging his death."

Kai gripped Beck by the shoulders and yanked him to his feet so he stood toe-to-toe with him. "Idiot."

"I— No, I wanted to help, too. To keep the mortal hunters from going after the wolves. And also, to find the one who killed my father."

"Noble. Idiotic," Kai barked. "Faery magic demands a return boon. What did you promise in exchange for such a monster?"

"I'm not sure. I promised the faery any return favor she should request."

Kai swore under his breath. The big wolf shoved his hands into his front pockets and turned away from Beck, eyeing the waxing moon framed by spindly birch trees that edged the iced pond.

"My mother and father," Kai began, "wanted children so badly they sought a faery's help. You know a werewolf can't have a vampire's child?" He turned a glance over his shoulder, and Beck nodded in acknowledgment. "So they needed some faery magic. But they promised a child in exchange for that magic. Each of them, on separate occasions, made that bargain with the same faery. My mother promised her firstborn. My father promised the second-born. Each had their own reasons. They had no idea Blu— my mother—would get pregnant with twins. It's a long story. Suffice it to say I was born cursed and ended up battling a faery for my life and my wife, Rissa's, life to fight that curse. You shouldn't have gone to the sidhe, Beck."

"I was desperate. I knew nothing about faeries save that they could work remarkable magic. I confess…" Beck glanced across the ground and swallowed hard.

"What?" Kai asked. "You asked for your father's life back, yes?"

Beck nodded, ashamed that his desperation had led him to such a request, but still clutching at the ache in his heart that had him wishing it could have been accomplished.

"No good magic can bring back the dead," Kai said. "You should be thankful the faery refused you that request."

"Yes, I know that now. And yet, the hunters are scared shitless to hunt wolves now."

"They won't be for long. Because you can't be the ghost wolf forever." Kai turned and approached him. "How long does it last?"

Beck shrugged. "Not sure. It's…"

He could confess that every time he shifted it was harder, more painful, and that he suspected it would slowly kill him. But he wasn't about to succumb to the fear of an unknown future.

"It'll kill you," Kai decided for himself. The man possessed wisdom comparable to Severo's knowledge. Beck respected him for that. "You better fix this, boy. You can love my daughter, and I suspect you might—"

"I do. I mean, we like one another—"

"Yeah? I know about Daisy and her liking men more than loving them. She's particular that way. Well, if it's like, then I won't have you dying on her. Fix this mess, Beckett. Or I'll fix you."

Kai strode off and around the side of the house. Beck heard the truck engine fire up and drive off.

Spitting blood onto the snow, Beck caught his head in his hands. He did want to fix this. And Daisy deserved better. But not until he'd had his showdown with the hunter.

He needed resolution. One way or another.

Malakai and Rissa Saint-Pierre had raised Daisy to be a strong, independent woman who did not require a man to complete her or make her happy. Happiness came from within. If a person couldn't be happy in and of themselves, then how could they ever be happy with another person in their lives?

As well, her parents had taught her that men respected women and never hurt them.

Daisy pushed back her welding mask to rest at the top of her head. She was no longer in the mood for creation.

Tugging off her leather gloves, she dropped them on the work bench then turned and leaned against it, her eyes unfocused on the wolf she was crafting from bicycle chains.

Beck had not hurt her last night. Physically, anyway. She even tried to convince herself that he had not hurt her emotionally when he'd literally pushed her away and told her to leave him alone.

She knew he had been trying to protect her from that ghostly werewolf within him that threatened to take over and destroy whatever was in its path.

Like her?

He worried about hurting her. And that troubled her. She didn't want him to have that worry, and she didn't want to fear him in any way.

Was he struggling with these issues as much as she was? Certainly he must be. He didn't need to worry about her while he was still grieving his father.

Maybe they'd gotten involved too quickly. Perhaps her father was right in an odd, roundabout way, that Beck wasn't the wolf for her.

She shook her head and set the mask aside. She couldn't deny her heart. Because this was the first man she'd actually worried over so much. That had to mean something. Like maybe he was worth the worry.

"He is," she said, shrugging down her suede work overalls.

Beneath, she wore black leggings and a long gray T-shirt. It was chilly in her place today so she wandered toward the bedroom and snagged a soft blue sweater to pull on over the T-shirt, then stepped into the bathroom to splash water on her face. It got sweaty wearing that welding mask.

Someone knocked on the door, and her heartbeats quickened. She knew who it was. She could scent him. But mingled with Beck's woodsy aroma was an out-of-place floral odor. Perfume?

Rushing to open the door, Daisy found a huge bouquet of red roses standing in the opening.

"Beck?"

"I'm back here. Somewhere."

The roses moved forward, and she guided them in toward the kitchen counter. The long-stem roses were already in a vase that Beck set on the counter. There must be three or four dozen, she guessed.

"They're so pretty."

"Better than blue?" He heaved out a sigh and splayed his hands. "I'm sorry about last night, Daisy. I shouldn't have been so quick with you. I—"

She touched the cut above his eye that was almost healed. She hadn't seen it there yesterday.

"Had a little scuffle," he offered in explanation. "Can you forgive me? I don't want you to get hurt."

"I understand. It was the ghost wolf, wasn't it?"

He nodded, shoved his hands in his front pockets and looked aside. Unsure about touching her? Or not wanting to?

Daisy couldn't stand there and let him get by without a kiss. She stepped before him, and with another stroke over the cut, she kissed him. It was an "everything is good between us" kiss. A promise that they were doing the best they could and that whatever roadblocks they encountered, she was in it for the bumpy ride.

His breaths softened and mingled within hers, and she sensed his heartbeat slow. Finally he surrendered to the embrace. Beck's hands glided up her back, pulling her in to meld her body against his. He was so warm despite having come from outside, where the below-zero temps had reduced the city to an icebox.

"From now on, whenever you tell me to leave, I will without question," she said. "I trust you know yourself and the beast within you."

"I hate having to deal with this beast. But the worst is that you have to deal with it."

"Then maybe it's time you did something about it?" Her conversation with Bella Severo popped into her brain. "Find the faery you made the bargain with and reverse it?"

He smirked. "Your father said the same thing."

He turned toward the couch, but she gripped his coat sleeve. "My father? What the heck?"

Beck shrugged off his coat and tossed it over the couch arm, then tugged her onto the couch with him. "Your dad stopped by my place not long after you left last night."

"But—why? And you were…"

"Not in the best mood or form. After you left I went out back to beat on the boxing bag. Tends to tame the ghost wolf when I work up a good sweat."

Daisy couldn't figure out why her father would go to Beck's house. Though he had called her this morning. Said he'd looked for her last night. She'd lied and said she was out shopping. Right. Because she loved to shop. Not.

"Did he know I had been there?"

"Of course. He could smell you."

"So he went to your place looking for me?"

"I guess so. We fought. Then we had a weird talk."

"You fought?" She couldn't believe this. Sitting up on her knees, facing him, her eyes veered to the cut near his eyebrow. "Beck, are you serious? You and my dad were throwing punches?"

"He came up behind me when I was punching the bag. I turned and threw a defensive punch before I knew who it was. Then he challenged me, and I was already worked up and itching to punch something, so…we shoved each other around a bit."

"A bit? You have a cut on your eyebrow that still hasn't healed. My dad is not someone you should mess with. And did you forget the fact that he's my dad?"

"Daisy, it's cool. We…had a moment. It's all good between us now. Mostly."

"What?" Unsure what to do—hug him or nurse him—Daisy couldn't bring herself to touch him. "Beck, you are blowing my mind with this. I so don't understand."

He bowed his head to her shoulder and nudged his nose up against her chin. The touch was so tender, so needy, she tilted her head beside his.

"Your dad knows how I feel about you now," he said, "and I know you're the most important thing in the world to him. His whole family is. He understands I would never do anything to harm them. I told him I was the ghost wolf."

"So you two beat each other up, then you had sharing time? I don't even know what to say to that. I can't believe Dad didn't mention anything when he called this morning."

"We came to a sort of gentleman's agreement to tolerate one another. At least, that's what I took away from it. Your dad is a good man. I respect him, Daisy."

"I know you do. I just didn't think I'd ever hear about the two of you hugging."

"I didn't say we hugged. Did I say that?"

"No, but your defensiveness makes me think that maybe you did." She smiled and kissed him quickly.

Whatever had gone on between the two, she was pleased Beck was in one piece. And only slightly wounded. Her father had certainly restrained himself.

"I was thinking of going out for a run this afternoon," she offered, thinking a change of subject was due. "It's so cold today. No one is out and about. But my wolf loves running over the crisp, iced snow."

"I can get behind that. And then we'll come back and warm up afterward."

"With hot chocolate," she agreed.

He kissed her cheek. "And sex."

"That's the best motivation I've heard for making the run short."

He stood and pulled her up into his embrace. "We could skip the run. Stay inside and make love all day."

That sounded even better. But if she got him out of the house on a run, there was a good chance they could go looking for the faery.

"To be honest, I could really use a run," she said. "It'll make coming in to warm up all the more fun. Yes?"

He kissed her in answer.

Chapter 24

"Mmm, my gorgeous werewolf."

A pale faery fluttered above the snow, her body draped with sheer fabric. Dozens of winged insects resembling white moths lazily waved their wings from within her finely braided yet flowing hair.

After Daisy and Beck had gone for a run in wolf form, they'd shifted back near a maple tree where they'd left their clothes, dressed, and then Daisy had suggested Beck try to call out the faery. A few kisses, a little snuggling and a pouty big-eyed plead had done the trick.

Beck hadn't spoken, but instead had closed his eyes and summoned the faery he'd called to after his father's death. And she had appeared quickly, in a burst of frost and sultry giggles. And white moths.

"Why have you come back to me, Beckett Severo?" the white faery cooed. "Are you not pleased with the gift I bestowed upon you for nothing more than the promise of a favor returned?"

Daisy lingered behind Beck, fascinated to look upon the gorgeous faery. Her wings had never looked so stunning. It was as if the white faery's wings were liquid and run through with rainbows flowing through her veins as the wings shifted slowly through the air. And even though the thermometer hadn't topped the freezing point, she looked a porcelain princess, alive with life.

"I am thankful for the gift you gave me," Beck said. "The ghost wolf has been successful in pressing back the hunters. The gray wolves in the area feel a safety that they haven't known since before the hunting ban was lifted."

"And were you able to achieve your foremost goal?" the faery asked. She hadn't regarded Daisy yet. Her violet eyes took in Beck as if she admired his strength and courage. And perhaps more than that.

"I know where the hunter who killed my father lives."

"Though your goal was not stated, I could read it in your soul, Beckett Severo. The ghost wolf must end the hunter's life," the faery stated.

"No," Daisy blurted out.

The moths about the faery's hair suddenly swirled into an angry tornado and aimed toward Daisy. She cringed behind Beck's broad shoulder.

With a sweep of a hand over her head, the faery calmed the raging insects that must be a part of her very being. "Do not listen to the half-breed whose curse will not allow her to decide whether she is wolf or faery," she said on an obvious sneer. "My brave warrior werewolf has not yet completed his task. Therefore I cannot request a return boon until you have."

She thought Daisy couldn't decide whether to be wolf or faery. What curse? That didn't make sense. Her father had been the one born with a faery curse upon his head.

"What do you mean by that?" Daisy asked. "I'm sorry, Beck, but I have to know if she senses something about me."

"Yes, I'd like to know, too." He clasped her hand and squeezed reassuringly. "Daisy is having, er, troubles with shifting."

"She was supposed to be born either wolf or faery. She must choose," the faery said curtly. "As simple as that."

"How do you know that?" Daisy asked. "I have brothers who are half-breeds. I've always thought—"

"As the firstborn child of Malakai Saint-Pierre, you shoulder remnants of the curse cast upon him by Ooghna. Your father was not to fall in love with a faery, or he would ransom his heart."

"But the curse was broken when my father killed Ooghna."

The faery snarled at Daisy, revealing pointed teeth. Perhaps she had known the warrior Ooghna, who had once been the Unseelie king's champion.

"Malakai Saint-Pierre murdered the warrior Ooghna. You are meant to be only wolf or only faery, but the curse lingers. Until you make a choice, you will ever struggle between the two."

"So it's as easy as that?" Beck asked. "She simply decides whether she wants to be one or the other?"

The faery nodded. "I thought you called me to discuss you? I do not owe this one any more than what I have revealed."

"I thank you," Daisy rushed out, knowing one should always appease the sidhe. "You've been a tremendous help. And you're right. We called you because Beck is suffering."

"I wouldn't say suffering. As I've said, I appreciate the gift. The ghost wolf is becoming difficult to control," Beck said. "I want to return the power to you, if I may. I don't want the beast to harm innocents."

"Is that so?" The faery's wings flitted back and forth before Beck and Daisy as she considered the wolf's request. "I see no malice in harming humans who claim murder as their goal."

"I do," Beck said. "As a creature of this realm, I cannot justify harming innocents."

"The hunter was not innocent."

"The humans are acting on morals that have been bred into them. Yes, it is a fear-based reaction to want to murder a wolf, but I don't think the ghost wolf can ever change that. And so…I've had a change of heart."

Drawing up her chin, the faery looked down her nose at the werewolf. "What would you give me in return for such a boon?"

"I, uh…"

Daisy placed her other hand over her and Beck's clasped hands. The faery noted their handhold, and again the moths showed their dismay. Daisy dropped his hand. Best tread carefully around this one.

"What would you ask of me?" Beck said.

"I'll take something that is important to you. Your wolf."

"No," Beck answered hastily. "I— No. You mean I would become merely human? Is that even possible?"

"Everything is possible."

"I suppose it is in Faery. But…my wolf. It's what I am. Is there something else? Anything?"

The faery sighed heavily and the moths swirled toward Beck, circling his head testily. Daisy could smell their spring scent, like raindrops on new moss. Only when one of the creatures dashed before her face, cutting her skin with a wing, did she step back and behind Beck again.

"Mind your place," the faery admonished Daisy. And to Beck she said, "The only other option is to take your firstborn."

"My— But I'm not even married."

"You will marry her," the faery said with bored assertion. "And you will have children. Most likely half-breeds, if she chooses her sidhe nature. Always a boon in Faery, mind you. Those are the two options I will give you to, in turn, remove the power of the ghost wolf from your frustratingly moral soul."

Beck glanced down to Daisy. He looked into her for the answer. But what did she know? And what right had she to tell him what was worthy of a trade? They were to be married? If so, then she would never hand over her first-born. But the faery couldn't possibly predict their future when their relationship was yet so new.

"I've always said making the wrong decision is more fun." He shook his head and regarded the faery. "But no. I'd never sacrifice my child."

"Then your wolf it is," the faery said with delight.

"No! I refuse to sacrifice what I am. I just…can't. I guess that means I'll have to deal with the ghost wolf on my own."

"Do not ever seek me again, werewolf," the faery said. "When you have finished what the ghost wolf desires, then I shall return for my favor."

Sweeping her wings forward once, the faery dispersed into thousands of white moths and soared away above the naked treetops.

"I'm sorry." Beck pulled Daisy against him.

"I'll be fine. We're going to be fine."

A kiss to her nose was warm in the icy air and made her smile. "I'll just have to live with this curse."

"No, you don't. Didn't you hear what she said? She can't ask for a return favor until you've completed your task. So don't ever kill the hunter, Beck. It's as easy as choosing to forgive."

He opened his mouth to reply, but only shook his head.

"Yes, forgive," she repeated.

"It's not as easy as you make it sound, Daisy. If I don't kill the hunter, the ghost wolf will kill me."

Sliding an arm around her waist, he walked her back to the truck parked on the gravel road outside the forest. Once inside, the engine running and the seat warmers cranked to high, Beck leaned over and kissed Daisy. "What are you going to choose?"

"What do you mean— Oh. You think she was right?"

"I have to believe she has some means to foretell things about us. And it makes sense. If your dad was cursed, you could carry remnants of that curse within you."

Daisy nodded. "I don't know. It's a weird thing to consider. One or the other? I'm wolf *and* faery. There are parts of my parents in me that I wouldn't want to sacrifice over the other."

"You did tell me you favor your wolf."

"I always have. But to think about giving up any part of me?" Daisy sighed.

"Maybe you should talk to your mother about it? She might be able to confirm what this one said. At the very least, you need to tell her about you carrying the remnants of the curse."

Weird how their lives had been so entwined with their parents'. Beck's mother coming to her to help her son. Her father going to Beck and possibly forming some kind of truce. And Beck suggesting she seek her mother's help.

Family truly was the foundation of everything that made life worth living.

"I'm glad you said you wouldn't give up your firstborn," she said as Beck turned onto the road and flicked on the headlights. The twin lights beamed through falling snow.

"How could I?"

"My grandparents both agreed to such a bargain."

"Your father told me."

"People do what they must when they are desperate."

"Then I guess I'm not desperate."

"What about giving up your wolf? That sounds worse."

"Don't worry. I'll always be wolf." He tugged her hand

to his lap and gave it a squeeze. "And I will like you if you are a wolf. And I will like you if you are faery."

She forced a smile. To make such a decision felt too ominous to think about. She just wanted to return home with Beck, strip away her clothes and make love with him until the sun woke them both.

Mugs bearing the dregs of their hot drinks imbued the air with sweet traces of chocolate. The mugs had been sitting on the nearby nightstand untended for over an hour. Some things were far better to pursue than chocolate.

Daisy rolled over and straddled Beck, knees on either side of his hips. He lay with his head off the pillow, eyes closed, mouth reddened from their long and erotic kissing session. She had come with him only kissing her lips and sucking her nipples.

Now it was her turn to bring him to the edge. Gripping his erection, hot and stiff in her fingers, she rubbed it against her moist folds, seeking to glide it over her clit, which yet pulsed from the delicious orgasm.

Her lover moaned and tilted his hips upward. She used both hands on him, one cupping his thick head, the other gliding up and down the shaft, twisting lightly, then pausing on the sweet spot just below the ridged head of it. That made him hiss and beg. "Please, Daisy."

With a wiggle of her hips, she slid down and took him in her mouth. One hand still held firmly the base of his majestic penis. She loved the thickness of him, the feel of his skin as she laved over it, tasting and teasing. His scrotum was tight against his body, and she sensed he was nearing release.

And Daisy realized that all her life she had strived to compete with men, to win, to prove herself better. She thrived by taking control, owning the win.

Yet now, with Beck literally at her command, she only wished to make him feel as amazing as it felt for her to be loved by him. (Make that liked by him.) She didn't need to best him. She wanted to share life with him.

Lashing her tongue over his cock, she sucked it in and served him the ultimate release.

The waning moon was framed in the window. They lay on their sides, content and basking in the cool light.

"I don't want to compete with you," Daisy said.

"Why not?" he asked with gasping breaths.

"I don't need to. I feel better standing on equal ground with you."

"I like the sound of that. But I'll still let you win at hockey."

She punched him gently and he overreacted, splaying out his arms and groaning. "First she gives me pleasure, then she beats me. I can't win!"

"You've won me. The punches are just a bonus, wolf boy." Daisy nuzzled her face against his neck and took in his heat and the aroma of his bliss. "You know what else I'm thinking about?"

"How many ways you can get your brothers to torment me?"

"I would choose my wolf," she whispered. "Because I feel most connected to my wolf."

"Your wolf is beautiful. So is your faery. Give it more thought. Don't rush into anything. I'll support you no matter what your decision. I love you, Daisy Blu. And that's beyond like in my world."

Chapter 25

"Wow." Daisy's mom, Rissa, curled up her legs on the leather couch that looked out over the backyard and the iced stream. Snowflakes fell like down from an open pillow, dusting the world with peaceful, glinting whiteness. "How long have you been having this problem, sweetie?"

"A few years. It's been mostly a nuisance, but lately the wolf insists on taking over my faery. And vice versa."

"I'm so sorry." Rissa stroked Daisy's hair, imbuing it with a faint trail of faery dust. "I wish you would have told me sooner."

"You know how I am."

"You tend to think something will go away if you just ignore it. Like that time you spilled paint on my sofa and turned the cushion upside down."

"Will you ever let that one go, Mom?"

Rissa laughed. "I guess not. Sorry. I've always thought of your wolf as one of the boys."

"Probably because I am one of the boys."

"You've had difficulty honoring your feminine side, sweetie. Your faery is the wise, gentle, healing and nurturing part of you. I so wanted you to excel with your healing studies, but you were more interested in playing with the boys." Rissa sighed.

"Did I have a choice?"

"Probably not. You know, when you were a baby your sidhe side was prominent, you flew all the time."

"I did?"

Rissa laughed. "Kai was always yelling to me, 'She's in the rafters again!'"

Daisy peered up at the rafters. She only remembered Kelyn fleeing for the wide beams when his brothers tried to gang up on him. Really? She'd flown a lot as a baby?

Her mother nodded. "I couldn't let you outside without a tether."

"You put a leash on me? I so don't remember any of this."

"Yes, well, when the boys came along you got competitive. You forgot the freedom of flight and dropped to earth, choosing to throw mud pies and race through the forest, and chumming around with your father all the time. You wanted to win his time. And you did."

"Wow. No wonder my faery feels so alien. I'm sorry, Mom."

"Nothing to apologize for. You're a bright, beautiful woman. I'm proud of the woman you have become."

"But apparently I'm not completely grown into myself." Daisy exhaled. "I've been so worried about trying to get a job lately, to prove to Dad that I am capable and don't need his help, when all my life it's all that I've done. Depend on him. And now this thing with Beck. Of course Dad would feel protective. Oh, Mom."

"Oh, sweetie, your father will survive this love affair just fine. You do what makes your heart happy. And your wolf. So the faery you spoke to with Beck said you have to choose. As simple as that? Choosing?"

"I guess so. But does it sound right to you?"

"I've grown distant from Faery. Haven't been there

since before I met your father. It sounds possible. I mean, that you carried remnants of Kai's curse with you. I'm so sorry about that."

"Don't worry about it, Mom. I'm sure it wasn't something that Dad could control. Besides, he broke the curse and won you. So it's all good."

"What does Beck say about it? You two are lovers, yes?"

"Yes. I adore him. He says he'll like me if I'm wolf or faery."

"Well, he should. My daughter is a very likable woman. So it's that serious, then? Like?"

Daisy nodded, a big grin filling her heart. "He's the one. I'm sure of it. But don't worry, we haven't bonded with our werewolves. Dad would freak, I know."

"I don't know. Kai's bark is much worse than his bite. You know that very well."

"Yes, and he did talk to Beck. He said Dad seemed okay with it all. But I'm thinking maybe Beck's head was spinning from one of Daddy's punches, and he probably misunderstood."

"Allow your father to surprise you."

"Fine. But now I have a lot of thinking to do. Because beyond my own problems, there's Beck and his ghost wolf. He needs to give it up before it kills him."

"Could you love him if he was human?" Rissa asked.

Daisy had also explained the faery's offer to take either Beck's wolf or his firstborn.

"I'm sure I could."

"A wolf would suit my daughter better."

"What if I choose faery? Then a human lover should not be so odd. It is only if I choose wolf and Beck sacrifices his that…" She turned to meet her mother's eyes. No words necessary. The two hugged as the snowflakes continued to fall.

"Promise you won't tell Dad about this?"

"Why? Daisy, if you have to choose between being wolf or faery, then we're all going to have to know. Your decision, whether or not you believe it, will affect the whole family."

"I know." Daisy sighed and tilted her head against the back of the sofa. It felt great to finally tell her mom. But now, the decision of which breed to choose. If it was really possible. "But for right now, let's keep it quiet. Until I decide what to do."

"What's that about not telling your dad?" Kai strolled in.

"Girl stuff," Rissa said quickly.

"I can handle girl stuff."

"No, you can't." Rissa kissed Kai, then turned to Daisy. "Go to Beck. I'll talk to your father."

"Thanks, Mom."

Bella tugged Beck into the kitchen and proceeded to lay out a spread of delicious cookies on the counter before him. As if she needed to bake to survive, Bella kept turning out the goodies.

She poured him a tall glass of milk while he tore into the hot-from-the-oven chocolate chip cookie that oozed out chocolate and was crowded with walnuts. He loved nuts in anything and everything.

"You should start your own business, Mom," he offered between bites of the decadent goodness and sips of cool milk. "I have never tasted cookies so good as yours. Or for that matter, brownies. And the red velvet cake. You could buy that little place on the corner in town that always seems to turn over at least every two years."

"There's a reason businesses don't thrive in that location," she said, sitting on the bar stool beside him. "The land is probably cursed. And bakeries tend to open in the wee morning hours to begin baking for the day. Can you see your late-rising mother managing a 3:00-a.m. wake-up call?"

"Probably not. You could start something new. Midnight Munchies."

Bella nodded. "I kind of like that. Now that you've put the idea in my brain, it'll never go away."

"So how's my little brother doing?"

"You think it'll be a boy?" She smoothed a palm over her belly. "I'd like a girl."

"Whatever it is, we'll love it like crazy." He kissed his mother's cheek and focused back on the cookie. One more bite. He pushed his plate toward the baking sheet, and Bella divvied up two cookies this time. "I think I'm in love, Mom."

"What?" Bella turned on the stool. "Really?"

"It's Daisy Saint-Pierre."

Bella grabbed a cookie and took a quick bite. She cast Beck a worried glance. Or at least, he thought it was worried. "Isn't her father the one who has it in for you?"

"He does, or rather, did. Now I'm not so sure. Well, you know Blu, Daisy's grandma, right?"

Bella nodded. "She's nice, but…loud. Out-there. That werewolf doesn't act her age. Her husband, Creed, is chivalrous, though. Severo looked up to him."

"Daisy has said her dad admired Severo."

Bella slid her hand over his and curled her fingers into a clasp. "None of that matters. What does is how she makes you feel. Do you love her?"

"I do. She's fun and smart. And she likes to feed me. You'll have to get her hot chocolate recipe."

"Yes, hot chocolate," Bella murmured.

"I proposed to her after drinking it."

"You—?"

"Don't worry. I wasn't serious. We were having fun. And fun is what we do. She's not like most of the girlfriends I've had."

"Sexpots?"

"Mother."

"Son, you do have a type. Anything blonde, leggy and willing to moon over you. You can't know how glad I am you never fell in love with any of those choices."

"How do you know I didn't?"

"Beck, really? I'll grant you a man's desire to fulfill certain needs, but you're too smart to give your heart to anyone less than exquisite."

"Daisy is exquisite, pink hair and all. Her mother is faery."

"So…"

"Don't do it, Mom. I can see the wheels turning in your brain. We're just dating."

"Yes, but when a wolf finds the one who makes his heart skip, then you may as well sign on for the long haul. So you could have werewolf faery babies, you know."

Not if he decided to succumb and give up his wolf. Which he'd thought he could never consider. But really? How selfish would he be to keep the ghost wolf and continue to harm innocents?

"Daisy is a half-breed," he said. "I've seen her wings. They're pretty cool. And one of her brothers is full faery. Man, that guy can deliver a punch."

"Don't tell me. Her brothers have roughed you up? Interesting. The family must approve of you."

"Strangest way of granting approval I've ever known. And her dad. He beat the hell out of me— Ah, I shouldn't have told you that."

"But you're okay?"

He nodded and finished the glass of milk. "I gave as good as I got. But get this. Malakai Saint-Pierre actually said if I married his daughter, then I'd have no choice but to join his pack."

"That's about as accepting as I've heard."

"Yeah. I've been wondering if I should give some serious reconsideration to the whole joining a pack thing. But it's a decision that would affect more than just me. If I did, it would involve you, as well."

"Let me tell you a secret." Bella pressed Beck's hand against her lips for a kiss. "Your father and I had discussed joining a pack, or even starting one, when you were growing up. We went back and forth over how it could be good for you."

"Dad considered as much?"

She nodded. "So don't feel as though you owe your dad some sort of unmade promise to never join a pack. He would be proud of you no matter what you do. So long as it doesn't harm others and makes you happy."

Beck tightened his jaw. Harming others. Inside he could feel the ghost wolf twang at his muscles. If he fulfilled his promise to his dying father, he would not stop until the hunter was dead. And Severo would never be proud of him then.

He caught his forehead against his palm.

"Beck? What is it?"

"I miss him," he whispered.

Bella rubbed a hand across his back. The soothing motion made him want to push it all away. He didn't know how to succumb to these emotions, and didn't want to.

Yet he had with Malakai last night. He'd broken down before the mighty wolf. It had felt oddly safe to do so.

But he couldn't allow his mother to see him weak. She was the one who needed the support right now. He turned and hugged her. "We're going to be just fine," he offered. "Pack or no pack. I'll take care of you and my little brother."

"I love you, Beck, but I don't want you to feel as though I am your responsibility now. I'm a big girl. I can do this."

"But you don't have to do this alone. I'll always be here for you. And don't forget that."

"I won't. And guess what? Dez invited me over for a girl's night this weekend, and I'm going. I'm feeling the urge to have a little fun, maybe laugh and gossip with the girls."

"You don't know how good that makes me feel, Mom." He kissed her temple. "One more cookie?"

Beck recognized the pickup truck in front of the Blue Bass, so he pulled over and wandered inside. Trouble threw darts at the board. Kelyn stood back, arms crossed, obviously losing. His brother made the bull's-eye and thrust up his arms in triumph.

To judge Kelyn's eye roll, he'd probably lived with his brother's antics so long that there was nothing he could do but accept the grandstanding.

Sliding up before the bar, he ordered a shot of whiskey. Beck sensed both brothers got a whiff of his scent. Hell, they'd scented him before he'd even entered the bar. Such casual ignorance of his presence must be an art form.

Beck wrapped his fingers around the shot glass. A dart landed on the bar an inch before the glass. He plucked it out of the varnished wood surface, twisted at the waist and threw. Bull's-eye.

Kelyn's approving nod resounded above Trouble's chuckle. The burly brother slid onto the bar stool next to him. He was wearing some kind of leather skirt again, lace-up biker boots and a puffy winter vest over a sweater.

The faery was, oddly, clad in jeans and a ripped T-shirt. No winter coat hanging on the hook near the door, either. Faeries must have excellent control over their body temperature.

"Still swooping my sister?" Trouble asked.

"Swooping?" Beck tilted back the whiskey shot to hide his grin. "Do you really want to know?"

"Nope. Heard my dad paid you a visit. You look all in one piece, so it must have gone well."

"He didn't tell you? I'm his new favorite son."

Trouble laughed and slapped Beck across the back, which burned more than the whiskey. "So how's it going tracking the hunter? If you don't get him, you know my brothers and I will. Right, Kel?"

The faery, who now tossed darts in practice with both hands, nodded.

"Hell, we know where he lives," Trouble said. "Let's go set his house ablaze."

"An eye for an eye isn't going to change things, man. It might even make things worse."

"How?"

"A revenge killing?" Beck reasoned, more with himself. "He only wounded your brother. He murdered my father. But even I can't justify taking a man's life."

"That crazy white werewolf you become would do it."

The man didn't know how right on he was. Beck clenched his fingers over the top of the shot glass. "I can't believe you would seriously consider killing another man."

Trouble leaned his elbows on the bar. "I'm no murderer. But the guy isn't like the usual hunters if he's using silver bullets and arrows. He saw us shift. And Kelyn said he acted as though he'd expected it. The man knows about our breed, Beck. That's not a good thing."

"I agree. But what does he know? And is he hunting

werewolves for notches on his shotgun, or does he have another purpose? Is he a werewolf hunter? We need more information on this guy. I don't even know his name."

"I gotcha covered. Kel!"

The faery strode over and sat on the other side of Beck. The bartender placed a tall glass of ice water before him and received an appreciative nod.

"Kelyn looked up the hunter's address online," Trouble said. "What was his name?"

"The land has been owned by the Marx family since the eighteenth century," Kelyn said. "Burnham wasn't even a town back then. But the property has been handed down on paper through the years. Last name listed as owner was a Denton Marx, but I don't think that's a current resident. Denton Marx has no online presence."

"That doesn't mean anything," Beck said. "I just fumbled online for the first time last year to look up info on starting up a garage."

"Yeah, well, as far as I know, whoever is living in the house now doesn't have a job, and may hunt for a living. Probably sells pelts and meat to the locals. I flew over his property and took a look."

"And?" Beck asked. The fact that he was seated between the brothers and neither had tried to rearrange his face was a miracle. Guess he'd won his way into the family's respect.

"There was a deer carcass hanging from a tree. Must have been a fresh kill. Saw a snowmobile that looked like something from another time, and a big shed that I assumed must be where he keeps his weapons and probably a freezer full of game. Some stretched rabbit furs outside the shed, as well. Either he's a pro, or he's so off the grid he lives off the land and is a complete ghost regarding an online presence."

"Sounds like a pro who is obviously looking for bigger game," Trouble said. "Uh, I have to ask… It's about your father, man."

Beck rolled the shot glass between his palms. "Yeah?"

"Was he in werewolf form when he was shot?"

"No, we were both in wolf shape. It was our usual weekend run in the forest. I chased the hunter off, otherwise my guess is he would have stuck around to claim his kill."

"So he didn't see him shift to human form after, uh…?"

"No. My father didn't shift until I'd gotten him to my mother's house. He uh…" Beck swallowed. "He lived that long after taking the bullet."

"Sorry, man," Kelyn offered.

"Yet that hunter used a silver bullet," Trouble said, "so he must have known what he was hunting. Does he think if he takes down a werewolf, it'll stay that shape so he can stuff it and mount it as a prize?"

"Dude." Kelyn shook his head. "That image gives me the heebie-jeebies. And I'm not even wolf."

"Yeah, well, all you gotta worry about," Trouble said, "is getting pinned like a bug by the wings, little brother."

"That is so wrong," Beck said. He managed a smile, and the brothers chuckled. "So what do we do?"

Trouble tilted back a swallow then asked, "Can you control the ghost wolf?"

"It's getting harder every time I shift. I don't trust myself."

"Maybe we can use the ghost wolf to draw out the hunter, then we move in for the coup de grâce."

"The what?" Kelyn asked.

"Hey, it's French. Grandpa taught me." Trouble stood and slammed a couple ten-dollar bills on the bar. "Let's talk about this tomorrow, eh? I've got a date."

Beck gazed down the man's attire.

"What?" Trouble tugged up the waistband of his skirt. "You never seen a guy in a kilt before?"

"Looks like a skirt to me."

Pain reverberated through Beck's jaw as Trouble's fist retracted. The wolf smirked and walked off.

Kelyn chuckled.

Not like he hadn't expected the pain, eh?

Chapter 26

Beck pumped lightly on the brakes as his truck slid toward the stop sign on an icy road. It had rained overnight, freezing the world to a gleaming sheen. He didn't have chains on his tires, but the automatic brake system was reliable. He slid to a stop, then slowly rolled through the intersection toward Daisy's street.

He'd been thinking a lot since leaving his mother's house. Should he sacrifice his werewolf to stop the ghost wolf from killing? It was an extreme sacrifice. But killing someone would be an unthinkable crime.

And to give up his firstborn? No doing. Especially if that child was also Daisy's.

Could the faery really have such knowledge? If she did, then Daisy also had a big decision to make. And Beck thought they could better decide together.

Parking before the three-story brick warehouse, he grabbed his coat, ran up the inner stairs and knocked on Daisy's door.

"Shoot," he muttered. "Should have brought flowers."

The door opened and Daisy jumped into his arms, wrapping her legs about his waist and kissing him hard. Dropping his coat on the floor, Beck walked inside with the faery wolf clinging to him.

She smelled like motor oil again, which meant she must have been working on her sculpture. And beneath the industrial top notes, he sniffed out her softness in a hint of chocolate on her skin and a dash of sweetness in her hair. Beck kissed from her mouth to her nose, and to her ear, which made her squirm in his arms.

"You always smell like candy."

"You like sweets."

"That I do. Are you working?" he asked.

"Thinking." She nodded toward the work space. "Firing up the welding torch always helps me think."

"I bet I can guess your thoughts."

She dropped down from his hold and kissed his chin. "You probably can."

"I thought I'd come over and we'd think together."

"That's awesome. I can use the extra brain. All right if I shower off the smell of work?"

"Only if I can join you."

After Beck toed off his boots, she led him into the bathroom where they stripped and headed under the steaming shower.

Slicking his hands over her skin, he mapped his desire across her breasts, down her belly and between her legs. She cooed and nudged up on her tiptoes to give him access. He liked the sounds she made when he pleasured her. Coos, moans and outrights gasps that insisted he either go faster or slower, or just that speed. Her pink hair slicked against his chest. She clung to his biceps and rocked her hips while he stroked her to climax.

As her body shuddered against his, he realized he wanted to hold her forever, feeling her pleasure, knowing her joy. And it didn't matter if he was a wolf or human. Her pleasure would always be the same. As would his.

Wouldn't it?

If he were not wolf, he could never bond with Daisy. Perhaps they could bond as werewolves and then he could sacrifice his wolf? What results would come of joining together in the deepest, most meaningful way possible for their breed, and then to walk away from the very nature with which he'd been born?

A hand about his cock twisted firmly. Beck gasped. She jacked him off, and he tilted up her face to kiss her wet lips. The shower spattered their faces, his shoulders, her hand sliding up and down his erection. She went faster, firmer, luring him to an edge he only wanted to jump off if she led him.

He gripped her hand, not stopping her, only following her lead. And he erupted, crying out a throaty surrender that felt so easy, too easy.

Far easier than surrendering his very being.

Still wet from the shower, Daisy's hair dripped onto Beck's shoulders. He sat on the bed against the pillows. She had straddled him and was rocking her hips, taking him deep inside her, in and out, back and forth. He'd slipped away to heaven, or that place called Above. It was all he could do to grip her derriere and guide her, but she didn't need the help. She knew what she was doing.

"I'm choosing wolf," she said. "No question about it."

Beck's eyes flashed open. "What? Oh, Daisy…"

"If I choose wolf, then we can be together as wolves. Assuming you don't sacrifice your wolf to get rid of the ghost wolf."

"I was thinking of doing just…that."

She stopped moving, his cock embedded within her. Pressing her hands aside his cheeks, Daisy studied her lover's arctic eyes. "But if you're no longer wolf…"

"I could still like you. Would you still like me?" He nudged her upward with a thrust of his hips.

Daisy rocked slowly now, aware he was close to climax and wanting to get him there, but this conversation was making her think. Too much. "I would. I…"

What would her father think of her loving a mere human? And why did she have to think about her family at a time like this?

Increasing her motions, Daisy squeezed her inner muscles about Beck's erection.

"If you were faery," he said, his eyes closed as he rode the pleasure, "a match with a human wouldn't be so odd, would it?"

She shook her head. Faeries in the mortal realm tended to hook up with humans simply because their kind were few and far between, and the appeal of something different, the mortal, was there.

"I don't care what you are," she said. "I just want you, Beck."

Did she? Was she being honest with herself? Why this heavy conversation right now?

Right. Because they'd both intended to discuss this. And it needed to be discussed. Just…

She stopped moving again and bowed her head to Beck's. He hummed deep in his throat and cupped her breasts. "This is good," he said. "Like this. I don't need to come. Just being inside you is right. I could live here, surrounded by you, your beauty and warmth. Your pinkness."

She giggled and kissed his neck. "You're too good to me."

"I want you to feel my love. My like. My want and need for you. It's only growing stronger. I like your independence. I like that you're not afraid to be yourself. You are proudly weird."

"I'll take that. Let's bond," she said suddenly, without thinking through the implications. "Tomorrow night. Let's go out by your place and do it."

"Daisy, you know that means we intend to mate forever?"

She nodded. "Do you want me?"

"Hell yes. But…"

"Don't say anything about family or if it's right or who we'll annoy if we do it. Let's just do this for us. And then whatever comes afterward we'll handle together. Bonded."

"I love you."

She kissed him. And it was a forever kind of kiss that wrapped about his heart and squeezed just firmly enough so that he knew the world and his future would be right. With Daisy Blu.

Beck wandered out of the grocery store, a ten-pack of paper towels hoisted over a shoulder and a heavy tub of kitty litter in the other hand. He set both in his pickup truck box.

He glanced to the man fishing about in his open car trunk, parked next to him and nodded. The guy sported a Vandyke beard to match his brown hair, which was pulled back with a leather tie. A leather coat hung on his thin frame, not a modern style but more fitted. It looked old. But not retro old, more like antiquated. Like something from a different century. Must be one of those role-playing sorts.

When the man's eyes met Beck's, something inside Beck thudded. He clenched his fingers into fists. He recognized him, but…how?

Inside, his muscles stretched along his bones. His heartbeats thundered. And his wolf growled.

And then he guessed. He had not seen the hunter in

the restaurant parking lot when Daisy and her brother had called him to track him down. The only moment he'd been close enough to mark the hunter's face was when he'd been wolfed out in the snowy field and had pushed the snowmobile down the ravine.

"It's him," he muttered under his breath.

Stretching his neck and fighting against the wolf that demanded release, Beck stepped around the back of his truck and toward the hunter. "Going out hunting?" he asked, because the man wore a bowie knife strapped at his thigh, above knee-high boots that also looked like something from time past. The knife reeked of animal blood.

Standing but four feet from the man, Beck winced. He forced his hands into his front jeans pockets and yet clenched his fists. Beyond the animal blood he scented the human. He was human, not some unknown breed. But Beck cautioned himself: werewolf hunters often were human.

"Later," the man replied gruffly. He briefly glanced at Beck. His attention was on sorting the contents in his trunk to fit in the bags of groceries. "You a hunter?"

"Not wolves."

The man jutted up his head and arrowed his gaze on Beck, his eyes dark and hollow. "What makes you think I hunt wolves?"

While he spoke English, he possessed a strange accent. Sounded like one of those pompous guys Beck had seen in costume dramas on TV.

"I, uh…was just talking about myself, man," he said. "Everyone in town is a hunter. You hunt deer?"

"Everything," the man said quickly. "Including wolves. I have one more kill, and then I'm finished with this town."

"What's wrong with Burnham?"

"It's not my home," the man said bluntly. Satisfied with how he'd arranged the contents, he closed the trunk.

"So a wolf will be your final kill?" Beck asked.

The man nodded. "Indeed."

"Wolves won't go near humans unless provoked. There's no reason to kill them beyond sport."

"There are many reasons."

"Why don't you enlighten me?"

The man drew his gaze up and down Beck. His hand glanced near the bowie knife, but he didn't touch the weapon.

"You one of those pro-wolf groupies I've heard about on the fancy television? Your DNR says I have a right to hunt wolves, so I hunt wolves. End of story. Why the long face? You have a pet wolf? Did I kill your pet?"

Beck lunged for the man's throat, gripping his neck. "You killed my—"

A sudden shooting pain in his shin stopped his angry tirade. Beck released the hunter, who had just kicked him with his steel-toed boot. In those few seconds of pain, his wolf battled for reign, yet his *were*self managed to grasp sanity.

Watch what you say.

"Get the hell away from me, you insolent," the hunter hissed. "You shall be glad when I finally kill that monster ghost wolf that's been stalking innocents. And then I can finally save her."

"Save who?"

"Not your concern. You got a bone to pick with me?" the hunter asked, his eyes carving into Beck's soul faster than the knife at his thigh could manage.

Beck shook his head. It wasn't going down like this. Not in a public place where anyone could witness his rage play out. Where he risked releasing the wolf and giving this hunter the challenge he craved.

Forcing himself to take a step backward, Beck shook his head. "No bones," he said. He got in the truck, fired up the engine and backed out of the parking space.

The hunter stood at the side of his car, watching as Beck drove away. Eyes keen and all-seeing. He'd seen something in Beck. But he couldn't have seen the truth.

Maybe.

If the man knew werewolves existed, there was no telling what skills he possessed to detect and hunt them. And yet something about the man disturbed Beck. Who was he trying to save? And how could killing a werewolf serve him that save?

"I have to take care of this," he said to himself. "Before he kills again. And someone I know."

"That's a lot of kitty litter for a guy who I know doesn't own a cat."

Beck unlocked the front door to his house. Daisy had arrived two minutes earlier and had decided a wait would be worth it. It was. They strode in and kicked off their boots, and Beck set the big yellow litter tub in the coat closet.

"Maybe I have a pet?" he said with a devious glint in his eyes.

"Right. A wolf with a pet cat. I don't believe it. Unless you have a girlfriend I don't know about."

"A familiar?" Beck pulled her in for a kiss that erased any thoughts she might have regarding Beck and a cat-shifting girlfriend. "Sunday and Dean made it work."

"Yeah, well..." She made a show of sniffing near his neck. "If I smell cat on you, I'm going to get jealous."

"Deal."

"I have nightmares about cats. Just so you know."

"Why?"

"Blade has owned a pitiful hairless cat for ages. Got him when I was a teen. You don't know terror until you've woken in the night with a naked creature that looks like a rat staring at you from your chest."

"Is that so? I vow to protect you from bald cats."

"And mushrooms, don't forget that."

"Right. Anything else I should add to my security detail?"

"The color chartreuse puts fear in me, too," she said seriously.

"Noted." Beck gestured to the closet. "The litter is for getting unstuck in the snow. Did I know you were stopping by?"

"No. Just thought…"

The feeling that she wasn't welcome suddenly washed over her. He did have his crazy don't-touch-me-or-I'll-wolf-out moments, but she didn't sense any tension in him. And they had discussed getting together tonight. To bond. He must have forgotten that conversation.

Yikes. She wouldn't bring it up unless he did. She didn't want to jump the gun. "If you have plans…?"

"I don't have plans. And even if I did, I'd cancel them if that means I get to spend time with you. You eat?"

"I had some leftover pizza that Trouble dropped off." She hoisted up the thermos she'd brought along. "I did bring hot chocolate."

Beck swept her into his arms and carried her into the living room. "I knew there was a reason for liking you. You've fed me your love brew, and now I'm completely and utterly head over heels."

He sat on the couch with her on his lap, and Daisy poured some steaming hot chocolate into the thermos cup for him.

"That is so good," he said after a sip. "I'm yours. Completely. Do as you wish with me." He spread out his arms across the back of the couch, opening himself to her. "Wait." He sat up abruptly, took the cup from Daisy and set it on the wood coffee table. "We were going to do something special tonight."

"I thought you might have forgotten."

"I've had so much on my mind lately, Daisy. I'm sorry. I spoke to the hunter earlier when I saw him in the parking lot outside the Piggly Wiggly."

Dread curdled in her gut. "What did you do?"

"We talked. No violence. Promise. Though my wolf wanted to kill the bastard."

"Did he know what you were?"

"I don't think so. He was…weird. He's going after the ghost wolf. Said it was his final kill before he could save some chick. I don't know what the hell that meant."

She placed her hands about the fist he'd formed and kissed his knuckles. "Tonight all I want you to think about is me."

"Easy enough."

"Will it be? If you shift to werewolf, won't the ghost wolf come out?"

"Uh…hell."

She hadn't considered that could be a problem, but it seemed Beck's werewolf was only able to shift to the ghostly-white form that had been scaring hunters huntless.

Beck blew out a breath and sat back. She slid a hand up under his sweater, seeking the heat from his skin. He placed his hand over hers.

"I want to take the risk," she said. "With your ghost wolf."

"Daisy, I… No. It could be dangerous."

"You won't hurt me. You've already seen me while in

your ghost wolf shape, and you walked away. And I'll be wolfed out, so it's all good."

"I don't know. I'm not the same werewolf I usually am. I don't trust myself."

"You said we could bond. I want that more than anything, Beck. To be yours. Bonded with you."

"I want that, too, but maybe we should wait until I can be rid of the ghost wolf."

Daisy nestled her head against his collarbone and closed her eyes. "Love should be daring," she said. "It should feel like we're racing through the forest over the snow and into the stars."

"It already feels like that."

She didn't want to push him. And then she did. Daisy wanted to challenge Beck to win her, to choose only her, to make her his.

He kissed her suddenly. It was an invitation into his heart, one she had answered many a time, yet this time it was tentative, a little unsure. She shifted her hips and straddled his legs without breaking the kiss. Beneath her hands his hard pecs pulsed with his movement. She hugged his hips with her knees. Pressed her breasts against his chest. Melded into him. Became him as their breaths entwined and their heartbeats raced alongside one another.

"If you want me…" She rose and stepped back from Beck, pulling off her sweater to reveal bare skin. She glanced to the patio door. "Then you'll have to come after me."

Dashing to the door, she opened it and skipped out into the chill air. Beck called after her, but she laughed and shimmied down her jeans. She would issue the challenge. She had to. Time was running out for them.

Chapter 27

His beautiful lover with the pink hair and pale skin scampered across the snow. Before reaching the pond, she shifted to wolf shape. She wouldn't stop there. She would shift to werewolf.

And his werewolf would go after her because instinct could not be ignored.

Standing in the open patio doorway, Beck pressed his palms to either side of the door frame. Inhaling the crisp winter air tinged with his lover's feral aroma, he felt the rise of his wild within him. And he let out a howl that was matched by Daisy's wolf.

"Don't hurt her," he said tightly as his body began the shift.

And the ghost wolf tracked across the iced pond, following the scent of the female. It held that scent in its nose, on its skin and fur and in its very being. She belonged to him. She was his mate.

Racing through the trees, the ghost wolf found the female werewolf, who stood bold and proud beneath the moon's glamorous shine. She howled.

The ghost wolf matched her longing cry.

Beck stared up at the ceiling. Morning beamed golden upon the log walls and felt more promising than it had for months. Daisy's scent filled his pores. The scent was tainted with a touch of dirt that he'd noticed on the sheets last night (probably from their wet paws) and pine from the forest (needles they'd tracked in on bare feet).

Closing his eyes, he smiled. Last night beneath the waning moon he had bonded with the woman he loved—and liked even more—and wanted to always have in his life.

Beck had sensed the moment his fears had been overwhelmed by desire. For his werewolf had gone after Daisy. The urge to mate had been fore, and while he only recalled bits now, he knew he had not hurt her. In fact, their werewolves had come together in a vigorous yet loving coupling. The ultimate bond. Howls had seasoned the night air, freezing above their heads and showering them with a sprinkle of faery dust.

Her faery had not come out, much to Daisy's relief, yet Beck had found faery dust on his skin and in his hair after shifting back to *were* shape.

He felt Daisy on his skin still, her warm body moving against his, her sighs entering his pores, her moans of pleasure harmonizing with his. They had given themselves to one another last night, and he wanted no other woman. Daisy Blu was his. He was hers.

If he had to battle each of the Saint-Pierre wolves—including the iron-fisted faery—he would fight and scrape until he was bloody and they understood how much Daisy meant to him.

Turning onto his side, Beck spread his hand across the sheet…but it was cool.

He opened his eyes to find Daisy's side empty. Thinking she might have started breakfast, or even thought to warm up the hot chocolate they hadn't finished last night, he padded naked from the bedroom out to the kitchen. Cold stove. He looked out the window. Her car was still here. Where had she gone?

He glanced out the back window. An eerie fog hung over the frozen pond. Had she gone for a walk? An early morning run?

If she had waited for him, he would have gladly gone along with her. Daisy did like her alone time. He understood that. It was an introvert thing. But it wasn't practical with hunters roaming the forest. Especially the dead-eyed Denton Marx.

Beck stepped out the back door and immediately picked up Daisy's scent. None of her clothing was lying about. She had probably padded out of the bedroom naked, as he had. Then he noticed something that made his heart drop to his stomach.

Wolf prints tracked across the snow-frosted ground.

Breath fogging in the chill air, he shivered. It wasn't from the cold that brisked over his skin, but rather the feeling of foreboding that tightened his veins and twisted.

Running across the surface of the pond, the loose snow did not promise sure steps from his human-shaped feet. He shifted midstride, and when his foot left the ground, it landed again as a wolf's paw. His senses increased in this shape, though his thoughts quickly ceased to grasp his *were* thoughts, so Beck kept only one thing in mind: Daisy.

The wolf landed on the snow-banked shore. It tracked for a long distance before the awful whining noise of another wolf pricked his ears and he smelled her frightened scent.

The wolf nearly flew over the snowy surface, sensing that this was another whom it must be near. A female he knew well. He had bonded with her; she was a part of him.

Dodging a thicket of wild grass, the wolf slowed as it picked up more scents. Smells of machinery oil and… menace.

Human.

The wolf slowed to a walking pace as it approached the scene. One of the female's back legs was caught in a trap. The wolf did not smell blood. She whined and struggled against the mortal means of harm.

He growled, showing his teeth as he caught sight of the human, who wore clothing in light colors that blended him into the pale landscape. He smelled of tobacco and oil. The human scent was familiar; he had encountered this one before. Yet now, the human did not approach the female, nor did he hold a weapon trained on her. Instead, he stood by, deadened eyes searching the area, as if in wait.

A trap, the wolf instinctually thought. One he must not go into on four legs.

Chapter 28

The ghost wolf came upon him quickly, shaking his body and stirring and stretching its bones. When fully formed, he howled and leaped for the hunter, who now held a weapon aimed toward him. He felt the touch of an arrow move through his fur, but it did not cut flesh.

Springing from his hind legs, he landed on top of the hunter's body. The weapon slid across the snow. The ghost wolf noted that the female struggling nearby had shifted. Another human caught in a trap? Wolf, maybe? He couldn't be sure. He only knew this human beneath his claws had taken something from him, and he would retaliate by drawing its blood until it ceased to live.

Clamping its maw onto the human's chest only gnawed the thick fabric that was not skin or bone. The werewolf shook the human, ignoring its shouts of fear. The acrid smell of urine spilled across the ground.

"No!"

Startled by the firm female voice, the ghost wolf released the human, but slammed a forepaw against its neck to hold it firmly beneath him. The wolf looked over at the human female, who struggled with the metal contraption and was finally able to pull free and roll away. She could not stand on the wounded leg, and flopped on the snowy ground.

"Beck, no!" she cried.

The wolf understood one of the words. It was related to him. He growled in warning at the female as she crawled toward him, dragging one leg. Only long, bright fur hanging down from her head, the rest of her was bare.

"Beck, this will not change things. Don't kill him!"

The human pinned beneath him kicked up a knee and managed to twist its body and attempt to crawl away. The werewolf stomped on its spine, stopping it as if an insect.

"Call it off me!"

"He's out of his mind in this shape," the female said. "Stop struggling!"

"And let it kill me?"

Beck's howl echoed through the forest and stirred up the crows perched high in the birch canopy. Wings flapped, and a dark wave swooshed low near where he stood.

Daisy dragged herself across the cold ground. Shivering from the pain tormenting her shin—her leg was broken—she bit down hard on her lip to redirect that pain. Her fingers clawed into the snow, and she reached out for the hunter's head. He was weeping now, facedown on the snow. He cried out a name: Sencha. Beck's monstrous ghost wolf crouched on top of him. The werewolf gripped the human about the neck and squeezed.

She couldn't allow him to make the kill. She knew it was not Beck inside the wolf that was calling the shots right now, but that the ghost wolf was fueled by the rage over losing his father. They were connected. Because she and his ghost wolf were now bonded. If it murdered, she would feel the pain of that crime ever after.

"Please." She slapped her hand over the werewolf's paw that squeezed tightly about the hunter's neck. "Listen to me. Look at me, Beck. It's me, Daisy Blu."

The wolf's grip loosened as its red eyes peered at her.
Up close he was all white, yet oddly transparent. As luminous as the moon. Faery magic at its worst.

"I love you," she managed through tears.

The scent of blood pierced the air. The hunter's blood.

Daisy gripped the wolf's paw with both hands and tore
it away from the hunter's neck. "You love me! For your
father's sake, let it go. Just stop!"

The werewolf reared to stand. Daisy saw the claws
swoop down before she could shuffle out of the way.
Razor-sharp claws cut through the snowy ground, and
the meaty paw slapped the hunter's body to the side as if
a mere doll. The man's body collided with an oak trunk.

Beck landed on all fours above her. Daisy rolled to her
back, instinctively putting up her hands to block an attack—

And then she breathed out, and put her hands down at
her sides, making herself lax beneath him. Just last night
this gorgeous, bold werewolf had bonded with her werewolf. She loved him, and she knew he loved her.

She just had to connect with that part of the animal's
brain that was still Beck.

"I like you," she whispered. She winced. The broken
bones were healing, but slowly.

The ghost wolf sniffed at her face, down her neck and
over her breasts. And then it whined that particular noise
a wolf made when it was showing submission to another.
Ears back, and head bowed, it crawled backward off her.

Straightening, it walked onto its hind legs over to the
hunter's weapon. Gripping it, the beast broke the crossbow,
and then the arrows, and tossed them aside. The hunter's
snowmobile was parked close. The wolf lifted it, and tossed
it toward the trees, where it landed in a crooked tangle of
branches five feet off the ground.

And then the ghost wolf surrendered to Beck's will. It

was the only thing that could truly push back the beast—Beck's determination.

Her lover shifted to *were* form, standing over the human's body. The hunter was not dead, but passed out from fear, and she suspected he'd taken a claw to the throat, but the blood was minimal.

Standing there, naked and stretching out his arms to fend off the final twinges of the shift, Beck yelled out in frustration. Probably anger, as well. And surely grief. He fell to his knees in the snow and yelled again, punching the air.

Tears froze on Daisy's cheeks. She bent to feel at her shin. It was nearly healed, but she couldn't walk on it. She wanted to run to Beck, to embrace him. To make his world a better place.

But the world was what it was. And bad things happened to good people. And good people tried to keep back the bad that wanted revenge. And today Beck had managed that.

"Beck?"

He twisted a look toward her, as if he'd forgotten she was there.

"It's going to be okay," she offered.

Stepping over to her, he bent and bracketed her face in his hands and kissed her deeply. "Sorry," he whispered. "So sorry."

"I was the one who went out on my own." She pressed a finger to his mouth before he could apologize again. His body shook with contained rage. "You wouldn't allow the ghost wolf to murder. You're a good man, Beck. And that is what makes your father most proud."

"Need to make it stop."

"The ghost wolf?"

"The…the pain." He pulled her against his bare skin, and they made body heat. "When will it stop?"

"When the time is right" was all she could say. Because she didn't know. "I'll be at your side all of that time. I promise."

He glanced to the hunter's prone body.

"He'll survive," Daisy offered. "It's just a scratch. Let's go home."

He lifted her into his arms, and walked them through the forest and to his house.

They would be all right.

As soon as the ghost wolf was vanquished.

Chapter 29

Beck raced toward his home, fighting the painful stretches at the back of his legs with every step. It felt as if he were midshift and trying to move on bones that hadn't completely solidified, wrapped by muscles that were too loose. By the time he reached the pond, he was thankful that Daisy hopped from his arms and limped toward the back of his house, his hand clasped in hers.

She dashed inside to the shower.

Now Beck could finally curl in on himself, there in the open doorway of his living room while snowflakes drifted across his shoulders. He wrapped his arms about his bent legs and held back a yowl that he suspected Daisy would hear even through the clatter from the shower. He cursed under his breath as his spine finally found its *were* position. But even as he stood, he wobbled, and caught himself against the door.

Breaths huffed out, panting. He did not feel exhilarated, but rather as if he wanted to drop in a sprawl and close his eyes forever. The ghost wolf had robbed him of vitality. But he would not allow Daisy to see his pain.

Closing the door, he forced himself to wander into the kitchen to make some hot chocolate for her, and by the time the shower had stopped, he was able to stand tall and wander back to the bedroom to kiss Daisy and tell her to go finish the drinks while he showered. He sat on the shower floor as the hot water beat on his aching muscles.

This had to stop. He'd put Daisy in danger today.

She was right. He'd never have to repay the faery a favor as long as the ghost wolf did not accomplish its goal of killing the hunter.

Beck wasn't sure the ghost wolf would allow him that restraint.

He needed to be rid of the monster within him. And the only way to do that was to either kill the hunter or the faery.

He couldn't live with either of those choices.

After drying off and pulling on some jogging pants and socks, he wandered out to the living room.

"The hot chocolate is done," Daisy said from the couch. "I was just resting my leg."

"You stay there. I got this."

Because she had had his back out there, Daisy had stopped his monster. When he'd been the ghost wolf he had known, somehow, that she would not guide him wrong. She had gentled his beast.

But tame it? He doubted that was possible.

"Wolf tamer," he whispered as he poured hot chocolate from the saucepan into two mugs.

"What was that?" Daisy asked as he returned to the couch and settled next to her. She embraced him and pressed her cheek against his bare shoulder.

"I called you wolf tamer." He turned to kiss her. She tasted fresh and sweet, and her wet hair spattered his face when he flicked it over her shoulder.

"The only place I want to tame you is in bed." She winked and kissed his nose.

"Yeah, but I appreciate that you gentled the ghost wolf.

Hell, Daisy, if you hadn't been able to do that…" He swallowed. Thinking of the consequences brought bile to the base of his throat.

He sipped the hot chocolate and handed her the mug. He would sacrifice his wolf. He had to. It was the only way to not kill.

They sat quietly, snuggled on the couch before the fire. The silence felt good, their bodies against one another, surrounded by the sweet tease of chocolate. Daisy set the mug aside. Leaning forward, she stroked her shin and ankle. It was completely healed. She had survived. Yet, even though she'd been in wolf form and could remember but smells and feelings about the event, she sensed the hunter had wanted to keep her alive.

To lure in Beck.

"Is it healed?" Beck asked, kissing her ankle. He stroked it lightly with his thumb, sending good shivers up her leg.

Daisy nodded. "That feels great."

Could the hunter have known Beck was the ghost wolf? Beck had shifted back to human form while the hunter had been unconscious. But Beck had said he'd encountered the hunter in town, and they had followed the hunter, Beck and her brothers nights ago.

Was the hunter something more than human to know about their breed and detect a werewolf while in human form? If so, he could prove very dangerous.

Had a werewolf harmed one of the hunter's own?

They were missing something about this hunter, and Daisy felt that whatever it was, it was the key to them solving this dilemma. As long as Beck knew he didn't have to kill Marx…

"No," she whispered. Being the ghost wolf would kill her lover sooner rather than later.

"What's that?" Beck whispered.

"I mean, yes," she said. "Keep doing that."

He placed another kiss to her leg. Sprawling onto his side, he moved the kisses down onto her foot and biggest toe, tendering them intently. If he did have a foot fetish, she wasn't about to argue against it. Lingering in his soft, stroking touch was beyond luxurious.

"I'm going to do it," he said, grasping her foot in his big warm hand.

"What?"

"Sacrifice my wolf."

"No," she murmured.

"I have to, Daisy. Unless I want to commit murder."

His confession hurt her. He had surely thought it over. And it was the right thing to do. But it was such a great sacrifice. And could she love a mortal?

She slid down to lie alongside him and kissed his mouth. It was so easy to be with him. She'd once thought that she would recognize a hero when he walked into her life. This one had loped in on four legs.

"I'll support you," she said softly.

"Do you think you could still like a guy who is just a guy? Not a werewolf?"

"I know I can. You are in me now. We've bonded."

"But will the bond remain when I'm no longer wolf?" He bowed his forehead to hers and exhaled. "Is it the right thing to do? I… What will I do as a human? It's so alien to me. Hell, my mother is vampire. I'm soon to have a little brother or sister that will likely be werewolf. And then I'll be the odd one, completely mortal. Is it even possible?"

"With the sidhe, anything is possible." She nuzzled her face against his chest. Comforting. Masculine. Tortured yet a survivor. All hers. And she intended to keep him in the form he should remain. "You're not one-hundred-percent sure. You can't do this, Beck."

"What? But you said…"

"I know what I said. But I can hear the reluctance in your voice. Feel it in your heart." She pressed a palm over his chest. "Kill the faery."

"What? No. Daisy?"

"My father once destroyed the faery responsible for cursing him."

"That was different. She was evil and cursed your parents. I *asked* for the ghost wolf. I can't take another life just because it didn't work out the way I planned it to. Really, Daisy?"

"You're right. I'm sorry. That was desperation talking."

She turned on the couch and snuggled her back to Beck's chest. He wrapped an arm across her stomach, holding her against his warmth.

He stroked her hair away from her face and kissed the curve of her ear. "Wolves and humans get along well enough. So do faeries and humans. Your parents are proof of that."

Daisy closed her eyes. It didn't matter what she chose to become. She'd mourn the loss of one half and rejoice gaining full control of the other. But as for Beck, his choice could destroy his life. Unless…

"I've been thinking about the hunter."

"I wish you wouldn't. The less time you afford Marx consideration the better."

Daisy turned her head to meet his gaze. "I don't think he's completely human. He knows too much."

Propping his chin in hand, he studied her eyes. "Maybe. But what will that serve us?"

"We could get the Council involved. If he's vampire or some other breed and he's hunting werewolves—"

"The Council would punish him and…I'd still be left with this monster growling within me. It doesn't matter,

Daisy. The fight is no longer between me and the hunter. I've got to stop whatever is inside me."

"But you have to stop the hunter, too. What about the gray wolves who populate the area? The entire state?"

"The wolves will continue to suffer as soon as the ghost wolf is gone. There's never going to be an easy way to make men stop hunting for sport. Even if we could get the DNR to reinstate the hunting ban, the wolves will always be in danger because kills are made and go unreported."

"Yes. But one less Marx is a bright spot for the packs, if you ask me."

"How do we learn more about him? Wait," Beck said. "I do know a local reporter."

"Who has no clue how to go about researching the man. I'll have Stryke look into it. He knows people who know things. It's worth a try, yes?"

He nodded.

"Can I stay overnight?" Daisy asked sweetly.

"I wasn't planning on letting you leave."

The next afternoon Daisy set down her welding torch just as a knock sounded on her front door. She sniffed, tilted her head. "Stryke?"

"Can I come in?"

"Yes. I'll be right there. Door's open!"

Her brother entered while she tended her equipment and slipped out of the work apron. Meanwhile, Stryke stuck his nose in her fridge, found a half pan of brownies and pulled it out. He was sitting by the counter, fork in hand, by the time she wandered over and grabbed the edge of the glass baking pan before he could spear up a hunk of treat.

"Use a plate, little brother."

"I was going to eat it all," he complained.

"Oh." With a shrug, she pushed the pan back toward him. "Fine. Those are a few days old anyway. They need to go today or get tossed."

"You have some whipped cream?"

She commandeered the Reddi-wip can from the fridge and handed it to him. "So I thought you were going to do some research for me?"

"Already have," Stryke said between bites. "Talked to Dez Merovech earlier. She's a—"

"I know, she's an ancient witch married to the vampire Ivan Drake. Beck's mom is friends with them."

"Dez is a wise witch who knows everything there is to know about spells and curses. Daisy, it freaks me out that you believe Dad's curse is still lingering in you."

"*If* I can believe what the faery said. But Stryke, it makes sense. I can't seem to get a handle on my wolf without my faery interrupting. And vice versa. So I do believe it. Some part of Dad's curse is keeping me from being fully…me."

"And what would you choose?" he asked, setting down his fork and giving her his attention. He had her father's deep brown eyes, and they were soulful, understanding.

"My wolf," she said without hesitation. "But I'd miss the faery."

"Well, if Dez knows her stuff, then maybe we can find someone to break that curse, or somehow lift the lingering remnants of it from you. Then you wouldn't have to choose."

"That would be amazing. And what about Beck's ghost wolf spell?"

Stryke pushed the brownie pan aside and placed his hands on the counter before him, palms down. "Dez told me there's a sort of witchlike person who isn't really a witch, mostly human, that is called a peller."

"A peller?"

"A peller is a breaker of spells and curses. They are rare. Some humans go through life without ever realizing their gift, or so Dez explained to me. They might even end up going down the wrong path, thinking they are psychic or like a ghost chaser or something like that."

"So if we find a peller, this person could break my curse? And lift Beck's spell?"

"Dez said it was possible. And she knew of a peller living close to Tangle Lake, probably Burnham. I guess he looked her up for help finding ingredients for a spell."

"What?" Daisy clasped her brother's hands, but his expression didn't lift to a hopeful grin as hers did. "Stryke, this is amazing. Who is it? When can we go to this person?"

"Daisy." He lifted her hand to his mouth and pressed her knuckles to his lips. "The peller is Denton Marx."

Chapter 30

Denton limped across the snow before the old shed that he had built so many decades earlier. Or had it been over a century earlier? He hadn't broken any bones, but when he'd landed against the tree after being tossed by the werewolf, his body had been bruised and battered. Though he could manage remarkable feats by any human's assessment, self-healing was not one of them.

He paused and reached out for the figment that stood so near, yet so far away. Her long dark hair fell over half her face. She was crying. For the love of all that was sacred, she was crying and he could but stand there and witness that silent pain.

"Soon, Sencha. I am close. I was right about the man and his girlfriend. They are both werewolves. I was able to use her to lure out the monstrous beast that he is. The people in the nearby town call it the ghost wolf. He will provide the powerful last step to the allbeast spell that I can then exchange for your release from the Edge."

He reached for her hair, but his fingers moved through the beautiful brown tresses as if she were a ghost herself. She did not acknowledge the touch. She could not. She was trapped in another dimension. One that she had feared someday falling into during her frequent trips through time.

"Soon we will be reunited," he whispered, tears falling down his cheeks. "And then we will go home. To the time where I was born to live. And the time where you are safe."

Beck arrived at Daisy's place just as Stryke was finishing off the pan of brownies.

"Lone wolf," Stryke acknowledged Beck after he'd kissed Daisy silly in greeting. "We were talking about you."

"Stryke knows someone who can break spells and curses."

Disappointed the pan was empty, Beck leaned against the fridge and asked, "And who is that?"

"The hunter who is after you," Stryke said. "He's a peller. Breaker of spells and curses."

"How the hell do you know that?"

"I talked to Dez Merovech."

The witch friend of his mother's. Beck knew Dez was all-powerful and revered within the witch community. She'd lived for something like a thousand years. If anyone knew something about Denton Marx, it would be her.

"So our only hope is a guy who wants us dead?"

"Life's a bitch, man." Stryke stood and kissed his sister's cheek. "I gotta go catch up with Trouble. You two want me to send him this way? You're going to need the full force for this one."

"The full force?" Beck asked.

"It's showdown time. You gotta make this peller guy work for you without getting killed in the process. Do you have any idea how to do that alone?"

"I just found out about this. Give me a minute to process, will you?"

"Yeah? While you're processing, I'm sending in the troops. Do not go near the hunter," Stryke said to Daisy, waggling an admonishing finger. "Even if Beck decides to go talk to him, you stay away. You understand?"

"Stryke, I'll be fine."

Stryke turned to eye Beck. "You know she'll try to jump into the fray. She's stubborn like that."

"She's not going to get hurt anymore." Beck pulled Daisy to his side and wrapped an arm across her shoulder. "You're right. This is showdown time. It's got to end today. I can't let the ghost wolf terrorize humans any longer."

"Give me an hour," Stryke said as he wandered to the front door. "I'll gather the troops and we'll meet?"

"I'll be waiting," Beck called.

As the door closed, he turned to pull Daisy into his embrace, but she shoved him away.

"I'm not some helpless pup you have to protect," she said. "I freed myself from that trap last night. And I stopped the ghost wolf from harming the hunter. You need me, Beck."

"I do need you. I need you alive."

"And I need you alive, Beck."

He pulled her to him, and this time she didn't resist, crushing her body against his and tilting her head to his chest.

"I'll have your brothers with me," he said. "I promise you I won't go into this alone. But you have to trust that I can handle this. Please, Daisy?"

She nodded against his chest. "I love you."

"Yeah? Well, I like you."

She chuffed out a weak laugh. "I like you more."

He kissed the crown of her head. He'd never tire of her candy scent. "I'll call you as soon as we've found Marx and talked to him. Promise."

"Fine. I'll…do something to keep myself busy."

"You could work on the sculpture. What about your article? How's that coming along?"

"It's almost finished. I'm going with a fictional slant. Ghost Wolf Really a Man Dressed In a Wolf Costume. I figure I can doctor up a blurry shot of it and maybe add a zipper?"

"Hmm, I like it."

"Yeah, but I can't focus on that right now. I was thinking about baking. It's more relaxing. I need to relax. Not think about you approaching a killer who wants to claim your head as his next trophy."

"Don't say that. It's all going to be great. I promise. Now, where was your brother headed?"

"To Trouble's place. I'll give you his phone number, then you won't have to venture into Trouble's lair."

"That bad, eh?"

"I don't think the guy knows the meaning of clean. It's safer if you don't tread his territory."

"Hey, me and Trouble are tight. Lately, he doesn't punch me quite as hard as he's capable."

She laughed. "Are you sure you want to claim me as yours? Because you know with me, you also get the whole pack. All four arrogant, rough and tough brothers. And the father."

"The Saint-Pierre pack will definitely keep me on my toes. If not humble. I'm in for the ride, Daisy Blu. You okay with that?"

"More than okay."

Half an hour after Beck had left, Daisy was up to her knuckles in flour, eggs and—no cocoa. She had only a tablespoon left and needed much more. So she bundled up in coat, cap, mittens and winter boots, and decided to walk the four blocks to the closest grocery store, which served an ongoing cavalcade of hunters during the winter season.

With a shudder, she strolled by a sign advertising deer cleaning and homemade sausage casings. Sure, she ate meat. It was her nature. But she never began a meal without blessing the source and thanking the universe for the gift.

Once in the baking aisle, she dropped a few extras in her basket. Vanilla, powdered sugar and those snowflake sprinkles looked interesting. Might be cute scattered on top of frosted cupcakes.

At the end of the aisle her senses, overwhelmed by sugary sweetness and spices, suddenly homed onto a familiar human scent. Woodsy and slightly old, like a smoky log cabin. She followed the scent past the cereal aisle and toward the natural foods section. Turning down that aisle, she sighted a tall man with hair tugged behind his head. He wore an odd leather coat and knee-high boots.

Daisy slipped around the end of the aisle, pressing her back against the canned tomatoes display. "It's him."

The hunter who was also the one man who could help her and Beck. And Beck and her brothers had gone off to find him?

She had left her cell phone at home. No way to alert Beck. Maybe she could talk to Marx? Beck had been adamant she not put herself in danger. But what harm could befall her in a supermarket? If anything, the hunter should beware her bite.

Decided, she swung around the corner. Marx stood before the spices, studying the label of a small glass jar. She strolled up to him, turned toward the spices and made a show of looking over the display from cumin to pepper to turmeric.

"I want to make you an offer," she said.

"You are quite the daring wolf," he said under his

breath. "I would have thought you'd keep your distance after the other night. Looks like you've healed well enough. I am pleased for that."

Aghast that he'd express such false condolences, Daisy almost swore out loud, but she suppressed her anger. "You were using me to lure in the ghost wolf."

"To much success."

"Your definition of success is lacking. We both got away."

"Yes, but now I know where to find my prey."

He made to turn away, but Daisy gripped his wrist. Twisting gently within her grasp, the man turned his gaze on her. His eyes were bloodshot. And black, almost demonically black. But he wasn't demon. Dez had said he was merely human.

"Why are you hunting werewolves?"

"Just the one wolf is all I need," he said. "Let go, little girl."

"Why? You afraid of me?"

He relaxed within her grip, his grin curling as he shook his head.

Daisy released him, and he remained before her. She had to look up to meet his eyes, but was not daunted by his height. "If you only need one wolf—and I don't know what for—then take mine."

"Ah? Sacrificing herself for the lover?"

"I'm a half-breed. I'm cursed. I have to give up one or the other. I'll give you my wolf, then I'll become completely faery."

He tilted his head at her. "Intriguing. Faeries can be useful—but…no. I have my sights on bigger quarry. And what I need might only be obtained from a dead werewolf."

She gripped his wrist again, but this time he tugged

away from her. "We can make this work," she pleaded. "I know we can. Then no one has to get hurt."

"It's too late for that," he said. He glanced around them, ensuring no one overheard their conversation. "I am concocting an allbeast spell. You won't understand, so I needn't explain my reasons for such a thing. Suffice it to say, I do this to save someone important to me. Now, I apologize in advance for any pain I will bring upon you for taking your lover's life, but it must be done to save my lover."

He swung around and marched off, leaving Daisy shaking in the middle of the aisle.

"The allbeast?" she wondered aloud. "I have to find Beck and stop him. Whatever Marx has planned, this can't be good."

Bella left Dez and Ivan's house and bundled into her SUV. Ivan had walked her out to the car, even though the sidewalk was shoveled and not icy. She'd spent a great afternoon with the couple, testing Dez's attempts at cheesecake (still not there yet) and listening to Ivan's plans for their new home in Venice. The couple loved Italy, and already owned a few houses around the world. Why not another?

It had all been going well until Bella had asked Dez, in the privacy of the kitchen after Ivan had excused himself to make a few business calls, what she could do to help Beckett.

Dez had explained to Bella what a peller was, a breaker of spells, and had mentioned that a Saint-Pierre had been asking the same thing of her. Was Beck in trouble?

Nothing her son and the Saint-Pierres couldn't handle, Bella had reassured her. And yet, Dez had gotten a worried look. She'd said there was a hunter in town who was also a

peller. His name was Denton Marx, and she sensed things
about him, but couldn't be sure what those things were.

"He's in the wrong place," Dez had said. "But I don't
know what that means."

She had warned Bella to be careful and to not interfere
with whatever her son was up to.

"Take care of the baby," Dez had said as Bella had
walked down the sidewalk on Ivan's arm.

Now, as she sat behind the wheel, thankful for the seat
warmers that heated her butt and back, she ran her gloved
fingers along the steering wheel. "I wonder if Beck knows
the hunter is someone who can help him break the spell?"

She tugged her cell phone out of her pocket. Shook her
head. "I'll stop by. A mother doesn't need an excuse to
visit her son."

Time to go straight to the source. Denton had lost all patience. And he couldn't bear to consider the Severo man's
lover had offered her wolf in exchange for his life. Severo
probably wasn't aware of such an offer.

A real man stood up for himself and for his woman.

Unfortunately for the woman, she would soon be grieving her lover's death.

Couldn't be helped. Denton had worked too long collecting ingredients for this spell to let emotions tumble it
now. Just one last element to the spell, and he could sum-
mon Sencha back into his arms.

When the allbeast was created it sought the Edge, its
natural habitat, and the only way for it to travel into such
a place was to replace another, who would then exchange
places with the allbeast. Sencha. And once and for all, they
could leave this horrible time for good.

He pulled the car down the gravel road to his cabin.
One last look at Sencha, then he'd go after Beck. On the

passenger seat sat a pistol, loaded with the specialized bullets that contained the nano-silver pellets. He'd gotten them more than a hundred years from now. As well, in the backseat, the crossbow with the same nano-silver-tipped arrows waited. He'd learned that he had to take the werewolf down while in werewolf form. The simple four-legged wolf form wouldn't do. He'd made that mistake once. Though at the time, when he'd shot the wolf in practice, he'd only thought it a natural gray wolf.

He noted the headlights arriving before the Marx homestead. The truck belonged to the Severo werewolf. Denton's heart raced as he shoved the pistol at the back of his pants and grabbed the crossbow. He had not invited anyone here. And yet, he shouldn't expect anything less than a showdown to the final breaths.

Breaths he would steal from the werewolf.

Aiming the crossbow, he vacillated between pulling the trigger and not. He didn't want to kill the man in *were* form. He needed to shift to that monstrous ghost wolf. But an arrow skimming his skin could be just the thing to anger him sufficiently.

Chapter 31

Beck sensed the hunter's decision to pull the crossbow trigger a nanosecond before it happened. He dodged, feeling the arrow skim the hair on his head. Racing for Marx, he slammed his hands against the man's shoulders, pushing him down onto the snow-packed driveway. The crossbow skittered across the slick surface.

A vehicle pulled up the long driveway, and Trouble's howl could be heard from inside the closed truck.

"If the Saint-Pierre boys get hold of you," Beck snarled at the man, "it's all over. What the hell do you want from me?"

"Your werewolf," Denton said. "I need a werewolf's essence to save her."

Beck followed the man's pointing finger. The sky was rapidly darkening, and the space between the cabin and the work shed looked over a vast field, backed by a thin line of pine trees. But he saw something move. Not an animal or bird. It was faint. Was it a woman?

"She's trapped in the Edge," the hunter explained. He kneed Beck in the ribs, but Beck maintained his hold on Marx's shoulder, pinning him to the ground. "I have a spell to release her. But I need a werewolf to complete it."

"So you want to kill me to save her?" Beck asked.

The brothers, all four of them, tumbled out from the truck. Trouble called for Beck to hold him; he was coming.

"Please," Denton pleaded. "She is my— Our souls belong together. She has been trapped for months."

"Yeah? Somehow I don't care to die today." Beck tugged the man upright.

Trouble lunged in and punched the hunter's jaw, splaying him out across the ground.

"Not this way." Beck shoved Trouble away from the unconscious hunter. "We're not going to kill him."

"I heard him say he needed you dead," Stryke said. The brothers filed beside Denton's body.

"He said something about a spell to save her." Beck thrust his hand toward the figment, which still stood off in the clearing. "Do you see her?"

"I do." Kelyn strode over the snow, his footsteps inaudible, right up to the figment of the woman. He reached through the air, aiming for her hair, but his hand went right through her. She didn't turn to acknowledge his presence. "A ghost?"

"I don't know," Beck said. "He said something about her being trapped in the Edge."

Blade hissed and took out a bowie knife, holding it in defense, not over the hunter, but as if he expected something to come out from the surrounding woods.

"I've heard about the Edge," Stryke said. "It's not a place anyone wants to visit. I'd take Daemonia over the Edge any day. What's she doing in there?"

"He said she was his lover. That their souls belonged together." Beck wandered over to where Kelyn studied the figment, but glanced over his shoulder. "Leave him alone, Trouble! Is there some way we can get her out?" he asked the faery as he joined his side. "That seems to be the hunter's goal. Said he needed a werewolf to complete the spell. She's…beautiful."

Kelyn shook his head. "From what you've told me, I suspect she's a wandersoul."

"A what?"

"A time witch. One whose soul wanders continuously through time. They can't stop. Not unless they find another soul worthy of their love."

"Soul mates?"

"In the truest sense of the term."

"You said she is a time traveler?"

"And the hunter might have come from another time, as well."

"I thought his clothes looked odd, like he was wearing a costume from another time. But what is the Edge?"

"It's another dimension." Kelyn waved his hand through the woman's figment. "Probably landed there instead of her goal time period. One of the dangers of time travel is falling into the Edge. The only thing that'll bring her out is some sort of exchange with an occupant in this dimension, I'm sure of that."

"Like an exchange spell? And that spell requires a dead werewolf."

Kelyn turned and strode back to his brothers.

Beck remained and walked around to stand before the woman. Ghostly and pale, she looked right at him yet didn't see him. Her hair was tangled and her clothing in tatters. The long dress was corseted, and the lace at her wrists hung in tatters. She'd been through hell; he could sense it from her eyes. They looked right through him. She'd given up.

"Another dimension and time travel? This is too weird for me. But if there was a way to save you…"

He placed his palm flat before her. If there were a means to let her know that he stood there, and was interested in helping her…

Beck glanced to the Saint-Pierre men, who stepped in a circle as the hunter roused and sat up. Another set of headlights revealed Daisy's car. But he saw two people in the front.

"This is getting out of hand." He marched back to the brothers. "Do not harm him," he warned, as he continued on toward Daisy's car.

When his mother got out of the passenger side, he swore under his breath. "What are you doing here?"

"I saw Daisy in town, and she said she was on her way to your house. But then we passed this property and I recognized your truck. Dez told me about the allbeast spell—"

"Mom? You shouldn't concern yourself with this. It's not safe for you here."

"Just because I'm pregnant doesn't make me incapable. Who are all these people?"

"Get back in the car, Mom."

Daisy popped out and strode up to Beck. She looked ready to run into his arms for a hug, so he stepped back and put his hands to his hips. Daisy stopped abruptly before him.

"We're here to support you," she said to him. "The man who killed your father lives here." She looked around his shoulder. "You must want to do the worst."

"I don't," he growled. "But your brothers just might."

"Beck," Bella said. "Dez said the man could help you."

"I know that. But trust me, I'm more valuable to him dead than alive." He turned and stalked away from both of them. It should have been him and Denton Marx tonight. Not the entire Saint-Pierre clan, and his mother.

Someone had to control this situation.

Trouble grabbed Denton, and just when his fist would have collided with his skull, Beck grabbed the wolf and yanked him to a stand.

"At least he has the courage to show me his anger," Denton mocked.

"Leave him," he ordered Trouble and the brothers, who had formed a ring around the hunter. "This is between him and me."

With a nod of his head, Trouble directed the brothers to step back. They did so, but remained alert and on guard.

"Daisy, stay back," Blade said.

"No." She walked up, Bella's hand in hers. "I want Mister Marx to take my wolf instead of Beck's."

"What?" Trouble barked.

"Daisy, you don't get a say in this," Beck warned.

"But I don't need my wolf," she insisted.

Bella nodded in agreement beside her. And Beck silently cursed his mother's newfound independence that should have waited for a safer time to show.

"The wolf is the one part of you that you identify with most," Beck argued with Daisy. "I won't let you sacrifice it."

"What's wrong with your faery half?" Kelyn asked his sister.

"I carry remnants of Father's curse," she explained to the brothers, who had been unaware of her struggles until now. "I can only be either werewolf or faery. I have to choose."

"You've always been more wolf," Trouble said. "And Beck is right. You're not sacrificing anything for this bastard."

"Do you not see her?" Denton pleaded, thrusting out an arm toward the figment. "Her name is Sencha, and she is my love, and she is trapped in the Edge. Her only hope is if I can complete the spell and send the allbeast to switch places with her."

"Not our problem, buddy. Most especially not worth murder," Trouble said.

"She looks so lost," Bella said quietly.

All the men's heads turned toward the vampiress, who cradled her swollen belly. Even the hunter regarded her. Denton gasped.

Noting his reaction, Daisy pulled Bella forward. "This is Belladonna Severo," she said to Denton. "Three months ago on a cold November night, she waited to tell her husband about the child she was carrying, but he never returned home. Instead, his son, that man you want to now kill, returned home with his father in his arms. He'd been shot by a hunter's bullet. A silver bullet."

Denton grasped Beck's gaze before then returning his attention to Bella. "Truly?"

Bella nodded and bowed her head, but then lifted it proudly. "I forgive you."

"Mother, you don't have to say that."

"I mean it," Bella reiterated. "Just because I can forgive does not mean I condone the act."

"But…" Denton's jaw dropped. "I took your husband's life?"

Bella nodded.

"I…" The hunter pressed his fingers over his gaping mouth. He shook his head and looked to Beck for confirmation.

"It was me who charged you that night you killed the wolf," Beck said. "I chased you away from my father's body."

"I hadn't known I had to kill the beast in werewolf form," Denton said quickly. "It was a wasted shot—"

Beck lunged for the hunter, landing them both on the ground as Bella screamed. The brothers formed a circle around the fallen men, shutting them off from the women.

"A wasted shot?" Beck felt his werewolf stretching at his spine. He dug his fingers into Denton's shoulders, but knew it was too late. "I won't do it!"

He shoved the hunter away from him. Beck crept away, his body shifting as he did so. "I have to get out of here. Daisy, don't let them—"

His werewolf came upon him so rapidly, his sweater tore away from his biceps and chest. Managing to step out of his boots, Beck landed on powerful hind paws with each step.

Daisy pushed Bella toward Blade, the safest place she could be right now. "Protect her."

Blade tugged the vampiress toward Daisy's car.

Daisy saw Denton pull a weapon from the back of his pants. "He's got a gun!"

Kelyn moved swiftly. The heel of his palm landed on Denton's shoulder just as the hunter lifted his arm to aim. The pistol fired skyward, the retort echoing across the snowy clearing.

Beck's werewolf howled. Claws scraped the air. The ghostly beast, eyes glowing red, stalked toward the hunter.

Trouble and Stryke grabbe d Denton by the arms and wrestled him into a secure hold while Kelyn took away his weapon and slid it under one of the vehicles.

"Please!" Denton cried. "He can save her!"

"You don't need the ghost wolf," Daisy insisted. "You can take my wolf. You only need the essence, yes?"

The hunter nodded. He glanced to Bella, huddled up against Blade's chest. "Yes."

At that moment the ghost wolf's claws cut across the hunter's chest. Blood oozed through his shirt.

"No!" Daisy raced to put herself between Beck and the hunter.

"Daisy, don't be stupid," Trouble said. "Get out of the way!"

"I'm not moving. He needs to see me. To hear me. Beck!"

The ghost wolf reared and swung around its arm, its claws aimed for Daisy. At Bella's scream, the werewolf stopped abruptly. It howled, lifting its chest and stretching its spine to call out to the moon.

"Hell, he keeps that up I'm going to shift," Trouble muttered. "Then it's all over," he said with a jerk of the hunter's arm backward.

Indeed, the air vibrated with aggression and werewolf pheromones. Daisy could feel the urge to shift, as well. Not because she wanted to hurt something, but rather because her bondmate called to her instinctual desire to mate. The situation had to be cooled. And fast.

She thrust out a hand, her palm landing the soft warm muscle strapping Beck's chest. "Feel me," she said. "Know me. Your bondmate."

Behind her, Trouble hissed. Well, he had to find out one way or another.

Teeth bared and claws at the ready, Beck's red eyes looked over her head. She knew he focused on Denton. The man who had destroyed his family. Now Marx relentlessly sought to take Beck's life. But it wasn't necessary if she could give him her werewolf. And she would. To save her lover.

Pushing both palms against his chest, Daisy sidled up next to the creature, sensing its need to pull away—and yet it did not. She would hold him until he knew her, and ever after.

Behind her, Trouble swore. Stryke told the oldest to pull it together. Her brother was shifting against his will. It was natural for a werewolf to want to shift when others around him gave off such aggressive vibes as Beck did.

She closed her eyes, curling her fingers into Beck's

chest fur and whispered, "I love you. And I like you even more. I am yours. Settle, lover. Feel my hands against your skin. Concentrate on that." If only she could heal him with her vita, but it was too weak even in faery form.

The ghost wolf slashed through the air above her head, and then his paw landed against Daisy's back none too gently. She chuffed out a breath.

"He's going to hurt her," Trouble said.

"No," Stryke warned. "She knows what she's doing."

Daisy spread her arm around the ghost wolf's massive rib cage and hugged him. The wolf let out a howl that was both mournful and triumphant.

Off by the car, Bella exhaled a sniffling sob.

"I will break your spell, wolf!" Denton shouted. "I will do it. I must. Sencha will... I'm sorry, Sencha."

Daisy glanced over her shoulder to the hunter, whose head hung miserably. Trouble shook off the wolf's ears that had already shifted on his head.

And suddenly the ghost wolf pulled her into a hug that lifted her feet from the ground. And he did not crush her; his embrace was so gentle it must take effort to be so careful in his form.

She grasped him by the neck and nuzzled her face aside his soft maw. "I love you."

She felt his body shift within her embrace. Behind her, Trouble blew out a breath and thanked the heavens he'd not shifted completely.

"Someone grab the guy a coat," Kelyn said as Beck's body shifted back to *were* shape, still clasping Daisy to his chest.

When her lover had completed the shift, he stumbled backward, landing in a snowbank and taking Daisy down with him. Ignoring the others, Daisy kissed him long and deeply. Surrounded by her bondmate's scent, she answered his need for her. To simply be there for him. And within his kiss she found safety and home and love.

"You talked me out of it," he whispered to her. "I wanted to kill him. But your softness, your sweet scent, it calmed me. I don't know what I'd do without you, Daisy Blu."

"Let's not consider what you would have done. You stopped the ghost wolf, and that's all that matters. Marx said he'd break your spell."

"Then let's do it."

Stryke tossed a coat toward Beck. It was too short to cover anything important, so Beck tied the arms about his waist for the time being. His jeans and sweater were shredded.

Stryke stepped beside Daisy and asked quietly, "Is this the tangle you wanted?"

"Oh, yes."

"Good going, sis. You almost got us all killed. You've just taken the lead versus all Trouble's antics."

"Normally that would thrill me. But now? I'm just happy Beck is alive."

"Your bondmate?"

She nodded. "I love him."

Bella rushed to Beck, and Daisy stepped aside to let his mother hug him. "Your father would be proud," she said to her son. "You did the right thing."

"What do we do with him?" Trouble still held Marx with an arm twisted behind his back, on his knees. "Did he really come from another time, Stryke?"

"Ask him."

Denton nodded. "This time is not my own. But I fear I shall never return to the eighteenth century if I cannot free Sencha. My time travel skills were depleted with the trip to the future to obtain the silver ammunition. But, as promised, I shall remove the curse of the ghost wolf from

Beckett Severo." He glanced to Bella. "It is the very least I can do for the suffering I have caused your family."

Daisy stepped up to the hunter. "You will return to your time. Because you'll take my wolf to finish your spell."

"No, Daisy," Trouble started, but Blade stepped up behind him, and with but a look, the troublemaker of the family conceded. "You can do what you want, I guess."

"I have to choose one or the other," she said. "I choose to help instead of harm."

"We must work quickly," Denton said. "Twilight is the best time to break a spell. But Beckett must return to his ghost wolf shape. It's the only way it'll work."

Chapter 32

Beck kissed Daisy while everyone around them faded into the distance. It was only he and his gorgeous faery wolf. The woman with whom he wanted to spend the rest of his life. The woman with whom his werewolf had bonded. The woman who made his heart laugh and his life worthwhile.

The woman who had made him stand up to the manifestation of his grief—the ghost wolf—and had helped him fight it. He would forever miss his father. But killing another man in vengeance would never serve his soul, or his father's memory.

And yet now to turn toward the hunter and ask for his help was as far from his understanding as possible. But it felt right.

Because Daisy in his arms was right. She had tamed his wild.

"We must hurry to use the twilight," Denton insisted. "Come, Beckett. Let us do this."

"I like you," he said, and kissed Daisy's forehead. "This is what's right for us." He clasped her hand. "Come with me."

And they strode after Denton toward the open land where the figment of the hunter's lost lover stood. Behind them, the Saint-Pierre brothers stalked as a protective crew that bracketed Bella. Beck felt with everyone he cared about present, it had to be right.

Breaking a spell couldn't do any more harm than he had already caused. Or so he hoped. It was Daisy giving up her wolf that frightened him.

Denton stopped and turned. Beck walked right up to him. The two assessed one another a moment. The man had killed in an attempt to save his lover. Selfish. And yet, Beck had come close to killing after his selfish request to become something that could scare mortal hunters. Perhaps they were more similar than he dared believe.

"Shift," Denton requested. "And try to control yourself. If you take my head from my shoulders, I can be of no help to you."

"Will it take long?" Beck asked as he toed off his boots and handed Daisy the coat he'd tied about his waist. Everyone present had already seen him naked, including his mother. "I don't have much control over the ghost wolf."

"I'll begin immediately," Denton said. "But she should stand back by the others. Manipulating magic can send off, er…sparks."

Daisy nodded, and stepped back beside her brothers.

"Dude, I've seen your ass more times than a man should," Trouble commented.

Beck flipped him off and turned to Denton. "All right, let's do this."

Daisy felt Bella's hand slip into hers. She slid up close to the vampiress as they watched Beck shift to the ghost wolf. Blade swore quietly as the monstrous creature reached full height and howled at the settling night.

Instantly Denton began a chant before the werewolf. Palms up and mesmerizing the werewolf into his stare, the peller spoke a language Daisy had never before heard. Wasn't Latin. She'd heard that enough times when around witches. Beck's werewolf grew transfixed, as if the man's words alone had bewitched him to a silent supplication.

An intense humming surrounded the two men and the snow stirred, whipping up around them. Daisy tightened her grip. Bella responded by whispering that all would be well.

"I hope so," she said. "I love him too much."

Bella smiled at her. "I know that feeling."

Suddenly Denton's body flew out of the snowy tornado, landing on the ground near the woman's figment. She didn't regard the goings-on, but merely stood there, as if against a wall, endlessly searching from another dimension.

Stryke took a step toward the fallen peller, but Blade stayed him.

And when the snow fell to the ground and Beck's werewolf stood there, shoulders arched forward and huffing, he was no longer the ghostly white wolf but a brown-furred werewolf similar to her brothers.

Daisy ran for him, and as the werewolf turned and opened its maw to growl warningly, it instead caught Daisy against its chest and hugged her.

An hour later, when the hunter/peller had finally come to after being spit out during the breaking of the spell, he nodded as if he had done well, and wandered toward the woman trapped in the Edge. He put up his palms before her, but his hands moved through her figment.

Beck hadn't let go of Daisy since he'd shifted back to human shape. Stryke had handed him a sweater and some pants. Bella had found the backpack with extra clothing Beck kept in his truck. He'd pulled on his pants, and then had grasped Daisy to his chest, never wanting to let her go.

"It worked," she said against his chest.

"I hope so."

"I know so. We won't believe anything but. Promise?"

He nodded. "I feel...not so exhausted. Like the great

drain of the ghost wolf is gone from me. But I wonder now what the faery whom I owed a favor to will think. Will she come after me?"

"We'll deal with that if and when it happens. Now it's my turn."

"You sure you want to do this?" Beck asked. "You can still sacrifice your faery."

"You said you'd like me as a faery."

"I will. I just don't want you to feel as though you owe Marx anything."

"I don't. I'm doing this for her." She nodded toward Sencha. "And besides, I'll always be bonded to you, no matter my form. I love you, Beck."

Daisy saw surprising compassion in Denton Marx's gaze. And she wasn't mistaking it as a desperate greed to get at her werewolf. He was a man who had lost his lover in the worst way possible. Sencha was trapped in some sort of no-man's-land that Daisy couldn't begin to comprehend. But if Stryke had said he'd take Daemonia, the place of all demons, over the Edge, then it was worse than the worst.

She grasped the peller's hands and gave them a reassuring squeeze. "I'm ready for this. Are you?"

He nodded. "I am truly sorry for the trouble I have brought to you and your family."

"I understand, and I can forgive you. Like Bella said, it doesn't mean I condone your actions, but I can see the reason you were driven toward killing."

He winced when she said that word. "Let us begin."

Beck stood beside her. Warmth radiated from his bare chest and sought hers beneath her coat. The guy needed more clothes, but as Denton had explained, this shouldn't take long. She merely had to release her werewolf and invite her faery to stay. Then they could all go home.

~~And she and her bondmate~~ could begin again.

Scanning her eyes across the waiting faces that stood thirty feet off by the vehicles, Daisy noticed that Trouble did not meet her gaze. He was disappointed she was sacrificing her wolf for the faery. Regret already made her shiver more with nerves than from the chill air. She loved being a wolf. But she hadn't given her faery a chance and, as her mother had said, it was her feminine nurturing side.

Could she abandon the tomboy that she had been all her life and become something else? This was going to be an awkward transition, she felt sure. As Beck had said, she could sacrifice her faery. She didn't need to help Denton by giving him her wolf. It just felt more right than anything. And if she had the power to save the trapped woman, then that was all that mattered.

"Will you step back beside the others?" Denton asked Beck.

Too late to back out now. Daisy nodded reassurance to Beck. Her lover kissed her, then whispered, "You can change your mind."

"No, I'm good. I have to give up one or the other. And you did say you liked my wings?"

"Like them. Love them. Adore them." He kissed her again. "I love you, faery wolf." And he wandered over to stand beside his mother, who wrapped her arms across his middle and tilted her head against his shoulder.

Marx held a glass container about the size of a peanut butter jar, from which he removed a cork stopper. "Say the words I've told you, and I shall capture your werewolf essence."

"So simple as that?"

He nodded, then shrugged. "As far as I know. Your werewolf is neither a curse nor a spell that I am able to break. I only have Sencha's grimoire that I studied for reference to capturing an essence."

He cast a look over his shoulder at the figment, who had wandered farther away, her head still bowed in sorrow.

"Right then."

Daisy straightened her shoulders and spread out her arms as she'd been directed. She closed her eyes, and before speaking, said a silent thank-you to her werewolf. It was all that she knew and was comfortable with. It had served her well and made her strong. Strong enough to face this new and unsure future.

"I release my werewolf willingly and with grace. And I invite my faery to reside upon my soul ever after."

The wind whistled through the trees. Snow swirled upon the ground, dusting up glittery whorls. The hush of Denton's breath was all Daisy could hear beyond the pulsing of her heart.

When would it—?

Chest lifting, her arms flung backward. Daisy felt as if she were being tugged upward by an invisible cord. The life essence sparkled before her in the air. Her insides flamed, then cooled instantly. That which sparkled swirled toward the open jar Denton held and landed within. He capped the container and nodded.

And Daisy dropped her shoulders and glanced toward Beck. His hands were spaded before his mouth in a hopeful clutch. She nodded at him and smiled.

"I think it worked," she said, though she didn't feel different. Any more faerylike or less wolflike. "I—"

A raging storm of white moths suddenly swooped over their heads. It moved toward Daisy, and when she realized what was happening, she screamed to Denton to protect the essence.

The white faery had returned.

Chapter 33

At the sight of the crazed storm of moths, Beck shoved his mother into Blade's arms and took off toward Daisy. Before he could reach her, the moths swirled in a tornado upon the ground and formed into the wicked white faery. The sidhe thrust out a hand toward him, which sent a bolt of moths against his chest. Felt like tens of thousands of volts pricking throughout his nervous system. Forced from his feet, Beck landed on the ground, but got up immediately and shook off the annoyance.

"You have reneged on our bargain, werewolf," the faery called.

Behind her, Denton stepped protectively before Daisy.

Beck had cheated the faery out of her boon. But that would have required he ransom his wolf. Become merely human. Or give up his firstborn.

"There must be something you can ask of me," he said, approaching cautiously. He wanted to get close enough to slip around beside the faery and grab Daisy to keep her safe.

"I wanted a werewolf! And I will have one."

The faery spun into a swirl of moths so thick Beck could not see before him. The snowy clearing filled with moths. The swarm's wings cut across his skin, drawing blood at his forehead and his bare chest. He heard his mother's scream. The brothers swore. And when again the moths narrowed into a focused figure of the faery, they streamed toward Denton and the jar of Daisy's wolf essence.

He would not allow Daisy's sacrifice to be used in a manner she had not intended. She'd wanted to help the hunter reunite with his lost lover.

Denton tucked the jar inside his leather coat, but try as he might to hold it closed, the flaps of his coat flayed wide and the jar lifted out of the pocket.

"No!" Beck called.

Thanks to the distracting shout, the faery turned her attention to Beck, and Denton was able to grasp the jar.

"Take my wolf," Beck called. He spread his arms wide. "It is only right you are granted the boon I promised."

"Beck, no!" Daisy shouted. She tried to move toward him, but a wall of moths blocked her. "Don't do this."

He'd snagged the faery's interest. Though she was not fully formed, her lower half busy with moths, he stood waiting as the sidhe moved toward him.

"It is a stronger, more vital wolf than that of the essence in that jar," he coaxed. And really, he was no man if he didn't live up to his bargains. For that, he knew his father would be proud. "Come take it if you dare."

Beck felt the entrance of the faery magic through his pores as pinpricks boring deeply, seeking the source of his very being. His essence. His wolf. The one thing that he was.

Muscles tightening in a reactive defense against the rape of his essence, Beck's fists formed and he thrust back his head to howl. His wolf cried out to the night, the howl long and unceasing. Crows stirred from the nearby trees, and a gray wolf a mile off answered the mourning howl.

And then it was gone.

Beck dropped to his knees. The storm of moths swirled about him, the wings scraping his skin raw. The fire of his werewolf had left his body.

Collapsing forward into the snow, he blacked out.

* * *

Beck woke. His head was nestled against something soft, warm and smelling like candy. Pink hair sifted over his face. A gentle hand stroked his cheek. It felt…safe. Loving. A teardrop splattered his mouth. He dashed out his tongue to taste the salted drop.

"Beck?" Daisy whispered. "You're back?"

He groaned and tried to sit up, but his body felt as though it had been worked over by the Saint-Pierre brothers *and* their dad. So he merely tilted his head toward the pink heaven and nodded.

"He's awake," he heard Daisy say.

"Thank God." His mother. She would never abandon her faith in the god she had worshipped as a human. Beck smiled. All was well? As good as it could be.

Then he realized he lay in the front of his truck, his head on Daisy's lap. The heater was blasting.

"He's good," Daisy said to someone else. Probably a brother.

"Let's head out," Trouble announced. "Stryke, what's the hunter up to?"

"Working with the spell," Stryke confirmed. "I still think we should steal Daisy's essence back for her."

"Boys," Daisy called out the truck window. "It's over. I made a choice. The peller has what he needs to rescue the woman and go home. And Beck…" she ran her fingers through his hair, and Beck shivered and snuggled up closer "…is going to be just fine."

Two days later

Just fine was a matter of opinion. Adjusting to his new human status was surprisingly bewildering. Beck had taken for granted simple things such as walking. While as a werewolf he had moved sinuously, with a grace he hadn't to consider, this mortal body seemed to fumble upon the earth. And he felt the clothes upon his body as cumbersome and itchy.

And he couldn't eat as much, which made him wonder if he'd grow thin and waste away. He'd only eaten a chicken leg, thigh, two wings and a breast tonight. Daisy had been surprised that he'd refused a second helping of red velvet cake.

They had made love for the first time since he'd become human this morning, tucked in his bed, snuggling together against the insistent cold. Man, did he feel the cold now. He could not walk outside without a shirt in this frigid weather.

And the sex. It had seemed the same to him. Spectacular. He and Daisy had kissed, hugged, touched, licked, stroked and…they'd both come a few times, as they usually did when making love.

But would she tell him if he was lacking now? What if he couldn't match the intensity she had known when bonding with his werewolf?

Her father had called right before they'd sat down to eat tonight. Daisy said Malakai wanted to talk to Beck. Of course her brothers had told her father that Beck had sacrificed his wolf. And he was sure one of them had mentioned that they'd bonded, as well.

Beck was pretty sure Malakai's offer regarding marrying Daisy and joining the pack would now be reneged.

He'd face that trial tomorrow at noon, when Kai had requested they meet.

High noon. Seriously?

Daisy hugged him from behind and kissed his ear. He reached back, grasping her hair and letting it slip through his fingers as she pulled away and took the dinner plate to the sink.

"What are you thinking about?" she asked over her shoulder.

That he wasn't going to like being human. At all. And that he hadn't scented her approach from behind, as he usually could. Hadn't gotten a whiff of her sweet candy smell until she'd been right there, kissing him.

"It's the talk with my dad," she decided. Turning, she leaned across the counter and took one of his hands. "It's going to be good."

"Is it? Can you honestly love a human, Daisy? I'm not sure I can deal with myself like this. I'm…nothing now."

"Don't say that. You are the man I like. Werewolf, human or otherwise."

"Says the faery who has suddenly developed a penchant for walking around the house naked."

"I haven't heard an argument from you yet." She stood back and fluffed the ruffle of the apron she'd tied over her bare body while making supper. It just covered her nipples and had distracted Beck so much that he had leaned over to kiss the plump side of her breast more than once during supper. "It's like I'm inside a whole new skin, and it wants to feel the world on it. I want to feel you on my skin." She winked.

How could a man bemoan his condition when his reality offered up a naked faery who loved him, cooked for him and wanted to have sex all the time?

A knock at the door startled Daisy upright. "I wonder who that could be?"

"Whoever it is, they are not going to see you like that." He jutted a thumb over his shoulder. "Go put some clothes on."

She spun around the counter, kissed him and skipped off toward his bedroom.

Beck rose and inhaled deeply. He couldn't get a scent

of who stood behind the door. Hell, he could barely smell the burning wood in the hearthfire.

Normally, by scenting out the unseen, he'd be able to sense danger. Or a simple visitor. Gripping the doorknob, he looked aside for a weapon. Wasn't so easy as slashing out a claw in defense now. He hadn't lost his strength, but—hell.

Beck swung the door open to find Denton Marx standing on the threshold, his hands cupped before him. He blew into his hands and rubbed them together. "It is wicked cold in this godforsaken century, do you know that?"

"I thought you'd be gone by now. The eighteenth century?"

"Seventeenth, actually. Might I be invited in, please?"

Beck stepped aside to allow the man in. He brought in a wave of cold that sent a wicked shiver through Beck's body. He quickly closed the door.

Daisy popped back in, clad in one of his flannel shirts and some tight black leggings. Her smile dropped at the sight of Denton. "What do you want now?"

"I have brought something for Beckett," Denton said.

"Where is your lover?" Daisy asked. "Didn't the spell work?"

The hunter bowed his head and clasped his hands before him. "I have not completed the allbeast spell. I have not all the ingredients. Rather." He met Beck's gaze. "I have them, but I don't wish to utilize them. I must find a replacement."

"For what?" Daisy asked. She joined Beck's side, her hand slipping into his.

"For this." Denton tucked a hand inside his jacket and brought out the glass jar that sparkled with Daisy's werewolf essence.

"Is that…?"

"It is, my lady. I combined all the ingredients, and was

prepared to uncork and add in the werewolf essence you so graciously offered to me when I felt her looking over my shoulder."

"Sencha?"

Denton nodded.

"I don't understand," Beck said.

"It was the first time we were able to communicate, of a sort, over the dimensions. She swept her hand toward this jar and shook her head. 'Not that one' is what I'm sure she was trying to convey to me. So." Denton offered the jar to Daisy. "I know you have no use for it, as I understand your condition was that you could either keep one or the other."

"Exactly," Daisy said, crossing her arms.

The hunter took Daisy's hand and placed the jar on her palm. He wrapped her fingers about the glass. "I thought you might make it a gift to your lover. If you so choose."

Daisy's bright smile beamed up at Beck.

"Wait." Beck couldn't help but feel elation at the idea of actually getting his werewolf back, but he wasn't stupid. "How can that work? It's not my werewolf in that glass jar."

"It is the *essence* of werewolf. When it once resided in your lovely Daisy Blu's body, her soul made the essence her own. Spinning about in this jar, it is but an essence waiting to be claimed and shaped by yet another soul. You can make it your own, Beckett."

"How do you know this?" Beck asked.

"I have learned much from Sencha and the study of her grimoires. If you doubt me, you have but to try it. If it fails, you have lost nothing. If it is successful…" The man's eyes glinted with promise.

Daisy held the jar up between her and Beck. He touched the glass, and inside, the sparkling essence reacted with a swirl.

"I will leave you two in peace," Denton said.

"Wait." Beck marched to the door, stopping the man with his hand on the knob. "You still need a werewolf essence to complete your spell."

"That I do." Marx did not meet his gaze. And if he had been werewolf at that moment, Beck felt sure he would have detected the sadness that crept about the man's heart. And the resolve that would push him to kill another wolf. "I have heard about a wolf that has been tearing cattle to shreds farther up north toward the boundary waters."

"Gray wolves don't tear cattle to shreds," Daisy commented.

"Exactly," Denton said. "Not unless it's sickly and an entire pack goes after it. These were healthy beef cattle. Farmers report finding only one set of overlarge wolf tracks. A werewolf like that might not be missed, eh?"

Beck lifted his chin, looking down on the man, who still dared not meet his gaze. He had tormented his family. Killed his father. And now he had offered Beck a second chance.

Stepping aside, he made room for the man to open the door and leave. He watched the hunter march down the drive. Daisy's hand slipped into his. And he heard his mother's voice in his head. *It was the right thing to do.*

Beck called out to the retreating hunter.

Denton turned. Waited.

The pounding of his heartbeat thundered in Beck's ears. His father's last breaths—he would never forget them. Yet at that moment he wished only to move forward.

"I forgive you," he called. "Go in peace."

Marx clasped his hands over his heart, bowed his head, then turned and got in his vehicle. Only when the headlights had receded did Beck turn to catch Daisy in his arms.

"How do you feel?" she asked.

Epilogue

Daisy didn't get the internship at the *Tangle Lake Tattler,* despite her exposé on the ghost wolf, which included a photo of the white beast with a zoom on the zipper down its back. Someone had done an extensive investigation into the unclaimed mineral rights in the area and had won the prize. Rocks had won over a man in a wolf suit? Go figure.

She'd stick to sculpting for now. Last week she and Beck had delivered the wolf sculpture to the Ely Wolf Sanctuary. And she'd received a commission for another work depicting a moose and using computer parts for the sculpture. It was a challenge she looked forward to.

Now the twosome stood in the spring-wet grass before Stephan Severo's grave at the back of the family property. Hands clasped, they silently held vigil.

"Forgiveness feels right," Beck said after a while. "I will never forget, but now I can move forward."

"We can move forward," Daisy said. "Will you tell me about the things you used to do with your father someday?"

"Yes. We can do one right now. Go for a run together. You want to?"

Daisy wiggled her shoulders and slipped off her shirt. Her wings unfurled beautifully. "Try and catch me, big boy."

* * * * *

"Lighter. I feel…lighter."

"I'm proud of you."

"He's out of our lives now."

She pressed the glass jar into his hand. "To our future."

Watch for Stryke Saint-Pierre's story next!

If you are interested in Michele Hauf's world of Beautiful Creatures, check out her website: michelehauf.com. You can also find her on Facebook, Twitter and Pinterest.

To read about the other characters in this book, find the digital books online. Bella and Severo's story is MOON KISSED, followed by AFTER THE KISS.
THE DEVIL TO PAY is Ivan and Dez's story.
RACING THE MOON is Sunday and Dean's story.
HER VAMPIRE HUSBAND is Blu and Creed's story.
MALAKAI is Malakai and Rissa's story.
And THE DARK'S MISTRESS is Kambriel and Johnny's story.

Discovering he's a father of a newborn, rodeo cowboy
Theo Colton turns to his new cook, Ellie, to help out as
nanny. But when Ellie's past returns to haunt her,
Theo's determined to protect her and the baby...
but who will protect his heart?

Read on for a sneak peek at

A SECRET COLTON BABY

by Karen Whiddon, the first novel in
The Coltons: Return to Wyoming miniseries.

"A man," Ellie gasped, pointing past where he stood, his
broad-shouldered body filling the doorway. "Dressed in
black, wearing a ski mask. He was trying to hurt Amelia."

And then the trembling started. She couldn't help it, despite the tiny infant she clutched close to her chest. Somehow, Theo seemed to sense this, as he gently took her arm
and steered her toward her bed.

"Sit," he ordered, taking the baby from her.

Reluctantly releasing Amelia, Ellie covered her face with
her hands. It had been a strange day, ever since the baby's
mother—a beautiful, elegant woman named Mimi Rand—
had shown up that morning insisting Theo was the father
and then collapsing. Mimi had been taken to the Dead River
clinic with a high fever and flulike symptoms. Theo had Ellie
looking after Amelia until everything could be sorted out.

But Theo had no way of knowing about Ellie's past, or the danger that seemed to follow her like a malicious shadow. "I need to leave," she told him. "Right now, for Amelia's sake."

Theo stared at her, holding Amelia to his shoulder and bouncing her gently, so that her sobs died away to whimpers and then silence. The sight of the big cowboy and the tiny baby struck a kernel of warmth in Ellie's frozen heart.

"Leave?" Theo asked. "You just started work here a week ago. If it's because I asked you to take care of this baby until her mama recovers, I'll double your pay."

"It's not about the money." Though she could certainly use every penny she could earn. "I…I thought I was safe here. Clearly, that's not the case."

He frowned. "I can assure you…" Stopping, he handed her back the baby, holding her as gingerly as fragile china. "How about I check everything out? Is anything missing?"

And then Theo went into her bathroom. He cursed, and she knew. Her stalker had somehow found her.

HARLEQUIN®

A *Romance* FOR EVERY MOOD™

Love the Harlequin book
you just read?

Your opinion matters.

Review this book on your favorite
book site, review site, blog or your own
social media properties and share
your opinion with other readers!

JUST CAN'T GET ENOUGH?

Join our social communities
and talk to us online.

You will have access to the latest
news on upcoming titles and special
promotions, but most importantly,
you can talk to other fans about your
favorite Harlequin reads.

Harlequin.com/Community

Facebook.com/HarlequinBooks

Twitter.com/HarlequinBooks

Pinterest.com/HarlequinBooks